Rachel Ward is a best-selling writer for young adults. Her first book, *Numbers*, was published in 2009 and shortlisted for the Waterstones Children's Book Prize. An avid reader of detective fiction, *The Cost of Living* is her first book for adults. Rachel is married, with two grown-up children, and lives in Bath.

THE COST OF LIVING

AN ANT & BEA MYSTERY

RACHEL WARD

SANDSTONEPRESS
HIGHLAND | SCOTLAND

First published in Great Britain by
Sandstone Press Ltd
Dochcarty Road
Dingwall
Ross-shire
IV15 9UG
Scotland

www.sandstonepress.com

The publisher acknowledges subsidy from Creative Scotland towards
publication of this volume.

ISBN: 978-1-910985-83-0
ISBNe: 978-1-910985-84-7

Cover design by David Wardle at Bold and Noble
Typeset by Iolaire Typography Ltd, Newtonmore
Printed and bound by CPI Group (UK) Ltd, Croydon, CR0 4YY

For Ozzy, Ali and Pete

1

The bottle wobbled with every movement of the conveyor belt.

'You'd be better off lying that down,' Bea said at the exact moment that the wobble turned into a nosedive. The woman made a grab for it. Too late. It hit the floor, glass and brown sauce exploding horizontally over a surprisingly wide area. The little boy started crying. The girl in the trolley seat clapped her hands and crowed with delight.

'Oh my God! Oh my God!' The woman crouched down by her son. 'Mason, are you hurt? Let me look at your legs.'

There was sauce splattered on the thick fleece of his jogging bottoms, but nothing worse.

'I'm so *stu*pid.'

'Is he all right?' Bea asked.

The woman was scrubbing at her son's legs with a used tissue.

'Yeah. Just in a mess. I can't believe—'

'It's all right,' Bea soothed. 'It's just an accident.' She pressed a button on her desk, lighting up the cube that identified her till. 'It's fine. Honestly. I'll get it cleaned up.'

'I can't do anything right. I can't *do* anything.'

The deputy manager, Neville, walked briskly towards them along the back of the tills, clutching a clipboard. As soon as he saw what the trouble was he swivelled on his heel and retreated to the customer service console. His nasal voice rang out through the tannoy system.

'Cleaner to checkout six. Cleaner to checkout six.'

The woman stood up, settling her son onto her hip. The sauce on his joggers made brown smears on her cream-coloured mac as she hitched him up.

'They'll be here soon,' said Bea. 'I'll get someone to fetch you a new bottle of sauce. Take the kids through. Sit down if you want. I'll do your packing.'

There were still a few items in the trolley. The woman's hands were shaking as she loaded them onto the belt. Her little girl was still clapping. 'Stop it, Tiffany. You're doing my head in.' She reached down to the bottom of the trolley for a tin of sweetcorn, squashing her son against the wire edge. His grizzling increased in volume. 'I'm just so stupid,' she said, her voice full of self-loathing. 'It's been that sort of day. Dave's right. I can't do anything.'

'Everyone has that sort of day. Luckily not all at the same time,' Bea said.

'I lost my wedding ring yesterday,' the woman confided. 'Dave went mad.'

She was gripping the handle of the trolley now, pushing it through to the packing area. Bea could see the pale line on her finger where her ring should have been.

'It'll turn up, I bet. By the sink? Or in it? Worth taking the trap apart.'

'It had better. My *wedding* ring. Dave's so upset. He thinks I'm ... ' The end of the sentence was lost as she dissolved into tears.

A tall, lanky youth was shambling towards them along the adjacent aisle, pushing a little cart with a mop handle poking up and an array of cleaning sprays, wipes and buckets on board. His progress was glacially slow.

Bea sighed. So this was the new recruit they'd been asked to 'welcome to the team' at the staff meeting. Ant Thompson. She remembered him from school. The last time she'd seen him, he'd been painting some railings in the park, wearing a hi-vis jacket with the words 'Community Payback' plastered across it. Big Gav had plumbed new depths with this one. Top management decision.

Eventually Ant got to the end of the aisle and looked along the row of checkouts. Bea waved at him.

'Here!' she said. 'Right in front of you.'

She pointed to the mess, which looked like it could have been featured in a cartoon with the word SPLAT! in the middle.

'Yeah. Got it.'

He stood looking at it for a long time, rubbing his stubbly chin with his index finger, like a professor of maths facing an insoluble equation on a blackboard.

'Brush the big stuff up first, then mop up the rest,' Bea said.

'All right. On it.'

He started unpacking stuff from his trolley. Bea returned her attention to getting the shopping scanned and packed. There was a copy of the local paper, the *Kingsleigh Bugle*. The headline caught her eye. 'Is There a Kingsleigh Stalker?' Bea frowned. There had been rumours doing the rounds for a few weeks about women in the town being followed at night, but nothing concrete. She bleeped the barcode and moved on to the next item.

'Ah,' she said to the woman, who was now dabbing her face and taking some deep breaths. 'The three for two on the four-pack of this is actually better value than the value pack.' She held up a packet of toilet paper. 'Ant will get it for you. And a new bottle of sauce. Won't you, Ant?'

'Huh?'

'You'll fetch three four-packs of loo roll and a brown sauce for this lady, won't you?'

He held his arms out wide, a brush in one hand and a dustpan in the other. 'What do you want from me? I'm not a chuffing personal shopper.'

'Please? Just to be nice?'

Bea creased her face into her smarmiest, sarkiest smile and batted her false eyelashes at him. He looked a bit confused for a second or two, then broke into a grin.

'Okay, but you'll have to tell me where to go. I haven't the foggiest.'

'Aisle three for the toilet tissue, aisle eleven for the sauce. Thanks, babe.'

His grin got wider. He dropped the brush and dustpan on the floor and set off.

'You'll get in trouble for that,' said a deep voice from the next till. 'You can't call people babe, babe, he'll have you for sexual harassment.' There was a volley of husky laughter.

Without looking over her shoulder, Bea called back, 'He should be so lucky. Anyway, you just did it to me. You flirting?'

This time she did turn around, and caught her neighbour's eye.

Dot, late fifties and beautifully quaffed and manicured, winked. 'You should be so lucky.'

By the time the shopping was packed and loaded back into the trolley, there was still no sign of Wonder Boy.

'He won't be a minute,' said Bea. Her customer was fumbling in her purse. She drew out a little wad of notes, ready to pay, but kept her purse open. Like a lot of people she had a photo in the plastic window where you can keep cards, a family snap – her, Mason, Tiffany and a smart-looking man in an open-necked shirt. A library card was peeking out of the other side of her purse, bearing the name 'Julie Ronson'.

At the other end of the checkout, shoppers kept approaching and then moving on, pulling faces at the mess on the floor.

Ant lumbered round the end of a shelf and headed back. Bea was relieved to see he'd managed to pick up the right stuff.

'At last! Thanks, b—' She stopped herself just in time. 'Thanks, Ant.'

She ran the items through the till and took the cash, while Ant started cleaning up.

'There we are,' she said, handing Julie her change. 'No harm done.' Bea smiled and Julie managed a watery smile back.

'Thank you,' she said. She put Mason down again and made him hold on to the trolley and they set off for the exit. Bea watched her go, then turned her attention to Ant, who was slopping soapy water around the floor with the mop. After a minute he ground to a halt, holding the mop with both hands and leaning his chin on top.

'You need to put your triangle out now,' said Bea. 'The wet floor one.'

'Okay. On it.' But he didn't move. 'I'm knackered,' he said. 'Don't know if I can hack this.'

'Shh, not in front of the customers. Go and empty that bucket in the drain outside.'

'Yeah. Right,' he said. He found the yellow warning cone and shambled off, leaving a good-sized puddle on the floor behind him.

When he'd gone, Bea clasped her hands together then turned them inside out, stretched and cracked her knuckles. 'Don't reckon he'll make it to Friday,' she said to Dot.

'Ah, don't be harsh. It's his first day. Remember yours?'

5

It felt to Bea that she'd always been there, although it was only five years since she started as a Saturday girl. She'd been full-time since she left school just after her A-levels, a couple of years ago.

'True enough,' she said. 'First days suck. If it's okay, I'll take my break now – it's only five minutes early – and no one's going to come near Lake Geneva for a while.'

'All right, doll.'

'You can't smoke out here.'

Ant was in the service yard, leaning against a wall, head back, blowing smoke into the drizzly air.

He grinned when he saw Bea. He knew there'd been a spark between them. She was a good-looking girl, too, with curves in all the right places. With her coat draped over her shoulders and that scraped-back ponytail, there was something about her, some old-school style.

'Can't leave me alone, can you? Can't keep away.'

She narrowed her eyes and nodded towards the 'No Smoking' sign directly above his head.

'I'm on my break. I wanted some fresh air,' she said pointedly. 'Not a lungful of second-hand smoke.'

He took another long drag, then dropped the cigarette end onto the concrete and ground it out with his shoe.

'Sorry.'

They stood side by side for a while, in silence, then Ant said, 'How did you do that thing with the bog roll?'

'What?'

'How did you know what was better value?'

She shrugged. 'Simple maths. You either divide the totals by the units to get a unit price, or multiply the costs up until you've got the same number of units. I usually do both ways, just to check I'm right.'

'In your head?'

'Yeah.'

He pulled a downward smile and nodded. 'Impressed.'

'I'm not just a pretty face, you know.'

He snorted.

'What?' she said, ready to start a fight.

'Nothing.'

They lapsed into silence again. Ant sighed and closed his eyes.

'I meant it about not hacking it. I dunno if I can do another three hours of this.'

It was Bea's turn to snort. 'That's what I said to Dot. Reckon you're a quitter.'

His eyes shot open. 'Shut up!'

'Well, what else are you if you can't hack seven hours work for one day?'

'Oh, come on, it's dead boring.'

'It's not that bad. It's what you make it, like most things.'

'So you're not bored?'

'Yeah. No. I mean, I try not to be. I try to be nice to my customers, save them a bit of money, have a bit of banter. It makes a difference. I like it. And there's staff discount on everything.'

'I don't get the discount. Not till I've done my probation.'

'There you go. Another reason to stick at it. Saves an eff-ton of money for me and Queenie.'

'Who?'

'My mum.'

'Queenie! What do you call her that for?'

'Revenge. She called me Beatrice after the princess. Minging name. So I call her Queenie. Trouble is, she likes it.'

'Ha! Mine's just as bad. With her it was Tony Blair.'

'Huh?'

'I'm Anthony, after Tony Blair. Things could only get better in 1997. Apparently.'

Bea started to laugh. 'Parents. What are they like?'

'Saddos with no imagination?' Ant was laughing now too. 'Anthony and Beatrice,' he said, shaking his head. 'Fuckin' 'ell.'

He held his hand up and, rather to her surprise, Bea found herself high-fiving him.

The door behind them blasted open.

'Anthony! What are you doing out here?'

A man stood in the doorway, almost filling it – the boss himself, Gavin. His white shirtsleeves were rolled up. One of his buttons had come undone revealing a swell of pale hairy flesh between the bottom of his tie and the top of his belt.

'We've been looking for you. You're needed inside. Eileen's going to show you how to stock the freezers.'

Ant looked at Bea and raised his eyebrows.

'I'm needed,' he said. 'Hate to tear myself away.'

'Come on! Chop, chop! I'm giving you a chance here. First day. A new start. Don't mess it up.'

Ant peeled himself from the wall and disappeared inside. Bea stayed in the yard for a few minutes more then went up to the staffroom. The rest of her shift dragged a little. There was the usual lull after lunch. Things picked up a bit around the end of the school day, with parents popping in to pick up some things for tea and kids doing their sweet and crisp run. At five o'clock, she handed over to Marcus gratefully. He was student at the university nearby and, like several others, he did three or four evening and weekend shifts to supplement his student loan.

'All right?' he said, as she logged out of the till.

'Yeah,' she said.

He sat down and started getting comfortable. His glasses slipped down his nose when he bent sideways to adjust the chair.

8

'Did you see the paper today?' he said, pushing his glasses up again.

'Something or nothing, I reckon,' said Bea.

'I dunno, I know one of the girls that got followed. You take care, okay?'

'I'm okay. I can look after myself,' said Bea. 'But thanks.'

She headed towards the back of the store. She'd pick up tea for her and Queenie on the way out, after she'd got changed. Wednesday today, so it was chicken and vegetable rice. Queenie liked routine. She fetched her handbag and coat from the ladies' locker room and went into the staffroom. Ginny, another checkout worker about Bea's age, was on her way out.

'New boy's in there,' she said to Bea. She rolled her eyes. 'He's in a bit of a mood.'

'Ha! First day blues,' said Bea. 'I think he's all right really.'

Ant was standing near the kitchen area, stripping off his branded polo shirt.

'Oi!' said Bea. 'Not in here. Go in the men's.'

'I don't want to be in this thing another minute,' he said. 'I hate chuffing uniforms.' He balled up the shirt and threw it into a corner. His body was so skinny Bea could see each one of his ribs. If I ran my fingernail up and down, he'd make a noise like a xylophone, she thought, although she had no desire to actually touch him. He caught her looking, though, and the grin was back. She did her coat up. Now he was perched on the edge of the one of the old beaten-up armchairs, watching her as he rummaged around in his pocket, apparently readjusting his groin.

'God! Stop it. There's ladies present, you know.'

He grinned. 'Unexpected item in bagging area.'

Bea gave him a withering look. 'Nobody's interested in your bagging area. Nobody.'

His grin remained.

9

'They're queuing up, girl. Join the back, if you want. I reckon that Ginny girl's interested for starters.'

Bea opened her mouth and stuck her fingers in making a retching noise. 'In your dreams,' she said. 'Seriously, take your hands out of your pocket or I'll report you.'

Ant sighed and reluctantly complied. As he brought his hand out, something fell onto the hard floor with a light, tinkling sound.

'What's that?' Bea asked.

'Nothing.' He moved his foot quickly, trapping something underneath.

'What's under your foot?'

She walked nearer to him.

'Nothing.' He tried to look at her, brazen it out, but couldn't meet her steely gaze.

'So move it.'

'Nah.'

She folded her arms across her ample chest. She could easily take him in a fight, or at least barge him away from whatever he was guarding, but then she'd have to actually make contact with him and, well, you didn't know where he'd been. No, she'd wait it out.

'Are you just going to stand there?' he asked.

'Yup.'

'Jesus.'

He moved his foot a few inches to the side to reveal a gold ring lying on the floor. They both swooped down to grab it and their heads clashed spectacularly. Bea ended up planting her bottom firmly on the floor, feet flying out. She went rolling backwards, like an upended turtle. Ant managed to put his hands down to stop himself and while Bea was righting herself, he picked up the ring.

'You little bugger—'

'What on earth—?'

Ears still ringing, Bea looked up to find Dot looking down at them both.

'We don't normally do the initiation ceremony until the second week,' she said. 'You're getting a bit ahead of yourselves. And why's he still got his trousers on? You're not doing it properly.'

She held out a hand to Bea and helped her up.

'Ha, ha. Very funny. We just ... I just ... bumped,' Bea said, dusting herself down. She was annoyed to see a big ladder in her tights.

'Hmm. Play nicely, you two.' She turned to Ant. 'You're coming back tomorrow, then? Don't let her frighten you off.'

Ant was rubbing his head.

'Yeah, I guess. I'm not a quitter.'

He and Bea exchanged looks. She watched him pocket the ring again. He put on a T-shirt, picked up his uniform from where he'd thrown it and sauntered out of the staffroom.

'Wait!' she said. 'Sorry, Dot. See you tomorrow.' She gathered up her bag and went after him. He was rounding the corner of the building when she got out of the staff exit.

'Ant! Wait!' He showed no sign of having heard her.

'Goddamn it.' She was going to have to run, something she avoided in the normal course of events. Huffing and puffing, she caught up with him halfway across the car park. She reached forward and tapped him on the shoulder.

'Didn't you hear me?'

He unplugged one earphone.

'Animal magnetism,' he said, grinning. 'Pheromones or something.'

'It's not you I want, Romeo, it's that wedding ring.'

'Bea, I like you and that. You've been a laugh today, but we've only just met—'

'I think I know whose it is.'

He kept walking.

11

'Yeah, so do I. Mine.'

'It's not yours, though, is it? *Is* it?'

She jabbed her finger into his arm. He stopped walking and turned to face her.

'It's my grandma's, okay?' he said. 'I keep it with me. It's sentimental.'

Wrong-footed, she wondered fleetingly if he was telling the truth. But this was Ant, wasn't it? Expelled from school. In and out of trouble before and since.

'That's really nice,' she said. 'Do you mind showing me?'

He pulled a face, but fished it out and held it in the middle of his palm.

'Can I—?' She picked it up and inspected it. On the outside it was a plain gold band, but there was some writing inside. 'So when exactly did your grandma get married?'

Ant shuffled his feet.

'1970?' he guessed wildly.

'You asking me or telling?'

'Telling.'

'So not the twenty-first of June 2008 then? Like the person whose ring this is.'

He puffed out his cheeks and blew out some air.

'Okay. It's not my grandma's. I found it. So it's mine. Finders keepers.'

'Where was it?'

'In one of the freezers. Eileen made me get all the chickens from the bottom, and then put in some new ones and put the old ones on top. I nearly got chuffing frostbite.'

'You were wearing gloves, weren't you?'

'Yeah.'

'Stop whining then. And the ring was in with the chickens?'

'Yeah. It had dropped down and was wedged in a layer of ice.'

Bea closed her hand around it. 'The woman who dropped

the brown sauce told me she'd lost her ring. She was so upset. I bet it's hers. I'll hand it in to Big Gav first thing tomorrow.'

His face darkened. 'Na-ah. I found it. It's mine. I could get twenty, well, a tenner for it down the Prospect. Give it here.' He held his hand out and beckoned to her with his fingers.

'No way. It's not yours. You can't sell it.'

'Do you know what they're paying me for this so-called great opportunity? Less than minimum wage.'

'It *is* an opportunity. Who else is going to give you a job round here? If you're good enough, they'll keep you on. Think about it. What's the alternative?'

'You sound like a probation worker. I was starting to like you, too. Thought we could have a laugh.'

Bea put the hand holding the ring into her pocket and clasped the strap of her bag with the other, pulling it into her body.

'Yeah, so did I, but I don't "have a laugh" with tea leaves.'

He looked at the ground and kicked at some loose stones.

'You're just like everyone else, after all. Labelling me. Writing me off. I'm not a thief.'

'That's a matter of opinion.'

She sniffed hard and stalked off in the opposite direction. She reached the main road and pressed the button at the crossing. A gust of wind caught the back of her neck. She shivered and turned up the collar of her coat. The traffic lights showed amber and then red. The green man at the crossing control lit up, but Bea stayed where she was. The driver of the car which had stopped for the lights sounded the horn. Bea glanced up and saw him gesticulating, palms up. He was mouthing something. Bea just shook her head, turned around and started running again.

She guessed that Ant lived somewhere on the ex-council estate, near the school. She jogged down an alleyway which led off the High Street and into the heart of the estate. She hadn't been this way for years – the alley was longer than she remembered.

About halfway along, she saw something blocking the light ahead. A figure, a man, was walking towards her. She felt a familiar frisson of alarm, made sharper by the words 'Kingsleigh Stalker' which were fresh in her mind. She checked behind her. It was as far to go back now as it was to press on. Why should she turn back? She had a right to be here. And this was just a bloke going for a walk. She shouldn't assume that all men were potential attackers.

As he got closer she could see that there was something walking alongside him, a dog of some sort, and she relaxed. A dog walker wasn't nearly as threatening as a man on his own.

She held her head up and kept walking. Everything was fine. A few metres away from her, the dog started barking and straining on its short leash. Bea stopped in her tracks. She could see now that its owner was only a lad, younger than her. He struggled to get the dog under control, swearing at it, and eventually gripping its studded collar and hauling the dog close to his legs.

''S okay,' he said. 'You can go past. He won't hurt yer.'

She skirted past them and jogged to the end of the alley. She decided to go left, rounded a corner and almost ran smack into Ant. He put his hands out to ward her off and ended up holding her shoulders.

'You again,' he said. 'This is getting silly. You're starting to creep me out.'

Bea needed a few moments to get her breath back. She stood in his arms-length embrace puffing and panting, mouth gasping like a fish out of water.

'Here,' she said, eventually. She held the ring between her thumb and index finger.

Ant let go of her.

'What are you doing?'

'Take it,' she said.

Slowly, he reached forward. His fingers pinched the other side of the ring, but Bea didn't let go. He pulled a little harder. So did she.

'I'm not like everyone else,' she said. A little rivulet of sweat trickled down the side of her face.

'No, okay. No offence meant.'

'So I'm giving this to you and I'm trusting you to do the right thing.'

'Take it back to work? Hand it in?' He blew out through his mouth, making a raspberry with his lips. A fine spray of spit reached Bea's face. She didn't flinch.

'Take it back to work,' she said, steadily. 'Hand it in. I trust you. I'm not like everyone else and neither are you.'

She let go of the ring.

'Goodnight, Ant. See you tomorrow.'

She turned around and started walking back towards the alley. When she was sure she was out of view, she extracted her hanky from up her sleeve and rubbed her face until it hurt.

Bea spent a restless night. As she tried to drop off to sleep she was haunted by her stupid impulsive behaviour. She had had Julie's ring in her hand and she gave it away! To Ant! What was she thinking? Let's face it, he wouldn't be back at work tomorrow, so then what would she do? Find out where he lived and go and see him? Plead with him? Buy the ring back herself? And what if he'd already got rid of it?

She tossed and turned, and when she finally drifted off, her sleep was tormented by twisted hobbity nightmares – a gold ring, dragons, dwarves, freezers and mops. She woke up at half past five in a hot sweat. As her eyes flicked open she remembered what she'd done.

'Stupid. Stupid. Stupid,' she said out loud, then looked at her alarm clock and groaned, and however much she tried she couldn't get to sleep again.

'You all right, love?' Queenie asked as Bea shuffled into the kitchen at quarter past seven. She'd set the table for break-fast like she did every day: boxes of cereal in a neat row, milk in a jug, bowls, plates, spoons and knives at the ready. 'Reckon you're a bit out of sorts, what with forgetting the rice yesterday, and now not sleeping. I heard you get up and go to the bathroom this morning. What was it? Five o'clock?'

Bea sighed. She loved her mum, but despite all the evidence over the years, Queenie had yet to grasp that Bea wasn't a morning person. What bliss it would be not to have to talk at least until after her first cup of tea. All she could manage today was a sort of grunt as she sat down opposite her and reached for the Rice Krispies.

Later, as she walked to work, she felt a twinge of guilt. Her mum probably wouldn't talk to anyone else until she came back from the supermarket in the evening. She should have made more effort. She'd try harder tomorrow.

In the staff loos Bea leaned close to the mirror. Her golden rule for bad mornings was to dab a good layer of concealer under her eyes, make the eyeliner thicker, add a jaunty flick at the corners and stick on bigger lashes. Despite the little pink veins sullying the whites of her eyes, she wasn't looking half as bad as she felt.

A cistern flushed behind her and one of the cubicle doors opened. Dot emerged, looking immaculate as ever – her uniform crisp, her hair lacquered to perfection, her nails glossy and red.

Bea had a sudden flash of insight that she was looking at her future. She wouldn't mind looking that good at

16

fifty-eight, but did she still want to be at Costsave?

'Rough night, doll?' said Dot.

'How can you tell? Do I look minging?'

'No, you look lush as ever, but you've got your megalashes on. I know you.'

'Yeah. Thank God for these babies.'

Dot washed her hands, then joined Bea at the mirror. 'You all right?'

'Yeah. Just couldn't sleep. The thing is, I did something yesterday—' She stopped. What was the point of telling her? The ring was gone, wasn't it?

'What?'

'Nothing. Doesn't matter.'

They walked into the staffroom.

'No sign of Ant, then,' Bea said morosely. 'What did I tell you?'

Dot tilted her head towards the corridor.

'He's in with Gav,' she said. 'Turned up five minutes before you did.'

Bea looked at her.

'Close your mouth, love,' said Dot, with a little smile of triumph. 'Slack-jawed isn't a good look on anyone.' She checked her watch. 'Time we weren't here. Ready for another day in paradise?'

They made their way onto the shop floor with everyone else. Even though it felt like she'd been here forever, even though it was a middle-of-the-range supermarket not Harrods, even though the first customer through the door would be Smelly Reg here to buy his Racing Post and a packet of fags like he always did, Bea still felt a tingle of anticipation in the minutes before the store opened. She made herself comfortable at checkout six, adjusted the chair back to where it should be, punched her ID into the screen and put on some hand cream. Beside her, Dot stretched out her arms and wiggled her fingers like a concert pianist preparing for bravura performance.

'All right, Gav?' Bea called out to their manager as he bustled along the row of tills towards the front door, a bundle of keys jangling at his waistband. He always liked to do the unlocking himself.

He winced visibly. 'Mr Howells, please, Beatrice. You know the rules.'

'Yes, Mr Howells. Sorry, Mr Howells.'

Dot raised her eyebrows and wagged a finger at Bea. 'Youth of today. No respect.' She winked.

Bea spotted Ant at the far end of the aisle opposite her. He appeared briefly, pushing his cleaning trolley towards the fresh veg section. He wasn't shuffling today. There was something jaunty about the way he was moving – it was almost a swagger. He glanced in her direction. She was embarrassed to be caught looking, but he grinned and gave her the thumbs up. Bea shook her head, smiling. He'd done it, then. Good for him.

The morning started slowly. Bea had a few of her regulars through – the ones that looked out for her and came to her checkout even if there wasn't a queue at one of the others. She liked to think of it as building a fan base. A smile here, a compliment there, went a long way. Some of the over-sixties liked to flirt with her. She didn't mind it up to a point, encouraged it even. It all helped to make the day pass more pleasantly.

She didn't see Julie until nearly lunchtime. She was pushing Tiffany in her pushchair with Mason trotting along beside her, trying to keep up as she powered up and down the aisles putting a few bits and bobs into a basket. Bea lit up her checkout number to summon the floor manager. It was Neville again today, clipboard clasped firmly, biro at the ready.

'The woman with the pushchair and the little boy, the one in the leather jacket—'

'Yes?'

'She lost her wedding ring, but Ant found it and gave it to Ga— to Mr Howells. Can you go and tell her?'

'Yes. Right.'

Julie was walking rapidly away from them. Neville ducked down the next aisle aiming to intercept her at the other end. Bea leaned sideways as far as she could, but she couldn't see what happened next. A couple of minutes later there was an announcement over the tannoy.

'Cleaner to management suite. Cleaner, Anthony, to the management suite, please.'

At lunchtime, Bea found Ant in the yard again. It wasn't drizzling today, but there was a cold wind whistling through the metal gates.

'You on your break too?' she said.

'Yeah. No. Bit of a nicotine top-up.'

She didn't bother pointing out the sign again.

'You brought it back then?'

'Yeah.'

'She was dead chuffed, you know. I could see when she came out of Big Gav's office. You did a good thing there.'

There was a pause, then, 'So did you. You made me think.'

'What?'

'You made me think what it would be like to be her. To lose something that means so much to you. Ach, sounds soft when you say it out loud.' He couldn't meet her eye, and instead looked at the ground and scuffed his toes in the gravel.

Bea looked down too. She was wondering what it would feel like to love someone so much you'd want to wear their ring. She wondered if it would ever happen to her.

19

'Mr Howells was well pleased,' said Ant. 'Treated me like some sort of hero.'

'Good. That's nice. You can't call him that, though,' said Bea. 'Everyone calls him Gav to his face, Big Gav behind his back. It's the rules.'

Ant grinned. 'I like those sort of rules. They're the sort I can sign up to.'

He held his hand up and, again, Bea found her hand moving to meet his.

The door to the store was open. The sound of the tannoy drifted out. 'Cleaning team to aisle four. Cleaning team to aisle four.'

'Uh-oh,' said Bea. 'That's not good.'

'What do you mean?'

'It's code. "Cleaner" is food spillage. "Cleaning team" is something biological – urine, vomit, and if you're very unlucky, poo.'

'You're kidding?' He searched her face, looking for tell-tale signs of a wind-up. Finding none, his shoulders sagged. 'Oh crap.'

'Very likely, mate. Welcome to paradise, Ant.'

2

'You're brave,' Ant said, grinning. He was leaning on Bea's checkout, having stopped on his way to do some litter-picking in the car park. He was kitted out with gloves, a thick, padded jacket with *Costsave* emblazoned across the front and back, and was carrying a black plastic bag and something that looked like long-handled tongs.

'What?'

'Sitting at checkout number six. Deano in Stores said the last four girls who sat there got knocked up.'

Bea sniffed. She smoothed down the skirt of uniform, even though it was perfectly crease free.

'I might not have any A-levels, but I do know that you don't fall pregnant by sitting on a chair.'

'What if I got there first and you're sitting on top of me?'

'You're actually making me feel sick now,' said Bea. 'You've given me the side effects of pregnancy without any physical contact. Impressive.'

'Perhaps you *want* to get pregnant. That's why you're sitting there. If so, I'm more than willing to oblige.'

'I'm sitting here because I'm not superstitious. I'm not going to get up the duff. This chair isn't special or magic or haunted. It's a chair.'

She spun it round for a full revolution to demonstrate its chair-like properties.

'I'm here if you're feeling frisky, Ant,' Dot called over. 'And I definitely won't get pregnant – I'm the wrong side of the change, so you'll be safe with me, love.'

The colour drained out of Ant's face. 'No, it's all right. I think I've just lost the urge.' He scuttled off towards the main door.

'Charming,' said Dot.

'Ne'mind, doll. Lucky escape, if you ask me. Would you really have liked it if he was interested?'

'I'm not past it, you know.'

'I know. But he's half your age, more than. That's a bit yucky, isn't it?'

'Maybe I fancy a toy boy. Besides, it's slim pickings these days.'

'You should put Bob-on-Meat out of his misery. He's been mooning after you for as long as I've been here.'

'I know, I know, but he's not, you know, very exciting, is he? Not my type.'

'He's got a pulse, hasn't he?'

'Cheeky cow.' No customers in sight, Dot swivelled her chair round so she could chat properly. 'Look at that sky. It's going to piss down in a minute. That'll dampen young Anthony down.'

'Lol. Something needs to.' Bea looked out of the window. It had certainly clouded over, and the sky was ominously dark to the west, over the High Street rooftops and the church tower.

'Missed you this morning, Bea,' said Dot. 'You on lates again today?'

'Yeah, here till ten. Queenie will have to get her own dinner tonight. I'll be keeping an eye on the lonely hearts club in aisle ten. Make sure there's no hanky-panky.'

Dot laughed and pursed her lips. 'Ooh, passion among the pot noodles.'

'Snogging by the stir in sauces.' Bea put her hands on her hips and wiggled a little bit in her seat.

'Sauciness by the steak bakes.'

'Mmm, I love Thursdays.'

Dot shuffled her chair a little closer, leaned towards Bea and lowered her voice.

'Do you ever, you know, hang about the ready meals when you're here on date night?'

'No!' She could see in Dot's eyes she didn't believe her. Perhaps she'd overplayed the outrage.

'Why not, babe?' said Dot. 'You might meet someone.'

Bea picked at a rogue spot of nail varnish near her thumbnail. 'I don't want to,' she said. 'Not the sort of creep who hangs out by the freezers in Costsave anyway.'

'Hmm. Maybe you're too picky. Maybe that's why . . . '

'Why what?' She looked up now, with a ferocity that told Dot she'd just crossed a line.

'Nothing,' she said.

'Why *what*? Spit it out, Dot.'

'Why you're single. I mean, you're a lovely girl.'

'Yeah, damn right, I am. I don't need anyone. And I don't need you poking your nose into my business.'

'Okay. Okay, I'm sorry, Bea.'

Her apology was too late. It couldn't cut through the atmosphere between them, an invisible wall between checkouts five and six. Dot slid her chair back and turned to face the next customer.

Bea busied herself with her customers too, but she was low on banter this afternoon and painfully aware of Dot's silent presence nearby. She had trouble making herself heard – the rain was lashing horizontally against the big windows a few metres away. She thought she sensed Dot glancing at her, but when she turned to look, her back was turned.

After ten minutes or so, Bea noticed Ant trailing through the main doorway to the store, dragging his litter picker behind him and leaving a small lake in his wake. Before he'd got more than a few metres, Neville pounced, sprinting from his customer service station and blocking his way.

'Not through the store like that, boy! Round the back. Round the back!' He was windmilling his arm dramatically, describing big circles in the air. Ant looked at him with an undisguised loathing. His hair was plastered to his scalp. Water dripped off his chin.

'You're kidding. I can't go out there again,' he said.

'You're not coming through the store. Out you go.'

Bea realised she was holding her breath. Was Ant simply going to punch Neville in his smug, overbearing face? But no, the lad's shoulders sagged, he put his head down and he turned around and trudged out of the shop.

'Thought Nev was going to cop it then,' said Dot.

'Yeah, me too. Some people'd pay good money to see that.'

They caught each other's eye. Bea wanted to hug Dot when she sent her a cheeky wink, but instead she just smiled and carried on working, happy that normal service had been resumed. It was coming up to her break. Kirsty was hovering behind her till, ready to take over. She was Bea's mum's age, dependable, cheerful, and quick – one of the shoppers' favourites.

'Phew,' she said. 'Thought I'd get washed away getting here today. I just beat the rain. Did you see young Anthony out in the car park? Talk about drowned rat.'

Bea smiled. 'Yeah. There's always someone worse off, isn't there?'

She eased out of her chair and headed for the staffroom. Ant had taken his fluorescent jacket off and thrown it over the back of a chair. His hair was still dripping, so were his jeans, which were saturated and shiny.

Bea reached into the cupboard under the sink and took out a tea towel.

'Here,' she said, holding it out towards Ant. 'Dry yourself off on this and then go and stand by the hand dryer in the loos. You can tip the thing so it does your hair.'

'Ah, cheers, Bea. I thought I was going to drown out there. Did you see what that tosser made me do? Walk all the way round?'

'Yeah. That's Neville for you. Rules is rules. Go on, go and get dry. I'll make you a cuppa.'

A few minutes later he emerged from the men's toilet looking a bit like a freshly laundered hedgehog.

'That's better,' Bea said with a smile, handing him his mug of tea. He sank down into an armchair, with his back to the door.

'Ta, mate. Aww, that's hitting the spot.' He held the mug with both hands and drank it quickly.

'Can't believe this place. I feel like a slave. How am I meant to say "yes, sir, no, sir" when my boss is such a dick?'

Bea's eyes grew wide as she saw Big Gav appear in the doorway. She looked from him to Ant and back again.

'Ant!' she hissed. Too late.

'Are my ears burning?' Gavin said, walking fully into the room. Ant's eyes nearly popped out of his head. His mouth fell open, just wide enough to put his other foot right in it.

'No, not you, Mr Howells. Neville – he's the—'

'He's your line manager. He's the one who reports to me and tells me whether we should keep you on or not. That one?'

Ant was slumped even further down in his chair now, defeated. He couldn't look at Gavin.

'Yeah. That's the one,' he said.

'I can't have you talking like that about any member of staff, let alone your manager.'

Bea winced. Was he going to issue an official warning?

'I'm going to pretend I didn't hear it this time, but don't let me catch you again.' He strode over to the kettle and started to make himself a cup of coffee.

Ant was still looking at the floor. 'Yes, Mr Howells. Thank you, Mr Howells.'

'Those trousers are still wet, aren't they?' His voice was softer now. 'Bea, have a rummage in the lost property cupboard. Get him some dry ones.'

When Gavin left the room, Bea told Ant where the cupboard was and to look for himself. 'I'm not his slave, or yours.'

'All right, but make me another cuppa, will you?'

She showed him her middle finger, but collected his mug and walked over to the sink.

Ant found some dry clothes. He held out the trousers and examined them. 'Who the hell loses their keks in a supermarket? Oh well.' He started peeling off his wet trousers.

'Oi! Not here! Do it in the men's toilets.'

He ignored her and although she looked away ostentatiously, she still caught a flash of his white shorts out of the corner of her eye.

'No peeping!' he said, in mock horror and, despite herself, she felt a hot blush spreading into her face. He put on the dry trousers. They were pull-on cotton khaki ones with an elastic waist, a bit too short in the leg for him. It wasn't a good look. 'There. All decent.'

He strutted around the room like a model on a catwalk, then threw himself back down on the sofa and started sipping his second cup of tea.

'Here,' he said. 'Deano said that Thursday is date night here. Was he just winding me up?'

'Nah,' said Bea. 'He's not what I'd call a reliable source, but it's true all right. It's not official, like we don't make announcements or anything or hand out roses at the door, but it's definitely a thing.'

'Seriously? So what happens? How does it work?'

'People just turn up and do a bit of shopping, but if they put a bunch of bananas in their trolley or basket it means they're single and shopping for something else too.'

Ant started laughing so violently he sprayed tea over a wide arc in front of him. 'Bananas? Love it.'

Bea smiled. 'I know. What are people like? It's quite sweet sometimes. Actually nice to see people talking to each other, rather than walking about wrapped up in their own little worlds.'

Ant wasn't listening. 'Bananas. Brilliant. What if you're a lesbo? Do you bung a couple of melons in there?'

Bea looked at him witheringly. 'Don't know. Shall I try it?'

Ant's jaw dropped open. 'What? Are you—?'

Bea raised her beautifully arched eyebrows and tapped her nose. Then without saying a word, she headed back to the shop floor.

The evening seemed to be dragging. Bea got on with all the girls on the checkouts but it was never as much fun without Dot there. She'd gone home at five, as had Ant, who had been back on general cleaning for the second half of the afternoon. He hadn't spoken to her, just given her searching, silent looks every time he passed with his cleaning cart.

This had pleased Bea greatly. She liked knowing how to press people's buttons and she had definitely got him rattled. One-nil to her.

By half past eight the store was well past the 'What's for tea?' evening rush. There were a few stragglers late home from work and a couple of frazzled parents pushing their sleepless baby around in a car seat perched on a trolley. It was a younger crowd than during the day.

Bea didn't know if her mind was playing tricks on her tonight but *everyone* seemed to be buying bananas. Not one basket or trolley was bananaless. She so wished that Dot was there to share the joke instead of being tucked up at home watching the telly.

But she wasn't at home. Because surely that was her, glimpsed nipping into the store grabbing a basket on the move and disappearing into the fresh fruit and veg. *Can't have been*, thought Bea. Dot never shopped in the evening. Like her, she just picked up what she needed at the end of a shift. No need to come back for anything. The shelves were blocking her view. It can't be, she thought. Then, Sod it, I'm going to look.

She signed off from her screen. 'I just need a wee. Can't wait,' she said to Kirsty.

'All right, love. You okay?'

'Yeah, just bursting.'

Keeping one eye on Neville at his service desk, Bea hurried along the end of the aisles and round the furthest set of shelves. As she did so, she caught a glimpse of someone disappearing around the opposite end; a well-turned-out woman, hair beautifully coiffed, belted mac, immaculate.

Bea scurried along the aisle. On her way past the bananas she noticed a man carefully selecting a bunch of large, organic fruit. He looked familiar but she couldn't place him. Just another customer, she thought. After all, she saw hundreds of people every day.

She didn't want to run and draw attention to herself so she walked as fast as she could. She grabbed the edge of the shelf to steady herself on the corner and peered round. The woman had gone. Damn! Cautiously, Bea walked past the aisles, checking each one. She ducked from shelf to shelf, stopping to look along each aisle like a cartoon spy. And then she saw her. It was quite clearly Dot, lingering by the freezers, pretending to read the description on one of the 'Best of' meals for one. She was carrying a wire basket which contained only one item – a bunch of bright yellow bananas.

'Oh, Dot, you're a sly one,' Bea muttered under her breath.

'Talking to yourself? First sign of madness.'

She wheeled round to find Ant standing behind her, uncomfortably close. She straightened up and took a step away from him, trying to reclaim her personal space. He, too, was carrying a basket with one banana in it.

'Oh God,' Bea groaned, 'not you too.'

'Why? Who else is here?'

Involuntarily, Bea looked down the aisle. It was empty. Dot had moved on.

'No one. No one you know anyway,' she said. 'What are you doing here? I thought you had girls queuing up for you?'

He pulled a face. 'I do. No harm in looking for fresh meat if it's there on a plate, is there?'

'Fresh meat? That's charming. Anyway, you're in the wrong place, mate.' Bea looked pointedly at the shelf next to them. 'You've got yoghurt and rice pudding here.'

He looked her up and down and seemed disappointed to see her empty-handed. 'Where's your basket?'

Bea sniffed hard. 'I'm not here for that. I'm *working*, remember? Just on my way to the staffroom actually.'

She started walking away from him. He walked alongside her.

'I don't need a minder,' she said. 'I know where it is.'

'I know. Just going to try my luck in the chocolate and snacks aisle. Perhaps I'll do a bit better with a box of Thorntons in my basket.'

'And a bag over your head.' Bea thought she'd said it

under her breath but apparently it had been loud enough to hear.

'Wow. That's harsh. Are you always such a bitch?'

She looked at his face. He was angry and hurt. She hadn't meant to sting him that hard. 'No. I'm sorry, Ant. It was just banter, I didn't mean . . . '

'Fuck off, Bea.'

He peeled away from her down the nearest aisle, 'Toilet Tissue and Cleaning Products'. I'd be a bit worried about anyone I picked up there, thought Bea, but Ant wasn't looking. He dumped his basket on the floor, and, head down, walked straight towards the door.

I've really hurt him, Bea thought. Damn. Typical Ant though, he could at least have put his basket back on the way out.

She walked along to the basket and picked it up. On her way to the fruit and veg section to put the banana back a man caught her eye. It was the guy with the organic fruit she'd seen earlier, the one she couldn't quite place. He smiled and looked from basket to basket.

'Snap,' he said and Bea felt her stomach lurch a little, but not in a bad way – a flutter, a tiny thrill. Blimey.

He was in his late twenties, well dressed in a nice suit, white shirt and tie. His dark hair was short at the sides, with a bit of a quiff at the front, held there by some sort of product. He was someone who looked after himself and Bea couldn't help noticing that he smelt delicious.

'Perhaps we're looking for the same thing,' he said. He wasn't smiling, but there was a softness around his mouth that said a smile wasn't far away. Bea found herself wondering what it would feel like if that face, that mouth, was closer to her. Closer. Touching . . .

'This is a staff announcement. All available staff to check-outs please. Staff to checkouts.'

The spell was broken.

30

'Ah, that's me,' she said. 'And I was just putting this back. For a friend.'

Now he did smile. 'Shame,' he said. 'Maybe another time.'

'Well,' said Bea, unable to stop herself, 'you know where to find me.'

She hurried away before he could see the full-on beetroot blush in her face. What the hell was going on? She flirted with the pensioners for a laugh, both men and women, but this was different.

She put Ant's banana back and walked quickly back to her checkout, putting the basket in the heap by the end of the conveyor belt. As she scuttled round to her seat she saw Neville approaching.

'Come and see me at the end of the shift, please, Bea. You've crossed the line this time.'

'I wasn't . . . I was just . . .'

'Not now,' he said testily, noting something down on his clipboard. 'At the end of the shift.'

He strode away.

'I didn't say anything,' said Kirsty. 'He spotted you himself. I'm sorry.'

Bea sighed. 'It looks bad, but it's not what he thinks. The thing is, I thought I saw – oh.'

The man in the suit was heading towards her checkout. They made eye contact and a little charge of electricity crackled up and down Bea's spine. He was only a few metres away when a woman in gym clothes nipped in front of him, plonked her basket onto the end and started unloading her stir-fry kit and packet of tofu.

'I'm free over here,' Kirsty called to him.

He smiled at Bea, shrugged regretfully and went over to Kirsty's checkout.

Bea turned her attention to her customer, who was radiating a heady mixture of sweat and perfume.

'Good workout?' she asked.

The woman smiled and nodded.

'Thursday night Zumba. It's the best.'

'Zumba? Is that the dance-y one? With music and the fancy footwork?'

'Yeah, that's it. It's fantastic. You should give it a try.'

As the words left her mouth, a look of mortification flashed across the woman's face. 'I didn't mean, you know, that you need to ... I just ... ' she spluttered, trying to look anywhere but at Bea's size sixteen self.

Bea blushed for her and for herself, painfully aware that Suit Guy was still within earshot at the neighbouring checkout. 'It's fine,' she said. 'I can take it – I'm a big girl.'

The woman bit her lip.

'Honestly, don't worry' Bea said. 'I have tried it, actually. It's bloody fast, though, isn't it? Found myself half a beat behind everyone else.'

'Oh, that's normal,' the woman said. 'Until you learn the routines. Everyone starts off like that. You mustn't let it put you off.'

'I'm here two out of four Thursdays, anyway.'

'You don't have to sign up. It's a drop-in.'

'Maybe, then.' She'd finished ringing through the shopping. 'That's £9.35. Do you have a Bonus Card?'

There were small queues building up now. By the time Zumba Woman had paid and gathered up her stuff, the next one was loaded up and waiting. Bea glanced sideways, but Cute Suit Guy had gone. She started processing the shopping. A bunch of bananas, an individual pizza, a bar of dark chocolate and a bottle of gin.

'Got all your major food groups covered there,' Bea said.

Her customer, a tired-looking woman in her thirties, gave her a wan smile.

'Yeah. Bridget bloody Jones, me.'

'I love that film,' said Bea.

'Me too.'

Later, when she'd received the regulation bollocking from Neville about leaving her station for 'unapproved reasons', Bea set off for home. She'd bought Queenie a box of Maltesers (normal price £2, reduced to £1) to make up for an evening alone. It was a twenty-minute walk through the streets and alleys she'd known her whole life. This morning's rain was long gone, and the wind had died down. She walked briskly along the wet pavements, thinking about the day's events, priming some stories in her head to amuse her mum. She might tell her about Dot's mysterious appearance this evening, and she'd definitely mention Ant getting drenched this morning and his run-in with Neville and Big Gav, but she'd keep Cute Suit Guy to herself. You need a bit of space if you're twenty-one and still living at home. And after all, it was nothing anyway.

She turned into the alleyway that led from the High Street to the estate. Halfway along she heard footsteps behind her. The words 'Kingsleigh Stalker' came into her head.

She tried to push them away. I've got every right to walk here without feeling frightened, she thought. I live here. These are my streets as much as anyone's.

The noise seemed to be getting closer. She picked up her pace. If I look round now, she thought, they'll know I'm nervous. It'll just make things worse. All her attention was behind her, on the unseen, the unknown. The skin on her neck and back was crawling at the thought of a stranger's touch.

This was silly. Just look. It was probably another woman, walking home from work like her. Don't look. Don't show any weakness, any sign of nerves. The end of the alleyway was twenty metres ahead.

Sod it. She clutched her handbag closer to her body and started to run.

She clattered out of the alleyway and turned right to skirt around the edge of the recreation ground. She carried on running for a while. Normally she'd go straight across, but it was exposed out there, lonely. She'd stay near the houses that led onto the green. She could run up to a front door, if she needed to.

Finally, with the breath painful in her lungs and sweat beading under her arms and between her shoulder blades, she slowed to a walk and allowed herself to look behind. The end of the alleyway was poorly lit. Did she see a shadow disappearing back into the alley? Something more solid, someone's back? Or was it nothing after all?

Fool, she told herself. Overactive imagination playing tricks again. She followed the path round to the other side of the park and then walked through the estate roads to the small 1960s terraced house she shared with Queenie. She let herself into the kitchen by the back door, which was unlocked as usual.

'All right, Queenie, it's only me,' she called out.

Her mum was in the front room, with the television on. News at Ten boomed out at a ridiculous volume. Without taking her coat off, Bea walked through.

'Oh,' her mum said, looking up as she entered the room. 'I didn't hear you come back.'

'I'm not surprised with that thing blaring out.' Bea grabbed the remote and turned down the sound a few notches. She was surprised to find her hand shaking. 'Here, these are for you.' She took the Maltesers out of her bag and handed them over. Her copy of the *Bugle* fell onto the floor. She picked it up and put it on the coffee table.

Her mum put her box of chocolates down and held Bea's hand in hers.

'What's up, love? You're trembling.'

'It's nothing. I'm fine.' But she wasn't. She was overcome with relief at being back at home. It was all she could do not to cry.

'No, you're not,' said Queenie and drew her down onto the sofa next to her and put her arms round her. 'What's happened?'

'Nothing. Really. Big, fat nothing. I'm being silly.' She should keep it buttoned. Her mum's view of the outside world was skewed enough without her adding to it. But she couldn't help herself. It all came blurting out. 'I thought I was being followed home, but I wasn't. Just gave myself a scare, that's all.'

'You were followed?'

'No. No, I just thought I was but I wasn't. I thought I heard someone, but when I turned around there wasn't anyone, or they'd gone the other way. It's all good, Mum, honestly.'

'You weren't walking down the alley?'

The *Bugle* was right side up on the table in front of them.

'Yes, but—'

'I've told you and told you not to walk there. Not after dark. Not anytime.'

'It's perfectly all right. I walk there every day. I'm okay, aren't I? I've got as much right to walk there as anyone—'

'Yes, you have, but there are a lot of nasty people out there, my lovely. It's all on the news – muggers, thieves, stalkers, rapists. This country's not like it was when I was your age.'

'It is, though, Mum. That's the point. It's exactly the same, it's just that every little thing gets reported. And that's what you see. All the bad stuff on the telly. They don't report the 99 per cent of people who are just going about their business, no trouble to anyone.'

Her mum shook her head and pulled Bea a little closer.

'Bless you, you're still so naïve. It's a nightmare out there, baby girl. It's not safe.'

She hugged her close and they stayed like that for a minute or two. When Bea got up she picked up the paper from the table and tucked it under her arm.

'Oh, is that this week's *Bugle*?' said Queenie.

'Yeah, but there's nothing in it. I'll put it in the recycling box.'

Queenie looked confused. 'Aren't you going to give me a chance to read it? Don't be daft. Hand it over.' She held out her hand.

Bea gave it to her and winced as Queenie unfolded it and spread it out on her knees.

'What's this?' Queenie said. 'Oh my God.'

'It's not really anything, though, when you read it. A few isolated incidents. It might not even be one person.'

Queenie was scanning the article, her face creased with concern.

'Bea,' she said, 'do you think it was him just now?'

'No,' said Bea. 'I don't even know if it was anyone. It might have been someone walking their dog, or nipping to the shops.'

'But they ducked back when they thought you might see them.'

'Maybe they ducked back when they realised their dog had done its business or they'd forgotten their money. It probably wasn't anything.'

Feeling calmer now and convinced that she'd imagined the whole thing, Bea disentangled herself and went into the kitchen to make their evening cups of tea. They watched the end of the news together and a documentary about pest control staff in inner-city London, then went to bed.

As she tried to sleep, Bea heard a droning in the distance which soon turned into the distinctive noise of the police helicopter. It was almost overhead, then moved away and circled back again. Probably after joyriders, Bea thought.

The noise seemed to go on for hours. In the end, Bea fired up her phone and looked at her Twitter feed. There were a couple of tweets complaining about the noise, but no explanation. She quickly typed a tweet: 'Whassup Kingsleigh? Why the chopper?'

She kept scrolling and refreshing and a few minutes later the first answer came through.

'3 cop cars at Westrope Avenue. Somethins kicking off.'

Westrope was only a few streets away.

Before long there was an official tweet from the regional police: 'Police helicopter assisting with a serious incident in Kingsleigh.'

Serious incident. She tried searching elsewhere on the Internet, but Twitter was the only place there was any news, and there wasn't much substance to any of it. Bea stayed awake until the noise overhead finally faded away. Somewhere between being asleep and awake, she remembered where she'd seen Cute Suit Guy before. The knowledge gave her a dull sinking feeling in her stomach, but she was too tired to be angry. That came when she woke up the next morning. It was the first thing she thought after she'd reached blindly for her alarm and switched it off. Cute Suit Guy wasn't so cute after all. And he had a name. Dave. It was his photograph in Julie's purse, the woman who had lost her wedding ring.

Bea groaned. 'I should have known. What a loser.' Though she wasn't quite sure whether the loser was her for fancying him or him for turning up at Costsave's date night with his bananas at the ready. Not classy, mate, she thought, even if your bananas are organic.

Dot caught up with her in the High Street. Despite the October gloom, she was wearing sunglasses. 'You all right, babe? I texted you this morning but you didn't reply.'

'Yeah, why wouldn't I be?'

'Girl got attacked up your way last night.'

Bea stopped walking and put her hand on Dot's arm. 'Oh shit. Is that what it was? I heard the helicopter.'

'It was on the local news this morning. Westrope Avenue, that's near you, isn't it? They didn't get anyone for it though. Not yet.'

'Do you know what time?'

''Bout half ten, they said.'

Bea felt her mouth go dry. 'Fuckin' 'ell.'

'I know. Looks like that stalker story was real. Shocking, isn't it?'

'It's not just that, Dot. I was followed last night, walking home. I heard someone and then I thought perhaps I'd imagined it, but now ...'

'God, Bea. Did you see him?'

'Not really. Maybe a glimpse of the back of him, disappearing back into the alley.'

'The alley? Oh, Bea!' Dot gave Bea a quick hug and they started walking again, arms linked.

They crossed the car park and headed round the side of the store to the staff entrance, then made straight for the ladies' locker room. They hung up their coats and put on their uniforms; polo shirts and branded nylon tabards over the top. Bea swapped her heavy flat boots for a pair of black ballet pumps. Then she got out her make-up bag and set it down by the mirror. Dot was there before her. With her dark glasses removed, she looked pretty rough.

'Blimey, what happened to you?' asked Bea.

'Up too late. Too much wine. The usual, love,' Dot said, rummaging in her make-up bag. Bea wondered if now was the time to admit she'd spotted her in store last night, but there was something defiant about the way Dot was dabbing concealer under her eyes. Better to leave it. They went into the staffroom, which was abuzz with news of the attack.

'Apparently it was a girl called Emma,' Dean from Stores said, tucking a length of greasy hair behind his ear. It was unusual for him to venture into the staffroom – he usually preferred to keep to himself in the loading bay or storage area, nibbling his home-made sandwiches and drinking tea from a flask. Seems like gossip had lured him in today, though.

'Emma Crosby?' Bea said.

'Yeah, think so,' he said.

'I know her. She was two years above me at school. God, I'm sure she was in the store yesterday. Is she ... I mean, what actually ...'

'Assault is what they're saying. Sexual assault.' Dean seemed to linger on the word 'sexual' emphasising each of its three syllables in turn. Bea shivered.

'There are some nutters out there,' said Ant, walking into the room. 'Disgusting. Tell you what, though, two coppers in uniform just came round the back into the store. I let them in. They were asking for Big Gav.'

A ripple of excitement spread around the room.

'Big Gav?'

'Ha! They've caught up with him at last!'

'Shut up, that's not even funny.'

'What do they want with him?'

Neville appeared in the doorway. He was holding his clipboard in one hand and the store keys in the other.

'Five minutes, everyone,' he said, like the stage manager warning of curtain up. 'To your posts, please.'

'Hey, Neville,' said Bea. 'How come you're opening up?'

'Mr Howells is in a meeting at the moment. That's all I can say.'

'Helping the police with their enquiries,' said Bea. 'That's what they call it, isn't it?'

'No, that's when they've got them down the station. Trust me, I know. I think they're just having a chat,' said Ant. 'God, I'm parched. I'll just grab some water.' He squeezed past Dot to get to the sink. 'All right?' he said quietly to her.

Dot didn't look at him, but she seemed to colour up a little under her thick layer of make-up. 'All right,' Dot said back, and quickly moved towards the door. 'You coming?' she said to Bea.

'Yeah,' Bea said back. 'I'll be right there.'

There was a copy of the *Bugle* on the coffee table. Bea went over and looked at the front page again. She felt cold inside, sure now that she'd had a near miss.

She took a couple of deep breaths and headed into the corridor. Ant was walking a little way in front, whistling. Bea couldn't place the tune. She was about to follow him down the stairs when she stopped. She should tell the police about what had happened last night.

Emma had been attacked. It could have been her.

3

Bea stood nervously outside Big Gav's office door. Her guts were achy and churning. She was just debating taking refuge in the toilet when the door opened.

'Did you want something, Bea?' Big Gav was looking pale and flustered.

'No. I mean, yes. I've got something to tell the police.' She looked past him to the two uniformed officers who were sitting at his desk with their backs to the door. Hearing her voice, one of them turned around. Bea recognised his freckly face and blue eyes. It was Tom Barnes, who had been to her primary school until his family moved to the other side of Bristol in year six. She'd always rather liked him. He was one of those nice, shy boys – the ones who don't call you names or pull your hair. He wouldn't remember her, though, would he? He smiled and stood up.

'Beatrice,' he said.

His companion, an older woman with neat short mousey hair, groaned and stood up too.

'Do you know everyone round here?' she said.

'No,' said Tom. 'Just the troublemakers.'

He took two steps across the room and held his hand out to Bea. He towered above her, which she wasn't expecting as they'd been about the same height back in the day. A bit discombobulated, but not wanting to be rude, her hand met his. His handshake was firm, his hand large and strong, warm but not clammy.

'Beatrice,' he said again. 'I don't suppose you remember me. Saint Stephen's in Cow Lane.' He smiled and his sandy skin crinkled at the outside corners of his eyes.

'I remember,' she said. 'Course I do. And it's Bea these days. Everyone calls me Bea.'

'Right you are,' he said. 'You wanted to see us. Do come in. This is Shaz,' he said, indicating the other officer.

'We can use this office for a while, can't we?' Shaz said to Gavin, who was lingering in the doorway.

'Yes. Yes, of course.' He made no sign of leaving.

'Thank you, Sir. We'll let you know when we've finished.' She stepped smartly over to the door and closed it firmly as Tom ushered Bea into Gavin's chair.

Bea felt a little thrill to be sitting at Big Gav's desk. It was neat and tidy, as you'd expect, almost sparse with only a lamp, a PC and keyboard, a phone and a framed photograph of Gavin's wife, Stephanie. His chair was disappointingly rickety and oddly uncomfortable. Good old Costsave, she thought. Cheap to the top.

'So, Bea, what did you want to tell us?'

Her nerves had dissipated with the unexpected pleasure of seeing Tom again, but now they came back.

'It's probably nothing. I don't know, and I didn't see anything but—' She paused, suddenly feeling foolish. She really did have very little to tell.

'It's okay,' Shaz encouraged. 'Anything you can tell us about last night, big or small, may help us.'

So she told them – about the alley and the footsteps, and not quite seeing who it was. If it was anyone. They questioned her closely about the time, which, as a creature of routine, she was able to pinpoint.

'Okay, that's really helpful. Emma was attacked about ten minutes after that.'

'She'd been to Costsave, hadn't she?'

'We can't discuss the details. You understand.'

'Of course. I didn't mean to pry.'

'We'd better not keep you any longer.'

She felt herself dismissed, but on the way out Tom said, 'Don't walk down that alley on your own. Better to keep safe. It was good to see you again, Bea.'

'Yeah. Likewise.'

When Bea opened the door, Gavin was lurking outside. He was sweating and he ran his finger between his collar and neck.

'Everything okay?' he said.

'Yeah.'

'Back to work, then.'

Bea walked downstairs and opened up her checkout. She was thinking about the walk home, the footsteps, her panic. She was thinking about PC Tom, too; how tall he was, his crinkly smile.

'You all right, doll? Where've you been?'

'Just told those coppers about being followed.'

'Oh, good idea. They tell you anything?'

'Nah, but I reckon she was here that evening. I remember talking to her. I'm gonna find Hermione at break time – see if she's got anything on the CCTV.'

'Hermione' was actually Anna who worked in the office. She looked nothing like Emma Watson with her short, straight blond hair and black-rimmed glasses, but she knew everything about Costsave's IT systems. Security, stock checking, personnel records, shift allocations – Hermione could skip her way through them with a few clicks of her mouse. As luck would have it, their breaks coincided so Bea took her cup of tea and sat next to her on one of the almost-collapsing sofas where Anna was eating fruit from a plastic pot.

'Hey H, how's it going?'

Anna pulled a face. 'It's all the drama today. Not the sort of drama I want to be part of though. Emma's friends with my little sister.'

Bea leaned forward eagerly. 'Do you know what happened then? Is she okay?'

'I dunno. They're being very cagey about releasing details, aren't they?'

'Mm. Have you looked at last night's CCTV?'

'No, but the police have. I had to find the footage for them. They're looking right now. I overheard them talking earlier. They think she may have been followed from the store.'

'Will they take the footage away?'

Anna popped a slice of apple into her mouth.

'S'all digital. I can just copy them the stuff they need.'

'So we could have a look together? Lunchtime or after work?'

Anna's eyebrows disappeared into her short fringe and she tutted. 'That would be inappropriate, wouldn't it, Bea? Illegal actually. Only us authorised people can view the tapes.'

'Oh, come on, H.'

'Why are you interested anyway?'

'It's personal. I know Emma as well, from school, plus I think the toerag followed me too.'

'Really? God, lucky escape. Look, I'll try and have a look myself. I can't promise anything, though. It's all go today.'

Back on the shop floor, Bea found it hard to settle. She was on autopilot as she scanned the shopping through. Lucky escape, she thought. Why was I lucky and Emma wasn't? Why should either of us have to put up with this?

Her fear and unease were rapidly turning to anger. She

found herself repeatedly trying to scan a reduced price bag of salad without success, turning it round, trying to stretch the plastic wrapping to make the bar code flatter. Her customer, a middle-aged man in a hurry, kept looking at her then checking his watch.

'Try typing in the number,' he said testily.

'Yeah, I know what to do. It *should* scan, though.'

'But it's not, is it? If something doesn't work, the smart thing isn't to keep trying the same thing.'

She stopped scanning altogether and stared at him. 'Thank you for that,' she said, very loudly and very slowly. 'I guess I'm just not smart enough.'

Dot glanced over her shoulder and frowned. Bea started feeding in the numbers beneath the barcode. 'Just trying to help. No offence, love,' her customer said.

Bea stopped typing for a moment, then after a couple of deep breaths, started again. She told him his total, processed his Bonus Card and bank card and willed him to get out of her sight.

'Nearly lost it there – that's not like you. Are you all right?' Dot said.

Bea was surprised to find she was close to tears. Dot was right. This wasn't like her. She was tougher than that. She took another deep breath. 'Yeah. I'm fine.'

She looked along her queue. The next customer was the Julie, the Wedding Ring woman, Dave's wife. Give me strength, thought Bea. Why couldn't you use another checkout? Why me?

She had both kids with her again. Mason was helping her put things on the conveyor belt, stretching up on tiptoes and reaching over the edge.

'That's a good boy helping your mum,' said Bea, forcing a smile onto her face. To Julie she said, 'Do you need any help with packing?'

'Yes, that would be great,' she replied. She rummaged around in her bag and brought out a tangle of reusable bags and put them in the packing area, then finished loading her shopping onto the belt. Bea noticed that there was a big plaster on her ring finger.

'Better safe than sorry, eh?' she said.

Julie looked confused.

'Won't fall off in the freezer again.'

'Oh, the ring. Yes.'

She didn't seem to want to talk. Not surprising with a load of shopping to get done and two toddlers in tow. Bea packed her shopping for her and told her the total.

'Have you got your Bonus Card?'

'Oh yes.'

Again, the purse was open and there was Dave's face looking out. Bea tutted to herself, but didn't say anything more than thanking her for the cash when she handed it over.

'And there's your change. Have a nice day.'

And on to the next one, a pensioner with just a sliced loaf, two tins of cat food and a meat pie in her basket.

She fumbled for the money, but didn't have enough cash. She slid the pie towards Bea. 'Put that back, then,' she said. 'I'll make do with toast.'

Bea frowned. For a moment she wondered about dipping into her own pocket and paying for the pie. She also considered letting the pie find its way into the woman's shopping bag unscanned. But it was a slippery slope. A good number of her customers couldn't afford all their shopping. Happened every day.

'Okay,' she said. She had a supply of little cards at her till advertising the local food bank. She slipped one into the woman's hand, who looked at it and handed it back.

'No, thanks, pet. I'm fine,' she said.

Bea watched her walk away. Her steps were slow and uncertain, but her back was poker-rod straight.

As she was watching, she heard the clump of heavy boots in unison. The two police officers were walking along the outside of the checkouts, deep in conversation. Bea felt a pang of disappointment as they passed by without Tom seeming to notice her at all. She started processing the next batch of shopping.

'Good afternoon. Would you like any help with packing?'

The tannoy spluttered into life. It was a female voice this time: 'This is a staff announcement. Would Bea Jordan report to the office, please? Bea Jordan to the office.'

Bea leant along the conveyor belt and put her 'Checkout Closing' sign out. She finished dealing with the customer she had and then signed out of her till.

'You're popular,' Dot said as Bea left her station.

'No rest for the wicked. I'll be back in a minute,' she said and scuttled across the shop towards the staff door at the back. She passed Ant on her way. He had a trolley full of bread and breakfast bakes.

'Ooh, restocking,' Bea said. 'You've gone up in the world.'

Ant scratched his head. 'It's not as easy as you'd think,' he said. 'You haven't got a minute, have you?'

'Nah, I'm off to the office, then I'm back on checkouts. Hasn't Eileen shown you what to do?'

'Yeah, but—'

'Just do that, then. Simples.' And she was off, through the staff door and up the stairs to what was laughingly referred to as the management suite – two offices off a grey corridor. She knocked on the main office door and went in.

Hermione was sitting at one of the desks. The other was empty. 'Close the door,' she said. 'If anyone asks, I was checking a discrepancy on your time sheet.'

'Oh, right. There isn't one, is there?'

'No, of course not. Look, I can't actually show you this, but I need to photocopy your time sheet, so ... ' Anna walked over to the photocopier by the door, and Bea quickly sat down in Anna's chair.

She looked at the screen, which was frozen on a grainy black and white image, and pressed 'play'.

There was an image of a woman entering the shop and picking up a basket. The camera was above her and Bea could clearly see the furry hood of her parka jacket and her hair drawn back in a tight ponytail. Emma.

The store layout meant that pretty much everyone walked through the fresh fruit and veg area first, unless they veered off left to the cigarette kiosk or determinedly aimed for another specific aisle. Emma wasn't one of those. She walked at a steady pace to the bananas and picked up a bunch. There were four men in the fruit and veg section. Bea froze the screen and peered closer.

'There's Ant,' said Bea. 'I know he was there yesterday. Look at him lurking there by the marrows – he couldn't be more obvious, could he? The other three are customers, I reckon. Who's she talking to? Can I zoom in?'

'Control-A it.'

'Oh,' said Bea. 'It's him.'

'Who?'

'He tried to chat me up. He's married.'

Anna nodded sagely.

'You don't seem surprised,' said Bea.

'I'm surprised that you are,' she said. 'Singles night at Costsave is just the place you'd expect to find married men looking for a bit of extra-curricular you-know-what.'

'Really?'

'Oh, bless you. You have much to learn.'

Bea pulled a face. 'I thought he was quite nice, there was something about him. Felt like a fool when I realised.'

'You didn't do anything?'

'God, no, just chatted.'

'Well, you're all right then. No harm done.'

Bea pressed play again. Emma was walking out of shot, so Anna showed Bea how to switch cameras to follow her progress. Bea had always known the cameras were there, of course, but didn't realise the detail they could pick up. She watched a woman casually put a half-bottle of booze in the inside pocket of her coat, before she went to the checkout with some cans of Coke. She also saw Bob-on-Meat scratching his backside. And she saw Emma, making her way around the store, Dot lingering by the ready meals, and herself talking to Ant and then him dumping his basket and storming out.

She was peering at the screen when she heard Anna say, 'Uh-oh, incoming.'

There was a shadow the other side of the frosted window in the office door. Bea jumped out of Anna's chair and Anna started walking back to her desk. As Gavin came in she was saying, 'So, I think you'd just put the wrong date on your sheet, because if that was the twenty-fourth instead then the shift rota and the time sheets match.'

'Yes,' said Bea. 'That must have been it. Slip of the pen. Thanks for sorting it out, Herm— Anna.'

Gavin gave her a quizzical look, but let her pass him in the doorway without comment.

'You're welcome,' Anna said, smoothly. 'See you later.'

As Bea went back to the shop floor she could hear raised voices in the bread aisle. She rounded the corner and saw Ant, Eileen and Neville standing by the sliced loaves.

'I'm disappointed in you, Eileen. You're meant to be supervising the boy, teaching him the basics. Stock rotation isn't rocket science. Even Anthony should be able to do it.'

Eileen was gaping at him, trying to get a word in edgeways,

49

her face red and flustered. 'I did tell him. Look at the date on the label. Near dates to the front, far dates to the back. I told you, didn't I?' Now she was looking daggers at Ant, who looked down like he was inspecting the floor, maybe hoping for a hole to open up and swallow him.

'Yeah,' he said, 'you did. It's not your fault. I'm just ... I didn't ... I dunno.'

Neville stared at him, nostrils flaring.

'That's it, is it? "I dunno." Give me strength. If you don't understand something, *ask*.'

Ant dragged his eyes up from the floor and looked from Eileen to Neville and back again.

'I couldn't, could I? Eileen was off—' Eileen's daggers turned to samurai swords 'off ... helping someone else, see?' He caught sight of Bea. 'Anyway, I did ask for help. I asked *her*.'

Three pairs of eyes now fixed themselves on Bea. She held her hands up in surrender.

'Whoa. Okay. He did ask me but I couldn't stop there and then, 'cos I'd been called to the office. I would've stopped on my way back ...'

Neville sighed a long and weary sigh.

'All right, all right. I've had enough. Eileen, can you stay and make sure he finishes the bread properly, please? Anthony, concentrate. And you,' he looked at Bea as if she was something stuck on the bottom of his shoe, 'you get back to your checkout. There are customers waiting.'

'Yes, I'm just going. I didn't even—' No point trying to reason with him. Bea marched down the aisle and along to checkout six. Dot looked up as she approached.

'You in trouble with Gav? Get the ruler out, did he? Six of the best?'

'No,' Bea said, settling down and logging on to her screen. 'Gav's fine. Just had a little run-in with Neville. He's being an ar—' Her first customer was right in front of her, so Bea

50

swallowed the word she'd been about to say and switched on her Costsave smile. 'Good morning. Do you need any help packing?'

At the end of their shift, Bea and Dot walked to the locker room together. Eileen was already in there, buckling up her coat.

'Bleurgh, that was a day, wasn't it?' Bea said.

'You're telling me,' said Eileen. 'He's nice enough, but that boy's useless. Even when I was standing over him, he couldn't shelve properly to save his life. Even my Dean can do that. I don't know what they teach them these days.' She picked up her handbag and headed for the door. 'Night, ladies. I'm back on Monday. See you then.'

'Have a good weekend, Eileen. Don't do anything I wouldn't do,' Dot called after her. 'How are you getting home?' she asked Bea.

'Walking, like usual. It's not quite dark yet.' Bea shivered, and Dot put a hand on her arm.

'Why don't you get a taxi? Shall we share one?'

Bea was tempted but part of her resented having to shell out and another part resented being frightened off the streets. 'Nah, I'll be okay. We can go to the end of the High Street together, can't we? Then I won't walk ... you know ... I'll go the long way round.'

They were on their way down the stairs when they heard a loud noise from the men's locker room, like a metal door slamming. They both stopped and looked at each other, and then turned to see Ant storming out of the room and bombing down the stairs towards them.

'Hey, hey, hey!' Dot shouted before he barged into them.

He shook his head angrily and said, 'Not now. I'm out of here. I ain't coming back either.' He was so clearly in a strop that the two women parted and flattened themselves against opposite walls to let him through.

'Ant,' Dot called. 'Don't do anything hasty, pet.'

Ant didn't answer, just flung his hands up as he reached the bottom of the stairs and blasted out of the side exit.

'That's that, then, is it?' Dot said. Bea didn't know if she was saying to her or to herself.

'It's probably nothing,' she said. 'He'll be back. What else is he going to do?'

They started down the stairs again when they heard someone else behind them.

''Scuse me, ladies,' said Hermione. 'Got a bus to catch.'

They flattened themselves again.

'See you Monday,' she called behind her. Then she too was out of the side door and gone.

'Let's get out of here before anyone else comes,' said Dot. 'It's like Piccadilly Circus.'

Queenie texted her as she was crossing the car park.

You walking home?

Yeah.

Not the alley. Keep your phone on.

Okay, see you soon. Xxx

When Bea tried the back door, it was locked. Her mum opened it from inside.

'Come in, love,' she said. 'I've been waiting for you.' She locked the door behind her.

'What's all this? Fort Knox?'

'I'm keeping it like that till they get him. We should keep it locked anyway, shouldn't we?'

'No, I mean, maybe. I don't know. Let's get the kettle on, and the oven. I've got the fish.'

Friday night – breaded fish and oven chips, and a couple of chocolate bars for pudding. When it was ready, they settled down in front of the TV. They watched the local news, like they did every day. Queenie gave a little squeak as a picture of Costsave came up.

'It's you, look!'

Bea flapped her hand at her.

'Sh, Mum, let's listen.'

It was a short item about the attack, clearly saying that Emma had been to Costsave that evening and that she may have been followed from there. There was more footage of her walking route home, including the alley, followed by the usual appeal for information. Bea put down her fork and pushed the plate to the far edge of the tray.

'I don't think I can eat the rest.'

'Come on, Bea. You've hardly touched your chips.'

'Nah.'

She took her tray into the kitchen and scraped the remains of the meal into the food waste bin by the sink. She stood for a minute, leaning on the worktop, thinking again about what might have happened. What had actually happened. Bastard, she thought. You're not going to get away with this.

She went back to the lounge and opened up her laptop.

The CCTV footage that she'd seen hadn't really shown her much more than she already knew. This is what she did all day; watch people, listen, observe. She had been there. She was a witness.

She started a simple Word file, listing the men she remembered seeing – staff and customers. She set about it systematically, trying to recall the evening as it happened, with her customers in sequence. Once she got started it was almost as if the memories were stored digitally in her head. One customer lead to another, the flow broken by her sighting and pursuit of Dot around the aisles.

It was easy to list the staff members on duty that night. The customers were more difficult. She didn't know most of the names, but jotted down descriptions.

'Any gossip? You on Facebook?'

Bea looked up. Queenie wasn't watching the TV any more. She was watching her.

'Huh?'

'You, typing away there. You missed the whole of The One Show. They had that actor on – you know, the one with the hair. I've been talking to you and you haven't heard a word.'

'I'm working.'

'Working?'

'Well, sort of. Working at something.'

'What?'

Damn, thought Bea. Don't get her involved. She won't like it.

'Working at . . . revamping my winter wardrobe. Online shopping.'

'Oh, right. Don't spend too much, love. Better to buy things you can afford outright, than get things on tick.'

'Yes, yes. I know.' Quick, distract her. 'You had your choccy yet? What's on now? *EastEnders*?'

'Ooh, yeah.' Queenie settled back down and gave her full attention to the TV again, and Bea got on with her sleuthing. She mentally got to the end of her shift and then pictured her walk home. This was more difficult. She closed her eyes for a minute to try and bring things into focus.

'That's not Top Shop, Bea.'

Bea jumped and slammed the laptop lid down. Queenie was standing by the side of her chair, looking down. Bea hadn't even noticed her coming over.

'That's a list of names. What are you doing?'

'It's . . . I'm . . .'

'Don't even try to lie to me. Just tell me the truth.'

Bea hesitated, but it was no good. She'd just have to fess up. 'I'm trying to find out who attacked Emma, who followed me.'

Queenie put her hand on Bea's shoulder.

'That's for the police to do, isn't it?'

'I know. I'm just . . . I want to *do something*. I don't want to be scared. I want to fight back.'

Queenie sat down on the arm of the chair and put her arms round Bea. 'I don't want you to be scared either,' she said, kissing her hair. The air around them was stuffy from the electric fire and heavy with things unsaid, unsayable. Words tiptoed to the edge of Bea's tongue and then retreated. How could she talk about fear with the woman who had let it disable her for years? Who found the outside so overwhelming she'd stayed inside.

They drew apart a little.

'The thing is,' Queenie said, 'if you try to track him down, love, you could put yourself in even more danger. I don't want that.'

'I'm not going to do anything silly, Mum. I'm going to find a name and then give it to the police. That's all. It's a small town. There are only so many people it could be. I want to prove he's not beaten me. I want to prove I'm smart enough.'

'You're the smartest person I know.'

'Hmph.'

'It doesn't matter about exams and certificates, you've got it all up here.' Queenie gently tapped the side of Bea's head. 'Not like me. Empty.' She balled up her hand and knocked on her own head, like she was knocking on wood. They both laughed.

'Don't be daft,' said Bea.

'Can't help it. Put that laptop away now. You've not had your Wispa yet. Do you want an old *Vicar of Dibley* or *Gardeners' World*?'

'Neither, really.' Her mum carried on looking at her – these were the only choices. 'Okay, *Dibley*.'

'*Dibley* it is.'

Bea watched for a while, then went upstairs to have a bath

and put on her onesie. When she went back down again, Queenie was asleep in her chair. Bea quietly opened her laptop again. She read through the list and replayed events in her head. She took the laptop up to bed with her, and kept looking at the screen, wondering about the people on her list. If Emma was sexually assaulted, the motive was obviously sexual. She tried to think who, out of her colleagues, would do that to anyone? They were an odd lot but she couldn't imagine any of them hurting someone. Maybe it was one of the customers . . .

By two in the morning, her head was spinning. The laptop was still open, the screen still bright, but by now she was so tired she couldn't see the wood for the trees. She turned the machine off, snuggled down under her duvet and tried to sleep. But there were too many questions jostling for her attention. How come Emma was attacked after she herself had been followed, when she had left the store before her? Was David, the married man, just sleazy or was he more sinister? Did Bob-on-Meat scratch his arse inside or outside his trousers? There was something else too, something about Ant . . .

She must have drifted off because she woke up the next morning with her head feeling like it was full of cotton wool. She dragged herself downstairs, wishing she'd left the laptop in the lounge last night and had three hours' extra sleep.

Queenie was up and about as usual. She poured Bea a cup of tea.

'Saturday today,' she said brightly. 'Sausage sandwiches. You won't forget to pick them up, will you?'

Bea sighed.

'Course not. I won't forget.' And then something from yesterday drifted to the front of her mind and she shuddered. 'Must remember I'm getting the pre-packed ones, though, Queenie.'

'Pre-packed?'

'I'm never going near Bob-on-Meat's sausages again.'

Later, as she walked through town, Bea caught sight of a familiar figure crossing the road ahead of her. He had his hood pulled up round his ears and his head down. She trotted a few yards to catch up with him.

'Hey! Ant! Wait up.'

Ant stopped but didn't turn around. She drew level with him.

'You going in to work, after all?'

He shook his head.

'Nah, heading home.'

She ostentatiously checked her watch.

'Wow, you lead an exciting life. All right for some. You *are* coming back, though, aren't you?'

He shrugged. 'No. Dunno. Maybe. Not due in until Monday. Gonna think about it.'

They walked along together.

'Don't let Eileen and Neville put you off.'

'I don't care about them.'

'I'm sorry I didn't help you.'

'Not your problem.'

Bea hesitated. Along with Bob's unsettling personal habits another thought had emerged from the fog of her brain. It was only a hunch, but ... 'Shelving isn't easy, especially if—' in for a penny 'especially if you can't read.'

Ant laughed. 'Shut up. What are you talking about? I can read.'

She peered round the edge of his hood. His face was colouring up.

'There's no shame in it, Ant. Maybe I could help you.'

He stopped walking and turned to face her. 'I don't need your help. I just got flustered yesterday, that's all. I don't need you on my case, all right?'

'I'm not . . . Ant—'

He stepped out into the road, desperate to get away from her, and then there was the sickening sound of tyres skidding on tarmac and the blare of a car horn.

'Ant!' she screamed. 'Ant, are you—?'

But he was away, darting round the front of the car, slapping its bonnet as he started running to the other side of the road. Bea watched the driver mouth obscenities, saw Ant disappear down the path to the park.

'God, that boy's got nine lives.' Dot had seen it all too. 'Was he hurt?'

'No, I don't think so. Quick on his feet, thank God. It was my fault.'

'You two fallen out?'

'Not really. I just said something I shouldn't. Or maybe I said it the wrong way. I was trying to help.'

'He'll get over it. He's very resilient.'

Bea looked at Dot. She was as bright as a button this morning. Was that extra blusher on her cheeks or just a healthy glow?

'Anyway, we're going to be late,' Dot said.

Bea checked her watch again. 'No, we're not.'

'Big Gav's called a staff meeting before work. Didn't you get the text?'

'Haven't looked. What time's the meeting?'

'Five minutes. We'd better get a wriggle on.'

As they set off along the High Street, Dot linked arms with Bea. Soon they were walking so fast Bea was almost forced to break into a run.

'Slow down, lady. I'm tired today. Didn't get much sleep.'

'Me neither. Come on,' she said, 'last one there makes the tea.'

4

'We all know by now that one of our customers was attacked on her way home from the store on Thursday evening. I hear that she is out of hospital now. Obviously, apart from sending our best wishes for a swift recovery, here at Costsave our first concern is staff and customer safety. I've contacted Head Office and spoken with the local police. The advice – and I'm talking about the female members of staff here – is not to walk home alone. Stick to well-lit paths, near housing, even if it takes a little longer to get home. Better safe than sorry.'

'Will the store pay for a taxi, if we've got no one to walk with?' This from Kirsty. Gavin looked a little flustered and pretended to check his notes among the bundle of paperwork he was carrying.

'Um, no. At least, it hasn't been discussed.'

'Maybe we should do a car share, like on the telly,' said Bob-on-Meat, who didn't look unlike Peter Kay if you took off ten years and added some hair.

'I'm not getting in a car with you, thank you very much,' someone piped up. A titter ran around the room and Bea thought, or at least I'd wipe the seats first.

'Okay, I'll look into that,' said Gavin. 'The next concern is the store itself. You may have seen us on the local news.

They say any publicity is good publicity. That's just not true. Takings were down 8 per cent yesterday on the previous Friday. I'm going to be keeping a close eye on things, but we need ideas on how to reassure people, keep them coming back, make them feel part of the family. Any ideas off the top of your heads?'

Silence. Bea fancied she saw a small ball of tumbleweed roll across the stained carpet and out of the door. She looked around the assembled staff and couldn't help running through the names on her list of suspects and noting the ones that were there. One of you, she thought. It could be one of you.

'Anyone? Come on, this is important.' Big Gav was flapping his arms now, trying to manually generate some sort of spark in his audience.

'We've got the Halloween promotion of course,' Neville said. 'Which personally I don't agree with, as you know.'

'What don't you agree with? Little kids dressing up and eating sweets?' said Bea.

'Trick or treat,' Neville said with a sneer. 'It's American. It's nothing to do with us. It's an excuse for kids to run riot and intimidate people.'

'I suppose you draw the curtains and turn the lights out and pretend you're not in, don't you?' said Dot.

'If you must know, my church runs an alternative evening – an evening of light. Maureen and I help at that.'

'Oh, well. Good for you,' said Bea, 'but the rest of us like dressing up. The kids round our way go mad for it.'

'Anyway, Halloween isn't for a week yet,' said Gavin. 'We need something sooner. I want you all to think about it and feed me your ideas by the end of the day. Write them down and put them in my in tray or pop in and see me. My door's always open, as you know.'

'Not always,' Bea muttered under her breath, as she and

Dot walked down to the shop floor. Dot smiled. 'Not after lunch when he's got his head down on that little pillow he keeps in his desk drawer. Have you seen it?'

'Yeah. Cute, isn't it? Crocheted, like something his granny made for him.'

'He thinks no one knows, but everyone does. Everyone. Bless.'

They chuckled to themselves as they took their places.

'Do you think people will stop shopping here?' said Bea.

'No. They still need bread and milk and bog roll. Where else are they going to go?'

'Out of town?'

'Yeah, if they've got a car. But they're probably going there already if they have, aren't they? I don't reckon we'll lose out. Anyway, people aren't daft. They know it's not Costsave's fault if someone got followed.'

'Not unless it was one of the staff.' The list was there again, at the front of her mind. All morning she kept a close eye on the milling customers, trying to spot any that were on her list. Halfway through the morning, she hit gold. A man in a tracksuit pushed one of the shallow trolleys around the end of the adjacent aisle and up the next one. The white double stripe on his jogger bottoms caught Bea's eye. One of Thursday evening's customers had been wearing the same, she was sure of it. She tried to remember any other outstanding features, while she processed the shopping in front of her.

'They're really juicy.'

The woman in front of her was saying something. Bea smiled. 'I'm sorry?'

'Have you tried these minneolas? They're really good. Sharp and sweet at the same time,' the woman said, brandishing a bag of oranges in Bea's direction.

'Oh, no. I don't eat much fruit.'

'Gotta have your five a day,' she said with a cheery smile and a mock-serious waggle of her index finger. 'Or is it seven now?'

'Do chocolate oranges count?'

The woman laughed. 'I wish.'

Bea had almost forgotten about striped jogger man, when she looked up and saw him approaching the checkouts.

Come to me, this way, that's right, she thought, trying to guide him in with the sheer power of her mind. He looked along the row and seemed to decide to head for a checkout further along, then looked again at Bea's conveyor belt. She made it jump forward, so that the gap at the back was bigger. That settled it, he steered his trolley into place beside it.

Result!

Once Minneola Woman had paid, Bea greeted the man in the striped joggers.

'Good morning, do you need any help packing?'

'Oh, um, no, thanks. I can manage.'

He was somewhere in his thirties, starting to go bald on top, with the remaining hair cut so short as to almost disappear. He had two piercings in his left ear and three in his right, and a bar through one of his eyebrows and underneath his tracksuit you could tell he was ripped. He moved down to Bea's end of the checkout and started putting the scanned goods into one of the bags he'd brought himself.

Bea wanted to talk to him, but, unusually for her, found herself lost for words. Then she noticed the logo embroidered in yellow thread into the tracksuit top. 'Local Leisure.'

'Oh,' she said, 'you're at the Leisure Centre.'

The man looked up from his packing.

'Yeah,' he said. He looked a little more closely. 'Don't think I've seen you down there, have I?'

'Ha, not since school swimming lessons. I never did get my twenty-five metres badge.'

'You'll have to come back, then. We do adult lessons.'

'Hmm, dunno. Maybe.' Not in a million years. 'Do all the staff there wear that?'

He looked down at his polyester top and bottom. 'Yeah. Why?'

Why? Good question. Why on earth would any normal person ask a question like that?

'Um, it just looks comfortable. Better than this anyway.' She pulled at her Costsave tabard, dismissively.

He smiled. 'Yeah. See what you mean.'

He thinks I look like a hippo, thought Bea. And then instantly, Urgh, God, haven't I got past thinking what people think of me yet?

'It doesn't have to be swimming. You could try the gym, or one of the classes. It's really friendly there.'

'Mmn, I'm not really . . . '

'The spinning class is good. I take that one, Sunday mornings and Thursday evenings. You should try it.'

Thursday evenings, thought Bea.

'Spinning? What, twiddling thread? Like weaving or something?'

He started to laugh and then looked at her pityingly. 'No. Spinning as in static cycling. Cycling indoors, with really loud music. It's intense, but fun.'

'Oh, that sort of spinning. What sort of music?'

'Nice fast poppy stuff. Something with a bit of beat. You'd like it.'

She pictured herself pedalling away intensely to a sound system turned up to eleven and felt clammy and uncomfortable.

'That'll be £24.34, please,' she said, changing the subject. 'Have you got a Bonus Card?'

He handed over his card, which she swiped. Then he pushed his debit card into the reader.

Bea cancelled the transaction, then pulled a face.

'I'm sorry it's not coming up on my machine. Can you try again?' she said.

He frowned and repeated the manoeuvre.

Bea shook her head.

'No good, I'm afraid. It does play up sometimes or the strips on the cards do. Here, let me.'

Bea took his card out of the machine and made a show of rubbing it clean on the hem of her tabard. She held it closer to her face, making a mental note of his name, Lee Jepson.

'That looks better,' she said, putting the card back in the reader and letting the transaction go through this time. 'That's got it. Sorry about that.'

'No worries,' he said. 'I'll see you down the Leisure Centre, shall I?'

'I'm not promising,' she said.

'Ask for me. I'll do your induction.'

He gathered up his bags and started walking away.

Induction, thought Bea. Sounds nasty. Nice guy, though. She used a biro from her pocket and wrote his name on the back of a money-off voucher.

'Your machine on the blink?' asked Dot.

'No,' said Bea, without thinking. 'I mean, yes. Yes, it is, piggin' thing.'

She tried not to catch Dot's eye, but too late, Dot was on to her.

'You're a sly one. You've got his name now, haven't you? And you know where he works. What a minx. Don't really blame you, though, he was a bit hot, wasn't he?'

'Shut up, Dot. It's not like that.'

'What did you just write down then?'

'Nothing.'

Dot leaned over and tried to snatch the bit of paper. Bea had hold of it and there was a brief tussle until Dot saw

Neville watching them and let go. Bea stuffed the paper down her bra.

'Gone,' she said and turned to her next customer, one of her regulars, Charles, a rather timid pensioner who always tied up his very good-natured golden retriever outside the shop. His eyes were nearly popping out behind his horn-rimmed glasses.

Bea patted her chest. 'Safe and sound,' she said and gave him a wink. Speechless, he made a show of putting his canvas shopping bag onto the packing area. Bea took pity on him and started bleeping his shopping through.

Later, when she was in the staff toilets, she retrieved the paper and studied it thoughtfully. Dot was right, Lee seemed like a nice bloke, but someone big and fit like him could easily attack and overpower someone. He was around on Thursday nights, too. Worth checking out the other male staff at Leisure Centre too, as Emma would have walked past there.

Repulsed as she was by the thought of exercise, she felt a shiver of excitement at the prospect of some real undercover detective work. What was it Lee said he taught? Spinning?

The penny dropped. She knew she'd heard it before: Gavin had talked about a having a fundraising spinathon in the store in November, to raise money for the store's charity, Kayleigh's Wish. Kayleigh was one of the 'Checkout Six Babies', who had been diagnosed with leukaemia when she was just past her first birthday. The store had already raised several thousand pounds and they were supporting her mum and dad, Keisha and Derrick, every way they could.

Bea flushed, washed her hands and checked herself in the mirror. Then she walked down the corridor and knocked on Gavin's open door.

'Come in,' he called. He looked up from his sheaf of papers as she walked in.

'Just a thought,' she said. 'You know the spinathon you were going to have for Kayleigh?'

'Yes.'

'It doesn't have to be November, does it? Why not move it forward? We'll get loads of publicity. I bet the *Bugle* will cover it, maybe even the *Evening Post*.'

Gavin's eyes lit up. 'That is a top idea. That is a *top* idea. Brilliant, Bea!' His eyes were shining now. 'I'd already talked to the Leisure Centre about it – they'll provide the kit, so if you get in touch and sort out a date with them. Start of the week's better for the local press, but that's too short notice. Maybe Wednesday would be okay. It'll be a rush to get everything organised, but I'll talk to Anna about the shift pattern, give you a few hours away from the tills.'

'Me? Why?'

'So you can get on top of things – the rota of staff volunteers to pedal, the collecting buckets, the sponsorship form. Anna can do the press release, so don't worry about that—'

'Wait a minute. I never said I was organising it!'

'You'll be brilliant—'

Brilliant? Me? thought Bea.

'Yes, but—'

'And it's a great opportunity for you. You're good on the checkouts – I've got no complaints – but there's more to you than that. Show me what you can do. This is your chance to shine.'

'But I, I mean . . . '

'You know Keisha, don't you? If you asked, maybe she'd bring young Kayleigh down for a photo-op. Come in to the office at lunchtime, Bea, and I'll get the file out for you. You can make a start!'

Bea tottered out of Gavin's office and into the staffroom, where she made a cup of tea, swirling the bag round with a spoon and leaving it in until the contents looked like treacle.

'All right, babe? You look a bit … shell-shocked. Loos in a state again?' said Dot.

Bea sank into the sofa between her and Ginny.

'No. No, I've just been – I don't know how to say it. *Gavined.*'

Ginny let out a squawk. Dot leaned in close. 'Gavined? Did he *touch you*?' she said in a hushed voice, almost a whisper.

Bea snorted so hard tea came down her nose. Heads turned as she wiped her face with a tissue. By the time she'd stopped laughing, pretty much everyone was looking at her.

'No, no,' she said, 'No. Not that. You might as well all know, Big Gav's asked me to organise the spinathon, and we're having it next week. So I'm going to be asking you to sign up for a stint on the bike – however long you can manage. We've got to cover the whole day, eight in the morning until ten at night.'

'I'll do it,' said Ginny. 'It's a great idea.' She was the athletic type, who was often seen jogging through the town in sporty gear on her way to or from netball or hockey practice.

'Really?' said Bea. 'That's brilliant.'

'Are you going to be doing it?' Dean from Stores had wandered in.

'God, no!' Bea shrieked, then looked around the room again. Half a dozen faces looked back at her, all oozing disapproval.

'I don't see why we should if you won't,' said Kirsty.

'It's for your own good,' said Bea. 'No one wants to see me on a bike, do they? I'll frighten the customers away.'

'Well, I'd pay good money for it. I'll put in a fiver if I can see you on that bike, sweating away in Lycra,' Dean said with an unpleasantly wolfish grin.

Bea pulled a face. 'I think a little bit of sick just came in my mouth,' she said, 'and I'm putting you down for a half-hour pedal.' The others weren't so easy to deal with and, to be fair, they had a point. By the end of tea break, Bea plodded back to her checkout with a feeling that she had been royally stitched up.

I've got four days, she thought, to organise this lot and get fit enough to cycle for ten minutes without making a complete show of myself. She groaned. It wasn't going to happen, was it?

At lunchtime, she sat at the spare desk in Hermione's office. The file on fundraising was fairly thick, but there were only a couple of notes about the spinathon including a copy of an email between Gavin and the Leisure Centre manager, which nominated Lee Jepson as the staff member to take the lead on it. Maybe this wasn't going to be so bad after all.

By the end of her hour, she had confirmed the date with Lee, sent an email to Keisha, and printed out a large sign-up sheet. She was pinning it up on the staff noticeboard when Gavin found her.

He looked at the notice and nodded approvingly. 'Smashing,' he said. 'I knew you could do this.'

'Go on, then,' said Bea.

'What?'

'Sign up. I will if you will.'

He took a pen from the top pocket of his jacket and wrote his name into one of the empty slots, then handed the pen to her. She signed too.

'I don't really know how this happened. I thought it was an ordinary Saturday today.'

Gavin put an approving hand on her shoulder. 'You made it happen. Your idea. Your work. That's what's good about my job. Bringing the best out in people.'

Bea was a bit taken aback, not used to such sincerity. Life at Costsave was normally fuelled by a diet of banter, cynicism and teasing.

'That's why I took on Anthony,' he continued. 'I know it won't be a smooth ride for him or us, oh, pardon the pun,' he said, looking back at the spinathon sheet, 'but if we can start him on the right track, he'll be set up for life.'

Bea wondered whether to tell Gavin about her suspicions about Ant and his problems with reading, but that would be overstepping the mark. Besides, she didn't even know if she was right, did she?

'I think he needs all the encouragement he can get,' she said. 'He was quite upset yesterday, got in a muddle, shelving.'

She silently cursed herself. Perhaps Neville hadn't told him about it.

'Well, get him involved with this, then. It'll be a confidence booster. Give him a job to do, or at least sign him up for a session or two. He's not due in until Monday, is he, so give him a ring or text him and tell him about it. His number will be in the personnel file – you've got my permission to access it.'

'Okay, thanks, Gav— Mr Howell.'

Bea put Ant's number into her phone but didn't ring him until she was walking home.

'Hey, what's up?'

'I need your help. Big Gav's got me organising a charity thing, a spinathon, next week.'

Silence. Then, 'What's that got to do with me?'

'He . . . I . . . thought you could help me.'

'I dunno, Bea, I don't know if I'll even be there next week.'

Bea's brain was whirring like a fruit machine, grasping for ways to make this whole thing less awkward. Why hadn't she thought it through before ringing?

'Look, at least come in until Wednesday. It'll be a laugh.'

'Nah, I've had it.'

'It's for Kayleigh, she's our charity this year.'

'Oh.'

Sensing a chink in his armour, Bea pressed on. 'You must know them. They live near you, don't they?'

'Yeah, our Stevo used to go out with Keisha's sister.'

'So you'll help?' She could hear him sigh.

'Yeah, okay. What do you want me to do?'

'Well, agree to pedal for a while for starters. I can sign you up on the sheet. Half an hour? More?'

'Whatever, Bea. I've been cycling all my life. I'm pretty fit.'

'You've got a bike then?'

'Course. Bit difficult cycling without one.'

Once again, Bea pictured herself pedalling at the front of the store while people pointed and laughed at her.

'Could you, I mean, could I have a go? I haven't been on a bike since I got too big for the little pink one with the streamers on the handles and jewels in the wheels I had when I was six.'

'Yeah, we've got a load here. Come round. I'm busy tonight but tomorrow's okay.'

'Okay, thanks. Two-ish?'

'Yeah. Number twenty-three. I'll look out for you.'

Bea ended the call, just as a text from Queenie came through.

Where are you? Are you nearly home?

Yeah. Five minutes.

Not the alley.

I know. See ya soon.

When she got home, the back door was locked again. She knocked and Queenie opened it.

'You're late,' she said. 'Should have been home four minutes ago, if your shift finished at six.'

Bea looked at her. The skin around Queenie's wrists was pink and raw looking. She'd been scratching again, her fingers worrying in tune with her mind.

'I was fine,' she soothed. 'Just walked slower than usual or something. You can't get het up like this, Queenie. It's not good for you.'

'I worry about you. Out there,' her mum said, locking the door again.

'I know you do, but you don't need to. I'm sensible. Listen, put the kettle on, I've got stuff to tell you. You'll never guess what happened today ...'

'Did you pick up the sausages?'

'Yes, course I did. And I got something else too.' Bea pulled out two minneolas from her bag.

'Oranges?'

'Minneolas. It's a cross between a grapefruit and a tangerine.'

Queenie wrinkled her nose. 'I don't know about that.'

'I sit there day in day out surrounded by food, and we only ever eat the same stuff. I'm going to start trying something new.'

'Not every day?'

'No, probably not. And you don't have to, if you don't want to, but it might be fun. Anyway, let's get these sausages under the grill and I can tell you all about the spinathon.'

'The whatathon?'

'Spinathon. You got the kettle on yet?'

While Queenie made a pot of tea, Bea told her about being ambushed by Gavin.

'He's all right, isn't he? As bosses go,' said Queenie.

'Yeah, people laugh at him, but I reckon he's pretty sound underneath the management speak.'

'What about that other business? You know, Emma.'

Bea suddenly remembered the scrap of paper in her

pocket, but she didn't need to get it out. She remembered the name. She'd add it to her Word file later.

'Everyone's still talking about it,' Bea said. 'Horrible business.'

They both fell silent, while the sausages hissed and spat under the grill.

'Brown or red sauce?' Queenie said.

Bea sighed. Why did she even ask? When had Bea ever not wanted brown sauce with her Saturday sausage sandwich?

Still, it would be ready soon, and then she'd open up the laptop. She could hardly wait.

'God, that's a lot of bikes! What did you do, rob a bike shop?'

As soon as she said it, she could have kicked herself. Ant's family, the Thompsons, had a bit of reputation in the town. Ant looked at her sharply and for a second, she wondered what he might do, then he smiled and said, 'No need to break into a shop, Bea. People leave bikes all over the place.'

He looked at her evenly and she couldn't tell if he was joking or not. She decided that for the purposes of this afternoon, he was.

'Here,' he said, extracting a bike from the sizeable heap piled into the lock-up garage. It was a purple-framed shopper bike, with a basket on the front. 'This should be about right. Our Danielle uses it, but she won't mind.'

He wheeled it out and propped it up against the fence, then fetched another bike for himself.

'Go on, then,' he said.

'What?'

'It's no good just looking at it. Get on.'

'Here?'

Bea looked around the tarmacked yard, with blocks of garages on three sides, and a narrow driveway leading out onto the estate roads.

'Good a place as any. Ride it round a couple of times before we go out.'

'Yeah. Right. Okay.'

She got hold of the handlebars and stood it upright.

'I don't know if I can do this.'

'Course you can.'

Ant closed the garage door and locked it. 'Don't want anyone getting their thieving mitts on that lot,' he said without a hint of irony. Then he turned his attention back to Bea. 'Do you want me to hold it while you get on?'

'Yeah. No. No, I can do this.'

Bea stepped through the middle and stood with one foot either side. Then she edged her bottom onto the saddle, relieved that she could still touch the ground.

'Bring one of the pedals up, start pressing down and you're away,' said Ant.

'Yeah. I remember. I've got this.'

Bea used the toe of her left foot to bring the pedal up, then put her foot on top of it and lifted her right foot onto the other pedal. She tried to push the left pedal, but it wouldn't move. She felt herself falling and heard Ant shouting at her, but she seemed frozen, unable to react. It was as if she was watching herself as she toppled sideways and crunched into the tarmac.

'Oh Jesus!'

She lay still trying to assess whether anything hurt, wondering whether somehow, if she tried really hard enough, she could make herself invisible, make this whole sorry episode go away. She shut her eyes. She felt Ant take the weight of the bike and lift it from on top of her. She heard him laughing. From the noise she could picture him doubled over, trying not to wet himself. She opened her eyes. She could see his feet in front of her. She let her eyes go upwards. He was doubled over, trying not to wet himself.

73

'Oh my God, oh my God. Are you all right?' The words made their way out of his mouth in bursts between bubbles of laughter. He held his hand out to her but she was too humiliated to take it.

'I can do it. I'm all right,' she said, huffily. She tried to sit up and realised that her left hip, knee and ankle hurt a lot. Her head did too. She put her hand up to her forehead and felt hard bits of grit sticking to her skin. She brushed them away crossly.

'Am I bleeding?' she said to Ant, who'd stopped laughing now.

'No,' he said. 'Not your head anyway, but you've scraped your ankle a bit.'

Bea looked down and saw bright red stippling on the knobbly bit of her ankle above the top of her sock.

'Oh,' she said. Hot tears pooled in her eyes. God, no, stop it, she thought. Don't be such a girl. But she couldn't stop them and they burst over the edge, spilling down her face.

'Hey, Bea, I'm sorry. I'm sorry I laughed.' Ant crouched down and put his hand on her shoulder. 'Come on,' he said, 'let me help you up. Let's have a look at the damage.'

This time she let him help her onto her feet. She dusted down her leggings, which were a bit torn on one side, then fished in her pocket for a tissue, but, finding none, wiped her eyes and snotty nose on her sleeve. She was beyond dignity now.

'I'm sorry,' Ant said again.

She shook her head. 'It's not you,' she said. 'I don't blame you for laughing. I'm just glad you didn't get it on your phone.' She looked at him. 'You didn't, did you?'

'No, wasn't quick enough.'

'Anyway, it's not that, it's everything.'

'Everything?'

'Everything.'

'Shit.'

They sat down, side by side, leaning against the garage door. Ant took a packet of cigarettes out of his pocket and lit one. He offered it to her, but she waved it away.

'What sort of everything?' he said.

'Home, work, life, I dunno.'

'Mm.' He took a long drag from his cigarette, tipped his head back and exhaled.

'I mean, I'm not normally like this. I just get on with things. I'm just being silly.'

'Nah. It's not silly.' He stubbed out the cigarette.

'I mean, everything's okay really. I just fell off a bike, that's all.'

Ant started to smile.

'Don't!' Bea snapped. 'Don't even—' Then she started to smile too, and it turned into a giggle and then a wave of hysterical laughter that was only one notch away from tears again. When they'd both calmed down again, Ant lit another ciggie.

'The thing is, you won't have that problem on Wednesday, 'cos the bike will be fixed. You won't have to balance.'

'No, but I'll still look like a peach on a cocktail stick. Bloody hell.'

'Nothing wrong with peaches,' Ant said. Bea could feel herself starting to blush. 'Except their furry skin.' He shuddered. 'Tinned peaches are all right, though, aren't they?' His voice trailed off as he saw Bea's tears welling up again.

'It's going to be a disaster anyway,' she said. 'I haven't got enough time to do everything. Big Gav wants us all in T-shirts with Costsave and Kayleigh's Wish all over them, and I've got to get some flyers printed and . . .'

'I can help you with the T-shirts.'

'Really?'

'My brother, Ken – one of his mates prints T-shirts. If we

work out how many and what you want on them, I can sort that out this evening. Have them ready by Wednesday.'

'That would be great.' Bea started to feel better already. 'How many brothers and sisters have you got?'

'Four brothers, two sisters. I'm number four, right in the middle.'

'Must be nice, though, all those people.'

'Yeah, sometimes.'

'It's just me and Queenie. Has been since Dad died.'

'Sorry.'

'What for?'

'About your dad.'

'Hmm, thanks. Six years ago, but it still hurts. I don't think that ever goes away. Queenie's not been the same since. She, well, she needs me more.'

'So, everything's not all right, really, is it? You've got a lot on your plate.'

'Yeah, I s'pose. So's everyone, though. Everyone's got something to deal with.'

'True that.'

'Like your reading?'

His face darkened.

'I told you, I'm fine. I'm not stupid, you know.'

'I know you're not. But maybe you need a bit of help. Maybe I could help you.'

He ground his cigarette into the tarmac with a viciousness which was nothing to do with extinguishing the embers.

'I don't need your help. I don't need anyone's help.'

A stiff breeze swirled around the yard. Bea shivered.

'Okay, okay. It's just that I need yours and I'd like to return the favour. That's all. Just remember that, okay? Can we put these bloody bikes away now and sort out the T-shirts?'

5

'Are you sure it should be here?' said Bea.

'Yes. You can't miss it. Everyone will have to walk past,' Gavin said.

He had moved the newspaper display to one side and the team from the Leisure Centre had started setting up the static bike directly opposite the front door.

'He's right,' said Lee, who was there with his stripy Leisure Centre tracksuit. 'It's a great spot.'

Bea's heart sank. She knew they were right. Everyone would have to walk past. Everyone would see. And that was the problem. Everyone would see *her*. She'd put herself down for the first half-hour stint. Now, everything was ready – balloons, banners, collecting buckets. It was all in place except the T-shirts. Despite his promises, Ant had yet to turn up with a single shirt, let alone the box of the twenty-four she'd ordered. At the moment she was wearing her Costsave tabard over a long black vest and her leggings. Today, and only today, trainers were allowed at work too.

'Okay,' she said and she stood back, by the fresh fruit and veg special offers, while they secured the bike and tested it. The first shift was starting to file onto the shop floor. Shelf-stackers, bakers, produce specialists and checkout staff all gathered around as Lee started pedalling slowly then quickly

77

built up so that his legs were firing like pistons. He'd stripped down to his T-shirt and Bea could see the tendons in his arms, as taut as cheese wires, as he gripped the handlebars and went for it. After a few minutes, he hadn't even broken a sweat. He wound down to a halt, then pressed the buttons on the panel at the front.

A little ripple of applause broke out among the watching staff. Lee did a mock bow and climbed off.

'That's all fine. I've zeroed it all.' He looked at his watch. 'Five to. Who's going to be first?'

Bea shuffled forward, hoping, even now, that there'd be some last-minute hitch which would stop this whole thing. But a hole didn't open up in the tiled floor, Health and Safety didn't suddenly swoop on Costsave to ban this farrago, and the fury of Lee's pedalling hadn't caused the bike to spontaneously combust. She was going to have to do it.

'Me,' she said. 'Thought I'd get it over with.'

'Go, girl!' someone called out.

Lee smiled and clapped her on the back, nearly knocking the wind out of her.

'Good plan,' he said. 'Do you want a warm-up?'

'No. No, I'll just, I mean, I think half an hour is going to be pushing it. I don't want to do a minute longer.'

As well as someone actually pedalling, Bea had scheduled two people to stand near the doors collecting money. Marcus, the student, and Joey were first up.

'Are we getting T-shirts?' asked Joey.

'Yes,' said Bea, 'but they're not here yet. Bear with us. I know they're coming.'

She checked her watch. One minute to eight.

Gavin was walking towards the front doors with his bunch of keys. He paused as he walked past Bea.

'Ready?' he said.

'As I'll ever be,' she said, pulling a face.

'I'm really proud of you,' he said. 'Of us. Of Costsave.'

Bea felt a little flutter of something she couldn't identify, swelling in her chest. She took a deep breath and climbed onto the bike, to the accompanying noise of twenty smartphones taking pictures. She glanced up.

'Oh, fuck off, you lot. No pictures!'

Her colleagues laughed, and carried on snapping.

'Here we go,' Gavin called from the door. Bea pressed down on the left pedal. It moved obligingly easily. Right. Left. This wasn't too bad. 'I declare the Great Costsave Spinathon open!'

Gavin unlocked the door and held it open for the first customer. Smelly Reg shambled in, his grubby brown coat flapping as he walked. He headed straight towards Bea and then stopped. He looked at her and then all around the semicircle of people watching her. Now, they were watching him. He seemed to be having trouble taking it all in. Bea kept pedalling while she watched him grapple with this unexpected vision.

He looked left and right, and then said, 'Where's the papers?'

Joey stepped forward.

'They're over there,' he said, pointing to the displaced island, 'but we're collecting for Kayleigh's Wish, if you'd like to—' but he was talking to Reg's back as he headed for his *Racing Post* and packet of fags. Bea caught a lungful of the familiar acrid 'Reg' odour wafting behind him.

'Okay, everyone, back to your stations,' Gavin said. He stood next to Bea, who was starting to feel uncomfortably warm and wondering what odour she'd be giving off in the next few minutes. She'd double-deodorised this morning and sprayed on an eye-watering amount of her favourite perfume, but even so . . .

'What time's the press coming?' he asked her.

'Half ten,' she said, amazed that she could still speak fairly comfortably. 'Keisha's going to bring Kayleigh and then they'll want you and a few of the staff too.'

'I want you to be in it.'

'Oh no. At half past ten, I'll still be lying down in the cool room. I'm not even kidding.' She could feel the warmth in her legs spreading through her body now. She was getting sticky down her back and under her boobs.

'Haha,' Gavin laughed, mirthlessly, 'I'll see you back here at about twenty past, then.'

Bea was really starting to feel it now, an ache in both hips, breath getting faster and more desperate. She'd been pedalling for ages – she must be at least halfway now. She checked the monitor on the front of the bike: 'Time: 2:15'. Two fifteen? Had Lee set the clock wrong, or something? She watched as it ticked up 2:20, 2:21, 2:22. Ah crap. It was right, after all. She'd still got twenty-seven minutes to go.

Now she knew. She didn't need to worry about attackers in alleyways. She could throw her list of suspects in the bin. She wasn't going to die at someone else's hands. She was going to die here in the foyer of Costsave, in front of half a dozen colleagues and Smelly Reg.

She leaned forward, resting her forehead on the handlebars and groaned.

'You all right? You're doing a great job.'

She sat up. Lee was at her elbow.

'Take it steady, that's the thing. You don't have to beat any land speed records.'

'I want to stop now. It hurts.'

'You can't stop. Keep pedalling. And keep smiling. You're doing great. Really.'

Bea groaned again. Underneath her tabard, her vest top was wringing wet now. Sweat was trickling from her hairline down her neck.

'I should've put towels out.'

Lee dived into his sports bag and brought out a navy blue Leisure Centre towel.

'Here,' he said.

Bea looked at the towel longingly.

'You can let go of the handles, Bea,' he said. 'Just remember to keep pedalling.'

'Oh, right.' She was actually gripping extremely tightly. It felt like her arms were holding her on there, but that wasn't logical, was it? She loosened her grip, and then let go, sitting up straighter. 'Oh, *right*. This is a bit better.'

She took the towel from Lee and wiped her face and neck, being careful around her eyes to try and avoid the smudged panda look.

More customers were starting to come in now. Many smiled as they saw her. The clink of their loose change in the buckets acted like a cattle prod – it reminded her what she was there for and spurred her on.

'Ha!' she said to Lee. 'Real money!'

She'd settled into a rhythm now. Although everything still hurt, she tried to detach herself from that, and just watch the numbers on the clock increasing and listen for the sound of coins on plastic. She found that if she made eye contact with the customers and managed a smile – even a grim imitation of one – they were more likely to dig in their pockets. Her regulars were the best contributors.

'Is that really you?' asked one, bringing her shopping bag on wheels closer. She was a pensioner with a tight perm and a sharp face, the sort of woman who would never shop without a list, and never deviate from it. In the heat of the moment, Bea couldn't remember her name.

'Yeah,' said Bea. 'It's me all right.'

'Good on you, girl.'

There was no noise in Joey's bucket, but Bea saw the folded note go in and pedalled a bit faster.

Towards the end of her half-hour, Ant turned up. He came through the front door, carrying a large cardboard box, which he dumped on the floor near the bike.

'Sorry,' he puffed. 'Could only pick them up this morning.'

By this stage, Bea was on autopilot, legs moving by themselves, brain dormant.

'I wanted to be here at the beginning, to cheer you on. Are you nearly done?'

Bea couldn't speak, but she nodded to the monitor. '28:16'.

'Wow! You've done it, Bea! You've done it!'

She relaxed for a moment, and her legs turned to jelly. Each turn of the pedal was suddenly impossible.

'I can't,' she murmured. 'I can't.'

'You can! You have!'

Lee stepped in closer, and a small crowd gathered.

'Go on, Bea. Go on! You're unstoppable!'

She fixed her eyes on the monitor, but surely it had stopped working. The seconds hardly changed, each one an agonising lifetime apart.

'Come on, Bea. You can do it!'

The crowd was counting down now. *Fifteen, fourteen, thirteen, twelve.* And a wave of nausea swept over her. She flushed hot and cold and unbearably hot again. *Eight, seven, six, five.* Bea started thinking of things to be sick in. The collecting buckets were out, obviously, but the flower stall wasn't far away. *Three, two, one.*

The world in front of Bea's eyes turned red aand then black. There was unbearable pressure in the back of throat, and a piercing shrill noise in her ears. A piercing shrill noise. Lee was blowing his whistle for her to stop. Multiple hands helped her off the bike and the next volunteer clambered on – Dean from Stores.

'Mm,' he said, 'nice warm seat.'

Bea wasn't listening. Her many helpers had lowered her to the floor and she sat there, enjoying the rather odd feeling of the cold tiles through her damp leggings. The cloth was so soggy, she wondered whether she had actually wet herself, but, to be honest, she was past caring.

Someone handed her a sports drink.

'Just sip it,' she heard Lee say.

She sucked on the bottle, and her mouth exploded with saliva at the first touch of the sweet liquid. She felt a bubble of euphoria. She was an actual Sportswoman, drinking a Sports drink because she had done Sport. There was a first time for everything.

She looked through the forest of legs around her. Dean was getting into his ride now, his spindly legs going like the clappers, his lank hair falling across his face as he leaned forward. He was no Bradley Wiggins but, bless him, he was going for it. She felt a surge of goodwill for everyone who had rallied to her call, who had helped her make this happen, her Costsave family.

'I bloody love you lot,' she said, leaned sideways and was sick on Lee's shoes.

Lee was surprisingly okay about his trainers, but Bea felt awful. She insisted on mopping them herself with one of the Leisure Centre towels. Afterwards she wondered whether that had compounded her disgrace, since Lee would presumably have to carry it back to work and wash it.

After a while, she was able to get to her feet. Dean was still going great guns, although there was a rather unsavoury hum around him. She noticed that the supporting players were starting to move their semi-circle a little further away from the bike. She craftily sniffed at her own pits – hot, sweaty, but not offensive, she thought, but can you ever really smell your own smell? She'd feel better when she'd had a shower and changed into her spare clothes.

Ant high-fived her. 'You did it. I knew you could. Joey reckons he's got about thirty or forty quid in his bucket already.'

'Let's have a look at these T-shirts, then,' said Bea. They crouched down either side of the box. The top was taped down. Ant tried picking at the tape, but Bea noticed that he hardly had any nails and the skin round the stumps that he had looked bitten and raw. 'Here, let me,' she said, and scythed through the tape with the edge of her glossy thumb-nail. She flipped open the top leaves of the box and picked out the first shirt. She held it by the shoulders and shook it out, spreading it face upwards over the top of the box. It was a striking bright pink with white writing, as they'd agreed.

She read it twice. And then again.

'What the hell's this, Ant?'

'It's what we agreed. What you wrote down on that paper.'

'It bloody isn't.'

'Why? What's wrong with it?'

His eyes ran over the printed words, but somehow they couldn't get a grip. The letters were just shapes, wriggling about on the material, not making sense.

'Cockslave, Ant. Cock. Slave.'

He focused on the company logo, and tried to sound out the letters. But he knew he didn't need to, because the look on her face told him he was in trouble.

'Oh shit.'

'Are these the T-shirts?' Joey said, walking over from his post by the door.

'No!' Bea stuffed the shirt into the box and slammed the top shut. 'No, they are T-shirts – but they've sent the wrong lot.'

'Oh, right.' He wandered away again.

'I'm sorry, Bea,' Ant said. 'I've stuffed up. I should've checked. I'll kill Saggy.' He was chewing the edge of his thumb, drawing blood. 'What are we going to do?'

'I dunno. We'll have to lose these. Can you take them back and get the money back?'

Ant looked panicky.

'These are legit, aren't they?' said Bea. 'I mean, it is a real company. You got a receipt and everything.'

'Not exactly.'

'You're shitting me?'

'I was helping you out.'

'Yeah. Big fat thanks. Everything else has worked. Everybody else is rallying round. But you—'

She was talking to the back of his heels. He'd picked up the box and was running out of the store. Legs protesting, Bea sprinted after him.

'You're not leaving, are you? I've got you down for the bike at one o'clock.'

'Yeah, I know. I'll be there,' he called back.

'Ant, you're actually meant to be—'

It was no good. He was gone. She walked back into the store. Kirsty and Joey rattled their buckets at her as she passed them while Neville was ready to pounce.

'I knew he wouldn't come to anything,' he said.

'Who? What are you talking about?' said Bea.

'That young layabout.' He pointedly looked at his watch. 'Half an hour late and now he's gone AWOL again. I know Mr Howells has got a soft spot for him, for some reason, but this is too much.'

'It's not his fault,' said Bea, quickly. 'He's doing something for me.'

'And you're management now, are you?'

'No. No, but Gav— Mr Howells has put me in charge of the spinathon and I asked Ant to do something urgently.

Talk to Mr Howells – he'll back me up.' Would he? Would it help if she crossed her fingers behind her back?

'I will talk to him.'

'Good. You do that.'

'In the meantime, according to my schedules, you're doing an hour on the checkouts, starting in fifteen minutes.'

'Yes. Yes, that's right. I'm just going to have a shower first.'

Bea bustled away as fast as her tired legs would let her. She showered and changed quickly so she could spend five minutes in front of the mirror fixing her face and hair. If she was going to have her picture in the paper, it was damn well not going to happen without make-up.

She checked on the spinathon on her way to the till. Everything was under control. Dot had taken over bucket duty.

'It's going really well,' she said. 'Proud of you, babe.'

As she was walking away, her phone bleeped illicitly in her pocket. Thought I'd put that on silent, thought Bea, hoping that no one else had heard. Sounded like a text coming through.

She settled into her station, punched in her password, applied her hand cream and took a sneaky look at her phone. A text from Queenie.

Can u ring me?

Come on, Queenie, you know it's a big day for me. Not now. She'd definitely get in trouble if she was caught using it on duty. She'd do it later. She put the phone onto 'vibrate', slid it back into her pocket and looked back along the row of checkouts towards the front door. There were pink balloons tied to each one, collecting buckets in the packing area on every checkout, and a cluster of balloons and banners around the static bike. It felt like the store was wearing party clothes. Today was a good day.

'Morning!' she chirped to her first customer. 'Would you like any help packing?'

'Yes. Yes, that would be lovely, thank you.' The voice was familiar, but subdued. Julie. Although it was overcast outside and threatening to rain, she was wearing sunglasses, and was holding one of her arms awkwardly, like it was in an imaginary sling. She noticed Bea looking. 'I've put my shoulder out,' she said. 'Can't really carry anything on that side.'

'Ooh, nasty, how did you do that?' said Bea. Then she caught sight of the black eye lurking beneath the side arm of the dark glasses and wished she'd kept quiet.

'I fell over. Silly, really.'

She had both the children with her, but there was no squealing from Tiffany today, who was sucking on a little plastic duck, and Mason was keeping his grabby hands to himself. Bea packed the shopping into bags and then got up to lift the bags into the shallow trolley. Then she sat down and took Julie's money. As she gave her the change, she lingered a little before handing it over, noticing that the plaster was still on her ring finger, a bit grubby and frayed now.

'You take care, now,' she said. 'If that arm carries on hurting, I'd take it to A & E, if I were you. Tell someone what happened.'

'Oh, it's fine. But thank you.' She examined the contents of her purse and dropped some coins in the collecting bucket.

'Thank you,' said Bea, 'that's very kind.'

'Poor little Kayleigh. There but for the grace of God.' She ruffled Tiffany's hair, then put her purse away and left, Mason trailing silently by her side.

Bea wanted to go after her, buy her a coffee, maybe give her a hug, but there was someone's weekly shop waiting to be processed, threatening to cause an avalanche.

'Good morning,' she said. 'Would you like any help with your packing?'

At a quarter past ten, Gavin walked past her checkout.

'Close up after this customer,' he said. 'It's nearly time.'

His hair was full of static electricity, dancing away from his head like it was underwater. He'd obviously spent some time in front of the mirror with a plastic comb.

A woman was heading towards them, her eye focused on the nice free stretch of conveyor belt behind Bea's current customer's shopping. Gavin stepped in.

'I'm sorry, Madam, this checkout's closing. Would you like to use another? Number four looks free.'

He placed a 'closed' sign on the end of her station, then adjusted his perfectly knotted tie and pulled the cuffs of his shirt a little further out from his jacket sleeves, before stretching his arms in front of him so the cuffs disappeared again.

'I'll see you there in a minute,' he said.

As Bea was dealing with her customer she sensed someone approaching her from behind. She glanced round. It was Ant, holding the box of shirts. He was breathing hard and sweating profusely.

'It's all right, Bea,' he said.

'I'll look in a minute,' Bea said. She finished up and logged off from her till. They stood to one side, near the window as Ant shook out a shirt and held it up. It was the same shirt, but the Costsave logo was just as it should be.

'It was Saggy's idea of a joke. He just did the top one. The rest were fine.'

'You're kidding?'

'No. Nearly pissed himself laughing when I caught up with him.'

'Some mate.'

'Ah, he's all right really. Shame I'll have to kill him after this, but there you go.'

'Okay, let's go with these. At least we've got them in time for the photographer. Thanks, Ant. You've saved the day.'

'Well, I ruined it first. Or at least Saggy did.'

'Nah,' said Bea, 'just a hiccup. Come on, I think Ginny's on at ten thirty, let's get her into one of these. And the two collectors at the door.'

They just had time to get everyone kitted up when Keisha arrived with little Kayleigh. She was in her pushchair, bundled up against the cold in a thick, padded coat with a rug round her legs. Her face, peering out of her hood, was pale and doll-like.

The female members of staff clustered around them. Those on nearby kiosks and counters left their posts to have a little fuss.

'Thanks so much for bringing her,' Bea said when she managed to negotiate her way through the throng. 'She's looking—' she couldn't bring herself to say well 'as cute as a button. Would she like a balloon?'

'Yeah, I'll tie one to her pushchair. She'll like that. Are the press coming?'

'They're here already,' Gavin said. 'From the *Evening Post*, no less.'

Lee blew the whistle to mark changeover time again and Ginny climbed on. She had her long, brown hair tied back in a ponytail and was wearing shorts. Her legs were fake-tanned to perfection.

'That T-shirt looks great on you,' Bea heard Ant telling her. 'I reckon you'd look good in anything.'

Ginny smiled with knowing modesty. She flicked her ponytail behind her shoulder and started to pedal.

The photographer, a short man with a receding hairline

and an unfortunate comb-over started to arrange the others around her.

'That's it. Can we get little Courtney as near to the bike as possible?'

'Kayleigh.'

'Sorry, isn't that what I said? Will she come out of the chair? Can you lift her up?'

Keisha started to look a bit flustered, but Gavin stepped forward.

'Let's leave her in the chair. Can we put her in the foreground? Will that work?'

The photographer didn't like his input, but gave in.

'All right, mate. Are you in this picture? Can you get to the back then? Tall ones at the back, shorter ones to the front.'

Bea hung back, watching the chaos, but Ant grabbed her elbow.

'Come on, Bea. You've done all this. You gotta be in it.'

He steered her into the group, next to Gavin, who beamed at her. Finally, after what seemed like hours, the photographer stood back and started snapping just as Kayleigh started to cry, prompting a chorus of clucking and cooing from all the Costsave ladies. But despite their and Keisha's best efforts, Kayleigh sobbed her way through the photo session – luckily for Bea as it turned out, as her phone kept vibrating in her pocket, right next to Gavin. Oh, Mum, she thought, if only you could have come down here and seen this, shared it with me. If only . . .

The photographer made everyone stay in their places while he wrote down their names, checking the spelling as he went. When he asked Bea's name, she had a flicker of recognition.

'I've seen you in here before, haven't I? Are you local?'

'Not any more, but I visit. My mum's in the bungalows by the Green.'

He moved on to the others, finishing with Ginny, who was still pedalling and starting to glow a little.

'Splendid,' he said, glowing a little himself. 'Have you ever thought of being a model? I could do some test shots for your portfolio. Here, let me give you a card.' He dug in his pocket and handed a business card to Ginny.

'I've got nowhere to put it,' she giggled, before propping it unsteadily onto the front of the machine.

Gavin was trying to talk to Keisha, but Kayleigh was crying too much for their conversation to go anywhere.

'I'm sorry, Mr Howells, I'm going to have to take her home. She's tired.'

'That's fine. I'm just so glad you could come. We're all behind you here at Costsave, you know.'

Her eyes filled with tears.

'I know,' she said, 'I can't thank you enough.' She looked around the store. 'I loved working here.'

'There's a job here for you, whenever you want it. You know that, don't you?'

She sniffed, hard. 'It won't be any time soon. She's in and out of hospital and she needs so much care. I could never put her in a nursery or with a childminder.'

'The offer's there, Keisha. Things change, you never know.'

She gave him a wan little smile. 'I appreciate that, Mr Howells. It's like a family here, isn't it? My Costsave family.'

Bea could see Gavin's chest puffing out with pride.

Keisha turned to her and gave her a hug. 'Thanks so much for all this, Bea. You're a star, you really are.'

Bea found herself too choked up to speak.

'Be careful,' said Keisha, and shook her head in a mock warning. 'Checkout six. You could be next. Get on the pill or keep your legs crossed.'

Bea opened her mouth to speak when Ant cut in, putting his arms round both their shoulders.

'It's all right. She's saving herself for me.'

'Oh, I've heard about you. Cocky, isn't he?' she said to Bea.

'Yeah. But he's not all bad,' said Bea. 'He did the T-shirts, you know.'

'Oh, wow, great job. Thanks.'

Keisha turned to tuck the blanket more snugly round Kayleigh's legs. Bea watched, then her eyes went idly beyond and rested on Ginny, still cycling in a fast and smooth rhythm. Damn, thought Bea, looks like a model, and fit too. Fit squared. The T-shirt was way too big for her, but she could make a black bin bag look glamorous. There was someone standing next to her, ogling. A skinny youth, with his trousers trailing halfway down to his knees. What would, no doubt, be an indecent amount of his boxers was hidden by the large bright pink T-shirt he was wearing, and Bea wondered for a moment if he was a new member of staff. Then her eyes focused on the logo on his chest and she realised who he was.

She dug Ant in the ribs.

'Ant,' she whispered furiously. 'Get him out of here.' She nodded towards Saggy. 'Quickly, before anyone notices.' Ant sidled though the crowd and Bea saw him catch Saggy's arm and start to lead him away.

Ginny pedalled strongly to the end of her session. As soon as she was off the bike, Bea tried to usher her away but her adoring fans (well, Dean from Stores) wanted a few more snaps of her posing by it. Bea noticed that she had left the photographer's card on the front of the bike. She picked it up and was about to give it to her when she thought better of it. She'd keep it until she'd written the details down, give it to Ginny later. Because she'd remembered where she'd seen

Kevin McKey before. She hadn't served him at her checkout, but she had seen him near the fruit and veg the night Emma was attacked.

Dot came over and took her aside.

'Bea, I think you ought to see this,' she said. She had her phone in her hand.

'I took a few snaps, you know, for the staff noticeboard. I'm not sure Big Gav's going to like this.'

The photo on her phone was of the group gathered around Ginny and Kayleigh. Dot must have been standing next to Kevin McKey to take it – it was a perfectly composed shot. It would look great in the *Evening Post*. Except for the lad at the side, leaning in with a massive grin on his face and giving the camera a cheeky two thumbs up. His hands framed the text on his T-shirt.

'Ant can wait his turn,' said Bea. 'I'm going to kill Saggy.'

6

Although her shift ended at four, Bea was intending to stay until the close of play just in case anything cropped up. She'd have something to eat in the café, then do some bucket-rattling. She stood in line at the counter, looking at the selection of cold food, then up at the board of 'hot specials'. Perhaps this was her chance to try something adventurous.

'Flo, what's that veggie thing like?' she called over to one of the servers, who was wrestling expertly with the coffee machine.

'Butternut squash lasagne? Very nice, Bea.'

'What's butternut squash taste like?'

'Haven't you ever had it?'

'Nope. First time for everything.'

'It's kind of smooth and sweet. In a good way.'

'Sweet? In a savoury dish? Oh. Can I have a bacon sandwich?'

Her phone pinged again. Queenie. 'RING ME.'

Bea sighed and dialled home.

'Where are you? Where have you been all day? Didn't you get my messages?'

'At work, Mum. I've been busy with the spinathon, remember?'

'Are you coming home now?'

'No, I told you this morning. I'm going to stay on until it's finished.'

'Bea, please. Come home.' There was a tremor in her voice. 'I've been holding on until now. Please, love.'

'Queenie, for God's sake. It's just today. It's only a few hours . . .'

'Please, love.' She was starting to cry and Bea felt like her insides were being scooped out.

'Has something happened? Mum—' she tried to make herself heard through the weeping at the other end 'what is it?'

'I've had a letter.'

'What sort of letter?'

'I'll show you when you get home.'

'All right. I'll come now, but I'll have to come back in later.'

She rang off and turned to Flo.

'Can I cancel that? I've got to go.'

'It's on the griddle now, love. Sit down and I'll bring it over in a minute. You look done in.'

'Nah. It's my mum – she's in one of her states. Tell you what, could you make another and wrap them up in some foil? We could have them at home.'

'All right, love. But sit down anyway. Sauce with them?'

'Brown, please.'

Bea sank down onto one of the hard wooden chairs at the nearest table. Flo wasn't wrong – she felt absolutely knackered.

It was already dark as she walked home. She'd tucked the aluminium foil bundles into her handbag and held it close to her body. Although the High Street was busy, Bea felt strangely vulnerable as she walked past the shops and pubs. She wondered if she saw people watching her out of the

95

corner of her eye. She walked on the road side of the pavement, keeping away from dark doorways.

I'm tired, she thought. That's all it is.

She turned out of the High Street and into the Green. Old people's bungalows were clustered on one side. As she walked past one row, she was sure she saw a curtain fall into place. Someone had been watching and didn't want to be seen.

She kept to the edge of the Green, near the houses and then took the long way around, along the path to the shops, rather than down the alleyway which had spooked her before. She couldn't help looking over her shoulder from time to time. There were a couple of dog walkers, and a gaggle of kids coming home late from school. Everything was normal. Everything was fine, even if it didn't feel like it.

She knocked on the back door and heard the key in the lock and two bolts sliding back. Queenie was waiting for her, her face blotchy, her eyes red and sore. She shut the door after her and stood there holding the key, turning it over and over in her hands. Bea was shocked by her appearance. Things hadn't been this bad for months.

'What on earth's wrong?' she said.

'Over there. On the table.'

There was a letter. It was still concertinaed from being folded into its envelope. Bea picked it up and tried to smooth out the creases. Her heart sank when she read the header. 'Department for Work and Pensions.'

She read on. The department were reviewing eligibility for those receiving benefits and would like to interview Mrs Jordan about her fitness for work. She was to ring the number given to arrange a mutually convenient time and date for the interview which would take place at the assessment centre in Bristol.

'What am I going to do, Bea? I can't go there, can I? They can't make me do that? What am I going to do?'

'All right, all right. Calm down. Let me put the kettle on and I'll read the letter again. Come on, Mum, sit down.'

The letter didn't improve on second reading.

'You'll have to ring them and explain about your . . . condition. They can come here if they want to interview you.'

'I can't ring them.'

'Of course you can.'

'But what if they won't—?'

'Then we'll get someone to talk to them for us. Your GP or Citizen's Advice or someone.'

'You'll ring for me, won't you? Tell them that I can't get there.'

'Yes. All right. I'll ring.' She checked her watch. Just after five. 'They won't be there now. I'll do it tomorrow.'

But Queenie wouldn't calm down. They talked round and round until their tea had grown cold. Then Bea remembered the bacon sandwiches. She opened her bag and produced the foil parcels. 'Look,' she said, 'we can't do anything about it this evening. Let's make a fresh pot of tea, watch the news and have these.'

'What are they?'

Bea unwrapped the foil and put the sandwiches onto plates. Despite the insulation, they were cold.

'Bacon sarnies,' she said, and then, to convince herself as much as Queenie, 'Yum.'

'What have you brought them for? It's chicken and vegetable rice on Wednesdays, you know that.'

'I just thought—'

'Why are you doing this to me, Bea?'

'I'm not *doing* anything. I brought you a bacon sandwich. You could just say thank you!'

'But it's Wednesday!'

'I know it's sodding Wednesday! And I know it should be sodding chicken and sodding rice, but it's not. Okay?'

'No! It's not okay! I don't understand—'

'For God's sake, Mum. Eat it or don't eat it. I don't sodding care.'

Bea grabbed her plate and took it through to the lounge, where she plonked herself down and clicked the telly on. She bit a good chunk out of the sandwich and started chewing. The tang of the brown sauce couldn't hide the nastiness of the cold, congealed fat. The meat itself was tough and stringy. How could something so glorious when hot be so unpleasant when cold? Would microwaving it help? But then she'd have to go back into the kitchen, which she wasn't prepared to do just yet. So she ploughed her way through it, bite by miserable bite.

By the time she got to the end, her stomach felt as heavy as her conscience. She hated falling out with Queenie, but sometimes, just sometimes she wished that things were different. She wished...

'Made you a hot one.'

Bea started awake. The plate that had been balanced on her knees fell onto the carpet. 'What?'

Queenie was next to the sofa, holding out a mug of tea.

'Fresh cup of tea. Peace offering. I'm sorry.

Bea reached down and retrieved her plate and put it on the glass-topped coffee table. It was all coming back to her now.

'No, I'm sorry. I shouldn't have lost my temper. I was just tired.'

'I know. You were spark out just now. And it's not your fault. I'd got in a state, hadn't I?'

'Yes, but—'

'You shouldn't have to deal with it.'

'I don't mind. Honestly.'

She took the tea from Queenie and put it next to her plate,

then held her mum's hands in hers and drew her onto the sofa next to her.

'We'll sort it all out, Mum. It'll be all right.'

'Will it?'

Queenie looked into her eyes, uncertain and yet trusting Bea to say the right thing, do the right thing, make everything better. Bea felt a sharp pang inside. When did she start feeling like the parent in this relationship? But she knew the answer, could trace it back to the terrible day six years ago, when the bottom fell out of both their worlds.

'You'll be there, won't you? When they come to interview me?'

'Yes, Mum. I'll be there.'

A little crowd gathered for the end of the spinathon. Bea had wondered whether it would just peter out, but all the staff still on shift left their stations for the big finale. Neville, Bob-on-Meat and Dean from Stores were there. Most of the checkout ladies were processing the last stragglers but a couple escaped from their tills early. Some had come back after an evening at home, including Ginny, who looked as fresh as a daisy. The Leisure Centre staff were there, too, including Lee.

Gavin was doing the final leg on the bike. Turns out his suit hid a multitude of sins: in jogging bottoms and T-shirt his full size was revealed. He was not a small man. It was clear that he was struggling to get to the finish line. His face was red, worryingly tinged with grey.

'He's really trying, isn't he?' Ginny said to Bea, looking towards him and covering her mouth with her hand. 'Can't be easy, being that, you know ... ' She left the word *big* hanging in the air, unspoken.

'We're not all skinny little racing snakes like you,' said Bea, without rancour. 'But everyone's mucked in, haven't they? Proper team effort.'

There were still ten minutes to go. The pedals were slowing. Gavin was gasping for air.

Policeman Tom found Bea in the crowd. He put his hand on her shoulder, making her jump. 'Can I have a word?'

What have I done now? thought Bea. Was it that sodding T-shirt, offending public decency?

He took her to one side and leaned in close.

'I've had First Aid training,' he said, 'and I think he's had enough.'

'Do you think he might keel over?'

'I think he should stop. Not good publicity for anyone if the manager is carted away in an ambulance.'

Bea went over to Lee, who was near the bike. She beckoned him close to her.

'Do you think he can carry on to the end?'

Lee shook his head.

'He started off way too fast and now he's not looking good. I did have a word in his ear, but he's determined to keep going.'

'Someone needs to tell him. He's not going to like it,' said Bea.

'No, but you're in charge, aren't you? Of the spinathon?'

'I suppose so.'

'Time for a substitution.'

Ant was skulking at the back of the crowd. Bea quickly threaded her way through to him.

'I'm going to take Gavin off,' she said. 'Are you fit to do the last ten minutes?'

'Me? I don't think I'm flavour of the month.'

'Just do it for me. I'll look after Gavin, take him away for a sit down, and you nip on and finish the job.'

'Yeah?'

'Yeah. Come with me now.'

They made their way to the middle of the gathering. Lee

and Tom stood nearby. She looked at both of them and they nodded. Okay, deep breath.

Gavin was still going, just. His head was hanging between his arms, his glasses slipping down to the end of his nose.

'Gavin,' Bea said, 'it's time to stop.'

He lifted his head a little to look at the monitor. He squinted his eyes, trying to make sense of it.

'Is it?' he said. 'I can't see the time on this thing.'

'Yes,' said Bea, firmly. 'You've done brilliantly. It's time now. Come on.' She put her hand on his arm and started to help him off the bike, then she turned to the crowd. 'Big round of applause for Gavin, everyone. Come on, show him some love!'

The onlookers dutifully complied with a burst of applause, some whooping, and a very piercing whistle. Bea and Tom led Gavin to a folding chair, set up near Customer Services.

'Is your wife – Steph – coming along? Do you want me to ring her?'

She wasn't sure if he'd heard her, then he muttered, 'No. No. Don't ring.'

'You sure?'

'Don't ring her. I'm all right.'

They handed him some water and draped a towel round his neck. Tom discreetly took his pulse. 'I'll take it again in five minutes, make sure you're recovering okay.'

Egged on by their own noise, the crowd kept going, encouraging Ant as he pedalled furiously, his legs becoming a blur.

Gavin was hunched over for a while. When he looked up he seemed confused.

'Why are they still cheering? What's going on?'

'Ant's just doing the last five minutes.'

'What? Didn't I—'

'You did brilliantly.'

'I didn't do thirty minutes, did I? I couldn't even manage that.'

He looked absolutely crushed. Bea did a bit of quick thinking.

'No, but it's not over yet. You've got five minutes to get your breath back and then lead the thank yous to everyone who's still here. I can't do that public speaking stuff. That's your job.'

'Oh, right. Right.'

He took another swig of water and started wiping his face and neck with the towel. He looked up at Bea. 'It's been a team effort, hasn't it?'

'Yes, Gav. It really has.' She beamed at him.

In the middle of the crowd, Ant looked like he was going for some sort of record. Tom took Gavin's pulse again and seemed satisfied. Bea waited until everyone started the countdown for the last thirty seconds.

'You okay to speak?' she asked Gavin.

'Yes.'

He stood up slowly. He was still flushed but he looked normally hot now, rather than worrying grey. The crowd parted to let him and Bea through.

When Lee blew the whistle for the final time, Ant climbed up onto the saddle and took a flying leap, like a triumphant jockey. He stumbled a bit on landing, but Dean and Bob were there to set him on his feet again.

Gavin waited for the noise to die down, then gave a short speech, thanking everyone for taking part. He reminded them about the reason they'd done it – little Kayleigh and her mum Keisha who were both, he said, part of the Costsave family. He thanked the Leisure Centre for providing the bike and their staff, and especially Bea for making it all happen. Bea felt herself colouring up as the cheers rang out for her. She did a little self-conscious curtsey and then stepped back into the crowd. She was so busy wishing she could disappear that she almost missed the last words from Gavin. 'I propose that we all move on to the Nag's Head. The first round is on me!'

Bea thought the roof was going to come off.

Neville bustled around with his clipboard, reminding everyone to log off from their tills and scrub down the counters like usual before they left. The off-duty staff mucked in. The last few customers were dealt with and escorted out, the shutters brought down on the freezers and fridges. Gavin locked the front door and people trooped back to the staffroom to get changed and collect their things.

As they filed out of the staff door, Dot linked arms with Bea. 'Coming to the pub? Don't think you'll have to buy a drink all night.'

Bea imagined the crush in the hot, sweaty room – condensation running down the windows, booze on everyone's breath and the waft of cigarette smoke every time someone opened the door. It had been a while since she'd been out. She was kind of tempted. But then she remembered Queenie and the letter, and she knew she'd be waiting for her, hovering by the back door until she got home.

'No,' she said, 'I'd better get back.'

There were howls of protest.

'Noo! Come on, Bea! This is your night.'

'Come on, Bea. Pleeeeease.'

'Ah, maybe one, then.'

A cheer went up. Her conscience pricked her, but it couldn't quite spoil the feeling of being the hero of the hour, as they swept along the High Street and bundled into the Nag's Head. Soon she was crammed into a corner by the bar with a vodka and tonic in her hand. There were multiple toasts and her drink was soon gone.

'Can I buy you another?'

She looked round. It was Dave, the married man. A movement in the crowd pushed him even closer to her. He seemed to stumble forward, pressing against her. He put his arm behind her and braced his hand against the wall, relieving some of the pressure.

'Busy in here, isn't it?' he said.

Close to, Bea could see a thin layer of stubble on his jawline. His eyes were brown and kind, and he had surprisingly long eyelashes. His face was only a few inches away from hers and once again she found herself imagining the gap closing, the feel of his mouth on hers. He had a nice mouth, not thin, but not too full. He's also got a wife, she told herself firmly. A wife who had a black eye this morning.

'So, what are you drinking?' he said. His arm had dropped to rest around her shoulders.

'Nothing. I've got to go, actually,' Bea said. 'I just popped in for one.'

'Ah, go on. One more won't hurt.'

'No, really – excuse me.'

'Bea,' he said. 'One drink.' The kindness had evaporated from his eyes. There was something steelier there now.

'How do you know my name?' she said. Despite the heat, a chill ran down her spine.

'You're not wearing it now, but you were last Thursday.' She must have looked confused. 'Your name badge,' he said.

'Oh, right.' She made a show of looking at her watch. It was nearly a quarter to eleven. 'Okay, I've really got to go now.'

'Boyfriend waiting for you?'

'Mum.' Damn! The minute the word was out of her mouth, Bea wanted to take it back. Not Mum, boyfriend. Big, fierce, imaginary boyfriend that would keep creeps like you away from me.

She wriggled away from him and squeezed through a gap in the crowd.

'You going, babe?' Dot said, as she passed her.

'Yeah. Better get back to Queenie.'

'Give her my love, then. See you tomorrow.'

'See ya.'

Gavin was near the door. 'Want another drink, Bea?'

'No, thanks, Gav. I've got to get off now.'

'Not on your own, surely?'

'It's only a few minutes, Gav. I'll be fine.'

'Okay, if you're sure. Thanks for today, Bea.' He high-fived her, and she reached for the door handle.

The air was shockingly cold after the warm fug of the pub. She pulled up the collar of her coat and set off. A few metres along she heard the swell of noise from the pub as the door opened again, but she didn't think anything of it. Her mind was focused on getting home, having a nice cup of tea and going to bed. It had been a very long day.

She turned off the High Street and walked past the bungalows. She thought she heard footsteps behind her. Well, it was the normal time for people to be walking home from the pub. Even so, she glanced round. The man, and she was sure it was a man, was in the shadows, between the pools of soft yellow light thrown out by the streetlights. He was about thirty metres behind her.

Okay, don't panic, she thought. Her legs protested as she increased her speed. The day's exertions had taken their toll. Oh God, she thought, I couldn't run if I had to. I just couldn't. She listened hard as she walked along. The man seemed to be keeping pace with her. Getting closer, even. Don't look. Don't let him think you're rattled. But she *was* rattled.

She was skirting around the edge of the Green now. The path was close to the rows of houses, but all the curtains were drawn, the doors shut and bolted. No one was around. No one could see her. There was an opening to a roadway between the houses. It would take her much longer to get home that way but a road felt better than a path right now.

She dodged sideways and hurried along. As she turned the corner, she couldn't help looking back. He was ten metres away now – a dark figure, wearing a hat or a hood which somehow shaded his face.

She turned another corner onto the main road into her estate, relieved to see headlights coming towards her.

'Bea!' The man behind shouted her name, as the car slowed to her pace and drove alongside. The streetlight picked out the fluorescent stripe down the side. The driver wound down his window. It was Tom.

'Bea!' he called. 'Get in!'

She ran around the back of the car and yanked open the passenger door. She swung into the seat and slammed the door shut.

'Drive,' she said. 'Just drive. There's someone . . . I think there's someone following me.'

'I'm a policeman,' Tom said. 'If there's someone there, I'll have him.'

They both looked in their side mirrors and then twisted round in their seats to look behind. There was no one there.

'We'll wait for a minute. See if he crawls out of the wood-work, although I should think the jam sandwich will have frightened him off.'

They sat for a little while. Bea leaned back in the seat and shut her eyes.

'You all right?'

Tom put his hand on top of hers. It was large, warm, reassuring. Bea just sat and enjoyed the feeling for a few seconds, then she opened her eyes.

'Yeah,' she said. 'Thank God you came along when you did.'

'I was in the pub,' he said, 'and I saw you leave. I just didn't like the thought of you walking home on your own.'

'That's really kind,' she said. Without really thinking about what she was doing, she turned her hand over so that their palms met. His fingers closed around hers, and this meeting of hands was something else now. A sort of conversation without words. And he was looking at her and she was looking at him.

'I'd better get home,' she said, and the spell was broken.

'Yes,' he said. 'Shall we drive around for a bit, see if we can spot this guy?'

'I don't know. No, really. I'd rather just go home.'

'Okay. I'll patrol the area when I've dropped you off.' He put the car into gear and drove off smoothly. 'Can you tell me anything about him?'

'No, not really.' Once again, Bea felt at a loss. 'It was dark when I looked back. He had a hood up, I think.'

'Tall? Short? Well built?'

'I don't know. Sorry, I'm a bit useless.'

'It's all right. If this guy's out there, we'll get him.'

'If?'

'If this was the one that attacked Emma. We'll get him. We won't stop until we do.'

'Did she say anything about the guy that attacked her? Was he wearing a hoodie too?'

'I shouldn't be telling you this, but she can't remember anything about the attack. She only remembers starting to walk home. The attack itself and five or ten minutes before that are blank.'

'Oh. Maybe it'll come back to her.'

'Yeah, the doctors say that might happen. You can't force these things though. So until then, we've got no description, no ID.'

'He needs stopping. Women should be able to walk home without being raped.'

'Emma wasn't raped, Bea. He hit her, punched her, but there wasn't anything sexual.'

'Oh, but I heard—'

'That's the trouble with the rumour mill, isn't it? People just make stuff up and it gets repeated like gospel. Anyway, we'll get the bastard, don't you worry. Is this you here?'

Tom was pulling the car up outside Bea's house.

'Yeah. Thanks, Tom. I mean it.'

She fumbled with the catch to release the seatbelt. He went to help her and their hands touched again.

'You were great today, Bea,' Tom said, and he leaned across and kissed her softly, just at the side of her mouth. Bea moved her head a little and her mouth met his. Two kisses. Three. Tentative. Gentle. They drew apart. Bea couldn't look at him. Wanted to, but couldn't.

'Okay. Thanks,' she said, and opened the door. Then she remembered, 'One thing. About the guy following me. He knew my name.'

'Right. That narrows it down. I'll go looking now. I'll radio the other cars, too, just in case. Goodnight, Bea.'

'Goodnight.'

She got out and closed the door. She walked slowly up the path and round to the back, partly because her legs would only just move, and partly because she was savouring her close encounter with Tom.

7

'Three and a half thousand pounds, Bea. That's amazing!' said Dot. Standing next to her at the mirrors, Bea hardly reacted. Dot frowned. 'What's up, love? You look like someone's taken your lollipop away.'

Bea leaned close. 'Don't tell anyone, but I was followed home last from the pub last night.'

'Followed? Again?'

'Yeah, he knew who I was, too. He called out my name, just before Tom turned up and I got in his car.'

'Tom? The dishy copper?'

Bea tried her very best not to blush, but saying his name, hearing it, thinking about the two of them in the car together made her go all hot – she couldn't help it.

'Here, you're blushing. You like him, don't you?'

'Maybe. Shut up.' She grew redder and hotter.

Dot grabbed a stiff paper towel and started fanning Bea's face. 'Love it!' she said. 'You go for it, girl!'

Bea grabbed the towel away from her and gently blotted her forehead.

'I'm not going for anything. There's nothing going on! I mean, we haven't . . . '

'You have. I know it.'

'Just a kiss.'

Dot's eyes lit up. 'Ooooh, I *knew* it. Is he a good kisser?'

'Shut up.'

But Dot kept looking at her, eyebrows raised.

'Yes, okay,' she admitted. '*Yes.*'

Dot drew Bea into a triumphal dance, waltzing her round the washroom. When they came to a stop, Dot gave her a little squeeze.

'I'm happy for you, babe. I really am. About time.'

'It might not even be anything, Dot, so don't say anything, okay?'

'Okay.'

Dot zipped her mouth up and then said in a muffled voice, 'Your secret's safe with me.' Then, unzipped, 'Come on, you're going to get a hero's welcome in the staffroom.'

Which is exactly what happened. A hero's welcome, Costsave style – a ripple of applause, some whistles and catcalls and a 'small token of appreciation' from management in the form of a box of Costsave Luxury Range Belgian Chocolates. An early edition of the local paper had come in and was proudly on display on the coffee table, open at page four. Bea anxiously studied the photo for Saggy's cheeky face and cheekier T-shirt, but thankfully an eagle-eyed picture editor had cropped him out. Everybody agreed what a cracking photo it was – a sea of smiling faces, Ginny looking like a supermodel on the bike and Keisha and a slightly tearful Kayleigh in the foreground.

'Brilliant, Bea, that's what it is,' said Gavin. 'Costsave is back on track. Anna's going to arrange one of those big presentation cheques and we'll get Keisha and Kayleigh down again for the handover. So, well done all!' Gavin started clapping, turning around and directing his applause to everyone in the room. The others joined in.

Ant slunk into the room, using the noise as cover for his lateness. Bea noticed he was looking flustered. They made eye contact and he started edging his way through the group towards her.

'Now,' said Gavin when the noise had died down, 'next up – Halloween. We're going to make it the best one ever for the store and the town. The local police will be coming in today to talk about it, and how to avoid last year's antisocial behaviour.'

'The Great K-Town Egg Riot?' Dean heckled from the back. 'Oh, man, that was classic!'

Gavin fixed him with a stern look. 'It was not "classic", Dean. It caused a lot of people a great deal of nuisance and distress. As you know, the perpetrators were never caught, but we'll be bringing in a strict no eggs to under-eighteens rule. Ask for ID if you have any doubt.'

Dean was still chuckling to himself.

'And if anyone is found selling eggs to under-eighteens, it will be a disciplinary offence.' He looked at his watch, 'Right, stations, everyone. Ant, stay here a minute. You were late.'

'Yes, I know, I'm sorry but I had to go a different way. The path was taped off by the cops and there was a white tent up. Something's gone on.'

There were murmurs of concern from the others, but Gavin wasn't going to be put off.

'You need to allow time to get here. It's important to all be here for the team briefings. You need to think "team", Ant,' he said, tapping the side of his head.

'Yeah, sorry, Gav— Mr Howells – it's just—'

'What?'

He and Gavin were causing a bottleneck in the doorway, the rest of the staff bunching up behind, ready to go downstairs to the shop floor. There was a bit of good-natured jostling – the mood was still buzzy.

Ant was standing on his tiptoes looking past Gavin across the heads of the group.

'What is it, Ant?' Gavin repeated.

'The tent,' he said. 'The tape.' He paused and scanned the crowd again. 'Has anyone seen Ginny?'

Her name rippled through the staff from the front of the queue to the back, and every single one of them fell silent. Gavin shot a look over to Anna, who pressed her lips together and nodded. Ginny was due on shift now.

Gavin cleared his throat and said, 'I expect she's off sick. Anna will ring from the office, just to check that she's okay. The rest of you go to your stations.'

The staff filed out and down the stairs. On the way down to the shop floor, Bea found Ant at her shoulder.

'Something's happened to her,' he said, keeping his voice low.

'You don't know that,' said Bea. 'She's probably slept in or got a cold or something.'

'She lives round the corner from that path.'

'So do lots of people. Did you actually see anything apart from the tent?'

Ant shrugged. 'Just a load of coppers in uniform and then a bloke in a white jumpsuit thing going into the tent.' Bea felt her stomach contract. 'There's a body there, Bea.'

'You didn't see one though?' She was trying to keep calm.

'No, but—'

'Don't jump to conclusions, then.'

'Okay, but . . . something else.'

'What?'

'I'm going to need your help, Bea.' She looked at his face. There was no mistaking the distress.

'What's up?'

'They've put me on picking – doing the shopping for online orders. I can't do it, Bea. Can you help me?'

'I don't see how I can. I'm stuck on the checkout. If you

112

bring it to my till at the end, I can check what you've got against the list. But that's about all I can do.'

'Can you tell me the first ten items and then I'll come back for the next ten?'

Bea sighed. 'We can try, but why don't you just own up? Tell someone why you can't do it.'

'I can't. People'll just think I'm thick.'

They were just outside the door to the shop floor now. Bea stopped walking.

'At least tell *me*. Say it.'

Ant looked at her. There was a sharp frown line between his brows. He licked his lips a couple of times.

'Bea,' he said, so quietly she could only just hear him. 'I can't read.'

Without saying anything, she put her arms round him. He felt rigid and unresponsive in her embrace, mortified by the words he'd just said out loud. Bea stepped back again.

'I'll help you as much as I can, Ant. We'll sort this out.'

Hard as they tried to sneak under the radar, Neville was soon on their case. After Ant had called by to see Bea for the third time, he swooped.

'Break time is when we chat,' he said to Bea. 'I'm going to have to report you to Mr Howells if you and Anthony keep stopping work like this.'

'We're not chatting, Neville, I'm helping him. He's really trying. He wants to get it just right. He doesn't know where everything is yet.'

'But Eileen is his supervisor on the shop floor. He should be going to her for advice.'

'Um, well, they didn't exactly hit it off, you must have noticed. It's not holding me up, I promise, and I'm happy to help. Don't get on at him, Neville, please. He's trying his best.'

Out of the corner of her eye, she saw Ant scoot into view.

He saw Neville, skidded to a stop and reversed, dragging his trolley out of sight. He waited until Neville had gone back to his station, then darted over to Bea without his trolley.

'What did he want?'

'He's onto us.'

'Not—?'

'No, just on at me to stop "chatting". I told him I was helping you find stuff.'

'I can't do it, Bea. I can't do this.'

'Ask Eileen.'

'I can't. She's a monster. She'll dob me in.'

'She's not that bad, Ant, just try.'

'I can't. I'm gonna . . . I'll just have to—' he looked around wildly 'hide in the bogs or something.'

'Don't do that, look at the stuff you've already got and guess what else she'd like. Bring it to my checkout, and I'll send you back for stuff if it's wrong.'

'I can't do that! I'm not a flippin' mind reader! How do I know what she wants?'

'Bags of rocket. Ripe and ready avocado. Soya milk. She's into alternative, healthy stuff, Ant. Give me the list. Yup, it's all here. Organic mince – that's in packets at the far end of aisle six – quails' eggs.'

'Quails' eggs? What are they?'

'Tiny little speckled eggs – look in the luxury foods section. Come on, Ant. You can do it.'

'I can't. I really can't.'

'That's it, you're both on report!' Neville had appeared without either of them noticing.

'Please, Neville, just give him a chance!'

'He's had plenty of chances. As have you. I will ask Mr Howells to issue both of you with an official warning—'

They wouldn't have to wait long. Bea could see Gavin

walking along the end of the aisles, looking down each one. She sighed.

'You can ask him now,' she said. 'He's coming our way.'

Neville bustled over to him. Bea could see him telling Gavin about all their shortcomings. He was enjoying this. Eileen joined their little group. She was nodding as Neville spoke and trying to get a word in. Put the boot in, more like, thought Bea.

Ant groaned and leaned his head onto Bea's conveyor belt. 'It's all over, isn't it?' he said. 'Just shoot me now.'

His anguish was real. Bea stretched forward and put a comforting hand on one of his shoulders.

'What's going on?' Dot hissed from the next till. 'What's happened?'

'I'll tell you later,' Bea hissed back, and then to Ant, 'Tell the truth, Ant. Gavin's a top bloke, for a boss. He'll want to help you.'

Neville, Gavin and Eileen walked over to Bea's till. Bea withdrew her hand from Ant's back.

'Stand up, boy,' Neville commanded. Ant stayed down.

'Ant, come and talk to me in the office,' Gavin said.

Ant groaned again, but didn't move.

'Come on now. This is silly. You're getting in the way of our customers. I want to hear your side. I'll listen to you.'

Ant tipped his head and squinted up at his audience. Gavin held his hand out to him. 'Come on.'

Ant unwound and stood up, but didn't take Gavin's hand. He smoothed himself down a bit and stared at the floor, shuffling his feet.

'I might as well just leave,' he said. 'I know how this is going to go.'

Gavin held his hand out again and this time gently made contact with Ant's elbow. 'Come on, come up to the office.'

'Um, Mr Howells, I think you're needed,' Eileen broke

115

in. She tipped her head towards the door. They all looked in that direction. Tom and his partner in crime-solving were heading their way.

Gavin looked at his watch. 'Ach,' he said, 'they're coming to talk about Operation Safe Halloween. I thought it was eleven thirty. Must have got my wires crossed.' He squeezed Ant's arm. 'Come and see me later. Just carry on here for the time being.'

Ant rolled his eyes at Bea, but she was focused on Tom, waiting for him to acknowledge her, make eye contact. She could feel herself blushing, feel Dot's eyes on her. Tom got closer. He was looking straight forward. For a moment he seemed to see her, but then it was like he was looking through her, to Gavin and the others. He came right up to her till and there was nothing – no flicker of recognition, no little sign. Her stomach flipped. Her face burnt. Yesterday meant nothing. She meant nothing to him. Why else would he ignore her like this? Shit! Damn him, then. And damn her for caring.

She glanced up at his face again. His pale freckled skin was blotched with pink patches. His Adam's apple was bobbing up and down.

'Constable Barnes,' Gavin said, with a Costsave welcoming smile, 'and Constable Sanders. Did we say ten for our Halloween chat?'

Tom swallowed hard. 'It's not that, I'm afraid, Mr Howells. We're here on other business. Can we go to your office?'

The smile fell from Gavin's face. 'Other business? Of course, of course. This way.'

He ushered them across the shop floor and through the door to the stairs. Neville trailed several paces behind them, not invited, but not able to leave them alone. Eileen looked daggers at Ant.

'You can't get away with this. The amount of skiving you

116

do is ridiculous. And you're encouraging him. I expected better from you,' she said to Bea.

'Eileen, it's complicated, it's—'

'Don't, Bea! It's nothing to do with you!' Ant shouted. 'It's me! I can't do this!'

'All right, let's all calm down. Not on the shop floor,' said Eileen.

'I'm trying my best! I just can't—'

'All right. All right. Take some time out. Go and help Wayne with the trolleys in the car park for a few minutes. I'll do this list.' She took the printout from Ant and started wheeling his trolley towards the Organic and Free From aisle. Ant watched her go, puffing out his cheeks and blowing out air through his mouth.

'This is too difficult, man,' he said. He headed through the shop towards the front door.

'What's going on with him?' Dot asked Bea.

'I'll tell you on our break. Can you cover for me for a minute? I need a wee.'

'Yeah, okay. We're not exactly busy, are we?'

Bea logged out of her till and headed for the staff door. She crept up the stairs and stood at the top, listening. She could hear voices coming from Gavin's office. She tiptoed closer to the door and pressed her ear against it, but could only catch the murmur of conversation, not the words. Then a sharper noise as a chair scraped back. She darted along the corridor to the ladies' loos and locked herself into a cubicle. After a decent interval she flushed and emerged, giving her hands a quick wash and dry, before going back out to the corridor. The door to the ladies' locker room was half-open. She could see figures inside. She went a little closer, and peered through the gap. The two police officers stood by as Gavin used his master key to open one of the lockers. Ginny's locker.

Bea gasped. Tom heard and looked round. The movement made the others look too.

'Bea,' Tom said. He shook his head. And Bea knew.

'No,' she said. 'No.'

She managed to reach a cubicle in the toilets just before she threw up.

8

Costsave stayed open for the rest of the day, but the whole place took on a different tone. Customers and staff conducted their business in a hushed, crushed way. The metal beams which on normal days made the shop look and feel like an industrial warehouse seemed to Bea more like the arches in a cathedral, a quiet space where people were lost in their thoughts as they wheeled their trolleys around, loaded and unloaded their shopping. The noise of the barcode scanner grated on her nerves until she didn't think she could take it any more.

Neville had retreated to the customer service desk and stayed there for the entire shift so Bea was able to help Ant complete a couple of online orders when he came back in from the car park. After that, he asked Eileen to be excused and she let him go back onto trolley duty outside until the end of the afternoon. No one had any appetite for a fight. They were all just trying to get through the day.

The two police officers called various staff members into Gavin's office, quizzing them about the day before. Bea kept an eye on the comings and goings from her checkout. Tom played it straight when it was Bea's turn. What was she doing yesterday? Had she noticed anything out of the ordinary during the spinathon or at the pub? What time did she leave the Nag's Head? His colleague raised an eyebrow when she told them both about getting into Tom's car, but didn't say a word, just carried on scribbling in her notebook. Bea thought Tom coloured up a little, but she wasn't sure.

'Is it the same person, do you think?' Bea asked. 'First Emma and now this?'

'We can't discuss the investigation,' Tom said.

'No. No, of course not.' But in her mind, Bea was already running through her list of suspects. She could cross-check them now, couldn't she? Who had been in the store both days. Who had been at the pub. Although, really, what business was it of hers? It was a job for the police, wasn't it? Even so, the thought of being busy, of actively trying to *do* something appealed.

As she was heading for the door, Tom called after her. 'I don't want you to walk home alone, Bea.'

She turned around. Was he offering her another lift? Was this his way of getting them together again? 'Is that what you're telling everyone?'

'It is actually, until we catch him.' A little bit crushed, she reached for the door handle, but Tom wasn't finished. 'I won't be done here, otherwise I'd give you a lift. Check in with me anyway. I need to know that you're safe.'

This was more like it. She nodded and smiled and made her way back to her station.

When clocking-off time finally crawled its way round, Bea and Dot got changed in silence. Ginny's locker was empty now, the door not quite closed. When they had shrugged off their uniforms and put on their coats, Bea glanced at the window. It was already dark outside and she shivered.

'Ant said he'd walk me home,' Dot said. 'He'll walk with you, too.'

'I wasn't going to go straight home,' said Bea, looking

over to Ginny's locker again. 'I thought I might take her some flowers, put some, you know, where ... '

Dot nodded. 'I was just thinking that. Some of ours or some nice ones?'

'Nice ones. Carol's shop should be open till half past.'

'Come on, then.' Dot linked her arm through Bea's. 'What were you going to tell me about Ant?'

Bea hesitated. It wasn't her place to say. 'It's just this problem doing his work. He should tell you really.'

'Come on, Bea. It's you and me. You tell me, and I promise I'll act surprised when he spills the beans.'

'It's just that he can't read, Dot. He never learnt at school.'

Dot's mouth formed a perfect O. 'That makes sense now you say it,' she said, 'but I never suspected. He's clever, isn't he? How he works round it. He's clever – but he can't read. Poor lad.'

'I think he should tell Big Gav, but he won't do it. Ashamed, I think.'

'Ah, bless,' said Dot. 'Nothing to be ashamed of. They won't sack him, though, will they? Although he might be on trolleys for the rest of his life.'

'Unless Costsave cough up and pay for lessons for him.'

'Do you think that's likely?'

'Dunno. It's definitely a good news story if they do,' said Bea. 'We won't know unless he gets up the courage to tell Gav.'

'Hmm, let's get him in a pincer movement. He'll be helpless.'

'I'm just going to pop in on Tom. He said to let him know how I was getting home.'

Dot's eyes brightened. 'Did he now?'

Bea couldn't think of a put-down. 'He's just ... being a gentleman.'

121

'Ah, that's nice. Think he might be a keeper, that one. I'll wait in the corridor.'

Bea knocked on Gavin's door; Tom came to answer it. 'I'm in the middle of things, Bea. Are you okay?' He looked tired. There were grey shadows under his eyes.

'Yeah, Ant's walking me and Dot home, so we'll be okay.'

He frowned. 'Will you be on your own with him?'

'Yeah, we'll probably go by Dot's first.'

'Do it the other way round. Make them walk to yours, then Dot's.'

She snorted, and then panicked that something might have flown out of her nose and onto Tom. 'It won't be Ant. He's not . . . no. Anyway, then Dot will be on her own with him, so what's the difference?'

He leaned a little closer. 'All the difference in the world,' he whispered. 'To me, anyway.'

Bea felt herself going warm again. She knew then that the kiss hadn't been a one-off. There would be another one. Oh yes.

Behind Tom she could see Bob-on-Meat sitting at the desk with his back to the door with the woman constable opposite, facing them. Their eyes met, and the woman didn't look away. It felt like she was sussing Bea out. Bea made to leave, and as she did so Tom reached out and his hand briefly touched hers.

'Be careful,' he said.

Dot and Ant were hanging about at the end of the corridor.

'All right, ladies?' said Ant.

'Yeah. You okay about coming with us to put some flowers down?'

'Course.'

The cold air hit them as they left the store. Bea wrapped her coat tighter around her and turned up her collar. As they walked past the recycling bins, they saw someone crouching down behind Tom's squad car. They heard the repeated click of a shutter.

'Jesus!' Ant darted ahead and shot round the side of the car. He tried to grab the camera from Kevin McKey's hands, and they tussled for a while before Kevin shoved Ant away. He staggered backwards, flailing his arms before he regained his balance.

'Push off, you little shit!' Kevin shouted. 'I'll get you for assault!'

Dislodged in the scuffle, strands of combed-over hair were flapping wildly by the side of his head. He looked like he was unravelling.

'You're out of order, you are!' Ant screamed back.

'It's my job! I'm reporting the investigation. You can't keep Costsave out of it. Everyone knows she worked here.'

'You don't have to take pictures of the girls who work here though. Creep! If you put them in your fucking paper, I'll have you!'

He jabbed a finger in Kevin's direction, inches away from his face. Kevin, holding the camera close to his body to protect it, backed away. 'All right, all right. It's not up to me anyway.'

'Well, tell whoever what I said. Don't print pictures of the girls. Got it?'

Kevin didn't reply. He was busy smoothing a hand from one ear right across the dome of his scalp to the other side. Enjoying its new found freedom, his hair sprang back again.

'Leave him, Ant. Let's get to Carol's before she closes,' Dot called out, and he came back to them. Dot and Bea linked arms with him, one either side, and they walked across the car park.

'Vultures. That's what people like him are,' said Ant.

Dot squeezed his arm. 'I know. Thanks for defending

us. You didn't need to, though. We could've had a word ourselves.'

Ant smiled. 'I was protecting him really. If you and Bea had had a go at him, he'd be wearing his balls as earrings by now.'

'True enough. Scumbag.'

'It could be him, you know,' said Bea, quietly.

'What?'

'It could be him. The man doing this. His mum lives near the Green, so he's around a lot of the time. He grew up here, so he knows all the alleyways.'

Dot and Ant stopped walking, pulling Bea to a halt as they did so.

'Are you serious?' Dot said.

Bea regretted blurting it out, but it was too late now. 'Yeah. He's on my list.'

'You've got a list?'

'When I was followed and Emma was attacked, I went through it in my mind and made a list of the blokes there that evening. That McKey bloke was one of them.'

'He is creepy,' said Dot.

'Yeah, but then so are a lot of people when you start looking. And maybe it's the ones that don't look creepy that we should be worried about.'

'It's always the quiet ones, that's what they say, isn't it?'

'Hmm.'

'Am I on it?' Ant said.

Bea swallowed. 'Yeah, but—'

'Shit. You don't really think . . . Do you?'

'No. Course not.'

'Because if you really think that I might be someone like that, do something like that, then I shouldn't be here now. I shouldn't walk you home, should I?' He was getting agitated now, disentangling his arms from theirs, stepping away then turning round to face them. 'But I can't leave you, because I know it's not me and I don't want either of you walking around while he's still out there and—'

'Ant. Ant! It's all right.' Bea walked towards him, put a hand on his arm. 'It's just a list. I don't think it's you. I'm pretty sure Dot and I are safe with you.'

'Yeah?'

'Yeah. Dot?'

'Of course. If I was at all worried, I wouldn't have . . . I mean we wouldn't . . . ' She stopped and sent a shifty look to Bea, checking if she'd noticed her embarrassment. 'You're a good person, Ant, that's all I'm saying. I'm very glad you're walking us home.'

'The cops don't think I'm a good person. They gave me a right grilling this afternoon.'

'Don't take it personally, Ant. They did that to everyone.'

She crooked her arm and held it out towards him. He grimaced and linked arms again. They set off down the High Street. 'Flowers by Carol' was halfway along, a tiny little shop, squeezed in between an Indian restaurant and a tanning place. The owner, in fleece, gilet and fingerless gloves, was taking in some of the buckets that formed the display outside.

'Not too late?' Dot said to her.

She turned around. 'Oh, hiya, Dot. No, I'm staying open later tonight. A lot of people are buying flowers for that poor girl.'

'That's what we're here for.'

She pressed her lips together. 'Feels a bit wrong taking people's money for something like this, but . . . '

'People want to buy them, Carol. They want to pay their respects. There's nothing wrong with that.'

'Yeah, I know. Do it every day, don't I, with funerals and that. Comes with the territory. This feels worse somehow.

125

Young girl like that.' They followed her into the shop. 'What would you like anyway?'

Dot and Bea decided to club together for a bouquet. They called Ant into the shop and he chipped in fifty pence. It was all he had in his pocket. While Carol wrapped the flowers in cellophane and tied them with raffia, Dot and Bea contemplated the blank card she put on the counter for them.

'I don't know what to write,' said Bea. She looked at Dot for help.

'What can we say? Rest in peace? Miss you? It all sounds, I don't know, it just doesn't say it, does it. Words can't really say what you feel.'

The card stayed blank. Dot and Bea looked at each other helplessly, then they both looked at Ant. He shrugged his shoulders.

'I didn't know her like you did. What will you miss about her?' said Ant.

'Her smile,' said Dot.

'Her cheerfulness, her optimism,' said Bea. 'There was nothing cynical about her. She was just a lovely person.'

'Yeah, she was. Like the sun coming out – she was like that.'

'Write that, then,' said Ant. 'They sound like good words to me. They do say what you feel.'

Bea wrote the card and Carol tied it onto the bouquet. They set off again, arms linked like before.

'You'll almost be home when we've done this,' Dot said. 'You won't want to walk back our way.'

'It's fine,' said Ant. 'No problem.'

The wind gusted along the street and they put their heads down and walked faster. Everyone else seemed to be doing the same. No eye contact, no friendly greetings. Everyone in a hurry to get home and lock the doors.

They passed a newspaper board outside the newsagents:

'Murder latest. Victim named.' They turned left at the roundabout at the end of the High Street and followed the road round until they reached the turning into Ant's estate. Bea was going to ask exactly where they were heading when she saw a cluster of people on the pavement fifty metres or so ahead of them, police tape visible in the gaps in between, sealing off the entrance to the alley.

'I don't know if I can do this,' said Bea.

'It's all right,' said Dot. 'We don't have to stop for long. Come on.'

As they got nearer to the alley it looked as if the pavement was twinkling as the streetlight was reflected off the wrappings of hundreds of bunches of flowers – a sea of plastic and petals.

'Oh,' said Bea, as the smell reached her: freesias and lilies and roses. The scent of a summer wedding wafting down the pavement on this cold, dark evening. She felt her tears coming and looked across at Dot. She was crying too. Between them, Ant was sombre-faced, taking in the scene.

They walked slowly forward until they reached the edge of the tribute. Bea bent down and added their bouquet. She stood up again and the three of them stood, heads bowed, for a moment or two. Bea fished in her pocket for a tissue. She dabbed at her eyes and blew her nose. Dot was doing the same. Ant had turned his back on them both and walked a few paces away. Bea turned to walk after him, but Dot caught her arm. She shook her head and mouthed, 'Leave him,' and Bea realised that he was crying too. So, the two women spent a few minutes reading some of the other cards. They were from family, friends, neighbours – an outpouring of love from the community Ginny had lived in her whole, short life.

When Ant rejoined them, they linked arms again and started walking back to the town centre.

They passed Eileen and Dean coming the other way, Eileen clutching a bunch of Costsave roses. They nodded to each other but didn't stop to chat. They walked in silence, past the end of the High Street, up to the Green. An old chip wrapper blew towards them and lodged on Bea's ankle. She kicked it off.

They crossed the Green and headed for Bea's estate. Rows of grey houses loomed out of the darkness like gravestones.

'Kingsleigh doesn't feel like Kingsleigh any more,' Dot said.

'Eh?' said Ant.

'I know what you mean,' said Bea. 'It's always been a bit dull. Nothing ever happens here. I like it like that.'

'That's not strictly true, is it?' said Ant. 'There was that time the travel agents got ram-raided.'

'Ha! They were aiming for the jewellers and missed,' said Bea. 'Classic. Only in K-town.'

'And the time those numpties were smashing the newsagents window with a sledgehammer and the frigging door was already open.'

'Again, only in K-town.'

'There was that stabbing in the chip shop, though, when we were at school,' said Ant. 'That was epic.'

'Epic? It was nasty. That's all anyone talked about for weeks at Costsave,' said Dot.

'But apart from that, it's not a bad old town, is it?'

'Hmm, not bad. And I never felt unsafe walking around. Not really,' said Bea. 'Not like now.'

'Me neither,' said Dot. 'It's just not that sort of place.'

'Maybe that's the point,' said Bea. 'Maybe everywhere is that sort of place. That's why I started investigating – I want that lowlife caught. I want Kingsleigh back to how it should be.'

'Just leave it to the professionals, Bea,' said Dot. 'Don't

start looking under stones and stirring things up. Just keep safe, babe.'

'Hmm, maybe.' She paused for a while, then, 'Ant, you should really tell Big Gav what's under your stone. Everyone forgot about it today, but it'll come back to bite you.'

Ant looked sideways at her, the whites of his eyes flashing in the streetlight.

'Shut up, Bea,' he hissed, and Bea cursed herself. She'd forgotten that Ant didn't know that Dot knew. 'Not now. Not today.'

'What not now?' asked Dot.

'Nothing,' Ant muttered.

'What is it?'

'*Nothing*. Just leave it, all right?'

'You in trouble, love?'

'No,' he said, sullenly.

'Yes,' said Bea. 'Tell her. Go on. Tell her, Ant.'

He breathed out through pursed lips and looked to the sky.

'Do you think I'm thick, Dot?'

'No. You're a smart lad.'

'Well, you're wrong. I am thick. So thick I can't even read.' His voice got quieter as he was speaking until the last four words were barely more than a whisper. But Dot had known what was coming, so she didn't need to humiliate him by asking him to repeat them.

'That's all right, love,' she said, evenly. 'Lots of people can't read.'

'Aren't you shocked?'

'No. Not really. School isn't for everyone, is it? Not everyone gets on there. My nan never learnt to read. There's no shame in it.'

'Well, I am ashamed. And Bea's on at me to tell Big Gav.'

'She's right,' said Dot. 'You'll get the sack if you don't.

You can't just refuse to do certain things, or mess them up. He needs to know.'

'He'll still sack me.'

'I'm not sure he can sack you for that. It's a thing, isn't it? Equal access or human rights or something.'

'I dunno.'

'Perhaps we could help you,' said Dot. 'Me and Bea could give you lessons.'

'You two?' said Ant. 'Are you kidding?'

'Yes, us two,' said Dot. 'And no, I'm not kidding. Bea, are you up for it?'

'Well, yeah, I'd give it a go,' said Bea. 'If you want. Ant?'

He'd turned his head away again. When he turned back his mouth was moving, but no words were coming out. Bea was shocked to see tears welling up in his eyes.

'You'd really do that?' he said, his voice a little unsteady.

'Yes, course we would.'

'Guys, that's just so ... I don't think anyone's ever been so ...'

Both women hugged his arms tighter. They were nearly at Bea's house now.

'I'll be all right from here,' she said at the end of her road.

'Na-ah, we'll see you to your door,' Ant insisted.

She said goodbye to them outside her front gate, giving each a little hug in turn. It felt right – it had been that kind of day.

'Thank you,' she said. 'I'll see you two tomorrow.' And then to Ant, 'You take care of her.'

He gave her the thumbs up. 'I will.'

Just before she went round the corner to the kitchen door, Bea glanced back. Dot was still holding Ant's arm. They both raised their free hands to wave at Bea, and she waved back.

Of course, although they'd managed to laugh it off, Ant

was one of the names on her list. And when she came to cross-check people at the pub, or at the spinathon, with those who were in the frame from Singles Night, Ant's name would still be there. She felt a little pain in her stomach, something twisting, digging away. Should she call them into the house, make up some excuse for Ant to stay here and Dot to get a taxi instead? No, she was being silly. Ant was a chancer, a bit of scally, but there was nothing nasty about him.

Whoever was out there, following girls, attacking them, leaving them for dead, was beyond nasty. There was evil inside them – something that made them step beyond normal behaviour that propelled them to cross a line.

Bea looked up again. Ant and Dot had gone. The space where they had been was softly lit up by the street lamp. It sent out a pool of light and beyond that was darkness. She'd lived in this road most of her life, but Dot was right: Kingsleigh didn't feel like Kingsleigh any more.

9

'Don't go upstairs, Bea. Sit with me.'

Bea sighed. She was worn out and numb from the day's events. But then she looked at her mum and felt her tired, sore heartstrings pulled again by the knowledge that Queenie had spent the day alone. So she sat and watched the news with her while they ate pasta parcels and sauce (it was Thursday), although in truth neither of them ate much, the food congealing on their plates as the presenter introduced the report about Ginny. A reporter stood by the taped-off alleyway leading out of the estate where Ant lived. She was wearing a red coat, with a patterned scarf tucked into the top. The wind hadn't died down at all – she kept having to scrape strands of hair away from her face.

'You'd have thought she'd have put a black coat on, wouldn't you? Showed a bit of respect,' said Queenie.

'Shh, Mum. I'm trying to watch.' They both listened as the reporter described the facts of the case. They were few and far between: Ginny's body had been found by a lad delivering newspapers in the morning. Although no official statement on the cause of death had been made, it was understood that Ginny had been attacked from behind. The area had been cordoned off and police had been making enquiries in the surrounding streets as well as at her place of work (cut to a shot of the front of the Costsave building) as well as the last place she was seen (The Nag's Head). They showed a map of Ginny's known movements which included her house, Costsave, the pub and the alley, and cut to a local police spokesman, in plain clothes, not uniform, appealing to members of the public to come forward with information.

'I wonder how much she'd been drinking,' Queenie said.

'What?'

'How much Ginny had had.'

'What's that got to do with anything?' Bea could feel her hackles rising.

'Well, if she was really drunk, she wouldn't be so aware of what was happening around her, she might not take so much care.'

Bea pointed the remote at the screen and froze it.

'Okay, stop right there, Mum. Stop. Right. There.'

'What?' Queenie seemed oblivious of the offence she was causing.

'Stop before you say "She was asking for it" because that's where you were heading.'

'Well, if you drink until you're incapable . . . '

'No! No, Mum. She was attacked in an alleyway. She was killed by some maniac. That's nothing to do with her and everything to do with the scum who attacked her.'

'I know, but—'

'But nothing. But nothing. End of.'

'Bea—'

'I was drinking, Mum. Was I asking for it, for that? Was I?'

'No. No, of course not, I just—'

'Oh, shush. Let's just watch the news.'

She pressed 'play'. Still struggling against the wind, the reporter wound up her report: 'There's an air of foreboding today in the little town of Kingsleigh. A serial attacker is walking among the people here, someone who knows the town, who knows the people. And the question on everyone's lips, "When will he strike again?" Now, back to the studio.'

'God, thought it was a news programme, not bloody *Silent Witness*,' said Bea.

'She's right, though, isn't she?' said Queenie. 'One injured, one dead. It's a serial killer. And they don't stop until someone stops them. Did you lock the door?'

'Yes, of course I did. But we don't know it's the same person. It could be a coincidence.'

'Oh, come on, Bea. It's the same man. Prowling around. Preying on girls like you.'

Bea wanted to shush her, tell her she was being ridiculous, but she was right. The guy was preying on girls like her. And she was pretty sure that he'd followed her, twice. He knew where she walked. It could have been her. She might be next.

Waves of panic surged through her, flipping her stomach over, making her heart race. She didn't want to show Queenie that she was rattled, but it was hard keeping a lid on her feelings. She hated feeling like this. She didn't want to feel helpless.

She put her untouched plate on the coffee table and reached for her laptop. She had to *do* something.

'What are you doing?' asked Queenie.

'Looking at my list.'

'Your detective one? It won't do any good. Leave it to the experts.'

'It won't do any harm. I want to do *something*.'

Bea opened the file. This was getting complicated, so she pasted the information she'd got so far into a spreadsheet and added a new column: 'Nag's Head'. She started going through the people she could remember being in the pub the night before. If they were already on the list from date night, she added a 'Yes' to their line. If they were new, she created a new entry for them.

'... not even listening, are you?'

She looked up and found that Queenie was looking at her, not the TV.

'Sorry, what?'

'I was saying that you should get a taxi to work and back. You shouldn't walk anywhere any more.'

Bea sighed, pressed 'save' and closed the lid.

'Have you won the lottery or something?' she said, then wished she hadn't. Finances were a touchy area.

'We'll find the money somewhere. Or just don't go to work until this is over. Ask for compassionate leave or something, or go on the sick.'

Bea could feel the steam rising. 'He's won then, hasn't he, the bastard who's doing this? If all the single women in the town don't go out, unless someone else can drive them, that's just giving in. What's the point?'

'The point is you'll be safe. My nerves are on edge every minute you're out of the house now, Bea. I don't know how much more I can take.'

The red patch of scratched skin on her mum's wrist was bigger.

'Mum, you've got to stop worrying. I'm taking precautions. I'm being sensible. I can't stay in like ... ' She tried to stop the last word coming out, but it was too late. They both knew what she had been going to say. Queenie seemed to collapse into the chair, her shoulders sagged and her head slumped forward.

'You don't want to be like me,' she said. 'No, of course not. Who would want to be like me?'

'Mum, I'm sorry.' Bea went over and put her arms round her. 'I'm sorry. I shouldn't have.'

'I don't want to be like me either. Do you think I like living

135

like this?' Queenie lifted her head up and Bea could see the tears forming wet tracks down her face.

Bea felt like she was dying inside – but at the same time there was a spark of hope. Maybe this was it. The breakthrough she'd been looking for. 'So let's *do* something about it. Let's see someone, talk to someone, get some help.'

'Who could possibly help me? It's too late, Beatrice. Too late for me.'

Bea wiped some of the tears away with her thumb, remembering Queenie doing the same thing for her when she was little. What did she cry about then? A scraped knee? A dropped ice cream? Six years ago, when her dad had died, they hadn't wiped the tears away because the next wave of them was never far behind. They had clung together, lost, and their tears had made damp patches on each other's shoulders, and their mascara had stained each other's clothes.

'Of course it isn't! We could start with your GP.'

'That quack? No, thank you. Do you remember how many times Dad went to see him? How many times he told him it was just indigestion?'

'I know. I know, but that one, Doctor Bennett, retired a couple of years ago. There's a nice new one, a woman. She's really sensible and kind. She'd understand.'

'And how would I get to the surgery when I can't even walk to the end of the front path? I can't do it, Bea. Don't try to make me.'

'She could come here. We could ask for a house call. Come on, Mum, how about it? We'll need a letter from her anyway for the benefits people. Let's make a phone call.'

'You want me out there, outside, when there's a maniac on the streets?'

'No! Of course not. I want you outside, doing the things you want to do. Going to the shops. Getting your hair done.

Going to the bingo or the cinema. I want you to have a normal life.'

Queenie's face closed down. 'I'll never have a normal life, Bea. You know that. How can I?'

Bea closed her eyes and rested her head against her mum's. People die all the time. It's the one inevitable, unavoidable truth. It's an everyday thing. But when is it ever okay to tell someone it's time to let go, to move on? She could never say that to Queenie. The words would turn to ash in her mouth and she'd choke on them.

'I loved him too, Mum. I loved him too,' she said and held her tightly. Queenie held her back and they sat in silence for a while.

Later, tucked up in bed, Bea returned to her spreadsheet. It was only a partial picture, but there were some obvious suspects – people who had been in Costsave on date night and at the Nag's Head or the spinathon the week before:

> Kevin
> Bob
> Big Gav
> Lee
> Dave
> Neville
> Dean

She looked at her lists again, and reluctantly added another name:

> Ant

It wasn't a definitive list, but it was a start. She studied each name in turn. Could she really see any of them as a killer?

She needed to put personal opinion aside somehow, be

more methodical. How did they do this on the telly or in films? There were three things, weren't there? She struggled to retrieve them from the back of her mind, but they wouldn't come, so she typed a quick search into Google and there it was: Means, motive and opportunity.

She added three more columns on her spreadsheet:

'Means – is he capable of killing Ginny?'

'Motive – Why kill Ginny?'

'Opportunity – did he have a chance to kill her?'

She then went through the list again, trying to fill in the columns. After twenty minutes or so, she still had one column completely clear – motive. Who on earth would want to harm Ginny, let alone kill her? She had been annoyingly pretty, almost perfect in a cheerleadery sort of way, but she was a nice person. Easy to get along with, down to earth. Bea felt her stomach flip again as she realised she'd never see her again. She was gone. She'd ended. Just like that. Someone had stopped her, mid-sentence.

Bea looked at the screen again, but it was blurred by the tears welling up in her eyes.

'Bastard!' she said. 'You bastard!'

She wiped her eyes with a tissue and blew her nose. She checked the alarm clock on the bedside table. Half past two. That terrible time when you've gone beyond sleepiness and have hours until the new day starts. She wanted to keep working on the case, but she'd hit a wall. She needed someone to talk it over with, another perspective.

Her phone pinged. Frowning, Bea reached for it. She'd left it near her pillow, charging from a power point under the bedhead. It had been pulled by the cord underneath the pillow and felt warm to the touch.

One new message.

Tom: You awake?

He'd messaged earlier in the evening to check that she'd

got home safely. Bea smiled and texted back. Yup. Can't sleep.

Wanna talk?

I'll ring.

No need. Look out ur window.

?

She got out of bed and went across to the window, which was at the front of the house. She parted the curtains in the middle and peered out. There was a car parked directly outside. It wasn't a police car, with its distinctive stripes down the side, but a dark saloon. Looking up at her from the driver's seat was Tom. He waved through the window.

Bea's phone pinged again.

Come on, come and see me.

Bea looked down at her Disney pyjamas.

I'm not dressed!

Even better.

You can come in. Too cold out.

Okay.

Come round the back.

Saucy!

Bea blushed, but there was no time for a suitable put-down. She could already see Tom opening the driver's door and there she was in nightwear suitable for a small child, with all her wobbly bits unconfined. She didn't have time to get dressed, so she chose her plainest, largest dressing gown and wrapped it firmly around her. She slid her feet into her slippers – pink, fluffy, Disney. Oh God, what on earth would he think of her?

She headed down the stairs as fast and as quietly as she could. She hoped he'd have the sense not to knock at the door. The last thing they needed now was Queenie joining the party. She unbolted the back door and turned the key in the lock. He was there, stamping his feet and blowing on his hands.

'Hello, you,' he said.

'Hello.'

He swooped in for a kiss, catching her by surprise, mouth open. His lips were cold and dry, his nose cold too, where it nestled against hers. But his tongue was warm as it explored her mouth, probing gently but insistently. She was too surprised to resist, didn't want to anyway. She moaned a little as he wrapped his arms round her.

'Mmn, you're warm,' he said, kissing her ear.

'And you're freezing, and you're bringing it in with you,' she hissed and she took his hand and led him into the room, shutting the door quietly behind him. For a moment, it was like someone had pressed 'pause'. They stood looking at each other, grinning.

'What's going on?' Bea said softly.

'I just wanted to see you,' he said, his voice too loud for the sleeping house.

'Shh,' Bea said, holding her index finger up to her lips. He lunged forward again, kissing her finger, sucking the end, then moving it away with his hand and kissing her mouth, hard.

For a minute or two, Bea was completely lost in the moment. Her senses were full of him – the sound of his lips on hers, his breath coming faster and louder, the scratch of his stubble against her face, his fingers somehow inside her dressing gown and cold through the material of her pyjama top, so cold they made her gasp when they explored further and found the bare skin underneath. He pushed her against the kitchen table, so that the edge was digging into the top

140

of her legs. Soon she'd have to sit down or fall backwards. She was surprised how keen he was, how insistent. It was unexpected but flattering, exciting too – but now a noise from upstairs brought her back to reality. Was Queenie just turning over in bed or was she getting up?

Suddenly it seemed a bit squalid, a bit wrong to be doing this here, now, with Queenie upstairs and Ginny lying in a mortuary somewhere. Especially Ginny. It was more than a bit wrong.

Bea wriggled her hand between them and pushed against his chest, at the same time pulling her face away from his.

'I can't do this, not today,' she said.

He didn't seem to have heard, and tried to kiss her again. His hand was still under her top, resting in the place where the curve of her waist met the curve of her breast.

'You saw her, didn't you? Ginny? How can you do this when it's been such an awful day?'

That stopped him. He sighed and drew back a little.

'It's my job, Bea. I see stuff, terrible stuff, every day. You learn to switch off. You have to or you'd go mad.'

Close up, she could see how some of the freckles joined up on his nose, how the tips of his eyelashes were white-blonde rather than ginger.

'I don't think I can,' she said. 'Switch off.'

'Bea—'

'I'm sorry. I can't. Ginny was my friend, she—' She reached inside her top and gently moved his hand away.

'Come on—'

'I can't.'

He breathed out sharply, almost a snort of frustration. 'I'll go then. I shouldn't have come here.'

'No, stay. Have a cup of tea. We can talk.'

He turned away and she thought he was heading for the door, but then he turned again and sat down at the table. 'Okay,' he said, 'a cup of tea. No sugar for me.'

While she filled the kettle and got the mugs ready, Bea self-consciously tried to set her clothes straight, pulling the hem of her top down and drawing her dressing gown tightly around her body. She was aware of him watching her, and felt somehow vulnerable – here, in her own kitchen, in her nightclothes – at a disadvantage.

She made the tea and put two mugs on the table, then sat opposite him.

'What was she like? Ginny?' Tom asked.

Bea found that she was happy to talk about her. 'Well, she was sickeningly pretty, and very sporty, but she was so nice with it. She wasn't one of those mean girls. She was everyone's friend.'

He clamped his lips together, shook his head. 'Doesn't make any sense, does it?' he said. 'Someone killing a girl like that. Perhaps she was just unlucky – wrong place, wrong time.'

'Do you think it was random then? It wasn't about her?'

He sipped his tea. 'We don't know. He may have known her, followed her. That's why we were interviewing people at the shop today. It could be a stranger, though. An opportunistic thing.'

'Not just opportunistic. If he was carrying a knife.'

'A knife?'

'They were hinting at a violent death on the telly. I guess he stabbed her.'

He didn't respond and Bea carried on, thinking aloud.

'Although that doesn't mean it was planned, I suppose. All sorts of people carried knives when we were at secondary school. It was a thing for a while, until most of them realised how stupid it was and Ricky Swales got caught out and excluded.'

'It wasn't a stabbing, Bea. He hit her with something.

142

From behind. Hit her on the back of the head with some-thing blunt. A hammer or something – we haven't found the murder weapon.'

'Jesus.'

'I shouldn't have told you that. It's not been made public yet. Don't say anything to anyone, okay?'

'No, of course not. That's . . . that's horrible.'

He looked down at his tea. 'Yeah, it's pretty grim. I have seen terrible stuff, but that was the worst. She didn't stand a chance.'

A little muscle was twitching beneath his right eye, and now Bea could see how pale he was, how tired. She reached across the table and put both her hands over his.

'I'm sorry, Tom. You've had a tough day. And I spoilt everything, didn't I?'

'No. No, not at all. I was being . . . it was all too fast anyway. I'm happy to just sit and talk. Honestly. It's good to talk to you, Bea.' He turned his hands palm upwards and they held hands properly.

'We should go on a date,' he said. 'Would you? I mean, would you like to?'

Bea smiled. 'Yes. That'd be lovely.'

'A meal out? A drink?'

Bea pictured them both with best bib and tucker on, sitting awkwardly across the table from each other, tumbleweed rolling in between.

'Okay. Nowhere too posh, though,' she said.

'Okay,' he said. 'Nando's?'

She laughed and his face fell.

'Too chavvy?'

'No, not too chavvy for me. I mean, look at me! I was just relieved you didn't say Maccy D's.'

'Or we could . . . nah.'

'What?'

143

'I was going to say, we could get fish and chips and just have a walk. Eat them in the park or down by the river. But, well, that's a bit naff.'

Bea stroked the back of his hand with her thumb. 'That's a bit *lovely*. Cold, though, at the moment.'

'How about Bonfire Night? Wrap up warm, watch the fireworks. The display's on the third this year, isn't it?'

'Yeah, that'd be great. Can't wait.' The clock on the wall behind Tom was showing a quarter to four. Bea tried and failed to stifle a yawn.

'Okay, I can take a hint,' Tom said. 'Time for me to go.'

'I wasn't—'

'I know. I was just teasing.'

He stood up, leaned across the table and kissed her forehead. Then he held her chin between index finger and thumb and gently tipped her face up so that he could kiss her properly. Gently, this time, on the lips, with nothing more. And she could feel herself melting again.

'Goodnight, Tom,' she said.

'Goodnight.'

She let him out of the back door and locked it behind him. She stood for a little while, leaning her back against the door, savouring the moment. The glass panels were cool against her shoulders. It was welcome for a minute or two, but then she shivered.

'Time for bed,' she said to herself. She walked to the hall, turning off the kitchen light as she went. She wondered if she'd be able to sleep, whether her senses would calm and her pulse would slow down enough for her to nod off. She put her laptop on the floor, but kept her phone on and near her, just in case there were any messages – not that she was expecting him to text, but, well, you never knew.

She drew the duvet up around her ears and snuggled

into the pillow, and this time she could feel herself slipping into drowsiness. She wasn't thinking about Ginny now. Instead she imagined herself walking hand in hand with Tom in the dark, him putting his arm round her shoulder, making her feel safe. She pictured them walking in step. Dot was irritatingly right – it'd been ages since she'd been on a date.

'Goodnight, Tom,' she said in a whisper and drifted into a deep sleep.

10

'So, we've decided that you playing detectives is a bad idea,' Dot said. 'Whoever is doing this is obviously a nutter and a really dangerous one at that. What if you find out who it is? What if they know you're going to identify them?'

She was one side of Bea. Ant was the other. They'd caught up with her on the High Street.

Ant nodded in agreement.

'I'm not gonna stop,' Bea said. 'He needs catching.'

'That's what we thought you'd say,' said Ant. '*So* if you're gonna to do it, we wanna help you.'

'What?'

'We'll be your sidekicks. We can do stuff.'

'Both of you?' She looked from one to the other.

'Yeah. Then you won't be on your own doing this. It'll be safer.'

'Two heads are better than one,' said Dot.

'Two and a half with Ant,' said Bea and was immediately sorry when she saw his crestfallen face. She reached out and ruffled his hair. 'I was teasing. Three of us – that's a proper team.'

'A crime-fighting posse,' said Ant, ducking away from her.

'I've never been in a "posse",' said Bea.

'Me neither,' said Dot. 'Do we need Stetsons and horses and guns?'

'What?' said Ant.

'Like the Wild West.'

'What are you talking about? Posse,' he repeated slowly and loudly like he was talking to someone hard of hearing. 'A gang, a crew, a massive. Do you know what I'm saying?'

'Massive?' said Dot. 'Are you saying I look big in this coat?'

Bea started laughing, and Ant clapped his hand to his forehead and spun away in mock agony.

'So, when shall we start?' said Bea. 'Lunchtime?'

The atmosphere at Costsave was still muted. It was difficult to ignore the empty locker, the mug on the shelf that wouldn't get used again.

As Bea logged on at her till, she sighed.

'I don't want to be at work, Dot,' she said, 'but I don't want to be at home either.'

'Yeah, I know what you mean.'

'It just seems wrong to be carrying on with everything, like nothing's happened.'

'I know. But what can you do? Ginny wouldn't want everything just to stop.'

Bea checked the change in the drawer of the till. She sprayed cleaner onto her conveyor belt and rubbed some antibacterial hand gel into her hands. She felt something tickling her neck just behind her ear. She put her hand up and turned around, then screamed. A huge foam hand was jabbing at her. Behind it, at the end of a long handle, was Ant.

'You little bugger!' Bea yelled at him. 'Get off me with that thing!'

Dot shrieked with laughter. 'Of all the people that shouldn't be let loose with the queue pointer. I thought they'd binned it.'

It was most people's idea of hell, the least popular job on the shop floor. Neville usually only brought it out of the Stores in the run-up to Christmas, when things were really busy and there was a danger of queue rage. Bea wondered if it was some sort of punishment for Ant but if it was, he was blissfully unaware of it. He spent the morning cruising up and down the line of tills, happily aiming the huge foam finger at the least busy operator.

Halfway through the morning, he scooted past Bea.

'You enjoying that?' she asked.

He grinned. 'I can do this,' he said. 'I can actually do it.' She was reminded of his agony the day before, the embarrassment of trying to deal with a list he couldn't read. Damn it, she thought, this is his life if we don't help him. Carrying a big foam finger. He needs to read.

At lunchtime they bought sandwiches and huddled round a coffee table in the far corner of the staffroom. Bea brought out her list of suspects from her pocket, unfolded and smoothed out the paper and handed it to Dot.

'You'll have to read it out,' said Ant.

Bea glanced round the room. Bob-on-Meat was reading *The Mirror* in one of the armchairs, well within earshot. Dean from Stores was making a cup of tea at the kitchenette.

'We can't do this here. Have we got time to go to the coffee shop?'

'Not really. Maybe if we're quick.'

They gathered up their things and headed for the door.

'Ooh, where are you going? Can anyone join in?' Dean called out, as they were bundling through the door.

148

'Just out for a bit,' Bea said, and disappeared before he could ask any more questions.

In the café just round the corner from the far end of the car park Bea read out the list. She left Ant's name until last.

'Well, it wasn't me. And if you think it was me, I shouldn't be here, should I?' He stuck his bottom lip out.

'I don't think it was you, Ant.'

'So cross me off the list. Here.' Bea had put a biro on the table. Now he slid it towards her.

Bea sighed. 'I can't, Ant. Not until I've got some evidence. An alibi. A witness who saw you somewhere else when the girls were being attacked.'

Ant looked at Dot and raised his eyebrows. She nodded briefly. Bea felt the glimmering of understanding, but dismissed it quickly. *No way. Really, no way.*

'I've got one,' he said. 'An alibi. A witness.'

He stopped.

'Good,' said Bea. She picked up her pen. 'So?'

'So what?'

'So, first things first, where were you after you left Cost-save the night Emma was attacked?'

He looked at Dot again. 'I was with her, wasn't I?' The pen dropped out of Bea's fingers. 'We were—'

'Talking,' Dot cut in. 'We were talking. All night.'

Ant broke into a grin. 'Yeah,' he said, 'we were talking.'

Their eyes locked and held each other and Bea suddenly felt like the greenest gooseberry in the fresh fruit and veg aisle.

'You two,' she murmured. 'I just didn't . . . I never . . . '

Dot looked at her sideways, bracing herself for Bea's reaction. 'I should've told you,' she said. 'Except there's nothing to tell really. We're just friends. Good friends now.'

Bea held up her hands. 'Listen, nothing to do with me. It's all good. It's just . . . I can't believe I didn't notice. I mean,

149

I'm meant to be observant. I'm trying to investigate – and I didn't see what was under my nose.'

'It's cool,' said Ant. 'Don't beat yourself up about it. Like Dot said, we're just friends, anyway.'

He reached for Dot's hand under the table and gave it a reassuring squeeze.

Bea tried not to stare. 'Right. Okay,' she said, pulling herself together. 'So you walked home together, did you? From Costsave to Bea's?'

'Yeah,' said Ant.

'No,' said Dot. 'Not all the way. You caught up with me on Orchard Avenue. I walked through the town centre on my own.'

'Yeah. Okay, whatever.'

'So there was ten minutes or so unaccounted for?'

'Yeah, but that was before Emma was attacked, wasn't it? Because she was attacked at about ten thirty, after you'd left work. So I'm in the clear. Right?' He nudged the pen again.

Dot nodded. 'He's right, Bea. Cross him off.'

Bea picked up the pen and put a couple of horizontal lines through Ant's name. 'Okay,' she said. 'Good. Great, actually. But how do we rule the others out? We can't interview them, can we? People will think we're mad.'

'We need to do stuff the police can't do,' said Ant.

'Like?'

'I dunno.' He rested his head in his hands. They sat in silence for a while, Bea doodling on the corner of the sheet of paper.

Then Ant sat up. 'What about you?'

'What do you mean?' said Bea.

'You were followed home twice. You've seen the guy. You know stuff no one else knows.'

'It was dark though. I didn't see much.'

'You don't think you did, but there's probably something

in there that you don't even know is there.' He tapped the side of his head. 'You might have the clue to finding out who he is.'

'I've been over it a million times in my head.'

'Tell us again, though, Bea,' said Dot. 'Tell us what you saw the first time.'

Bea tried to take herself back to that evening. She remembered looking behind her, but what she saw was indistinct.

'Just someone following. Getting closer to me. One person, on their own. I can't remember any detail. Can't see anything in my head.'

'Give it a little time,' said Dot.

Trying harder didn't make the image any clearer. This was hopeless.

'There's nothing there. I can't—'

'It's okay. Don't get stressy,' Ant said. 'Stop trying to see it, what did it feel like? Walking home. Being followed. What were you feeling?'

Bea looked at him. Was he getting some weird sort of kick listening to her? And now, in her mind's eye, the list of names again. She'd only crossed him out on Dot's say-so. Was that right, though? Was this part of some sort of sick game?

'What was it like?' Ant said again, and suddenly Bea was back there. Her heart was speeding up. The skin on the back of her neck was crawling. *Don't look back. Stay calm.* But she had broken into a run, hadn't she? And looked back when she was in the open, by the side of the Rec. What had she seen? A shadow disappearing back into the alleyway. Was that it? A shadow. The head and body one dark shape.

One dark shape.

'They were wearing a hoodie,' she said.

'Yeah?' said Ant. His own light grey hoodie which he'd put on over his Costsave uniform, was half-unzipped, the hood down. Bea tried not to seem as if she was looking at it.

151

'Yeah. I'm sure. I didn't really notice it, take it in, but it's true. I saw him ducking back into the alley, and he was wearing a hoodie.'

'So that's gotta rule out some of our suspects, hasn't it?' said Ant.

'Does it?' said Bea. 'Doesn't everyone own one? All the people on our list? Let's see. I can't imagine creepy Kevin in one, or Neville. Or Bob.' She laughed at the thought.

'He's got a dressing gown with a hood,' said Dot quietly.

'What?' said Bea.

Ant was looking from one woman to the other and back again, his mouth gaping. 'His dressing gown?'

'Oh Jesus, Dot,' said Bea. 'You didn't, did you?'

'Only the once, after the Christmas party two years ago.'

'No wonder he's mooning after you. He's tasted that sweet honey and wants some more.'

'Bob?' Ant managed to close his jaw long enough to splutter. 'Really? You were boning Bob the Butcher?'

Dot reached for his hand again under the table. He moved it pointedly away.

'Just once. That's all,' she said softly, then to Bea, 'I'm not going to apologise. And don't you get all holier than thou, Madam, that was the year you got off with you-know-who.'

Now Ant was looking at Bea.

'Who?' he said.

'None of your business,' said Bea. 'It's got nothing to do with this. Neither, I'm pretty confident, has Bob's dressing gown. The thing is, most people own a hoodie – or other hooded clothes,' she said looking at Dot significantly. 'Not everyone was wearing one the night I was followed.'

'What about the second night?' said Ant. 'When Ginny was . . . did you see much then? Was it the same person?'

'I didn't see much at all. I just heard him call my name.'

'What was his voice like? High-pitched? Low?'

'I don't know. Just ... ordinary. I don't know. God, this is useless. We're running out of time, too. We've got three minutes to get back to the mother ship.'

'Oh blimey. Come on,' said Dot.

They scraped back their chairs and left, scuttling over the car park towards the staff entrance.

During the afternoon, Bea enjoyed watching Ant shepherding customers to the tills. Quite a few of Bea's regulars ignored his increasingly insistent pointing. Time was one thing they had plenty of and they didn't mind waiting a bit longer for a chat with Bea. Ant seemed to take their actions personally, walking up to them and wafting his big foam hand in the opposite direction.

'It's all right, love,' said Norma, as she balanced her wire basket on top of a sturdy tartan bag on wheels, 'I'll wait here.'

'But it's quicker over there. Till number eight. There's no queue.'

The finger drooped a little and came perilously close to the top of Norma's purple rinsed perm.

'Ant! It's okay. She's fine here,' said Bea. 'Take your finger over there, please.'

He retreated, tutting to himself and muttering, 'Can't help some people.'

Later Julie, with Mason and Tiffany in tow, came to Bea's till. There were two snail trails running from Mason's nose; Julie wiped them away with a tissue. In the trolley seat, Tiffany was rubbing her eyes and whining. Bea noticed that the plaster had gone from Julie's ring finger, but the skin by the ring looked weird. She tried not to make it too obvious that she was looking, just sneaking a glance now and then as Julie reached into the trolley and loaded the shopping onto the conveyor belt. There was a layer of almost clear stuff between the ring and her skin, and the surrounding skin was being pulled every time her finger moved. It was almost like the ring was attached. Like it was glued on.

Bea beeped the shopping through and started putting it into bags. Mason stood with his hands over the metal edge of the table, watching her. The snail trails had seeped back down Mason's top lip. Without really thinking, Bea fished a tissue out of the packet under her till, reached forward and wiped his nose.

'Oh, you shouldn't have to do that! I'm sorry,' Julie said, darting back from the far end of the belt.

'It's okay. It's that time of year, isn't it? Coughs and colds.'

'It's just one thing after another with these two. You don't want to catch it, though, do you? His cold.' She peeled Mason's hands away from the edge.

'It's okay. I reckon I'm pretty immune to most things that pass through here.'

Julie looked distressed to the edge of tears.

'Honestly,' said Bea. 'It's okay.'

She finished processing the shopping and together they packed the last of it. Julie heaved the bags back into her trolley and paid. The photo of Dave was still in her purse. He was wearing an open-necked shirt in this picture. He'd always been wearing a business suit when Bea had seen him. In the store on date night. In the pub after the spinathon. He'd been there, but suited and booted. Definitely not a hoodie.

Julie paid in cash, as usual. As Bea handed over her change, she fought the temptation to catch hold of her hand, have a closer look at her ring finger. It was odd – but it was none of Bea's business, was it? The little family set off for the exit, Mason holding onto the trolley. He glanced back as they passed the newspapers and magazines and Bea caught the glint of his top lip, wet with snot again.

Five o'clock approached and it was dark again beyond the big plate glass windows at the front of the store. The women on her shift got changed in silence. The door to Ginny's locker was slightly ajar. Everybody noticed. No one wanted to shut it.

'Shall we walk together again?' Dot asked. 'Ant wants to.'

'Yeah,' said Bea. 'I've got to buy Queenie's tea on the way out, though.'

'We'll wait out front.'

Bea went back onto the shop floor and straight to the fish section in the frozen food cabinets. She picked out a packet of breaded cod fillets and then walked to the meat aisle labelled 'Sausages, Bacon and Pork'. Unfortunately, it was within sight of Bob-on-Meat, who was still on duty at the fresh meat counter at the back of the store. He noticed her as he was chopping up bones on the board at the back next to the bacon slicer. The cleaver sat easily in his big hand. As he brought the blade down onto the carcass, splinters of bone and flecks of flesh danced and scattered.

He tipped the smashed up chunks into a bag, placed it on the scale and then printed off a price label. 'There you go, Madam. That'll make lovely stock.'

'The best,' his customer said, putting the bag in her trolley. 'Thanks, Bob.'

With no one else waiting, Bob called out to Bea. 'Here, you don't want that packaged stuff, you want some of mine.'

Bea winced, replaced the packet of branded bangers and went up to Bob.

'Late one tonight, Bob?' she said.

'On till eight,' he said, ruefully. 'I'll miss half the football. I'm recording it, but it's not the same.'

'Nemmind.'

'Yeah, but I wanted to, well, make sure Dot got home

okay. I don't like the thought of her walking on her own. Or you either,' he added hastily.

'It's okay, Bob, we're both walking with—' Bea stopped conscious of a crack opening up in the thin ice beneath her feet.

'Walking with . . . ?'

'With Ant. Ant's walking us home.'

'Oh. Him.' Bob's face darkened, like his own personal cloud had moved overhead and cast a shadow. He made a visible effort to pull himself together. 'What can I do you for anyway, love?'

'I was just going to get some ordinary sausages.'

Bob pulled a face. 'You don't want that pap,' he said, nodding to the cabinet. 'Women like you need proper meat.'

'What would you recommend?'

'These ones. A nice thick sausage, all pork, bit of black pepper. How many, love?'

'Four. Two each.'

He placed the sausages on a layer of plastic on the scales, printed the label and put them in a bag. Then popped a couple of slices of bacon in with them. When Bea took it from him, the price was ludicrously low, half what it should be.

'Bob?'

'Shh,' he said, and winked at her. 'Mates' rates.'

'Ta, but—'

'Off you go. Give my regards to Queenie.'

'Thanks, Bob. Goodnight.'

'Night, love.'

Bea paid at the self-checkout and joined Dot and Ant outside.

'Get a move on, slowcoach,' said Ant. 'I'm freezing to chuffing mintballs here.'

156

They headed across the car park.

'So, are you going to work on the case this evening?' Ant asked Bea.

'Yeah.'

'We could join you.'

'I don't know,' said Bea. 'Queenie isn't all that comfortable with company.'

'She knows me though, Bea, doesn't she?' said Dot.

'Yeah, but—'

'But she doesn't want oiks like me in her house,' said Ant.

'It's not that, Ant. She's . . . you know . . . she has trouble . . . '

'It's all right. I'm only teasing.'

'Anyway, you can't blame her, can you?' said Dot. 'I mean, you're only just house-trained.' Ant tipped back his head and barked like a dog.

'Shh, for goodness' sake.'

'I'll ask Queenie about you two coming round. She might actually enjoy it. It won't be tonight, though.'

'Fair enough. What are you going to do tonight?'

'Reckon I'll go through my lists again. I could text you if I come up with something.'

Ant's shoulders rounded a little. Bea could feel him withdrawing.

'Oh, sorry. Texting's no good, is it?'

'No good to me. Send me a picture. Or just ring,' he said.

'Yeah.'

They were nearly at Bea's house.

'You are going to Dot's, aren't you? I mean, you will walk Dot right to her house,' asked Bea.

'Yeah. Course.'

Both Ant and Dot couldn't look each other in the eye, and Bea was sure he was planning to keep her company further than her front door.

'It's just that ... I shouldn't tell you this, but Tom said that Ginny was hit with a hammer or something like it.'

'Oh God.' Dot's hand went up to her mouth.

Ant whistled and shook his head. 'That's gross. That's really sick,' he said. 'When did he tell you? During your interview?'

'No.' God, why didn't she just say yes? What was wrong with her? 'He just came round for a chat, last night after work.'

Ant narrowed his eyes. 'He came round to yours? Your house?'

'Yes.'

'After work, that must have been pretty late.'

'Yes, he's ... he's a friend, Ant. We were at Cow Lane together.'

'There must have been two hundred kids at that school. You don't invite them all round to yours every night, do you?' he said.

'No, course not. He's a friend, okay? Okay?'

'Not really.' Ant was increasingly agitated – hopping from foot to foot, flailing his arms around. 'He's not human, Bea. He's a pig.'

'That's a disgusting thing to say. He's just a bloke, a nice bloke, who happens to be a policeman.'

'No one "happens to be a policeman" – he chose to join up. He chose to put that uniform on. He's one of them.'

'Don't be so stupid. They're not the enemy.'

'They are in my house. That's exactly what they are.'

Dot put a hand on his arm. 'That's enough, Ant. Calm down.'

'I just don't get it,' he said. 'How anyone could be *friends* with someone like that.'

Bea started walking away from them. 'We don't all have your fucked-up view of society. Some of us think the police are there to keep us safe.'

Ant let out a kind of snort, and Bea kept walking. She was only a few yards from her front gate.

'Night, doll,' Dot called out to her.

She turned around. 'Night.'

Nothing to Ant. He was only a year or two younger than her, but boy oh boy, did he need to grow up, Bea thought. She wondered again about what went on when Dot closed the front door behind them. What was she doing with such an immature kid, young enough to be her grandson? She could picture her with someone like Bob, cuddled up on the sofa together watching *Antiques Roadshow* or *Gardener's World* or something. They'd be good together. But Ant?

'Fish today, Queenie,' she called out as she went through the kitchen door. 'Get the oven on. Bob-on-Meat says hi. He only charged me half price for the sausages for tomorrow.'

'Ah, Bob. We used to see him down the club, every Friday. Seems like a lifetime ago. What's his Fiona doing now? She went to uni, didn't she?'

Queenie made the tea while Bea put their fish and chips in the oven. They chatted happily while they waited for it to cook, enjoying the smells wafting from the cooker. For a few minutes, it felt reassuringly normal, chewing over other people's lives, the day-to-day gossip that oiled the working of the day. When the food was ready, they took their plates into the lounge to eat in front of the telly and somehow the spell was broken. There was another report on the news about Ginny's murder. The post-mortem had been completed but the results weren't going to be released until the inquest opened.

'It'll be the funeral next,' said Queenie. 'Have they got a date yet?'

'I dunno,' said Bea. 'Don't think so.'

She looked at the food that remained on her plate and put down her knife and fork.

'What's up, love?'

'I can't eat it.'

'Not even the fish? Give it here, then.'

11

'This is doing my head in,' said Bea. 'All of it. Spreadsheets, lists, maps, timelines. It's too much.' She had eighteen men on her list and names for only eleven of them. 'The thing is, the killer needn't necessarily have been in the store or the pub. They could have been roaming the streets outside, looking for a victim. The common element might not be Costsave after all.'

'So, we're looking for anyone, anywhere? That's impossible. Unless you're the police,' said Dot.

'Yeah, it's impossible. But I keep wondering if there's a sort of pattern. When you think about the girls being followed, then Emma, who was a customer, and then Ginny, who was staff – it feels like it's all coming closer to Costsave. I think the killer has a link to the store. What if he is on my list? It's worth looking at, isn't it? But even that's too much.'

'So, that's what we're here for,' said Ant, as they walked past the newsagents, the only shop open on the High Street this early. 'To take some of this on.'

'But you can't. I mean . . .'

'You mean, I can't tweak your spreadsheet. 'Cos I'm stupid. Yeah, fair play, but I can look at CCTV footage – that's just watching telly, right? I've got a fucking degree in that. Or I can take some of your suspects and see what I can find out about them.'

'That's it!' said Dot. 'Why don't we split up that list of yours? Each takes three or four people.'

'O-kay,' said Bea, thinking on her feet. 'We'd have to be careful who had who, though. Like, no offence, but I couldn't really have you investigating Bob, for example, seeing as you know him so well.'

'Knew him. Once,' said Dot. 'But point taken.'

'So how are we going to do this?'

'I've got my list here.' Bea rummaged in her pocket. 'Okay, you could do Gavin and Neville, Dot. Poke about, see what you can find out about them.'

Dot nodded.

'And you could do Bob and maybe Lee from the Leisure Centre. Do you ever go in there?'

Ant pulled a face. 'Nah. But I suppose I could do.'

'So that leaves Kevin the photographer, and Dave the creep.'

'You shouldn't do Dave the creep – he's hit on you before,' said Dot. 'You don't want to follow him around. He might think you're encouraging him.'

'So why don't I do him, if you show me who he is on the CCTV?' said Ant. 'In fact, give me all the ones outside the store. I'll use my contacts.' He winked.

'Who are your contacts?'

'It's better that you don't know.'

'Okay,' she said, dubious. 'So, are we sorted? I'll do Kevin and Dean from Stores. We'll work on our people and report back tomorrow lunchtime?'

'That doesn't give us very long.'

162

'How long do you think it will be before the psycho attacks someone else? How long have we got?'

'Good point.'

In the locker room, Bea looked in the mirror. She hadn't worn the megalashes for a few days now, had hardly put any make-up on. It had seemed disrespectful somehow, to be tarting yourself up when one of your friends had died. Like they didn't matter. She had to admit, though, that she looked pretty rank this morning. Without make-up, her eyes almost disappeared – they became piggy little things sitting above big pouchy cheeks.

Beside her, Dot drew on a cupid's bow in bright, red lippy, while further along Eileen dragged a comb through her hair

'You look fab, Dot,' Bea said. 'Love that colour on you.'

'Thanks, babe. Got to look good for my public. You can borrow it if you like. You look tired, darlin'. Not sleeping?'

Bea groaned. 'God, when anyone tells me I look tired, I feel ten times worse.'

'Sorry, babe. I didn't mean—'

'No, it's all right. I do look tired. I gotta fix this.' She started rummaging in her bag and took out her make-up basics; foundation, concealer, eyeliner, mascara, lipstick, blusher. Then she set to work. A couple of minutes later she looked more like herself again.

She was zipping up her make-up bag when the dark vertical slit of Ginny's open locker caught her eye.

'I'm sorry, girls, I'm going to have to do it.'

Bea took a couple of steps towards the locker and pushed the metal door. It stuck in the frame. She pushed harder. The top of the door went into place, but the door bent in the middle, as the bottom failed to move.

'What the—?'

Bea opened the door again and looked down. There was

something there, a bit of card or paper. She leaned over and picked it up. It was a business card. 'Kevin McKey – photographer.' His contact details were there, not the ones for the *Evening Post*. These were his personal email and a mobile phone number.

'What is it?' asked Eileen.

'A card. From that press photographer. He gave it to her at the spinathon.'

Dot shrugged. 'She was stunningly pretty. You can't blame him.'

'Blame him for what?'

'I dunno. Chatting her up?'

'Kevin? He's old, no offence.'

'None taken, but it doesn't mean he wasn't interested.'

'True. Or maybe it was professional. He wanted to take more pictures of her?'

They looked at each other, each reading the other's mind.

'Throw it in the bin,' said Eileen. 'She doesn't need it now, does she? Here, I'll do it.' She made to take the card from Bea's hand, but Bea closed her fingers around it.

'No, it's okay,' she said. 'I'll keep hold of it.'

'What for?' said Eileen. 'Do you fancy yourself as a model?' There was a sneer in her voice that Bea didn't like one little bit.

She slipped the card into her pocket. 'Yeah,' she said. 'Why not?'

Dot joined in. 'Yeah, why not, Eileen? Bea could easily be a model. She's gorgeous.' She came up behind Bea and ran her hands down her sides, emphasising her curves and tickling her as she did it. Bea buckled forward, squirming and giggling.

'Get off, Dot, you sex maniac. That's harassment, that is!' She turned around and grabbed Dot's hands to fend her off.

'Can anyone join in?'

Dean from Stores was hovering just outside the half-open door, looking into the women's changing room.

'No,' said Bea, firmly. 'Really, really not. I only let my best bitches touch me like that.' She and Dot let go of each other's hands and high-fived each other, laughing.

'Get out, Dean. You shouldn't be looking in here!' Eileen shouted at him.

'Yeah, all right, Mum. You're all weird anyway,' Dean said and trudged away towards the staffroom. Bea noticed a magazine sticking out of his coat pocket. It was rolled up, with the back cover facing outwards. It was starting to unwind, though, and she could see the top corner of the front – a bronzed shoulder, a pert bosom, an erect pink nipple. Nice recreational reading. Was that what kept him in Stores most break times?

She, Dot and Eileen went to make themselves a quick cuppa before their shift started. Ant was already in the staffroom, talking to Dean.

Big Gav followed them into the room, with Neville trailing in his wake. Immediately, Gav was besieged by people asking for the day off to attend Ginny's funeral. He held his hands up and flapped them, palm down, to try and suppress the noise. 'I'll talk about the funeral in a minute, but first we need to be clear about tomorrow: Halloween. We all know about the trouble last year and we've taken steps to prevent that. From today we're enforcing the "no eggs without ID" rule and Anna will be bringing round signs to stick up at all the tills. And please, be mindful of your personal safety when going home. I'm talking to the women here. Don't walk home alone. I'm serious about this. I shall be on duty until close of play tomorrow and I want each of you to find me and tell me how you are getting home. If you haven't got anyone to walk with, Costsave will pay for a taxi for you.'

A ripple of surprise went round the staff. The women

made approving noises. Bea was expecting some outrage from the men, but none of them said anything. Ginny's murder, so close to home, was playing on all of their minds. No one wanted their friends, colleagues, wives or daughters to be next.

'Right, the store's looking spookily great, thanks for your efforts. Let's make it a good one tomorrow.'

A couple of people clapped but the applause petered out almost before it started. They knew what was coming next.

'Okay, Ginny's funeral. As you have obviously all heard, the funeral will take place on the second. Neville?' Gavin turned to Neville to detail the leave arrangements.

'We will be applying normal rules to leave for that day,' he said, to howls of protest. He raised his voice above the throng. 'You must fill in your leave cards and submit them to the office. We will be maintaining full coverage of the daytime shifts. Applications will be dealt with on a first come, first served basis.'

There was chorus of tutting and complaining and then a stampede as people headed out of the staffroom and towards the office. Bea watched them go.

'We've got no chance,' she said to Dot. Then to Gavin, 'Everyone wants to go. You can't expect people to work that afternoon.'

'I sympathise. I really do. But Costsave isn't just a shop, Bea, it's a public service. Our customers rely on us. We can't let them down.'

'Half of them will be at the funeral, Gav.'

'It's company policy to open seven days a week, except for Christmas Day and New Year's Day,' sniffed Neville. 'No exceptions. And it's *Mr Howells* here, Beatrice.'

'Are *you* both going?' she asked.

'Of course,' he said. 'I mean, we haven't sorted out managerial cover yet, but—'

'I'll be there,' said Gavin. 'Representing the company.'

Neville looked discomfited. He pretended to be making a note on his clipboard.

'Have you put your leave card in?' asked Bea. 'Because if you haven't, you're at the back of a long queue.'

The line to the office stretched back as far as the staff-room door. There was a bit of pushing and shoving going on, bad temper and frustration spilling out. Gavin took a deep breath in and a long breath out. 'We don't need this,' he said. 'Things are bad enough and we've got to get through Halloween first. Neville?'

'Shall we have a special Management Team meeting?' said Neville, making a note on his ever-present clipboard. They pushed past the end of the queue and edged their way down the corridor.

'You going to join the queue?' Dot asked Bea.

'Nah. What's the point? We'll have to do this another way,' said Bea. She tapped the side of her nose and they went down to the shop floor together, with the sound of Neville trying to disburse the crowd ringing in their ears.

Ant was back on pointing duty. He was happy in his work. As she was signing in to her till, Bea beckoned him over.

'I might need you later,' she said. 'Keep watching me.'

'Okay,' he said.

Smelly Reg was first in as usual, but there was quite a crowd with him, waiting for the doors to open and surging in when they did. These were people who knew what they wanted: fags before work, forgotten ingredients for school cooking lessons, milk for the morning cereal. They made a beeline for the section they needed and then straight to the checkouts. Some of them didn't even bother with baskets.

'Did you find everything you need?' Bea asked her first customer, a young lad with paint-stained overalls and big workmen's boots on.

The lad looked puzzled, then replied, 'Yeah.'

She asked the same thing of her next customer, a woman in a nicely tailored black coat. 'Did you find everything you need?'

'Yes, thanks. And more,' the woman chuckled, slipping the bar of honeycomb chocolate into her handbag.

When there was a bit of a lull, Dot swizzled her chair round. 'What's your game?' she said.

'What do you mean?'

'Did you find everything you need?' Dot mimicked in a high-pitched sing-song voice.

'I'm being helpful.'

Dot's beautifully drawn in eyebrows shot up towards her hairline. 'If you say so.'

Later, when the serious shoppers were in, trolleys piled high with the weekly shop, Bea struck lucky.

'Did you find everything you need?' she asked.

'Well, I couldn't find any Chinese Allspice,' said a woman with a shearling coat and Ugg boots. 'But you don't always have it.'

'Oh, I'll get someone to check for you.' Bea looked around for Ant. He was lurking near the cigarette kiosk, his pointing finger drooping by his side. Bea waved at him and he shambled over to her.

'Can you check Stores for Chinese Allspice?' she said.

'Do what? Chinese Whatspice?'

'It's a little jar of, well, spice. Go and have a look in Stores for it. 4772 is the code.' She nodded to him meaningfully and the penny dropped.

'Yeah, right. Got it,' he said. 'Look after this for me.' He hefted the foam finger over the conveyor belt to Bea. She propped it up behind her.

Ant walked swiftly to the back of the store. Dean was one

168

of the names on his list. Now he had a reason to do some snooping. He keyed the code into the double door and went through to Stores. There were racks of boxed-up products, a row of metal open-sided carts, massive numbers of plastic bottles of soft drink shrink-wrapped with more plastic, bags of rice and pasta piled high. It was chaos, but organised chaos.

Ant didn't bother looking at the shelves very closely. He made his way quickly but quietly along the shelves to the far end of the room. There was a gap between the wall and the end of the shelves. He tiptoed towards it and peered through. There was a sort of den in the corner – a couple of plastic chairs, a makeshift table made from an upturned crate and some pictures of topless women Blu-Tacked to the wall.

He thought he could see something through the holes in the side of the crate. He checked behind him then lifted up one side. There was a row of beer bottles and a heap of magazines. The magazines were definitely top shelf material, or maybe under the counter. You dirty bastard, he thought to himself. He replaced the crate and retreated from this grubby little nest.

As he walked back towards the door to the shop floor, he heard a noise. A tap. Or maybe a crack. He eased his way along the rows of shelves, until he spotted Dean. He had his back to Ant and obviously hadn't noticed that he wasn't alone.

Ant tiptoed nearer. There it was again. Crack! And now he could see what Dean was doing. He watched as he opened up a box of eggs and hit one with the handle of a screwdriver. Then he shut the box and put it on a growing pile.

If he sneaked away now and got caught, Ant thought, he'd look suspicious. Better to brazen it out. He cleared his throat noisily and was gratified to see Dean jump and drop the screwdriver on the floor.

'Chinese Allspice,' he declared. 'Have you got any lurking out here, Deano?'

'Chinese Whatspice?' Dean said, standing up and trying to surreptitiously kick the screwdriver behind the pile of boxes. Ant pretended not to notice.

'Allspice, in a little jar,' said Ant, like he'd always known it. '4772.'

'Um, I'll just check.'

He darted away leaving Ant looking at the pile of rejected egg boxes, some of them with dark stains seeping through their cardboard. Dean came back shaking his head and, without comment, Ant went back to Bea's checkout.

As Bea gave him back the foam hand, she hissed, 'Did you find anything?'

Ant tapped his nose. 'Later.'

At break time, Bea made mugs of tea for Ant and Dot. They huddled in the corner.

'So?' said Bea. 'What did you find out?'

Ant leaned further forward. 'Well, he's got a nasty taste in reading and he's up to something with eggs.'

'Eggs?'

'I saw him deliberately breaking them. What's that all about?'

'The little bugger,' said Dot. 'If there's a broken egg in a box, the whole lot gets rejected as waste. I bet he flogs them off to his mates.'

'Should we rat on him?' asked Bea.

'I dunno,' said Ant.

'We'll have to decide quickly before he's got boxes of ammunition to all the toerags in Kingsleigh. Does he know you know?'

'Don't think so.'

'What are you plotting over here?'

170

All three of them looked up to find Neville looming over them.

'Nothing,' they said all together, in blatantly unconvincing unison.

'Did I hear you mention eggs?' he said.

Dot winced.

'Yes,' said Ant, and Bea bit her lip so hard she thought she'd drawn blood. 'Yes. We were just saying the ID thing is a good idea.'

Neville narrowed his eyes, wondering for a moment if he was being teased.

'I mean, who wants to clear up that mess, eh?' said Ant. 'Not me.'

Neville's face relaxed. 'No. Exactly. Good,' he said, and, slightly at a loss, he stalked off.

Bea high-fived Ant. 'Nice one,' she said.

'I was free-styling,' he admitted, 'but it's true, innit? If there's a mess tomorrow, I'm going to be back to the mop and bucket. Screw that. I reckon we should dob Dean in.'

'Let's think about it, shall we?' said Bea. 'Maybe we should just have a quiet word with him. Let him know that we know.'

'Give him a chance to do the right thing, like you did with me? Yeah, I like that,' said Ant.

At the end of the day, Ant and Bea found Dean in his 'den', lounging on one of the plastic chairs with his feet resting on top of the crate. He heard them coming this time.

'Bea,' he said, looking round. 'This is a pleasant surprise.' Then he saw Ant coming to stand next to her. 'Oh. Twice in one day. What are you doing here?'

'We want to talk about eggs,' said Bea.

'Do you want some?' Dean said. 'Didn't think you'd be into that, but Ant—'

'I'm straight now,' said Ant. 'I've seen the light.'

'So what is it? What do you want?'

'You were seen earlier,' said Bea. 'You were deliberately cracking eggs, so they can't be sold. It's you, isn't it, who supplies the kids in the town. You did it last year and it's the same again.'

Dean fired daggers at Ant, then tipped his chair back in a show of nonchalance.

'I don't know what you're talking about,' said Dean.

'I want you to stop selling or giving out the eggs, and I want you to take those pictures down. If you do that, I won't tell Big Gav. If you don't . . .'

'Ooh, I'm scared,' said Dean, grinning all the time.

'I'm serious,' said Bea. 'I'll do it. The town was a fucking mess last year. If the police traced the eggs back here, it's not just trouble for you, it's Gavin that'll take the heat.'

'Nobody's going to trace anything anywhere. There are no eggs,' said Dean.

'Shut up. Ant saw you.'

Still grinning, he held both arms out wide and shrugged. Ant pushed past Bea and marched back to the place where he'd seen Dean at his work. There were no leaking boxes in piles. The screwdriver was gone. The only eggs were stacked neatly on the shelves where they should be. He peered into a couple of boxes. Six perfect eggs. No breakages.

He went up and down the room, looking for damaged eggs, but they were gone.

Back in the den, he and Bea were waiting in awkward silence.

'Where have they gone?' Ant demanded.

'There are no eggs. There were never any eggs. I don't know what you're talking about.'

Ant was red in the face, glowing from his frenzied search and the frustration of failure. 'You lying shit,' he said.

'You like me really,' Dean said.

'If there's trouble tomorrow, I'm going to bring it right back here to you,' Bea said. 'Come on, Ant. Let's get out of here.'

She turned on her heel, but not before Ant had kicked one of the chair legs from under Dean, sending him sprawling onto the concrete floor.

'I'll kill you,' Dean shouted after them. 'I'll kill you, Ant. You're dead!'

12

'What have you come as?' Ant said to Neville. He himself was wrapped up head to toe in toilet roll. Ends were trailing left, right and centre and Bea fervently hoped that he was wearing something decent underneath as it was more than likely going to be on display by the end of the day.

'You know I don't agree with all this Halloween nonsense,' Neville sniffed, picking at an imaginary hair on his Costsave uniform.

'What do you mean? You've come as a muggle, haven't you? I think it's great. You could win, Neville. Good job,' said Bea.

'I haven't—' Neville stopped abruptly when he realised Bea was taking the piss.

'It's a bit of fun, that's all. And it's for charity. Where's your heart, Nev?'

'Not that it's anyone's business, but I've given my contribution to Anna already. I paid *not* to dress up.'

'Okay. Fair enough.' Bea adjusted her headband. The sparkly cat ears had seemed like a bargain when she'd spotted them in the pound shop, but she already had little sore patches where the ends dug in. She'd wear them for as long as possible, though, as the short black dress was a bit boring without them and no one would see the cat's tail sewn onto the back when she was sitting at her till.

'Who's judging, anyway?' said Dot, looking up from applying another coat of green lipstick. She'd gone the whole hog with her witch costume including sticking Rice Krispies to her face to make nastily convincing warts.

'Gav, I think,' said Bea. 'It's not the winning, though, it's the taking part.' She glanced at Dot who was smoothing down her black silky dress, and smiled to herself. 'You look great, Dot. Think you've got it in the bag.'

'What about me?' said Ant, holding his arms out and doing a twirl.

'I think your chances just went down the pan,' said Bea.

'Otherwise, you'd be flushed with success,' said Dot.

He pulled a face. 'Haha, very funny.'

'What are you three plotting?' said Eileen as she walked past.

'Sorry?' said Bea.

'Heard you've been poking your nose in where it wasn't wanted.'

Conversation in the room quietened as people sensed that something interesting was going on.

'I've not been poking my nose anywhere, Eileen. I did go into the Stores yesterday but as far as I know it hasn't been declared out of bounds. It's not your son's private property.'

'Well, no,' she sniffed.

'So there's no poking and no plotting. No unless you're doing it. Or do you just stick to stirring?'

Eileen looked as if she was on the edge of replying, then changed her mind. She sniffed again and disappeared towards the locker room. There was almost an audible sigh from everyone else, though whether it was relief or disappointment, it was hard to tell.

The atmosphere on the shop floor, however, was more

upbeat than it had been for days. It was like everyone had been given permission to lighten up a bit, after the shock of Ginny's murder.

Tom and Shaz walked through the store mid-morning. Bea saw him coming. He lagged behind by her checkout and stopped long enough to say, 'You look purr-fect.'

She blushed, pretended to stroke her whiskers and said, 'Mi-aowww.'

He caught up with Shaz and they went up to Gavin, who was waiting for them.

'Halloween or Ginny?' Dot asked, as they disappeared through the staff door.

'Dunno. Perhaps I'll find out later.'

'Have you two got plans?'

'No, but you never know.'

Dot reached backwards and gave her a little dig in the ribs. 'I've been thinking, Bea,' she said, 'it's good that Gav said they'd pay for taxis and that, but do you think there's anything fishy about it?'

'What?'

'Well, if we tell him our travel plans, he'll know who's with who, won't he? He'll know if anyone's on their own.'

'Yeah, and he'll pay for a taxi for them. I think he's just ruled himself off our list.'

'Unless it's some sort of double bluff.'

'You're getting worse than me, Dot. It's Gavin we're talking about. It'd be fishier if he was offering lifts himself, wouldn't it?'

'Yeah. Yeah, it would.'

Bea peeled the headband off, and grunted with relief. 'God, I can't wear these ears any longer, I'm that sore.'

'Ooh, you've got really red patches. They're evil those things, aren't they? I'm not sure I'm going to be able to keep this hat on all day.'

176

The Halloween specials kept selling well through the morning.

'Have you got any pumpkins?' a harassed mum asked, trailing a tired toddler behind her.

'We've sold out of the big ones,' said Bea, 'but we've got little ones for a pound. There are some in with the fresh veg and some at the end of aisle ten.'

'Thanks.'

As she talked to the woman she saw another watching her. She had scraped-back hair and large hooped earrings. There was something about the way she was looking that rang alarm bells with Bea, but before she could say anything to Dot or even reach for the button to summon Neville, the woman was making a beeline for her. But it wasn't Bea she had in her sights. It was Dot.

'It's you, isn't it?'

'I beg your pardon?'

'You're the one, the one who's been seeing my Anthony.'

Bea apologised to her customer and swivelled round in her chair. She could just see past Dot's tall black hat to her accuser who was standing by Dot's till, jabbing one hand towards Dot's face.

'I don't know who you are,' said Dot steadily. 'If you want to buy something please put it on the belt here. Otherwise, there are people waiting.'

'Don't come all hoity-toity with me. You're a cradle-snatcher, a paedophile, a pervert! That's what you are.' She was shouting now, and people were starting to look. 'How old are you? Sixty? Older than me. Old enough to be my mum! It's disgusting.'

'Can we talk about this somewhere else?' said Dot. As she logged off her till, Bea could see her hands shaking.

'Dot,' she said, 'shall I get someone?'

'It's all right. I'll deal with it,' said Dot.

177

'It?' screeched the woman. 'It? How dare you?'

Bea pressed the button at her station to summon Neville and the checkout number on top of the pole started flashing.

Ant came skidding round the corner, loo paper flapping behind him.

'Oh no! Mum! What are you *doing*?'

'Stay out of this, Anthony. It's between me and her.'

'Don't be stupid. It's nothing to do with you. Nothing. I'm nineteen, Mum.'

'And she's about a hundred! If she was a man, I'd have the police out.'

'No, you wouldn't. I'm *nineteen*! I can do what I want.'

'Not when you're living under my roof, you can't.'

'That's easily fixed.'

'What? Don't you dare.'

By now there was quite a crowd gathering. Other customers had stopped to look, but were keeping their distance. Neville came scurrying over.

'What's going on?' he said, looking around.

'It's nothing, Neville,' said Ant. 'My mum's just going.'

'Your mum.' He looked at her with renewed distaste. 'Madam, is there a problem I can help you with?'

She turned her attention to him, and, instinctively, he moved his clipboard from under his arm to across his chest, like a shield.

'Yes, you can tell this slag to leave my son alone.'

Little spots of colour appeared in Neville's cheeks. 'If it's not a customer service issue, then I will have to ask you to leave the store.'

'I'm not going anywhere. Not till this pervert apologises to me and promises to get on her broomstick and stay away from my son.'

'For fuck's sake, Mum—'

The spots of colour had joined up now – Neville was red-faced with rage.

'That'll do,' he barked. 'I want you all off the shop floor!'

'I'm not budging.' Her mouth was set into a thin straight line. Her earrings were quivering with indignation.

'In that case, I'm calling the police.' He took out his phone and started dialling.

Ant clapped his hands to his forehead. 'Come on, Mum, let's get out of here.' He took hold of her elbow to guide her away, but she jabbed it upwards sharply almost catching his face.

'Jesus! Behave yourself, Mum!'

'I'm not going!'

'You fucking are. Do you want me to call Dad?'

'He thinks the same as me. You should be ashamed of yourself.'

She raised her hand now, ready to slap him, but in a flash Dot leaned across the desk and grabbed hold of her wrist, stopping it in mid-air. 'That's enough,' she said.

The women's faces were close now. They stared at each other, like two boxers in the ring, just before the first punch is thrown. Each was focusing on the other so intently that they didn't notice the crowd parting and the two police officers walking through.

'Mrs Thompson,' Tom said. 'Bit early for this sort of thing, isn't it?'

Dot and Ant's mum both turned their heads. Dot let go of Mrs Thompson's wrist. Her pointy hat had taken on a rakish angle in the melee.

'Let's take this outside, shall we?' said Tom. 'I'll walk with you.'

He breezed through between the checkouts and swept Ant's mum out of the packing area and towards the door.

'I'm sorry,' Ant said to Dot. 'I can't even—'

'It's all right. It's not your fault,' she said, but Bea could see one of her Rice Krispie warts dancing as a little muscle twitched in her cheek. She was close to tears. 'Neville, do you mind if I take a few minutes?' she said.

'No. No, of course not.'

Dot left her station and started to walk towards the back of the store, her cloak billowing out behind her. Ant trotted beside her, apologising over and over again. At the far end of the aisles, Bea saw Bob-on-Meat step out from behind his counter. He said something to Dot, but she didn't stop walking and Bea guessed that the tears were flowing now.

At lunchtime Anna told Bea that Dot had gone home. Gavin had agreed to call it 'sick leave'. Ant was missing too, but he was AWOL. He'd have some music to face in the morning. Bea wondered whether he was with Dot or his mum. She made a mug of tea then sat down and texted Dot.

> You ok?
>
> > Yeah. Thx, doll.
>
> Do you want me to come round after work?
>
> > No. I'm fine. Licking my wounds. See you tomoz.

Dean slunk in, his wolfish grin almost lost within the wide-mouthed Joker make-up plastered onto his face.

'I hear I missed all the fun,' he said.

'It wasn't fun for Dot, though, Dean,' said Eileen. 'That woman was tearing into her.'

'Well, she had it coming, if you ask me. I mean, *her* and *him*. It's disgusting.'

'We don't even know if it was true, do we?'

'No, but—'

'I knew he was trouble.' Bob was joining in now. His 'costume' seemed to be little more than his normal white coat with some extra streaks of blood added. 'I could've told

180

her. I *did* tell her. Lovely woman like that getting mixed up with a little runt like him.'

Eileen turned to Bea. 'You know, don't you? You're pals with both of them. What's going on?'

'It's none of our business, that's what.'

'But *him* and *her*!'

It was too much for Bea. 'So what if she's seeing him? Good luck to her.' She left her tea on the table and stalked out.

She met Gavin in the corridor. The bolt in one side of his neck had fallen off. She wondered if anyone had told him, but decided not to.

'Bea,' he said, 'how are you getting home tonight?'

'I was walking with Dot and Ant, but they've both gone missing.'

'Okay, so is there someone else you can walk with?'

'I dunno.'

'No one?'

'I'll be fine. It'll be busy out there with all the kids out and about.'

'You mustn't walk on your own. Look, I'll drop you off there, shall I?'

Bea looked at his round, open face. He was a nice guy, Gavin. Then she remembered what Bea had said the night before. What if he was using his show of concern to find out who was walking home alone?

'There's no need to go out of your way,' she said. 'I could book a taxi, like you said at the meeting.'

'It's not really out of my way. A couple of minutes, that's all.'

Her phone pinged – a text coming in. She quickly checked it. It was from Tom.

What time do you get off?

A quick reply: 8

Meet you in the car park at 8. Police escort home?

She smiled. 'It's okay, Gav,' she said, nodding at her phone. 'A friend's going to give me a lift.'

'Ah, that's great,' he said, and he sounded genuinely pleased. 'Let me know if things change, though. I'm serious about this. We can't have any more ... incidents.'

The afternoon couldn't go quickly enough for Bea. The firework display seemed a long time off. She'd been hoping to see Tom before that.

At a few minutes after six, a small vampire peered over the side of her desk. He had a pale white face, dark circles round his eyes and his hair slicked back. His plastic fangs were causing a bit of trouble. Instead of being attached to his upper teeth, they were balancing on the end of his stuck-out tongue.

'Oooh, scary,' Bea said, recognising Mason under the face paint.

'Trick or treat,' he lisped and the fangs fell out of his mouth and onto her conveyor belt.

'Sorry,' his mum said, scooping them up and putting them in her pocket.

'Heeyyy.' Mason started to squeal, but Bea swooped in.

'It had better be treat, hadn't it?' She fished under the counter and produced a lolly. Mason took it greedily.

'Thank you,' Julie said, 'that's kind. Say thank you to the lady, Mason.'

'Fankoo,' Mason said, the lolly already unwrapped and stuffed in his mouth.

'Better have this for the little 'un,' Bea said and handed another lolly to Julie. Their hands briefly touched and Bea saw that the sticking plaster was back on Julie's ring finger.

There were a couple of marks that looked like cigarette burns on her wrist.

'You all right?' she said, without really thinking.

'Course she is.' Bea hadn't seen that Dave was behind them. He put his hand protectively on his wife's shoulder and she flinched. He was in civvies today – tracksuit bottoms and zipped-up hoodie. He watched his wife get her purse out of her bag, then said, 'No, darlin'. I'll get this,' and paid using his debit card. Bea studiously tried not to look at him, but as she handed over the receipt their eyes met and he winked. Bea cringed but said nothing. Feeling slightly sick, she watched him pick up their bag and head towards the door.

Trade was slowing down now. Perhaps it was the Emma and Ginny effect. Perhaps it was Halloween. There were still people picking up things for dinner and a few harassed parents with tired children in tow. Now and again, a gang of dressed up teens swept through. All the staff eyed them warily, checked their ID when they asked for cigarettes, cider or eggs, but there was no trouble in the store.

'Bit late for you to be out,' Bea said to Norma.

'Ran out of my winter warmer,' the woman said, placing her hand protectively on the half-bottle of whisky lying on the belt between a packet of cheese slices and a small sliced white loaf. 'Wish I hadn't, though. There are kids out there with eggs.'

'In the car park?'

'No, around the town. Little hooligans. I'm going to get straight home and shut the door. I don't believe in this trick or treating. We never used to have it. I blame America.'

'It's okay if it's little kids dressing up and eating sweets, though. Not the other stuff.'

'You look very fetching anyway, with your whiskers. Let me find some change.'

Norma scrabbled in her purse and found a few coppers. 'Oh, you don't have to,' Bea protested. She knew the money wasn't really 'spare'.

'It's for little Kayleigh, isn't it?'

'Yes, but—'

'Here you go. God bless, darling. See you soon.'

'Goodnight. You take care.'

It was people like this that made her job worth it, Bea thought. Some people might look down on her being a checkout girl, but what did they know? Sometimes it felt like the best job in the world. The fracas with Dot had unsettled her, and she hated being here with the station next to her empty one. But Dot would be back tomorrow, and before then, she had a date with a rather hot cop.

13

Bea checked her watch. Three minutes past eight. She scanned the car park, but couldn't see a police car anywhere. Maybe he was in his own car. It was some sort of dark-coloured saloon, wasn't it? Her phone was ominously silent. No new messages. She walked slowly along the rows of cars to the far corner where the path cut through to the café and on to the High Street. Five past now. It was only five minutes. The stormy weather of the last few days had been replaced by clear skies and a cold, crisp stillness. Bea could see stars beyond the yellow sulphur glow of the streetlights. She stamped her feet to keep warm. Eight minutes past. And then her phone pinged: On a call. Sorry. Get a taxi. Txx

Bea sighed. Duty calls, she thought. This is what you've got to expect if you date a cop. Was it worth it? She'd find out at the firework party, if he didn't stand her up.

She set off walking. The High Street was bright and busy with a steady stream of traffic and plenty of people around. The newsagent was still open, as were the takeaways and the Indian and Italian restaurants. She passed the open door of the Methodist Church. A banner across the entrance advertised their 'Festival of Light'. Inside, she could see families sitting at tables eating soup and baked potatoes. She caught sight of Neville with an apron on, carrying a tray full of mugs. He glanced over to the door and nodded when he saw her. He raised his eyebrows and tipped his head, inviting her in. She smiled and waved to him, and walked on.

Further down the street, the owner of Mumtaz Restaurant was scrubbing his front window as Bea passed, washing away the egg splattered across the glass.

'Little toerags,' Bea said to him and rolled her eyes.

'Nothing personal. They've done all down the street,' he said. 'Their parents should know where they are, what they're doing, but these days . . . '

It was true, streaks of egg on windows and doors would greet most of Kingsleigh's shop owners tomorrow morning.

'Bloody Dean,' Bea muttered.

The shops thinned out at the end of the High Street, and it got progressively quieter. The entrance to the Leisure Centre was the other side of the road. Lee was standing outside. He waved at her, and she crossed the road.

'Haven't seen you in the gym yet,' he said.

Bea pulled a face. 'No. Been busy.'

'Induction only takes half an hour. You can find half an hour, can't you?'

'Not tonight,' she said.

'No. Not tonight.' He looked up and down the street. 'I'm meant to be running a five-a-side comp, keep the lads off the street and out of trouble, but no one's turned up. Well, I had three, but I sent them home. Might as well take this in.' He folded up an A-board advertising the event and tucked it under his arm. 'See you later, Bea. Take care.'

'See ya.'

Bea crossed over the road again. As she turned off into the side street, she wondered whether she should stop where it was busier and ring for a taxi, but righteous indignation overtook her. Why should she faff about and have to wait in the cold? There were a lot of people out and about tonight.

Safety in numbers. It wouldn't take her long to get home.

Pumpkin lanterns dotted the suburban street. Some were straightforward, ghoulish faces, others clearly the result of templates and a lot of adult patience. On one hedge, two distorted faces spewed a mess of seeds out of their gaping mouths. On another, a head was cruelly stuck with pins and nails.

Bea heard a click and looked to one side. Kevin, the photographer, was crouching down in a gateway. His lens was pointing at her.

'Oh,' she said, 'it's you.'

She pulled her coat more firmly around her.

'Sorry,' he said, straightening up and stepping out of the shadows. 'Did I scare you?'

He had a dark anorak on. It was zipped up to the top, but the hood was down.

'No,' said Bea.

'On your own?'

It was perfectly obvious that she was.

'No,' she bluffed. 'I'm meeting some friends.'

'That's all right then. I can walk with you, if you like. Until you find them.'

'Don't you need to take some more pictures?'

'I've got what I need,' he said. 'A few groups of kids dressed up. Some lanterns. All that sort of thing. Same every year. Don't think my editor would notice if I just sent in last year's pictures. I can do this stuff in my sleep.'

He started walking in the direction Bea had been heading, and she had no real choice but to walk with him.

'You don't sound very thrilled with it. What would you rather be doing?'

'Oh, don't get me wrong. I like this small-town stuff. It's a good gig. But the photos I *really* like taking are a bit more . . . artistic.'

They had turned off the main drag now and were heading for the bungalows near the rec. Bea was relieved to see the unsteady beams of torches from a group of trick or treaters not too far ahead of them. She glanced behind. There was no one following.

'Yeah?' she said, casually. 'Like landscapes and things, the sort of stuff you see in the posh Sunday paper magazines?'

'Ha, no, not landscapes,' he said. 'People.'

'Oh, right.'

'People like you, Bea. Good-looking. Fun.'

Bea's heart was racing now. If she was a real detective she would play along now, wouldn't she? See what she could get him to reveal, but her skin was prickling with discomfort and her hackles were up.

'Fun,' she said. 'Some people use that word when they mean fat.'

'Not me,' Kevin said. 'I just meant fun. You're up for a laugh, aren't you?'

'Sometimes,' said Bea. 'Not recently, though. This is you, isn't it? You said your mum lived in one of these bungalows.'

'Oh, yes,' said Kevin. 'Right here, but I'm happy to walk you home if you've given up on your friends.'

Bea was glad it was dark, so he couldn't see her blush at her lie being exposed for what it was.

'They'll be at the pub. The Jubilee,' she said, naming the pub at the other side of the rec. 'I'll go there now. They'll be expecting me.'

'I quite fancy a pint. I'll join you, shall I?'

The trick or treaters had moved out of sight, into one of the side streets. The thought of walking across the Green alone with Kevin made Bea feel sick, but she couldn't think how to get out of it. Then she heard another noise – someone rapping on a window. She turned her head towards the sound and there was a woman standing in the front room of the nearest bungalow. She was pointing at Kevin and gesturing. He rolled his eyes.

'Mother,' he said. 'She's spotted me. I'd better go in. Here, I'll give you my card. It's not for the paper, it's for my private work. I'd take some shots for free – you wouldn't have to pay.'

'Oh, great. Thanks.' Bea took the card, identical to the one she'd found in Ginny's locker. 'Goodnight, then.'

'Night.'

She hurried along the path, glad to get away from him. There was no one ahead and no one behind. It would only take her a minute or two to cross the rec. She wondered if she'd actually be safer going straight over the middle, but instinct kept her to the path round the edge. She could hear voices as she approached one of the paths off into the estate. She had butterflies the size of small birds battering their wings against the inside of her stomach.

Voices, plural, she thought. That's okay. It's the someone on their own that I need to worry about. Somebody quiet.

She pressed on. As she passed the entrance to the path people swirled out towards her. They weren't really wearing costumes, just black hoodies and jeans, trackie bottoms and tops, but all their faces were covered by masks. They were cackling and shrieking, jeering at her, moving constantly.

They're just kids, she told herself. I probably know them. But they weren't little kids, they were as tall as her, taller some of them. And all boys.

'Trick or treat,' they chanted.

'Neither, okay?' Bea said. They were getting in her way now. She was trying to keep walking but she was forced to slow right down, was almost at a standstill. The masks bothered her. She hated not being able to see their faces, apart from the glint of their eyes through the little holes.

'Reckon it'll have to be a trick,' one of them said, from

189

behind his *Scream* mask. Bea thought she recognised the voice. 'What's it going to be?'

There was laughter. Six of them and one of me, thought Bea. Shit. She couldn't outrun them. Nor could she fight all of them off if it got physical.

She'd stopped walking. They were circling closer now, their masked faces looming in at her, taunting her. Someone touched her bum. She spun round and the laughing got louder. She had the sense of everything getting out of control, slipping away from her. She had to act now.

She scanned the carousel of faces until she saw the *Scream* mask coming round. Quick as a flash she grabbed it and pulled as hard and she could. The elastic holding it on stretched and then snapped.

'Aargh! Jesus, fuck!' the boy screamed. He clapped his hand up to his eye.

'Ken Thompson!' Bea shouted. It was one of Ant's younger brothers. 'I thought it was you.'

'Huh?' Ken said. The others had stopped circling now.

'Ant's going to skin you when I tell him what you're up to.'

'Shut up. I'm not up to anything.'

'Are you shitting me? Picking on people who are walking on their own. After what happened to Ginny. You should be ashamed of yourselves. You and your pathetic little mates.'

They were shuffling their feet now, looking down at the ground. Bea noticed that most of them were carrying plastic bags.

'Now take those sodding masks off and you can walk me to the shops, like gentlemen.'

Amazingly, one by one, the masks came off, propped up on the top of their heads or held sheepishly in their hands.

'Come on,' she said. 'I don't want to hang around here any longer.'

They walked together towards the lit row of shops.

'You won't tell Ant, will you?' said Ken, who was by her side.

'I dunno. Are you going to go home now?'

'It's a bit early.'

'You got school tomorrow, haven't you?'

'Yeah, but—'

'Pack it in for tonight, then, and don't spook anyone else on your way home.'

They were at the shops now.

'Okay. Will you be all right from here?'

'Yes. Thank you.'

She watched them turn back to the rec. They seemed to be arguing. One of the lads hit another one with his mask and there was a bit of a scuffle. Someone ran ahead and another reached into a bag and threw something at them. A white shape flew through the air and shattered on the path by their feet. An egg.

Let them take it out on each other, not the unsuspecting public. Little shits, thought Bea. But as she walked along her road, she found that she was shaking. Little shits they might be, but they had scared her badly.

Most of the pumpkin lanterns had gone out now, the candles burnt down to a stump. There were only one or two sending guttering light out onto the pavement. From along the road, she couldn't see a lantern on her front gatepost. It must have burnt out too, she thought. But when she got to number twenty-three, she saw that there wasn't a pumpkin at all. She looked up the path to the house. All the lights were off, even the outside one that Queenie always put on for her to help her safely round to the back door.

'What the—?'

She went through the gate and followed the path round to the back of the house. She had one hand on the wall to guide her as even though she knew the way well enough, it was tricky in the dark. She got to the back door and tried the handle. It was locked. She knocked on the door and then listened. No lights came on. No sound of footsteps coming to the door. 'Oh God,' she muttered. 'Something's happened!'

She knocked again, louder this time and started shouting. 'Mum! Queenie! Open up, it's me!'

She stopped to listen again. Her phone started vibrating in her pocket. She took it out. The screen was a bright rectangle. 'Queenie calling.'

She accepted the call.

'Mum, where are you?'

'At home. Is that you outside?'

'Yes. Of course it's me. I've just told you it's me. Open the frigging door.'

'Okay.'

Bea could hear movement inside, then the liquid sound of the key turning in the lock, and the thunk of both bolts being undone. Finally, the door opened an inch or two and she could see Queenie squinting out at her. When she recognised her daughter she opened the door further. 'Come in, then. Quickly.'

Inside the kitchen Bea couldn't see a thing. The only light was a ghostly glow from the door to the living room, cast by the TV.

'Mum, what's going on? What are you doing, sitting here in the dark?'

'I don't want anyone knocking at the door.'

'But we always do Halloween. It's one of our things.'

'Not this year. Not with that maniac out and about.'

'What about the pumpkin I brought home? Have you carved it?'

'No.'

'I've got two bags of sweets.'

'So? We'll work our way through them, or you can take them back to work.'

'This isn't like you. We always . . . when Dad was here . . .'

'Don't, Bea. Don't bring him into this.'

'But, Mum—'

'Did you lock that door?'

'Yes, but—'

'Come into the lounge then.'

The television screen cast eerie shadows across the ceiling.

Bea could hear the high-pitched sounds of another gaggle of teenagers outside in the street. The noise got nearer. They were coming up the front path.

'Mum?'

'Shh.' Queenie held her finger to her lips. 'We're not here. Not at home to strangers.'

'They're just kids, Mum.'

Someone knocked on the door. Queenie sat, motionless, in her chair. The visitors rattled the letterbox. Even though Bea knew it was trick or treaters, the butterflies were back in her stomach. Another barrage of knocks made Bea jump despite herself.

'God,' she said, 'this is worse than answering the flaming door. It's giving me the creeps. I'm going.' She got up from her chair, but Queenie lunged forward and grabbed her.

'No!' she shouted. 'Don't open that door!' Her fingertips dug into Bea's arms and there was real anguish in her voice.

'Okay, okay,' said Bea. She prised her mum's hands off her. 'Let's have a cup of tea.'

They sat out the evening, pretending to watch the telly while really listening to every noise outside. Voices, footsteps, laughter, screams.

As they were going up the stairs to bed, Queenie said, 'I've got a date, you know. For my interview. The third.' The day after Ginny's funeral.

'Okay, mum. I think that's my day off. I'll check. I'll get the time off if it isn't.'

Before going to sleep, Bea got on her laptop and typed in the web address on Kevin's business card. The 'people' he liked photographing were all women, mostly young. Very young. The images in his gallery were fairly tasteful, bare backs and no nipples, but Bea wondered what images didn't make it onto this shop window.

She went back to her spreadsheet and thought back over the day. She couldn't rule Kevin out. Far from it. Dave was still in the frame too, especially now she'd seen him in his hoodie and sweats.

What about Dean? He liked the sort of pictures Kevin took, and he was quite blatantly the supplier of eggs to the locals, but that didn't make him a killer, did it?

She closed the lid of the laptop, but the images and words were imprinted on her brain. There when she closed her eyes. There when she opened them. The sounds of the evening stuck with her too. Those boys and their voices. Kids' screams and laughter.

She dozed fitfully and woke with a start. She'd been asleep and dreaming, except she could still hear screaming now. Her mind tried to focus. This wasn't kids messing about on the rec – it was coming from inside the house.

'Oh God! Mum!'

She threw off her duvet and ran out of the room. Her mum's room was the other side of the bathroom. The screams made Bea's blood run cold. It wasn't just noise, she was shouting words, 'Get out! Get out! Get him out of here!'

'Mum! Mum!'

The bedroom door was open but the room was dark. Bea raced in. She could just make out a pale shape on the bed, her mother sitting up.

'Mum, it's me!'

The screaming didn't stop.

Bea crouched by the bed and put her hands on her mother's shoulders. 'It's me. It's all right.'

'Get him out!'

Bea fumbled for the light switch at the side of the bed. The light was blinding. As her eyes readjusted she scanned the room, expecting – dreading – to see someone else there. But there was no one. The room was exactly as it always was: a dressing table with a mirror, a hairbrush and some bottles of scent; and two wardrobes – one for her mum's clothes, the other for her dad's, still there after six years, untouched.

'There's no one here, Mum. It's fine. Everything's fine.'

Queenie stopped shouting, but there were tears pouring down her face now. Her hair was tousled. Bea took a tissue from the box on the bedside table and wiped the tears away. She smoothed her hair, and a familiar queasy feeling overtook her. The tables were turned again. She was parent and Queenie was the child.

'Can you see now? There's only me and you. We're fine. Everything's fine,' Bea soothed.

Her mum found a tissue of her own and blew her nose. 'I heard something,' she said, her voice trembling. 'Saw something. Someone. Here, in this room.'

'There was no one here when I came in. There's no one else in the house.'

'Are you sure?'

'Yeah. Well, I haven't checked the whole house. I'll do it now.'

'No!' Queenie clutched her again. 'Don't go down there. What if he's still there?'

'Who? Who do you think it is?'

'Him. The one who's been attacking people.'

'Don't be silly. He's been doing it outside in the street, not breaking into people's houses. I'll go and make us a cup of tea, shall I? And check the house while I'm about it.'

'Don't, Bea! Let's ring the police!'

Bea sighed and stood up. 'I'm not ringing the police because you had a nightmare. That's all it was. Bloody Halloween got to you. I'll be back in a minute.'

Despite her brave words, Bea felt sick as she stood at the top of the stairs looking down. She couldn't hear anything, because, of course, she told herself, there was nothing to hear. Even so, what if there was someone there? What should she do? Scream? Hit them? There's no one there, she told herself firmly, and switched on the landing light.

Downstairs was just as they had left it. Bea padded into the kitchen and checked the back door – still locked and bolted. She made two mugs of tea and heated up two microwavable bags in the shape of cuddly owls, and retreated upstairs again with everything balanced on a tray.

Queenie was still sitting up, still looking confused and lost.

'Here, Mum,' Bea said putting the tray on the floor. 'Here's an owl for your feet and a nice cup of tea.'

She lifted up the bottom of the duvet and put the warm bag in.

As Queenie sipped her tea, she seemed to come back to herself.

'Ahh,' she said, smacking her lips a little. 'That's better. I'm a silly old fool, aren't I?'

'No, Mum. Everyone has bad dreams sometimes.'

'I never hear you in the night. Well, not shouting out. Snoring, maybe.'

'Shut up, I don't snore!'

'Says you.'

Bea sat on the side of the bed until both mugs were empty. The bedside alarm clock was showing nearly ten past four. She took her mum's empty mug and put in on the tray.

196

'Right,' she said. 'Time for lights out again. You're okay now, aren't you?'

'Yes,' said Queenie. 'But could you sleep here, just for tonight?'

They'd slept in the same bed for a couple of months after Bea's dad died. They had both needed the comfort to start with, but in the end it was Bea who had decided to move back to her own room. Was this a step backwards?

'Okay,' she said. 'I'll just turn the lights out.'

'Leave the landing light on, love. Just tonight.'

'Okay.'

Bea switched the bedside light out, then walked around the bed and climbed in. She lay on her right side facing away from her mum, who was still sitting upright. After a few minutes, Bea turned over. She could see in the soft light cast from the landing that Queenie's eyes were still open.

'Mum,' she said. 'Lie down, for goodness' sake. You'll never get to sleep like that, and neither will I.'

Queenie turned her head, and Bea saw the faint glistening of fresh tears on her face.

'Mum,' she said softly. 'Come on.'

She held her arms out, and Queenie shuffled down the bed. She curled up with her back to Bea who curled up too, her legs parallel to Queenie's, one arm around her stomach, the other hand stroking her hair. And sure enough, Queenie's breathing became slower and more regular. She stopped sniffing and her body relaxed. Soon, she was asleep, leaving Bea wide awake, but too scared of waking her to move.

The house was quiet and would be until the heating pipes started creaking when the boiler fired up in a couple of hours' time. There were no footsteps on the pavement, but now and again the soft purr of a car passing in the road. At one point, a car seemed to stop outside with its engine idling. Bea craned over her mother's sleeping bulk to see the clock.

Five thirty. She wondered if it was Tom, finally back from whatever call he'd had to go on instead of driving her home. Her phone was in her own bedroom, otherwise she might have sent him a cheeky text, find out if it was him. Maybe she could tiptoe to the window, peek out.

She moved her arm away from Queenie's waist and started to slide away from her towards the edge of the bed. Queenie groaned and turned over. She flopped out an arm and pulled Bea closer. Bea rolled her eyes to the heavens and gave in. She was here for the night. Her mum's breath was warm against her neck. Instead of disgusting her, it was soothing, and now, finally, she found herself drifting off. She was almost asleep when she heard a car door open, the telltale sigh of the gate on its hinges, and footsteps on the path. Her heart started racing, jumping about in her chest. Someone was in their front garden, getting closer to the house. Her breath was coming fast now too and she strained to hear what was coming next. The letterbox rapped once, twice, and then the footsteps retreated.

A car door slammed and then the engine revved up and the car was away. Bea listened until she couldn't hear it any more. An over-enthusiastic paper boy? A meths-soaked flaming rag? For fuck's sake, I'm never going to sleep! she thought.

'Sorry, Queenie,' she whispered and slithered out of her mum's grasp. Queenie protested and shuffled about, but was settled again as Bea headed out of the bedroom. She crept downstairs. There was a square of paper on the floor by the front door. She picked it up. It was, in fact, a rectangle, folded in the middle. She opened it up. It was written in red biro in capital letters. Five words.

'MIND YOUR OWN BUSINESS, BITCH.'

14

Gavin was scrubbing the front windows with a broom and big bucket of soapy water when Bea got to Costsave the next morning. She was on her own as neither Dot nor Ant had materialised on the High Street like usual. Perhaps Dot was still lying low.

'Been demoted? You must've done something really bad.'

Gavin spun round. His forehead glistened a little from his efforts with the broom. 'That's a bit below the belt. Wouldn't expect that from you, Bea.'

Bea's stomach lurched. 'I d-didn't mean anything ... ' It had only been a bit of gentle teasing.

He dipped the brush into the bucket. 'Anyway, I was first in, Bea. Can't have people seeing the store like this, especially if the eggs came from us.'

Her stomach gave another little flip. 'Did they?' Did he know something? Had someone turned Dean in?

'Where else? The farm shop was in lockdown, apparently. No one else has big quantities of eggs.'

She still couldn't bring herself to tell him about Dean, but she could at least drop a heavy hint. 'You could check the stock levels, I suppose, look at breakages.'

He turned to face her, eggy suds dripping off the end of his brush. 'Yes. I'll ask Neville later.' He let the brush stand on the ground and leaned against it, puffing a little. The brush handle put Bea in mind of a pole propping up a washing line.

'Do you want me to finish that, Mr Howells? I don't mind.'

He wiped his forehead with the back of his hand. 'No. I'm nearly done here. Thanks, though, Bea.'

Inside, Bea got changed and touched up her make-up. She checked her watch. Dot was definitely going to be late. She was about to send her a text when Anna came into the locker room.

'Ant's just rung,' she said. 'Dot's in hospital.'

Bea heard herself gasp. 'What? What's happened?'

Please God, not Dot. Let her be all right.

'Broken her hip, apparently. In a fall. Ant's with her.'

'Oh my God. Is she okay?'

'He didn't say much. She's having an operation now. He said he'd ring again when he knew more.'

'Is it the Royal United?'

'Yeah. Ward 10, he said.'

'I'll go after work, get the bus. Bloody hell.'

'I know. What with that and Gavin.'

'What?'

Anna lowered her voice. 'Got turned down for promotion yesterday. Don't tell anyone, but he's a bit down about it.'

'Oh shit. I just opened my mouth and put both feet in.'

Bea told Anna about her exchange with Gavin. In spite of herself, Anna started to laugh.

'God, only you, Bea!'

'I didn't mean to. I didn't know, did I?'

'I know. That's what makes it funnier. Poor Gavin. Having a bit of a rough time of it. Don't tell anyone, though. Mum's the word.'

The day dragged slowly by without Dot at the next checkout. A broken hip? She could be gone for ages. Bea sat with Eileen and Anna at lunchtime but Eileen was busy with her Sudoku and Anna had her nose in a book. Dean came in to make a mug of tea. She caught him looking at her and wilted inside as he strutted over towards her.

'Get home all right last night, did you?'

'Yes, thank you. How nice of you to ask.'

'No trouble on the way?'

Then she knew: he'd set up Ant's brother and his stupid friends to ambush her. He'd armed them with eggs. She'd felt a little guilty about pointing Gav in his direction, but not any more. He deserved everything that was coming to him.

She struggled through the afternoon. On her way out, she rang Queenie to let her know where she was going. Queenie was put out at the thought of a pizza from the freezer for tea, but she understood Bea's reasons and asked her to send Dot her love.

'I'll see you later, Bea. You take care coming home.'

Dot was sitting in a high-backed blue plastic chair by the side of her bed. Her face lit up when she saw Bea. Ant was sitting in another chair, with his head propped up in his hands. His face had a shiny, unwashed look about it and there were dark rings under his eyes.

'Ant, you look knackered,' said Bea. 'Have you been here all day?'

He didn't answer.

'Seriously,' said Bea. 'Go home. Get some sleep. It looks like you need it.'

'Dot?' Ant said.

Dot smiled at him. 'It's fine, love. You've done so much today. Go home. See your mum. Get some sleep.'

He dragged himself to his feet, then leaned down and kissed Dot on her cheek. She cupped his face with one hand. 'I'll see you tomorrow, darlin'.'

'Okay,' he said. 'If you're sure.'

'I'm sure I'm sure.'

'See ya, Bea,' he said, and trailed out of the ward, scuffing his toes as he went.

'Blimey,' said Bea. 'He's wrecked. I thought you were the one in the wars, but I'm not so sure now. Anyway, you're up! I thought you'd be lying in bed with your leg in the air.'

'Bea! Come here, darling!' She held one arm out and gathered Bea in for a heartfelt hug. When she let go, Bea sat on the chair vacated by Ant.

'They make you get out of bed really quickly,' said Dot. 'They're sadists, Bea. I'm not joking.'

'Does it hurt?'

'Not as much as I thought, but I think I'm still dosed up to my gills.'

The room was swelteringly hot. All the windows were shut.

Bea took off her coat and put it over the metal end of the bed. She unwrapped her scarf and flapped the top of her blouse. 'Warm in here. Can I have some of your water?'

'Yeah, sure.'

Bea took a clean cup from the stack on Dot's table on wheels, and poured out some water from the plastic jug. She drank the whole lot quickly and poured out some more.

'So,' she said, 'how on earth did you break your hip?'

Dot looked at her steadily. 'Silly me. I fell over in the middle of the night. Need to take more water with it or something.'

'And what happened then? Did you have your phone on you? How did you get help?

Silence for a beat, then, 'Well, Ant was there, so he called an ambulance.'

Bea narrowed her eyes. 'Ant was there.'

Dot started fiddling with the tape which kept the cannula on place on the back of her hand. 'Yeah.'

'So that was handy,' said Bea, casually. 'Ant being there.'

'Yeah. Don't know what I would have done without him.'

Bea couldn't help seeing her list in her mind's eye. The names of the men. Ant's name. And he'd looked dreadful just now – tiredness? Maybe guilt too.

She got up and walked round the bed and then back again drawing the floor-length curtain with her.

'What are you doing?' said Dot.

Bea pulled her chair closer to Dot's. She leaned forward and took hold of Dot's hands in hers. She lowered her voice.

'Dot, did he . . . did he *hurt* you?'

Dot looked shocked.

'No! No. He wouldn't. He's not like that.'

'Dot, you can tell me if he did. You *should* tell someone.'

'He didn't hurt me, Bea, not intentionally.'

'I've read it in my magazines, women always blame themselves.' The image of Julie's face flashed into Bea's mind – her face and the weird, puckered skin around her wedding ring.

'Stop it, Bea,' Dot said, bringing Bea's attention back to the hospital room. 'You're barking up the wrong tree, love. He would never hurt me.'

Bea let go of Dot's hands and picked up the cup again. She had a sip of water. 'So?'

Dot took a couple of deep breaths. 'Okay, you mustn't tell anyone, right?'

'Of course not.'

Another breath. Dot closed her eyes momentarily, almost as if she was praying. Bea had another sip. When Dot opened her eyes she said, 'We fell off the bed.'

Bea sprayed water out of her mouth in a perfect arc. It landed on the blanket on Dot's knees in a shower of spitty rain. Bea grabbed a tissue and started dabbing at the wet patches. It gave her something to do while she tried to compose herself.

When she finally looked up, Dot was squinting at her through half-closed eyes, shielding herself from Bea's reaction.

'You fell off the bed while you were *at it*?' Bea hissed.

Dot nodded and beckoned her closer.

'It was the first time,' she whispered. 'We hadn't even done it before. Just held hands and had a little snog. It was his mum that made it happen.'

'His mum?'

'He was so mad with her after she came into the store, he came round to see me and I was upset and he was comforting me and I was comforting him and, well, this happened.'

'Wow.'

'So I guess she was right, after all. Stupid for me to get involved with someone so young. I'm not cut out for it.'

'Well, it was bloody bad luck for this to happen the first time.'

Dot smiled ruefully. 'Yeah. First and last, I reckon. I'm not going to be spreading these legs for some time.' She winced as she shifted in her chair. Without her make-up, she looked every one of her fifty-eight years. Still lovely, to Bea's eyes, but definitely a woman of a certain age.

'You know your list? I know you put a line through Ant's name, but I don't think you crossed him off in your head, did you? 'Cos I was his alibi and we were, you know.'

'Yeah. I'm sorry, but ... '

'The thing is I've known you much longer than I've known him. You're my friend, Bea, my proper friend. I like Ant, but he's, you know, a boy. If it was a choice between you and him, it would be you every time. And so I wouldn't lie to you. He was with me when Emma was attacked. God's truth. You can take him off your list for real.'

'Okay. I will.'

'Thank you,' said Dot. Her face seemed to be getting greyer. 'Have you made any progress?'

'Yes! I wanted to report back to you two. Haven't eliminated anyone yet but I've got some new info.'

Dot shifted in her chair again and winced a little. 'I think I need to get back into bed.' She shut her eyes.

'Shall I fetch someone?' said Bea.

'No, if you just help me get out of this dressing gown and shuffle across. Don't need to bother the nurses, they've got enough to do.'

'Okay, if you're sure.'

Bea helped Dot ease her arms out of her dressing gown in the chair. Then she supported her as she got onto her feet, taking as much weight from her as she could. Dot shrugged off her gown and took the couple of steps over to the bed.

'Move those covers,' she said.

Bea held onto Dot with one hand and turned the sheets and blanket back with the other. Dot sat on the bed slowly.

'Can you lift my feet up together and help me swivel round? Gently, though.'

Before too long, she was safely tucked up. Bea adjusted the pillow behind her. Dot closed her eyes. The effort seemed to have exhausted her.

'I should go,' said Bea.

Dot opened her eyes again. 'No, it's all right. I'm okay, just a bit tired that's all. You wanted to tell me something. Report back.'

'Yeah, but ... '

Dot nodded. 'If I close my eyes,' she said, 'I'm still listening. Carry on.'

'Okay, so that Dave was in the store at the start of the evening. He was there with his whole family and he winked at me. They were right there, Dot. He's disgusting.'

'Scumbag.'

'And something else. He was wearing a tracksuit.'

'With a hood?'

'Yeah.'

'Put an asterisk by his name,' said Dot. 'Known sleazeball, opportunity, hoodie-wearer. He's got to be in the frame.'

'Okay.'

'What else?'

'Last night, I met Kevin the photographer on the way home. He walked along with me, gave me the right creeps. He gave me one of his cards, like the one Ginny had and I checked out his website. He likes taking photos of girls, young girls, Dot. He's pretty sleazy.'

'Well, you can tell that just by looking at him.'

'Yeah.'

'Does he wear a hoodie, though?'

'He's got a dark green anorak. That's got a hood.'

'Asterisk,' said Dot.

'Then really early this morning, someone put a note through my door. I've got it. Look.'

She brought out the piece of paper and handed it to Dot.

'Charming,' Dot said.

'Mind what business, though? Do you think it's the killer?'

'Who knows we're investigating? Have you told anyone?'

'No. Just us three. And my mum. She sends her love, by the way.'

'Maybe it's our friend Dean. Wants you to keep your nose out of his little scams.'

'The whole town was covered with egg last night. Little shit had already shifted those eggs when I went back with Ant.'

'Yeah, Ant said he floored him. But I've been wondering...'

'What?'

'Someone ratted on me to Ant's mum. It could only have

been one of my neighbours or someone at the store. Could it be Dean taking revenge?'

'I wouldn't put it past him. I think he got some of his mates to try and frighten me on the way home. I wasn't going to tell you.'

'You were on your own?' Dot rolled her eyes. 'Sorry, that was 'cos of me, wasn't it?'

'No, it was my own silly fault. They were only kids anyway, including one of Ant's brothers. I sorted them out.'

'Someone needs to sort Dean out.'

'I was going to tell Gav, but then maybe Eileen would be better. She'd give her baby boy what for, wouldn't she?'

'Yeah. Unless she's in on his little schemes.' Dot's face was grey. 'The pain's coming back,' she said. Her hand groped around the covers.

'What do you want?' said Bea.

'The buzzer that calls a nurse. I can't find it.'

There was a white plastic box on a cable trailing down the side of the bed. Bea reached for it and held it up. 'This it?'

'Yeah. Thanks, doll. Can you press it for me?'

Bea pressed the red button. It looked like the sort of thing that might start a nuclear war, but instead a nurse came along within a minute. She had purple-dyed dreadlocks tied back in a ponytail and a kind way about her.

'Oh, you're back in bed,' she said.

'Yeah. I'm just tired and I need some more painkillers.'

The nurse checked the record sheet at the end of the bed. 'Yes,' she said. 'I'll get you something.'

While they waited, Dot closed her eyes again. Bea wondered if she was asleep this time, but then she said, 'Bea, whether it was Dean or whether it was someone else, that note, I don't like it. Perhaps you should stop your detecting. Just look after yourself and Queenie.'

'I'm not going to put myself in any danger.'

'Aren't you? Walking on your own?'

'Yes, but that wasn't because I was following a trail, it just happened.'

'Well, it mustn't. Not while all this is going on. Get your Tom to give you a lift, or get a taxi.'

'Hmm, Tom always seems to be busy. He was my Plan A yesterday, but he stood me up. That reminds me, though. Gav offered me a lift.'

Dot opened her eyes. 'Did he?'

'Yeah. When I said that I'd planned to walk home with you.'

'Gavin,' Dot said. 'Gavin ... there was something Anna said.'

The nurse was back. She injected some clear liquid into the cannula attached to the back of Dot's hand.

'I'll do your obs while I'm here,' she said, and took Dot's temperature and blood pressure. 'Lovely,' she said, writing the results down. 'Is there anything else you need?'

'No, ta. I'm fine now.' And it was true. Bea could see that the grim tension had gone from Dot's face. Her eyes kept closing and opening, then closing again.

'There was something, Bea,' she said. Her voice was quiet and drowsy. Bea leaned forward. 'Something I wanted to tell you about Gav.'

'Yeah? Anna said he'd got turned down for promotion. Was that it?'

'I can't 'member.'

Her eyes were closed now. Her breathing was slow and regular.

'Dot?'

She was gone – eyes shut, mouth open, the hint of a snore as she breathed in and out.

Bea gave Dot's hand a little squeeze. 'I'll come back tomorrow,' she said. She gathered up her things and walked out of the ward, down the long corridor towards the lift. She was so busy thinking about what Dot was trying to tell her that she didn't see Bob-on-Meat until he was only a few feet away.

'Hello,' he said, half-hiding a bunch of tulips behind him, looking for all the world like he'd been caught in some shameful act. 'I was just going to see Dot. If she'll see me?'

'She's asleep, Bob. She's just nodded off.'

'Oh.' He looked crestfallen.

'She got really tired. Couldn't keep her eyes open.'

'Maybe I could just leave these.' He brought the flowers out into full view.

'I don't think they're allowed flowers in hospital any more. Something to do with infection.'

'Oh.'

'We could check with a nurse. I'll walk back with you, shall I?'

'No. No, it's okay. If she's asleep anyway. I'll come back another time.' He turned around and started walking towards the lift with Bea. 'She probably wouldn't even want me to visit. Seems to prefer the company of other people.'

Bea winced inside, hoping it wasn't showing on her face.

Back on the ground floor, they walked past the atrium café.

'Do you want a coffee, Bob?'

He looked at her like it was a trick question and Bea realised that they had rarely, if ever, had a proper conversation before.

'No, it's okay,' he said. 'I'd better get back.' As far as Bea knew, he lived on his own, in a flat on the outskirts of town. What did he have to get back to? 'I can give you a lift, if you like. Save you waiting in the cold.'

'Thanks, Bob.' But as soon as the words were out of her

209

mouth she realised their folly. What the hell was she doing getting a lift from a man on his own? One of the names on her list? Once she got in the car, that would be it, wouldn't it? He could drive anywhere, stop anywhere. She couldn't think of a polite way to get out of it, though. Oh shit, she thought, I'm going to have to go through with it. Okay, how to make it safer? Think, Bea, think.

They were nearly at the car park now. She took out her phone.

'I'll just text Mum I'm on my way,' she said. 'Tell her you're going to drop me back in K-town.'

'How is she?' said Bob, seemingly unruffled by this tactic. 'Haven't seen her for ages.'

'She's, um, she's fine. Doesn't go out much.'

'Used to have a right laugh at the social club with her and your dad, and me and . . . well, before Moira left.'

'Yes, she mentioned it the other day. Good times.'

'Good times indeed. Here, this is me.'

He took a bunch of keys from the pocket of his leather jacket and clicked the locks open. He opened the boot and put the bunch of tulips inside. Bea pretended to send another text, while noting the registration number down as a memo on her phone, then she got in and buckled up.

'Traffic shouldn't be too bad. We're going the other way to most people, aren't we?'

'Yeah.'

He started the engine and moved smoothly out of the car park and along the feeder road towards the main gates. Ahead, Bea could see the bus stop where she should be right now. There were a lot of people waiting – the shelter was full and the queue was spilling along the pavement.

'Looks like the buses are up the creek anyway. The queue shouldn't be that long,' she said. Then, 'Wait! Stop! Can you pull over?'

210

Bob checked his mirrors and pulled into the kerb just past the stop.

'What is it?' he said. 'Are you okay?'

'It's Ant,' she said. 'He's in the queue. Must have been there ages. It's okay to give him a lift too, isn't it?'

Bob groaned. 'Him? Really?'

'Yes. Thanks, Bob.' She wound down the window. 'Ant! Ant!' He didn't appear to have heard so she pinched her finger and thumb together and put them up to her mouth to give an almighty whistle.

'Oi! Bea! That'll do,' Bob protested.

This time Ant heard. He looked their way and his face brightened when he saw Bea. He jogged along the pavement and leaned down to her window.

'Get in,' she said.

He looked past her to Bob and the smile dropped from his face.

'Um, it's okay,' Ant said.

Bob sighed. 'Don't be soft, lad. Get in.'

Ant opened the back passenger door and climbed in. 'Thanks very much, Bob. That's very decent.'

'You been to see Dot?'

'Yeah.'

Bea saw Bob looking at Ant in his rear-view mirror. She wondered what was going on in his head. A tiny muscle was twitching beneath his left eye, but whatever emotions he was wrestling with, he kept to himself.

'Put your seatbelt on, then,' he said.

As they set off back to Kingsleigh it started to rain. Bea found the red taillights of the cars in front and the white headlights coming towards them mesmeric, blurring and sharpening as the wipers swept back and forth. She lost track of where they were and was surprised when the car turned off the bypass and started travelling through the outskirts of the town. She realised that no one had spoken for a long time and desperately tried to think of something to break the silence.

'Hope it doesn't rain tomorrow,' she said.

'The funeral,' said Bob. 'Bad business. Young girl like that.'

'Have you got the time off, Bob?'

'Yes, but I think that Gavin should close the shop. Everyone does. It only right, isn't it, that we should all get to pay our respects? I reckon we should just close the shop ourselves, give him no option.'

'Direct action.'

'Something like that.'

'What do you think, Ant?' said Bea.

'I dunno,' said Ant.

'Shall I drop you here?' said Bob. 'You live on the Rushton estate, don't you?'

'Oh, um, no, it's okay. You can drop me at Bea's or wherever you're dropping her. I don't think they want to see me at home at the moment.'

'Hmm, I saw your mum in the shop yesterday.'

'Yeah. You and half the town.'

Bea fancied she saw a wisp of tumbleweed blow through the car from the back seat. Awkward.

'Come and have a cup of tea at mine, Ant,' she said. 'I'll introduce you to Queenie.'

'Okay. Ta.'

'You, too, Bob, if you like. I'm sure she'd like to see you.'

'No, that's okay. I'd better get on.'

Bob took Bea and Ant right to Bea's door. As they clambered out of the car, Bob called out to Ant.

'There are some flowers in the boot, Ant. Fish them out, will you? You can take them in to Bea's mum for me.' Ant leaned over the back seat and retrieved the flowers. They said their goodbyes to Bob and watched as he drove away down the street.

'I don't have to come in if your mum doesn't like visitors,' said Ant.

'Where else are you going to go?' said Bea.

'Back to Dot's, I suppose. I've got her key.'

His shoulders were sagging and he looked done in.

'Come and have a cuppa.'

As they walked up the path, Ant said, 'Did you see what was in the boot of his car?'

Bea shrugged. 'Nope.'

'There was a blanket over it, but it didn't cover it all up.'

'What?'

'A toolbox. One of those metal ones where the top folds out.'

'So?'

'Tools, Bea. Screwdrivers, pliers – hammers. He carries them around with him.'

Bea stopped walking.

'Oh shit,' she said. 'Bob?'

Ant raised his eyebrows. 'Could be.'

'We need to get into the car. Have a look. See if there's any, you know, blood on them.'

'Or if they look suspiciously clean,' added Ant, and Bea nodded her approval. He was starting to think like a detective, too. 'How are we going to do that?'

'Dunno,' she said.

'Or, and I hate saying this, we could tell your ginger friend,' said Ant.

'Tom?'

It's nothing, though, is it? Not worth telling the police. Perhaps we could just borrow Bob's keys one lunchtime?'

'I like the way you're thinking, Miss Marple. I'm up for that.'

She shivered. 'I was crapping myself getting into the car with him. What a relief when I spotted you at the bus stop!'

'You're telling me. I was freezing my nuts off out there. Anyway, that's why I stayed in the car. So you weren't on your own with him.'

'Thanks, mate. You definitely deserve a cuppa for that.'

The back door was locked. Bea knocked and Queenie opened up. She backed away when she saw Ant standing in the doorway.

'Oh!'

'Mum, it's all right. This is Ant, from work. I've told you about him.'

'I didn't know you were bringing anyone here.'

'No, I didn't tell you. It's a spur of the moment sort of thing. Bob gave us a lift from the hospital and we both ended up here.'

'How is Dot?'

'She's not too bad.' Bea beckoned Ant into the room, knowing that her mum would be too distracted by one of her favourite subjects – other people's medical problems – to worry too much about him. 'They'd made her get out of bed already.'

'Really? But she had the operation this morning, didn't she?'

'Yeah. Seems cruel, doesn't it?'

'And was it painful?'

'Yeah, she was dosed up on painkillers, though. When they gave her some more, she went to sleep.'

'Ah. Nasty business. She's not that old, is she? Same age as me.'

Ant was standing just inside the door, not knowing where to put himself.

'Sit down, then,' Queenie said. 'You're in now. You all right?'

He sat down at the kitchen table. In the harsh fluorescent light, his face looked even more pinched. He ran his hands over the top of his head.

'It's been a long day,' he said.

'Have you eaten anything?' said Queenie.

'Yeah. No. I dunno. I think I had a sandwich or something at lunchtime.'

She bustled over to the toaster and put two slices in. Without asking what Ant wanted, she buttered them up and cut some thick slices of cheese on top, with a dollop of pickle on top.

'Here,' she said. 'Try this.'

Without seeming to look, Ant started cramming the food in.

'Mmm,' he said, through a full mouth, 'this is good.'

He washed it down with the sweet tea that Bea made and after a few minutes, he started to look a bit more human. As the food hit his system, his eyelids became heavier. 'I'm knackered,' he said.

'Better get off home, then,' Queenie said.

Ant hung his head.

'Nah, not yet. Bit of a domestic, if you know what I mean.'

'Trouble?'

'Yeah. You could say that. I should go though. Leave you ladies to it.'

He started to get to his feet, but swayed a little and had to hold onto the table. Queenie stepped towards him, put her hand on his shoulder.

'Tell you what, why don't I put some blankets and a spare pillow on the sofa for you? Make up a little bed.'

'Ah, cheers, Mrs Jordan. That'd be ace.'

Bea and Ant looked at each other as they listened to Queenie go up and down the stairs.

'She likes you,' said Bea. 'God knows why, but she does.'

Ant smiled. 'Mums do like me. Except for mine.'

'Don't be daft. She loves you, Ant. She was just worried about you. It'll all blow over.'

'Yeah. S'pose.'

'Go and see her tomorrow.'

'Maybe. Perhaps I'll go after the funeral.'

'While you're at it you could sort your brother out, too.'

'My brother? Which one?'

'Ken. He and his mates jumped out at me last night when I was walking home.'

'Oh God.'

He pinched the skin between his eyebrows, shut his eyes briefly. Bea wondered if it was all too much for him.

'They were the eggers, too. I saw them throwing some when I'd seen them off.'

'That figures. Little shit.' He sighed. 'I need to go home, don't I? Teach him some manners.'

'Tomorrow,' said Bea. 'Tomorrow's soon enough. I had a bit of a run-in with Kevin, that photographer, as well last night. He's definitely still on the list.'

'Yeah?'

Bea told Ant everything she'd told Dot earlier.

'And now we've got Bob's box of tools, too,' said Ant.

'It's almost too much information, isn't it?' said Bea. 'But it feels like we're getting closer now. Closer to whoever did it.'

'Does it? It just feels like a mess to me.' He rubbed his head again and blinked strenuously. 'I'm too knackered to think about it.'

'You'd better get your head down then.' She smiled. 'Still can't believe Queenie let you stay. It's a miracle.'

'She's nice, your mum.'

'Yeah. She has her moments.'

She went to put a beanbag in the microwave. 'Do you want a hot owl?'

216

Ant looked at her like she'd lost her mind. 'What is *that*?'

'You put it in the microwave and it stays warm for ages.'

He puffed a long breath out of his mouth. 'Course I don't. I'm not a *girl*.' But when the microwave pinged, Bea handed the owl to him. He held it to his stomach. 'Yeah. Okay, that's really nice.'

Bea smiled and put a second owl in to warm.

She left Ant bedding down on the sofa and went upstairs. As she pulled the duvet up around her shoulders, her phone pinged.

A text from Tom:

Goodnight, sexy. Xxx

Night. Xxxx

She stared at the screen until it shut off. When she closed her eyes, she could still see the bright rectangle, imprinted on her eyelids. That's what Tom is, she thought, a bright light in this dark, dark world. She wanted the thought to stay with her but instead she found herself thinking about Bob, his large hands bringing the cleaver up and down on the chopping block. She heard Ant switch the light off downstairs and realised she was listening for other noises too: cars, footsteps, the rattle of the letterbox. She lay on her back with her eyes open – listening, thinking – and she knew that sleep was a long way away.

15

On Monday afternoon at half past two, the Costsave family started gathering in the churchyard of Saint Swithin's, joining Ginny's real family and friends, and people from the town who hadn't known her but wanted to pay their respects. There had been no need for rebellion in the end. Staff had arrived for work ready for an act of mass resistance but were met with a black-edged notice Blu-Tacked onto the front door: 'As a mark of respect to a much-valued colleague, Ginny Meldrum, this store will be closed from 2.00pm until 6.00pm. We apologise to our customers but hope that you will understand.'

There were press and television crews lurking about too, although they kept a discreet distance. Gavin and Neville were already there when Bea arrived. They were welcoming their employees, shaking hands with them. It was both formal and somehow very inclusive.

'Good to see you,' Gavin said to Bea. She felt a bit odd holding out her hand to him, but he took it firmly with both of his, enclosing it, like it really meant something to him.

'Glad I can be here,' said Bea. 'What changed your mind?'

'It was Dot,' he said. 'I rang her last night and she said that her dearest wish was that everyone could be allowed to come here today. I couldn't really say no, could I?'

'No, I suppose not.' said Bea. 'It's a shame she can't be here too.'

'She'll be thinking of us, though. She told me that.'

Saint Swithin's was used to witnessing funerals peopled by mourners wearing something bright, or the loved one's favourite colour, especially when the deceased was someone young, but Ginny's family had made no special requests about dress code. They had let it be known that they wanted this to be a celebration of her life, but as the dark-dressed mourners arrived it was clear that celebrating was too much to ask. Everyone seemed crushed by grief. There was a palpable air of shock.

Keisha joined the group, with little Kayleigh in her push-chair. The tot was wearing a rather smart navy coat, with navy ribbons in her hair. She looked tired, burrowing her head into the corner of her seat and sucking her thumb.

'I wanted to be here,' Keisha said. 'But I'll sit at the back, take this one out if she starts fussing.' Keisha looked tired too.

'How's she been?' asked Bea.

'So-so,' she said, and Bea wondered what that really meant. 'I'll take her in. It's a bit cold out here.'

Now Bea spotted another little group making its way up the path, with a young woman in the middle. Emma. It was the first time Bea had seen her since the attack. People were looking at her and then looking away. Everyone was aware she was there, but no one knew whether to approach her or what to say.

Bea left Gavin and walked up to Emma. She was wearing a black scarf on her head, tied at the back, but a pale edge of bandage escaped from one side. Bea's stomach went soft at the thought of the wound underneath.

'Hi Emma,' she said. 'Good to see you.'

Emma looked startled for a minute then her face softened.

'Bea,' she said. 'How are you?'

Bea pulled a face. 'I'm fine,' she said. 'How are *you*?'

'Oh,' said Emma. She looked sideways at her mum, who was looking anxiously back at her. 'I'm doing okay. It's hard.'

'Of course.'

As she was talking, Emma looked around her. Normally Bea hated talking to someone who was constantly on the lookout for anyone more interesting. But Emma's expression was haunted: she was scared to be out, among people again.

'It's good that you're here.'

'Yeah. Thanks.' Suddenly Emma's eyes seemed to focus on one person.

'I *know* him,' she said.

'Who?' said Bea, turning her head and scanning the crowd.

'I've seen him somewhere before . . .'

There were literally hundreds of people gathering. Without thinking Bea whipped out her phone and started taking pictures. She'd snapped three or four when she felt a hand on her forearm, gripping and pulling her own hand down.

'What are you doing?' hissed Neville. 'Show some respect.'

His face was close to hers. She could see a little white ball of spit at the corner of his mouth.

'I'm sorry,' she said, then turned back to Emma. 'I'm sorry, Emma.'

But Emma was clutching her mother's arm. 'I want to go home,' she was saying. 'I want to—'

'It's all right,' her mum said. 'We're here now. Let's go in.'

'Don't leave me. You won't leave me, will you?'

'No. Dad and I are right here. We won't leave you.'

Mum on one side, Dad on the other, they walked past Bea up the cobbled path and though the large arched doorway into the church.

'Fucking 'ell, Bea. Were you taking a selfie with Emma?'
Dean was next to her now.

'No! Of course I wasn't.'

'You had your phone out. Let's see.' He made to take her
phone and Bea plunged it into her pocket, keeping her hand
firmly round it.

'Go away, Dean,' she said.

'You took a selfie! I love it,' he said. He looked around for
someone to tell and spotted Joe lurking nearby.

Bea sighed.

'You all right?' Another voice in her ear, but this one was
welcome. Tom. She looked round and there he was, in full
uniform, buttons gleaming, shoes spotlessly shiny.

'Yes,' she said. 'You couldn't just arrest that little git over
there, could you?' She nodded towards Dean who was in
animated conversation with Joey.

'What for?' said Tom.

'Just being annoying.'

Tom laughed. 'I'd be busy all day if I locked up annoying
people. Anything else?'

Supplying eggs to hooligans, thought Bea. Inciting intimi-
dation. But she couldn't bring herself to turn him in. Besides,
did she really have any evidence?

'No,' she said reluctantly. 'What are you doing here
anyway?'

'Part of my role. Community policing. Be seen. Be
supportive.' He was standing a foot or so away from her,
legs apart, hands behind his back. He too was looking
around which she minded, badly. She wanted him to look at
her. 'And keeping my eyes and ears open.'

'Huh?'

'The killer often comes to the funeral. Didn't you know?'

'Is that a real thing? Does it actually happen apart from
on the telly?'

'They like to feel close to the action. Watch the family.'

Bea shivered. 'That's horrible.'

'Don't worry. Nothing will happen here. It's perfectly safe.'

'I know, but just the thought of it, that someone here could be the one ... ' She looked around again at the sea of people in dark coats. She tried to memorise the faces, fix them in her mind. At least she had a few photos. Maybe the killer was caught on camera.

'Shall we sit together in the church?' she said.

'Better not,' said Tom. 'I need to sit at the back, so I can observe. Better mingle too, put myself about a bit. I'll catch you later, yeah?'

'Okay.'

He looked so smart in his uniform. Young, but somehow authoritative. She resisted the urge to stand on tiptoes, plant a kiss on his cheek. This wasn't the place or the time, was it? And he was on duty.

There was something about his body language too, the way he'd kept his distance from her. No sign of anything other than a friendly chat between the community copper and one of his locals. He didn't want anyone to know about him and her. Which she supposed was fine. Although a little part of her wanted to hold his hand, announce their relationship on Facebook or shout it from the top of the church tower, there was an equal thrill in keeping things a delicious secret.

Tom moved away through the crowd. Bea watched him go, forgetting for a while that she should be scanning the crowd for suspects.

'What did *he* want?' Ant was threading his way towards her now, shaking his head. He was wearing skinny jeans and a dark jacket that looked like it belonged to someone else.

'Nothing. Just saying hello.'

He snorted with disgust.

'Give it a rest, Ant. You don't like him. I do. End of.'

He held both hands up in self-defence. 'Okay. Anyway, I've been hearing things about you. Tell me you didn't take a selfie.'

'Of course I didn't!'

'Ha! That's funny, 'cos everyone here thinks you did.'

'Well, I did take some photos, but not selfies.'

'Are you nuts? What of?'

'The crowd. I was talking to Emma and she went sort of funny when she spotted someone.'

'Who?'

'I don't know, but I snapped the view, so maybe I can work out who it is.'

'That may be smart sleuthing, but it's kind of sick.'

'I know. I feel a bit queasy about it, but you know, it might be the one thing that ties all this up. Stops it happening again.'

There was a low murmur of chatter in the churchyard, but at the first sight of the hearse pulling up at the lych-gate an eerie silence fell. People watched as the coffin was taken out and hoisted onto the shoulders of the pallbearers. A huge arrangement of flowers sat on top – pink and white roses. It's real, thought Bea. It's really happening.

'We'd better go in,' Gavin said softly, moving around the edge of the group and shepherding his flock towards the church. The Costsave crowd trailed in together, filling four pews that someone had saved for them.

Sitting waiting for the coffin to be carried in, Bea felt tense. It wasn't until the procession started down the middle aisle that she realised why she was feeling so bad. She hadn't been to a funeral for six years. That time, she'd been sitting at the front and her dad had been inside the coffin. She started to feel hot all over.

'I don't think I can do this,' she whispered to Ant.

'What's up?'

The palms of her hands were clammy.

'I don't feel very well. I want to get out of here.'

There were three other people between her and the aisle.

'You can't. Sit still,' said Ant.

The coffin was in place. The service was about to begin. The building seemed to swim in front of Bea's eyes. She was going to faint.

'Take some deep breaths.' He reached across and held her hand.

Bea breathed in and out as slowly as she could and somehow she got through the service. She stood up for the hymns and knelt for the prayers, and Ant guided her through it and held her hand.

Outside, the hearse set off for the crematorium. Word passed among the crowd that they were all welcome at the nearby British Legion Club for a drink and some food. The Costsave crew looked to Gavin, who nodded his assent. The store could stay closed for a little while longer.

'You okay now?' Ant asked.

The cold, fresh air felt soothing against her skin. She was feeling almost normal again.

'It was your dad, wasn't it?' said Ant. 'You were thinking about him.'

She looked at him sideways, surprised by his sensitivity. 'Yes.'

'I was thinking about my nan and grandad, and my other nan. And my friend from school, Motty, died in a car crash. He was seventeen. You can't help it, can you? Funerals remind you of other funerals.'

For the first time, tears welled up in Bea's eyes. 'No,' she said. 'You can't help it. And Ginny, of course.'

Now she was properly crying.

'Hey,' Ant said, 'it's okay.' He put his arms round her and

she rested her head on his shoulder and sobbed.

She heard Dean's unwelcome voice. 'Bloody hell, Ant. You don't mess about. I've been trying to crack her for years.'

'Fuck off, Dean,' Ant said. 'All the way off and then a little bit further.'

He hugged Bea a bit tighter, until her sobbing subsided. She wiped her eyes and blew her nose.

'I'm sorry,' she said.

'Don't be.'

'Dean's a dick, isn't he?'

'Yeah.'

She looked around and found several of her colleagues looking at them. Bob-on-Meat and Gavin looked away when she caught their eye. Anna sent her a sympathetic smile and beckoned to her, inviting her to join the others in the walk across the road to the Legion. Just beyond her, Tom was frowning. He, too, quickly pretended that he hadn't been looking, turning instead to the vicar who had conducted the service. But Bea felt a little something – maybe a flutter of triumph – because she was sure she'd seen jealousy in that look. He might want to keep things under wraps for now, but he definitely wanted her.

'Are you coming to the Legion?' said Ant.

'I dunno.'

'Come on, it's free food.'

'I'm not sure I'm hungry.'

'Five minutes.'

'Okay.'

They were among the last to leave the churchyard. Almost unseen, a little huddle of people walked behind them. Emma and her parents had waited in the church until everyone had gone. Glancing behind her, Bea saw them turn right outside the gate, and walk towards the car park, instead of joining everyone else.

Once across the road, near a wooden bench by the bus stop, Bea tapped Ant's arm.

'I'm going to sit here for a minute.'

'Okay. I'll sit with you.'

'No, it's all right. I'll come to the Legion in a bit, once I've got myself together.'

'Sure?' He looked doubtful.

She smiled. 'Sure.'

She smoothed her coat underneath her, sat down and took out her phone. She looked in the gallery and selected the most recent image – a sea of heads and shoulders. Not the best picture she'd ever taken but at least, more by accident than design, it was in focus. Bea tapped on the screen to expand the image and then slid her finger left and right, up and down, examining the faces, the backs of heads, the profiles. There were familiar faces from Costsave – Gavin, Neville, Bob, Ant, Dean and Joe. Lee from the Leisure Centre was almost unrecognisable in a dark coat instead of a tracksuit. He was there with a gaggle of colleagues, all those who had been involved in the spinathon. Tom was in shot, his ginger hair standing out in the crowd. And then there was something odd. Something round, like an eye looking straight at her. She zoomed in further and found herself looking into a lens. Above the body of the camera, a wisp of long hair trying to escape from the grease plastering it down to Kevin's domed, bald head. She hadn't been the only one taking pictures.

She got up and walked to the Legion. The 'do' was being held upstairs in the function room. As she entered the room, it was clear from the noise that some people were taking full advantage of the free bar. She searched the crowd for Ant and spotted him skulking in a corner, nursing half a pint of what looked like cider.

She made her way over to him. 'Ant, look at this picture.'

He squinted at it. 'What am I looking at?'

'Well, it could have been any of them, but I think the man Emma spotted was Kevin. Look, he's pointing the camera straight at her.'

Ant peered closer, then enlarged that section of the photo. Bea watched over his shoulder. Neither of them saw Dean coming.

'Looking at that selfie?'

'Go away, Dean,' said Bea.

'Don't know why you're hanging around with him. He likes them a lot older. Gets turned on by a Zimmer frame, don't you, mate?'

Ant handed the camera back to Bea and stood up.

'She's asked you to go away,' he said. 'And now I'm telling you.'

'It's a free country, mate. I'm all right here.'

'No,' Ant said, pushing Dean in the middle of his chest. 'You're not.'

Dean stumbled backwards. 'You can't tell me what to do,' he said, straightening himself up and coming back towards Ant.

A frisson of excitement rippled round the room. People were looking, pointing. Some were walking towards them, others were trying to get away. Over by the bar, Ginny's dad got wind of the trouble. Bea saw him putting his arm round his wife and steering her in the opposite direction.

'Stop it, both of you,' she said. 'Not here, for God's sake.'

They weren't listening, both immune to anything except the stirring blood in their ears and their surging adrenalin.

'I can't tell you what to do,' said Ant. 'But I can tell everyone what you actually do – ripping off the shop, threatening people, telling tales.'

He shoved Dean again, hard, but this time Dean grabbed his hands and they started wrestling. Bea tried to cut in between them.

But the Costsave squad swung into action. The boys were hauled apart from each other by Bob and Gavin. Dean tried to shrug Bob off, but he stayed with him as stumbled out of the room, closely followed by Eileen who looked like she was ready to handbag him in the car park. Ant was heading after him, but Gavin stood in his way.

'Don't go out there yet. I don't want any more trouble. I want to see you in my office at six o'clock sharp,' he said, seething, and then he went to find Ginny's parents to apologise on behalf of the store.

Ant found the end of his half and drained it, then went to the bar to get another one.

The rest of the staff were abuzz.

'What was all that about?'

'It was like two stick insects fighting over a leaf.'

'Little idiots.'

'I'd cheerfully take a swing at that Ant, but not here. That's completely out of order.' The last comment was from Bob.

Bea kept quiet. She sidled up to Ant, who was by the window now, working his way through his cider.

'All right?' she said.

'Yeah,' Ant said. 'Wish I'd knocked his head off.'

'Someone will one day. Not here, though.'

'I heard what Bob said, as well. Reckon I'm not welcome at Costsave any more.'

'He's just jealous,' said Bea. 'You know how he feels about Dot.'

'Will you come with me to see Gav?'

'Yeah, if he'll let me.'

'Thanks, Bea.' He drained his pint and set the empty glass on the windowsill. 'Let's get out of here. We've got things to do.'

'What things?'

Ant turned his back to the room and drew his hand out of his pocket. He unfolded his fingers to reveal a silver ring with two keys on it, sitting in his palm.

'Bob's?' Bea mouthed silently.

Ant nodded. He put his hand back in his pocket.

'How did you? I mean . . .'

Ant looked towards Bob's coat, hanging over the back of a chair, several tables away.

'Easy,' he said. 'They'll all be here until a few minutes before they're due back at the shop. We've got half an hour. You coming?'

'Yeah. Okay. Should we leave separately?'

'Nah. We're mates, aren't we? Everyone knows that.'

Ant and Bea threaded their way through the crowd, their departure inevitably noted and commented on. They crossed the Legion car park and headed to the alleyway that led to Costsave. Bob's car was at the back of the store in the staff parking area.

'What about CCTV?' asked Bea.

'No one's there right now, are they? And they're only going to look at the footage if they notice anything wrong when they come back. We're just opening a car boot and closing it again. No damage. We'll be fine.'

Bea kept her head down anyway, in a feeble attempt to stay anonymous. 'Have you got any gloves?' she asked.

'No, but we don't need them.'

'Well, better if our prints aren't all over here, isn't it?'

'Have you got some?'

Bea held up her hands and their black, woolly gloves.

'You do it then.'

Ant took out the keys and handed them to her. She clicked open the boot and pushed the door up. A smell wafted out, but Bea couldn't place it.

'It's too dark,' she said. 'Hang on, there's a torch on my phone. Here, hold this.'

Ant shone the thin beam into the boot. The toolbox was still there, partially covered by a blanket. Bea moved the blanket and opened the box. The smell was stronger. She could taste it now – there was something metallic about it that made her think of blood.

'What are you doing? Get on with it,' Ant hissed and Bea realised that she had frozen.

'Right. Yes.'

She looked at the top layer of tools. They were mostly small: mini-screwdrivers, a metal tape measure, some pliers, a pencil and a plastic handled knife.

'There's a knife,' she said.

'Yeah, well, it's a toolbox. We're looking for something heavier, aren't we? Lift up that tray.'

She held the long handle and lifted the metal tray out of the box and put it in the boot.

'Shit,' she said.

There was an impressive collection of larger tools in the main body of the box: wrenches, large screwdrivers, hammers.

'Shine the light a bit closer, can you?'

They both leaned in further and Ant held the torch inside the box. Bea sifted through the tools. There were three hammers. One was a solid, plastic mallet, the others were ordinary claw hammers. There seemed to be discoloration on one of them – the blunt end had a dark stain, but Bea couldn't be sure if this was part of its design or not.

'That one,' she said. 'Has that one got blood on it?'

Suddenly they heard a noise behind them. They both jumped. Ant dropped the phone. Bea looked over her shoulder. There was something moving along the side fence. It was low, below the line of car bonnets. Someone was creeping up on them.

'Fuck's sake, Ant. Get my phone. Let's go!'

230

'Wait! Wait a minute!'

'No! Let's get out of here!'

'No, wait, look!'

Bea watched as a fox jumped onto a car bumper and then up onto the fence. Almost before she'd seen it, it had disappeared to the other side. She looked all around. There was nobody, nothing else there.

'I want to get out of here anyway,' she said. 'At least we know he's keeps a hammer handy. And that might or might not be blood on it.'

'I'll take a picture with the flash, shall I? Evidence. How do you do it?'

'Give it here.'

Bea took the phone. She had to take off her gloves to switch to camera mode. She took a couple of photos. The flash lit up the car boot.

'Right, let's get it back to how it was and scarper. Oh shit, where's my other glove?'

She switched the phone back to the torch function. The glove was on the ground. Her hand was shaking as she picked it up and put it back on and she was swearing like a trooper.

'Come on, Bea, keep it together,' said Ant. Bea took a deep breath and put the top tray back in the tool box, then the blanket on top of that. She tried to place it at the right angle, silently cursing that she hadn't photographed the whole thing first.

'Are we done?' said Ant.

'Yeah. Think so.'

She pulled the boot lid down until there was just a small gap, then put all her weight into closing it quickly.

'Let's get out of here.'

They walked out of the staff car park and round the side of the store. Bea checked her watch. It was twenty to six. The evening staff would be back soon to open up.

231

'What are you going to do with the keys?' she said. 'You haven't got time to go back to the Legion.'

'I'll wait for him to come in to work and put them back in the men's locker room.'

'Can you do that?'

'Yeah. If there's a problem I'll go back and drop them near the car. It'll look like they fell out of his pocket.'

Neville was first back to Costsave. Ant and Bea followed him in and went upstairs. Bea refreshed her make-up in the ladies' while Ant skulked in the staffroom. Just before six, Bea waited for Ant outside Gavin's office. Ant came sauntering out of the staffroom and gave Bea the thumbs up and a nod and a wink. Mission accomplished. Keys back where they should be. They stood in silence until Anna told them they could go in.

Gavin was seated behind his desk. They were not invited to sit down.

'I don't want to know what it was about,' said Gavin. 'I'm looking for an apology and I'm going to give you an official warning.'

'Can you do that?' said Bea. 'It wasn't at work. It wasn't at Costsave.'

Gavin sent Bea a hard look. 'We were all at the Legion representing Costsave. What Anthony did was a disgrace.'

'So why isn't Dean here?' said Ant.

'He will be. One at a time.'

'What does a warning mean?'

'It goes on your record. It's like a yellow card. The next time you are in trouble, it's dismissal. No questions. No comeback.'

'Shit.' Gav raised his eyebrows, and Ant said quickly, 'Sorry, sir.'

He started biting his lip and Bea wondered whether he was going to cry but instead he blurted out, 'Do you think I should go anyway, Sir? I mean, I'm not cut out for it, am I?'

Gavin put down his pen and sat up straighter in his chair. 'Is that what you really want? To quit?'

'Yeah,' said Ant.

'No,' said Bea at the same time.

'Let him speak, Bea,' said Gavin.

'I'm not good for anything, just cleaning and doing the pointer at the checkouts. I'm not even very good at that.'

'You *are* good at those things, which is great because they're valuable roles in this business, but I believe you can do more than that. I always have believed in you. That's why I was so disappointed today.'

Ant was biting his lip so hard, a little bead of blood appeared.

'Tell him, Ant,' said Bea.

He shook his head.

'Tell me what?' said Gavin. He looked at Ant. 'Tell me what?'

'I'm never gonna be able to do the things you think I can do,' said Ant, head down, eyes down, talking to the floor, 'Because . . . because I can't read.'

Gavin pursed his lips and a low whistle came out. He was silent for a few seconds, although it seemed much longer than that.

'You can't read,' he said. He closed his eyes and rubbed his fingers in the sockets. Then he opened them again and said, 'I should have guessed. Sit down, both of you. Come on.'

They sat opposite Gavin.

'You knew?' he said to Bea.

'Yeah, I was going to try and help him learn, but we haven't got started yet. I've been helping him with reading lists and labels and things.'

Gavin sighed. 'To be honest, considering you can't read,

233

you've done very well. You've shown a lot of initiative covering up and coping.'

Ant still looked as if the ground was opening up underneath him, about to swallow him up.

'I don't want you to quit, Ant. You've got a right to be able to read and write. Costsave has a responsibility to give you the training you need to do the job.'

Ant raised his head a little and squinted at Gavin. 'Yeah?'

'Yes, Ant. I'll escalate this to the regional office.'

'What does that mean?'

'I'll ask them if they will fund some lessons for you.'

'Oh, right. That would be great. Unless I'm just too thick.'

'Trust me, you're not. You can read, Ant. You will read. None of this excuses what happened earlier, though.'

'No, Sir. I'm very sorry for that. Very sorry.'

'That's good to hear.'

'He was asking for it, though.'

'Ah!' Gavin held his hands up. 'Don't spoil things.'

'He's not a great role model,' said Bea.

'We can't like everyone we work with.'

'It's not that, he's . . . ' she paused. 'He's not loyal to you, Gavin, or to Costsave.'

'Well, I'll be the judge of that,' said Gavin. 'Off you go, now, both of you. I'll make sure you're on appropriate duties until I can get that training sorted. And, Ant?'

'Yeah?'

'Don't let me down.'

16

'We want to help you get back to work.'

The woman from the assessment agency, Ms Norcross, hadn't touched the tea that Bea had made her. Bea had put too much milk in it, a slip of her nervous hands, and now a thin skin was forming on the top as it sat cooling on the coffee table in front of her.

'I'm fifty-seven and I haven't left my house for six years,' said Queenie.

'We haven't seen a report of any recognised medical condition.'

'I don't go to the doctors.'

'I'm on the case,' Bea cut in. 'I've asked a GP to call here and do an assessment.'

'But we don't have one now?'

'No.'

'So, let's start from where we are now, how you are today. I'm going to ask you a series of questions.'

Queenie was holding onto her wedding and engagement rings, twisting them round and round her ring finger.

'It was my husband,' she said. 'He had cancer. Pancreas, then bladder and bowels. Liver. I left work to care for him, and I never went back. I couldn't.'

'I understand,' said Ms Norcross in a voice that

contradicted her words. 'But we need to talk about whether we can help you back to work now.'

Queenie wasn't listening. 'I just couldn't face seeing people, having them ask me things, or not ask me anything. I couldn't go back to my job 'cos that would be like saying that everything was the same, that he didn't matter, that he'd never mattered.'

'Mrs—'

'Out there, everything's just carrying on, but I can't be like that. I can't just pretend to be okay.' Her hands were shaking violently.

'Mum. Mum.' Bea put her hands over Queenie's. 'It's all right. You don't have to go over it all.'

'But I do. Nothing's changed. I'm just the same. I can't go out there. I can't just get on with it and get a job. That's what she's here for – to tell me to stop all this – but I can't.'

'Mrs Jordan, I'm here to help. Now, do you need a break or shall we start the interview?'

Somehow they made it through to the end of the questions. Queenie was asked about a typical day, a good day and a bad day, about her mobility, her lifestyle, her medication. After a couple of hours, her inquisitor switched off her tablet and put it in her briefcase.

'Thank you,' she said, a little wearily. 'What happens next is that I write a report and then the department will let you know their decision.'

'What are you going to say in your report?' Queenie asked.

'I'm afraid I can't tell you at this stage. You'll hear the decision within two weeks.'

Bea showed her out. She closed the front door firmly and stood for a minute with her back leaning against it, then she gathered herself and walked through to Queenie in the kitchen.

'We need to get that letter from the GP,' she said. 'Back you up.'

Queenie was sitting where she'd left her, twirling her wedding ring and staring into space.

'They're going to cut me off,' she said. 'Then it'll be down to you. That's not fair, is it? I can't ask you to pay for every-thing.'

'It won't come to that, we're going to sort it.'

'Did you see her face when I was talking?'

'Yes, but you can't tell anything from that. It's her report that matters. Anyway, if the worst does happen, it won't be that bad. We'll manage.'

'How much do you earn?'

'You know how much I earn.'

'And how much are our bills?'

'Mum, stop it.' Bea perched on the arm of the chair and put her arm round Queenie's shoulders. 'We're going to be all right. We won't have to stop our luxury lifestyle – we'll be fine.'

'You'd be better off without me. I'm just dragging you down.'

'That's just silly talk. What would I do without you? We're a team, aren't we?' She gave her shoulder a little shake. 'You and me.'

'Not much of a team. What do I bring? I'm just a burden.'

Bea took a deep breath. They'd had this conversation too many times before. Whatever Bea said, it didn't seem to help, but that didn't mean she wouldn't keep trying. 'Mum, you bring *you*. You're my mum. You're Queenie. You don't have to bring anything else.'

Bea's phone pinged.

'Who's that?'

Bea didn't even look. 'It doesn't matter.'

'It might be something important.'

'Okay.' Bea picked up her phone. It was a text from Tom.

Pick you up at 6.30?

Despite herself, Bea felt a little tingle of excitement tickling her stomach lining.

'What is it?' asked Queenie, wiping her nose with a flowery hankie.

'Tom.'

'Tom the policeman?'

'Yeah.'

'And?'

'Nothing really. We were going to see the fireworks tonight, but I don't have to go.' Bea was amazed how light and easy her own voice sounded.

'Why wouldn't you go?'

'Well, because ... you know. We've not had a very nice day, have we? I don't mind staying in.'

'Don't be daft. I'll be fine. It's a date, is it?'

'No. Yeah. Sort of.'

'That's a yes, then,' Queenie said. 'You go out, have a good time. What are you going to wear?'

'God, I don't know. I hadn't even thought.'

Her normal Bonfire Night gear consisted of a thick vest and three layers of wool, not the most romantic gear. Was that what was needed, though – something romantic? She remembered the feel of his hands through her clothes as he pressed her up against the kitchen table. God, she thought, definitely lose the vest.

'I might go and look, see what I've got that's clean.'

'It's all clean,' Queenie sniffed. 'I do at least keep on top of the housework.'

'I know. I know you do. You make this a proper home.'

'Go on. Go and get ready. Don't want to keep the man waiting.'

Despite a couple of hours of intensive sifting, trying on, shortlisting and discarding, Bea wasn't ready when Tom turned up. She howled in anguish when she heard the doorbell. Queenie shouted up the stairs, 'I'll get it. Hurry up!'

Bea heard the door open and Queenie saying,

'Oh, aren't they beautiful?' she said. 'Bea will love them!'

Tom replied, but, agonisingly, his voice was too low for Bea to make out the words. She decided to leave the lip liner and just apply lipstick for speed. Two sweeps of neutral pink – nothing too obvious – and she was done. She pressed her lips together, then blotted them on some tissue. One last check in the mirror and she headed for the stairs.

'No. No, I'll stay in,' Queenie was saying. 'I can see the fireworks from the bedroom window anyway. Don't have to get cold that way. You kids go and have fun. But Tom?'

'Yes?'

'Thanks for asking. And thanks for the flowers.'

Queenie turned round as she heard Bea on the stairs. She was holding a bouquet of flowers in crinkly cellophane and looking a little flushed in the face.

Bea was wearing jeans and a woolly jumper, but it was only one layer and it was a fine-knit, slinky black one, which clung to her curves and was thin enough to reveal the outline of her push-up bra. Behind Queenie, Bea noticed with satisfaction that Tom was taking everything in. She picked up her scarf and coat from the stair post.

'More flowers?' she said to Queenie.

'I know.' Queenie beamed. 'I could start a flower shop this week.'

'Right,' said Bea, winding the scarf round her neck and slipping her arms into her coat. 'Are we ready?'

'I am,' said Tom.

'I've got my phone, Mum,' said Bea.

'I'll be fine. Have fun,' said Queenie and shooed her out of the door.

Bea followed Tom down the front path to his car. He clicked the locks and went round to the passenger side to hold the door open for her. Bea smiled and tried to get in as elegantly as she could. There was an awkward silence between them as they set off through the estate. Bea was glad the radio was on, babbling in the background. Radio One. She approved.

She looked sideways at Tom, then out of the front and side windows. Something caught her eye. In the wing mirror, she could see someone cycling along the pavement, pedalling furiously, head down. Now they were looking forward, waving an arm.

'Tom?' Bea said. 'I think there's someone chasing us.'

He checked his rear mirror. 'You mean that bike? I could have him. On the pavement. No lights. Little idiot.'

Bea turned round in her seat and looked over her shoulder. The bike was about ten metres away. The rider's hood had come down and she could see now that it was Ant!

'Tom, stop! It's Ant. From the shop. He's trying to flag us down.'

'Ant Thompson? I was right, then. It *is* an idiot. That whole family are crooks.'

'Ant's not a crook. He's my friend. Can you stop a minute, Tom?'

Tom made a show of checking his watch. 'We'll miss the fireworks if we don't get a move on, Bea.' He accelerated away and Bea watched as Ant got smaller in the wing mirror and then was lost to view as they turned into the next street.

'Tom?' she protested.

'We're having an evening to ourselves, aren't we? I've

been looking forward to this, Bea. You and me. It's taken long enough.'

You and me. Bea liked the sound of that. Whatever Ant wanted could wait until tomorrow. Bea caught Tom glancing her way and she smiled.

'Eyes on the road, soldier,' she said, but she didn't really mean it. She liked him looking at her.

'Having said that, I asked your mum to join us.'

'Really? That was nice.'

'She said she didn't want to play gooseberry.'

'Would she have been? Playing gooseberry.'

'Hope so.'

Bea could feel the colour rising in her face. 'She doesn't go out much anyway. Well, she doesn't go out at all.'

'What? Never?'

'Not for six years.'

Tom frowned. 'Seriously? She needs help, then.'

'I know, but I can't force her to see someone, can I? And now the Social want to cut her benefits off.'

'Bea, I'm so sorry. What can I do to help?'

'That's really sweet. You don't need to do anything. I've got it covered.'

Tom parked in the far end of the rugby club car park. They got out and he held her hand. It was a cold, clear, crisp night. Perfect Bonfire Night weather. He started leading her away from the entrance to the rugby ground.

'Where are we going?' asked Bea.

'You'll see,' he said. They cut down a path that skirted the field. It was dark, darker with every step they took away from the floodlights at the ground. Tom took a metal torch out of his pocket and shone it at the ground ahead of them. Bea thought she heard someone walking behind them, but when she turned around she couldn't see anyone, just the dark shape of the hedge one side and the fence the other.

Tom stopped. 'There's a stile here,' he said. 'Careful.'

He went first and offered a hand to help her over.

'It's very dark,' she said.

'Don't let go of my hand, then,' he said. 'I'll look after you.'

It was more open on the other side of the stile and Bea realised they'd come to the bottom corner of the park. The path was tarmacked here and it was easier to walk, but she still held his hand. There was a brook to the left of them. A couple of minutes later they reached the lake that fed it. During the day, it was thronging with ducks and seagulls, but now it was quiet – a body of black water disappearing into the dark. They walked along the edge, following the path as it curved round to a little hump-backed bridge.

'Here,' Tom said in the middle of the bridge. He stopped walking and turned out the torch.

'Here?' said Bea. No bonfire. No hot dogs. No one else at all.

'You'll see. Couple of minutes to go, I reckon. Stand here.' He turned her around too and placed her in front of him. Bea looked across the water towards the bright white floodlights at the ground. The noise of the crowd drifted through the still air towards them. Bea shivered.

'Cold?'

Tom wrapped his arms round her, linking his hands in front and drawing her closer. She could feel his breath in her hair. She leaned back a little, so his chin was resting on the top of her head. If she turned a little and tipped her face up, and if he tipped his down to meet hers . . .

She jumped as her phone started trilling in her pocket.

Tom tutted. 'Leave it,' he said.

She drew some cold air in through her teeth, then reluctantly said, 'I can't. It might be Mum.'

She fumbled to get the phone out. The screen was

brilliantly bright in the darkness, the caller ID clear: 'Ant calling.'

'I'm sorry, Tom,' Bea said. She was about to swipe the screen to accept the call, when Tom reached for the phone and pressed, 'Reject.' The noise stopped. After a couple of seconds the screen dimmed.

Bea was speechless. She was outraged at what Tom had just done, but so surprised she didn't know what to say. If it was anyone else, she'd tell them to eff off, but this was Tom, the man who gave her butterflies when he said her name, who made her feel something she hadn't felt for a very long time . . .

'Really,' she spluttered. 'Really, you shouldn't have – it's my phone.'

'I meant what I said, Bea—' and once again the butterflies took flight inside her 'I want you to myself this evening.'

'But—'

'Shh, look!'

The floodlights had been switched off. For a moment K-town seemed to hold its breath and then a volley of muffled reports announced the first rockets of the evening. Moments later they exploded into life, with ear-splitting noise and a dazzling array of stars, bursting, blossoming, moving outwards, ever outwards, until they disappeared, their place taken by more and more and more. And every point of light was echoed in the still surface of the lake, so that the colour, the movement, the drama seemed to fill Bea's field of vision. It was magical. It made her feel like a little girl again, seeing the fireworks for the first time, perched on her dad's shoulders – entranced and a little bit scared, but knowing all the time that she was safe. Her dad had got her.

'It's beautiful,' she squealed and started laughing.

Tom unlinked his arms and stroked one side of her face,

moving her hair away, and leaned closer, his mouth next to her ear.

'I knew you'd like it,' he said, and his mouth came closer still and he kissed her – on her ear, and her cheek and her neck. Bea didn't feel like a little girl any more, but she did feel safe – here with this man, on their own in the dark. She could hardly hear the fireworks above the sound of her own breath and his. She turned a little at the same time as he did and she put her hands up around the back of his neck as he undid the buttons on her coat and slid his hands inside around her waist. She closed her eyes as his cold hands explored her body: the small of her back, and then down, undoing the button of her jeans. His fingers were inside her knickers.

'Not here,' she said.

'Yes. Here.' He was still kissing her, breathing hard and fast.

She tried to move away a little, slow things down. 'I'm not standing in the park with my jeans round my ankles,' she said. 'Let's find somewhere better.' He was holding onto her, still trying to pull her close. 'Tom,' she said loudly. 'Let's find somewhere better.'

Now he stopped. He took his hands out of her clothes and held both her shoulders. 'Sorry,' he said. 'I just ... you're so lovely, Bea.' He kissed her again, tenderly, and she knew everything was okay. He listened to her. He was a good man. She was a lucky woman.

The fireworks had stopped, but they could just see the orange glow thrown out by the massive bonfire at the far end of the rugby field.

'Good fireworks,' Bea said. 'And this was the perfect place to see them.'

'Were there fireworks?' said Tom. 'I didn't notice.'

She pretended to hit him. 'Silly. Come on, let's go.'

They held hands again as they walked back by the lake and the brook, then negotiated the stile and followed the path to the car park. As they got nearer to the rugby ground, they could hear the crackle from the fire as it sent sparks spiralling up into the dark.

'I love this time of year,' said Bea.

'Me too.'

Again, Tom opened the passenger door for Bea. While he was walking round to his side, she did a quick check in the passenger mirror – hair and make-up were in pretty good nick considering. She ran her finger under her eye to fix some smudged eyeliner.

'Shall we go to yours?' she said as he started the engine.

'My flatmate's in. Bit awkward,' he said.

'We can't go to mine. Maybe eventually, but not . . . ' Not on a first date. She didn't need to say it out loud.

'It's okay. I know somewhere.'

He eased the car out of the car park and headed away from the town centre. It only took a few minutes to move from suburbia to country lanes. No streetlights. No other cars. He pulled off the road onto a farm track, tucked the car into a gateway and killed the engine.

'We'll be fine here,' he said.

'Here? In your car?'

'In the back. More room there.' He could see the doubt on her face. 'It's all right. It'll be fine.'

He leaned over and released her seat belt.

Later, they lay in each other's arms. Their clothes were mostly still on because it was so cold. Tom was on the seat, but Bea was half on him and half hanging in mid-air. She wrapped her legs round his in an effort to stop her falling bum first into the gap behind the front seats.

'This feels so right,' Tom said.

Bea, clinging on for dear life couldn't bring herself to agree. 'Mm,' she said.

'Everything. Coming back to Kingsleigh. Meeting you again. It's all perfect. It's like it was meant to be.'

Bea's underwear, which she'd hitched up to stop her bare arse getting frostbite, was digging in to the top of her leg. She wriggled round a little but that made it worse.

'Well, some things could be better,' she said. 'We need a place to go.'

Tom smiled. 'We're all right here, aren't we? It's going to take a while for me to get my own place. Need to get a promotion first.'

'Is that on the cards?'

'I want to get out of the uniform.'

'Ooh, steady.'

'No, I mean permanently. I want to be a detective. Detective constable. Then sergeant.'

'How do you do that?'

'You can apply, but if I could feed the squad some useful stuff it might help. You know, to do with this murder case. They need all the help they can get, as far as I can see.'

'Do a bit of detecting yourself?' Could Tom be another partner in crime-solving? She couldn't see him teaming up with Ant.

'Yeah. Information gathering. Local knowledge.' He paused and then said, as if the thought had just come to him, 'Is there anything you can think of at Costsave? People acting oddly?'

'Haha, they're all pretty odd at Costsave, trust me.'

'Yeah, but is there anyone who makes you feel uncomfortable? You know what I mean?'

'Well,' she said. 'There are some people who worry me more than others, but I don't—'

'Anything you can tell us could be useful. We're talking about murder here, Bea.'

'I know.' She took a deep breath. 'There's a guy in Stores. Dean. He's on the fiddle – at least I'm pretty sure he supplied the local kids with eggs from the store at Halloween. I don't know if he'd attack anyone, but he's pretty sleazy.'

'Okay. Anyone else?'

'No. I don't know. I'm not even sure about telling you about Dean.' And she wasn't sure, at all. In fact, it felt like she'd done something very wrong. She'd stop there before she did any more damage.

He stroked her hair. 'It's okay. I'll treat everything as confidential.'

She shivered again.

'I'd better get you home,' said Tom. 'Before you catch your death.'

17

The clear Bonfire Night skies had led to an icy cold morning. Bea was trying to hurry across the rec but the path was caked with frost, and slippery. She was late, having spent five minutes too long getting her hair and make-up just right. If Tom just happened to call in to Costsave today, she was damn well going to look her best – megalashes, pillar box red lipstick, perfect foundation with a hint of shimmer. She was looking down, being careful where she put her feet, so didn't see Ant cycling up to her until he skidded to a halt.

'Careful!' Bea shouted.

'Ha! Sorry! Brakes are all that good. Not too clever when it's icy.'

He climbed off and wheeled the bike around, falling in beside her.

'Why didn't you pick up my call last night?' he said.

Bea sighed. 'I was on a date, Ant. I just wanted a night off.'

'With that copper,' he sneered. 'That's what I wanted to talk to you about.'

'I know you don't like him, but, honestly, Ant, what's it got to do with you?'

'I like you, Bea.' He coloured up and she started to smile. 'Not like that. Not that you aren't – oh, fucking hell – we're mates, aren't we? You've been really good to me. I've appreciated it.'

'Yeah, course we're mates. So?'

'So, I wanted to tell you some stuff, stuff that a mate would tell you.'

'About Tom?'

'Yeah. You see, I've been doing my research. The people we agreed I'd suss out.'

'You had Bob, Lee and Dave.'

'Yeah, I know and I've got some stuff on them. Do you want to hear it?'

'Yes, of course, but—'

Now Ant was off. 'So,' he said, 'turns out Bob is a bit of a handyman. He does odd jobs for little old ladies, his customers.'

'Half a pound of sausages and a shelf putting up?'

'Something like that. He's changed some light bulbs for a woman in our street, and one of my nan's friends had him put up a fence that had blown down. He's some sort of knight in shining armour to the old biddies of K-town.'

'Let's walk and talk. We're cutting it fine already. Okay, so that's why he's got all those tools in the boot of his car.'

''Zactly.'

'Who knew? Doesn't mean he isn't our man.'

Ant tipped his head sideways. 'I think it shifts him down the list though.'

'Yeah, maybe.'

'Lee at the Leisure Centre seems like a good guy, too.'

'Yeah?'

'Volunteers as a footy coach for the under-elevens. Got a Duke of Edinburgh gold award at school too, whatever that is.'

'Oh, still that doesn't mean—'

'. . . that he's not our man. No, I know.'

They were passing Kevin's mum's bungalow now. Bea looked at the front of the house. The curtains were drawn. No lights were on.

'I haven't got anything on that Dave, though,' Ant said. 'No one knows him or knows anything about him. But I have got something on Tom.' Ant screwed up his face.

'So? Spit it out.'

'Ah, Bea, I don't know how to tell you.'

They'd entered the High Street now. He turned away from her.

Bea was starting to get impatient. 'Just tell me.'

'Okay.' He turned back to face her, and his face was so serious she felt a stab of anxiety under her ribs. Whatever was coming, this was for real. 'Word is, he didn't choose to come to Kingsleigh. He was moved. Inappropriate behaviour. He wasn't charged with nothing, it was all hushed up.'

'So what did he do?'

'He had sex with a woman while he was on duty. He banged her instead of arresting her. That's what they're saying anyway.'

Bea tried to process his words. She didn't like them, wanted them not to be true.

'But no one really knows,' she said, clutching at straws. 'It's just gossip.'

He held his left arm out wide, while still holding on to the bike with his right hand. 'I got no evidence, if that's what you mean, but that's what everyone's saying.'

'Who's everyone?'

'People I know who live over in Carlswood where he was based.'

Bea shrugged and puffed out some air. 'It's gossip, Ant.'

'There's something else.'

They'd stopped walking now, and were standing by

the crossing over to the Leisure Centre. Ant scuffed at the ground with his scruffy trainer.

'Go on,' said Bea.

'Has he told you he's single?'

'Yeah. No. He hasn't actually *told* me.'

'You haven't been to his place, though, have you?'

'No. He said his flatmate was in and it was awkward.'

'Yeah. Yeah, it would be. He lives with his girlfriend ... and their little boy.'

Without thinking, Bea raised both hands and shoved Ant in the middle of his chest, so that he let go of his bike and staggered backwards. Both he and the bike hit the metal railings.

'Oh, fuck off, Ant. That's not true. You don't like the guy, I get that, but you don't need to make stuff up about him. That's just sick.'

Ant got his balance again, but stayed hunched down holding his arms up in front of him as protection.

'Bea, I haven't made it up, I swear. I know you like him. I didn't want to tell you, I just wanted you to know what you were getting into.'

'So why not tell me before I went out with him?'

Even as she said it, she knew she was being unfair.

'I tried. I even came up to your place last night, but I was too late. You didn't see me. And then I rang.'

She stepped back from him, her arms limp at her sides.

'But you've only had one date, haven't you?' Ant continued. 'So if you wanted to just walk away, it's no biggie. Right?'

'Right,' she said, numbly.

Ant unwound his arms and peered at her. 'I'm sorry, Bea. I really am.'

'Yeah. Whatever.'

'But it's all okay, isn't it?'

She didn't reply and Ant pressed his hand to his forehead.

251

'At least it would all be okay if you hadn't done the deed,' he said. 'Bea—'

She needed to get away. She barged past him into the road without looking. There was the screech of tyres as a four-by-four hit its brakes. Ant grabbed his bike and ran after her, waving their apologies at the driver.

'Bea, what can I say?'

She blanked him. He darted in front of her, peering at her face.

'Bea, I'm so sorry. The guy's a scumbag.'

'Just leave me alone, Ant.'

'I never wanted to upset you.'

'Honestly, I just need some space.'

'Bea—'

'Fuck off, Ant! I fucking mean it!'

She carried on walking at a furious pace – maybe if she was quick enough she could leave all this behind her. Ant followed at a safe distance, all the way to Costsave. By the time he'd locked up his bike she'd disappeared upstairs into the women's toilets.

She shut herself in a cubicle for a long time. She didn't want to cry, but somehow her anger and humiliation combined to spill out of her in unstoppable hot, fat tears. She wiped them away with the back of her hand and felt angrier still at the grey, diluted mascara smearing her skin. She was a mess.

When she'd stopped crying, she emerged from the stall and used wipes and tissues from her bag to clean her face. As she peered into the mirror above the sinks, she was painfully aware of the lack of Dot. If only she was here to commiserate.

She couldn't think of anyone else she'd like to confide in – although maybe a cuppa with Hermione at lunchtime would fit the bill. After a final inspection in the mirror, she walked along the corridor to the offices. Anna's desk was empty. Bea tapped tentatively on Gavin's door.

'Is Anna in?'

Gavin looked up from his desk. 'Ah, Bea!' he said. 'No, she's going to be away for a few weeks. Come in.'

Bea went into his office and stood near the door. 'What? Has something happened?'

'She's got a secondment to Head Office, working on our national staff database. She spotted it on the website and asked if I'd recommend her.'

'It's all a bit quick, isn't it? She never said anything.'

He was holding his biro between his first two fingers and tapping it against his thumb. His desk seemed tidier than ever.

'They needed someone straight away. It was right up her street. I didn't want to lose her so suddenly, but I didn't want to stand in her way. As you know, staff development is very important to me.'

'Wow, well, good luck to her, I suppose. She's coming back, though, isn't she?'

'Yes, she'll be back. But it does leave me with a problem. And I was wondering whether you'd be able to help out, Bea.' He stopped tapping his pen and pointed it towards her.

'Me?'

'You know I see potential in you. You did a great job with the spinathon, everyone said so.'

Bea narrowed her eyes, half-knowing what was coming next.

'So, I wonder if you'll fill in for Anna for the next three or four weeks.'

'Full-time in the office?'

'Not quite full-time. Neville and I will cover the confidential stuff. But you could do the routine data entry, dealing with leave forms, sickness reports, all that sort of thing.'

'I'm not sure about the computer systems. Not sure at all.'

'There's a very clear manual, and central IT have a very good helpline.'

'I don't know, Gav. I'm happy on the tills, and we're already struggling with Dot in hospital and, you know, Ginny.'

'Let me worry about the staffing. Did I mention the honorarium for acting up? Extra responsibility. I haven't worked it out, but it'll be about £200 a month.'

'Seriously?' Bea thought of Queenie's disappearing benefits. The money would definitely come in handy. 'Can I think about it?'

'Of course. Give me your answer at the end of the day.'

Bea made her way down to her checkout. Now that she might be leaving it for a while she savoured the start-up routine; switching on the till, logging on, wiping the screen, the keyboard and the conveyor belt, checking for bags, a quick squirt of hand sanitizer and she was ready. Kirsty was next to her at Dot's till.

'Have you heard about Anna?' Bea said.

'Yeah, looks like she's headed for big things.'

'Bit sudden, though. Had she said anything to you?'

'No. P'rhaps she was keeping it under her hat until it was all agreed.'

'Maybe.'

The store was open. Bea could see Smelly Reg making a beeline for her till. His familiar twang reached her several seconds before he did. Maybe there'd be some advantages to working upstairs in the office!

Halfway through the morning Bea noticed a couple of police cars pulling into the car park. They stopped in the disabled bays nearest the front door. Tom was one of the officers getting out and she felt herself going hot and cold. She didn't want to see him. Couldn't deal with him. Not yet. Perhaps she could make a break for the loos and stay there until the coast was clear.

'Look at that,' her customer said. 'They're after someone.'

Bea turned around and saw Tom and three other uniformed guys jogging round the side of the store. A ripple of excitement spread across the shop floor. Bea carried on bleeping the shopping in front of her.

'You've missed a two for one on these tissues. Do you want to go and fetch another box?' she said.

'Oh. I don't know. I've got all this packing to do.'

'Don't worry. I'll get someone to fetch it. Ant!'

Ant was staring out of the front window, his giant foam finger by his side.

'Ant!'

Her voice startled him and he looked round, then sauntered over.

'Can you fetch another box like this, please?' She held up the tissues.

'Yeah. Okay. Did you just see that outside?'

'There was nothing to see, was there. Not really.'

Ant whistled through his teeth. 'There is now. Oh my days – they've got someone.'

Everyone in the shop turned to the front window, and watched as Dean from Stores was bundled into the back of one of the patrol cars.

'Dean? Oh crap,' said Bea, but no one heard her above the sudden screaming from the wines and spirits aisle.

'Oi! That's my son!' Eileen tore past the checkouts and skidded out of the front door. She slammed her hand against the front window of the police car. Officers got out of the car behind and went up to her, trying to talk to her and then physically moving her away from the front car, which moved off slowly and left the car park. She was still shouting, trying to shrug them off. Neville left his post at the customer service desk and went to join them. He stood at the edge of the group, trying ineffectually to make himself

255

heard. Eventually, the constables let Eileen go. Neville spoke to her, but she turned away angrily and headed back into the store. There were thunderclouds above her head as she steamed towards the back door.

'All right, Eileen?' Ant said, as swept past him. Bea hardly dared look, but couldn't help herself.

'He hasn't done anything! Not my Dean,' Eileen shouted. 'It's victimisation! I'm going down to the station. I'll get him out of there.'

She disappeared through the staff door.

Ant looked at Bea. 'That's that then,' he said. 'I had him down as a complete tosser, but I'm a bit surprised . . . '

She frowned and said, 'Shh, not in front of the customers.'

But around her, it was all anyone was talking about. They'd arrested the murderer. The Kingsleigh Stalker had been caught.

'Weaselly little bloke, wasn't he? Do you know him?' a woman in a shiny mac was asking Kirsty at the next till.

'He works here,' was all Kirsty would say.

Eileen reappeared, this time in her 'civvies' and accompanied by Gavin.

'Keep me posted,' Bea heard Gavin say as he walked her to the front door. 'Take as much time as you need.'

The officers stayed behind to search the Stores, which were declared out of bounds.

'No shelf filling. No checking for items not on display. Just for a few hours,' said Neville, going down the line briefing the checkout staff. 'If we don't have an item, a courteous apology is the best we can do at the moment. Apart from that, it's business as usual.'

At lunchtime the staffroom was still buzzing. Ant was all ready to join in the fun, but Bea dragged him away and they headed for the café across the car park instead. Ant was grinning as he tucked into a big plate of beans on toast. Bea couldn't even bring herself to order any food. She sipped at the eye-wateringly strong tea in her mug, and looked glumly at the menu.

'I'm sorry about, you know, Tom,' said Ant. 'You're better off without him, though.'

Bea put her mug down.

'I can't even think about him. Not yet.'

'What is it, then? What's up? I thought you weren't even talking to me.' Bean juice spilled out of the corner of his mouth and he wiped it with a paper napkin.

'It was me, Ant. I got Dean arrested.'

'What?'

'Last night, I told Tom that Dean was shady. Twelve hours later ... ' She raised her eyebrows.

'Well, he is shady.'

'Yeah, but is he a killer? Or have I just caused someone a whole lot of trouble who doesn't really deserve it?'

'He deserves everything coming to him, that git.'

'What if isn't him?'

'I dunno. Shall we look at your list again?'

'I think I might be done with my list, Ant. Everyone's right. We shouldn't be meddling with this. We should leave it to the police. I think I've done enough.' She took her precious piece of paper out of her pocket and crumpled it up in her hands, then dropped it on the table. 'I've made a mess of things and Dot's in hospital. I think it's time to declare our crime-fighting adventure over.'

'Hmm, shame. But maybe you're right. What about covering for Anna?'

'I reckon I should do it. Stop playing detective and concentrate on my job here. Who knows, perhaps Big Gav's right and I have got potential for better things.'

'Course you have.'

Bea looked at him, but he was being perfectly sincere.

'I know my limits,' said Ant, 'but you, you could do anything you wanted. I don't really understand why you're on the checkouts.'

'What do you mean?'

'You're brighter than all the others put together. Why are you even in Costsave? You could have an office job somewhere, earn some decent money.'

'I'm not that bright, Ant. I failed my A-levels.'

He pulled a face. 'Exams,' he snorted. 'I didn't even turn up to mine. What subjects did you do?'

'English, French and Maths.'

He whistled through his teeth. 'Jesus,' he said. 'I said you were brainy, didn't I? That's serious stuff.'

'Yeah, but like I said, I failed.'

'Have a go at Anna's job, then. See how you get on.'

Bea swilled the last of her tea round in the bottom of the mug. 'Yeah, I reckon I will. Thanks, Ant.'

'What for?'

'Being nice.'

'Ha, don't get called that very often. So we're friends again, yeah? You've forgiven me for telling you about Tom?'

Bea scowled. 'I don't even want to hear his name. Wanker.'

Ant pressed his lips together sympathetically.

'Walk you home tonight?'

'Yeah, if you don't mind waiting. I'd better go and give Gav his answer.'

'No probs.'

At the end of her shift, Bea got changed and put on her coat. She could hear voices coming from Gavin's office. She slowed down and stood listening, just outside the door.

'Things are really stretched now, Gavin. We don't need to be carrying any dead wood.' The nasal voice was unmistakeably Neville's.

258

'Dead wood?' Gavin replied.

'That lad, Anthony. He's not good for anything.'

'I've identified particular development needs for him, Neville. Head office are dealing with my request for the training.'

'Care to share that with me?' There was a testy edge to Neville's question. 'What's wrong with him?'

'There's nothing "wrong", Neville. That's not a helpful attitude. It's not the Costsave way. I'll tell you when it's all approved.'

'It feels like Costsave is falling apart. With Ginny . . . gone, and now Dean arrested. The place is going to the dogs.'

'Dean's only being questioned. No charges yet, remember. I know it's not looking good for him, but innocent until proven guilty.'

'Innocent? Huh. That's one thing he isn't. I looked at the egg stock records. There was huge variance in the percentage loss through breakage around Halloween.'

'Can you put that in a written report to me, please, Neville? There are other things I'm not happy about. There was the fight at the Legion. And when I went down to look at the Stores with the police, it was clear that Dean wasn't adhering to our equal opportunities policy.'

'The pictures in his "den"?'

'You knew about them?'

Neville sniffed loudly. 'I did. We'd had words about it.'

'And there were magazines too.'

'Magazines? Disgusting. Poor Ginny.'

'They haven't charged him yet.'

'But with that attitude to women . . .'

'Let's wait and see.'

There was the scuffling sound of a chair moving backwards. Bea realised she was about to get caught listening. She crept back along the corridor a little way, then walked normally towards the door, knocking as soon as she reached it. Gavin and Neville looked her way.

'Ah, Bea, come in. Sit down. Neville's just going, although you can stay if you want to, Neville.'

'It's all right,' said Bea. 'I only popped in to say yes. I'll give it a go.'

Gavin beamed at her. 'Great. That's great, isn't it, Neville?'

Neville forced himself to crack a smile.

'Yes,' he said. 'Of course, although how we're going to cover the tills . . . '

'We'll manage. We could offer the students some more hours. Have a look at it tomorrow, will you, Neville?'

'Yes. Well, good night.' Neville stalked out of the office. Bea was about to follow in his slipstream, when Gavin called her back.

'Thank you, Bea, and welcome aboard,' he said. 'I'm looking forward to working with you. You can do this. You've got management potential, Bea.'

Bea scuffed her feet on the carpet. 'Don't know about that, but I'll try my best.'

The phone on the desk started ringing. Bea tipped her head to the door, but Gavin held up his hand. He picked up the phone.

'Gavin Howells. Yes. Yes. I see. Okay, thank you.'

He replaced the receiver but kept his hand on it for a little while.

'It's Dean,' he said, and Bea's stomach fluttered. 'The police have let him go without charge. He's got a cast-iron alibi for the night Ginny was killed. He was with his mum Eileen.' He blew a long breath out through pursed lips.

Bea couldn't own up to listening in before, so she searched for something neutral to say.

'Well, that's good then, isn't it?'

Gavin leaned forward in his chair and rested his elbows on the desk. He pinched the skin at the top of his nose.

'There are some ... disciplinary issues to deal with. But that's not what's bothering me.'

'What then?'

He looked up at her and his face was haunted. 'We've all lost someone we loved, Bea. This place, this family, is suffering. If he didn't do it, Bea, who did?'

18

The next morning when Bea saw a hooded figure cycling across the rec towards her, she thought at first that it was Ant again. But as they got closer, she realised her mistake. She looked around. There were a couple of schoolkids about twenty metres behind, and a rotund, elderly dog walker the other side of the grass. Would any of them help her? She got her phone out of her pocket and dialled Ant's number.

The cyclist stopped on the path ahead of her, blocking her way.

The phone was ringing but no one was picking up. Bea took a deep breath.

'Dean,' she said.

'All right, Bea.'

His lank hair was spilling out of his hood. He had dark circles under his eyes, and his skin had the unhealthy shine of accumulated grease. She waited for him to say something else, but he just stood there, looking.

'On your way to work?' she said. She stepped off the path to go round him. He jerked the handlebars of the bike and turned it around.

'No,' he said. 'Got a phone call from Gavin first thing. Told me not to come in. I'm suspended while they consider my future.'

'Oh. Right. Sorry to hear that. I'd have gone back to bed, if that was me.'

She started walking towards the High Street. There'd be more people there. Safer. Dean pedalled his bike slowly beside her, looping around her, weaving in front and behind.

'Gone back to bed with that copper?'

Her stomach flipped. 'What copper? What you talking about?'

'You were *seen*.' A little bit of spit landed on the path in front of her. She kept walking.

'Seen? Seen where?'

'Going off with that carrot top, in his car, from the fireworks. You and him. A copper and his snitch.'

'Dean, I didn't say anything to him. We were on a *date*.'

'And they came for me the very next day. They were "acting on information".'

'It wasn't me.'

He stopped the bike in front of her again.

'I don't believe you, bitch.'

Bitch. *MIND YOUR OWN BUSINESS, BITCH.* It had to have been him.

'Believe what you like. Excuse me. I've got to get to work.'

She sidestepped again, but he shot out an arm and held onto her.

'And I haven't, because you've spoilt it for me.'

'Let go, Dean, or I'm calling the police.'

His grip got stronger. He leaned in so his face was closer to hers. 'It's not me, I'm worried about. It's my mum. I've never seen her so upset. You can't do that to her. No one does that to her.'

'Dean, I told you. I haven't done anything.'

'We love our mums, don't we? We don't like them getting hurt.'

Bea's breakfast – Coco Pops and a slice of toast – formed a solid ball in her stomach. 'Is that a threat?'

'No, Bea. Why would you think that?'

'I haven't done anything to you. You stay away from me and mine, okay? Do I make myself clear?'

Dean was smiling now, that familiar wolfish grin. He'd got to her and they both knew it. He looked at his watch.

'Tut, tut. You'll be late.'

He let go of her arm and she darted past him. Again, he pedalled along beside her.

'You can go now, Dean. I got the message.'

'I'll make sure you get there safely. There are some nasty people about at the moment.'

'It's okay. I can look after myself.'

'Yeah?'

'I'd rather you left me alone.'

'Keep your friends close and your enemies closer, Bea. I'm not going anywhere. It's a free country.'

'All right, Bea?' They both turned round to see Ant running towards them. He caught up with them. 'Thought I could smell rotten eggs – reckoned there was some trouble at the sewage works, but I was wrong. It was right here.'

Bea was tempted to hug him, but instead she linked her arm through his. Dean looked at him with disgust. He bumped his bike off the edge of the pavement and started cycling in the road next to them.

'Can I borrow your brolly, Bea?' Ant said.

Bea looked up at the clear sky overhead.

'Sure,' she said, handing it over.

'Ta.' Ant took the umbrella and in one swift movement poked it into the spokes of Dean's front wheel. The bike ground to a halt and Dean toppled sideways onto the tarmac.

'You fucking idiot!' he shouted. 'That's assault, that is. I could have you for that.'

'Do want the number?' Bea said and held out her phone.

'Fuck off!' Dean said, picking himself and the bike up. Ant and Bea left him to it.

'You okay?' said Ant.

'Yeah. He knows, though.'

'Knows what?'

'That I told Tom. Bloody hell, Ant, this just gets worse. He's on the loose, hating my guts, and he's not even the killer. There's someone else out there. Someone on my list.'

'Forget your list, Bea. We agreed to let it drop, didn't we?'

'I don't think I can, Ant. It feels personal. And now I'm going to be in the office, I can look at the CCTV, the customer records, staff time sheets.'

Ant sucked some air in through his teeth. 'Be careful, though, mate. Don't let Gav or Neville catch you snooping. They wouldn't like it.'

'I know.'

'Which reminds me, I've got something on Kevin, that photographer.'

'Yeah?'

'He doesn't just visit his mum's house to be nice. He's got a studio there. Keeps all his kit, lights and that in a shed in the back garden.'

'How do you know?'

'My brother Stevo's ex-girlfriend's friend told him. She wants to be a model and had some pictures done. Cost her two hundred quid and they weren't all that, apparently.'

'So he's a rip-off merchant.'

'Bit more than that – he asked her to take her top off.'

'Did she?'

'No.'

'So, it was all okay.'

'Sort of. Who asks a fourteen-year-old to take their top off? That's not right, is it?'

'She was *fourteen*?'

'Yeah.'

'Perv.'

He nodded.

They'd reached the staff entrance.

'So, I'll see you at break time then,' said Ant. 'Enjoy your morning in the office.'

'Thanks.'

She didn't need to use a locker today. She hung her coat on the back of the office door and walked over to Anna's desk. There were a few sheets of paper in the top of a stack of trays, some pens in a pot next to the computer screen, a photo of two cats, and that was it. Anna ran a tight ship with a neat desk. Bea tentatively pulled the chair out a little and sat down. Could she really do this? What was it she was meant to do? She smoothed down the side of her skirt and one of her nails caught in the fabric. She reached into her handbag and took out a nail file and started tidying up the offender.

'Settling in, I see.' Neville was standing in the doorway.

'It's important to look the part,' said Bea. She was actually really pleased with her outfit today – pencil skirt, blouse with a bow at the neck and a little cardigan to go over the top.

Neville sniffed. 'Mr Howells will be through in a minute to go through your work plan for the day. While you're waiting you can collect the post and check the answer machine. The post box is—'

'I know. Inside the side door. I'll go now.'

She went downstairs and emptied the post box. As she was walking along the corridor to go back upstairs someone barged past her.

'Dean! You're not meant to be—'

'I'm collecting my stuff, okay? Clearing my locker. I'm allowed to do that.'

'Yeah. Okay. Right.'

Back in her office, she opened the letters and put the envelopes in the recycling bin. She read the contents but couldn't do much with most of the letters, so she listened to the answer machine. There were three new messages, all for Gavin. She noted the names and numbers on the lined pad next to the phone and then looked around for something else to do. The drawers of her desk were locked. She searched the desk top for the key, then started looking around the whole office.

Hermione was smart, really smart. If she didn't carry the keys with her, where would she hide them? Bea tried under the plant pot on top of the filing cabinet and behind the framed print of a Welsh beach that hung on the wall. No joy.

Rather than bothering Gavin, she sent a quick text to Anna.

Hey Hermione, hope you're enjoying your new job. I'm filling in for you. Yes, me! Where are the keys to your drawers?

She waited less than a minute for the reply.

Ha! Wondered if they'd ask you. Congrats! Key to top drawer is stuck underneath desk w Blu-Tack. Other keys in drawer. Passwords, etc. in file marked Health and Safety 2014 no one looks there. Any probs just txt. Good luck!

Thanks, babe. You too. Don't forget us, will you. Xxx

Bea reached under the desk and found the key. She unlocked the top drawer, and, sure enough, there were a couple of bunches of other keys, along with some scissors, a stapler, some paperclips, a small tube of hand cream and a tin box marked 'Petty Cash'. She spent a few happy minutes testing the keys and unlocking the filing cabinets. When she found the Health and Safety 2014 file, she returned to the desk and fired up Anna's computer.

'Right,' she said, rubbing her hands together. 'I can do this.'

She checked Anna's list of passwords and logged on, then examined the alarming array of icons that filled the screen.

'One thing at a time,' she muttered and was about to select the first one that looked interesting when Gavin came in.

'Oh,' he said, 'you're on the system already. I was coming in to help you with that.'

'I used my initiative,' said Bea. 'Texted Anna.'

'Anna? You've been in touch with her?' His voice was conversational, but he was jiggling his hand against his leg.

'Yeah, she told me where the desk keys were and the password file.' The jiggling carried on. 'That's okay, isn't it?'

'Yes. Yes, of course,' he said. 'Well done. Easier to ask me first, though, than bother Anna. I'm right next door.'

'Well, you are the boss. I'm sure you've got better things to do than hold my hand. I mean— I didn't mean—'

He held his hand up to halt her stumbling apology.

'It's okay. I am the boss, but I like to think that we're all colleagues here. And I'm happy to help you while you settle in. That's part of my job. An important part.'

He grabbed a chair and trundled it over next to Bea, so he could see her screen too. Close to, Bea could smell his aftershave which wasn't quite masking an underlying hint of unwashed armpit.

'That's what's so nice about working here,' she said. 'You really want people to get on. You care.'

'Yes. Yes, I do.'

268

'I couldn't help overhearing you talking about Ant with Neville yesterday. I wanted to thank you. For dealing with his problem so sensitively.'

Gavin smiled. 'I know the staff laugh at me when I talk about the Costsave family, but I really believe it. And families look after each other. Ant's not a bad lad. And if he's given a chance and the right support I think he'll make something of himself.'

'I agree. He's sharp. He just hides it well sometimes.'

'You've taken him under your wing, haven't you? I appreciate that.'

'We're mates now.'

'Might be a good idea not to get too pally, though. If you're going to join us on the management side.'

'Well, I never thought that I would—'

'You need to start thinking that way. I believe in you. Be ambitious for yourself.'

'Maybe.'

He reached over and rested his hand on top of hers. Surprised, she glanced at him. He smiled and gave her hand a reassuring squeeze.

'Right,' he said. 'Let's get started. We need to keep on top of the basics. You need to compile daily reports on stock levels and sales and email them to me. I'll show you how to do that – it's very straightforward. You'll also be the first port of call for routine staff issues: holiday forms, sickness reporting, that sort of thing. You can report them to Neville and then keep the records up to date and liaise with staff. There are some routine health and safety things, too. Inspections, reports. I'd like you to get involved with those. Okay?' He looked sideways at Bea, who had started to glaze over. 'I'm sorry. It's a lot, isn't it? Let's start with the routine stats. I'll show you. No, better still, I'll tell you and you do it. You need to click on the "Stock" icon . . .'

Gavin talked Bea through some of the daily admin tasks. After compiling a couple of reports, he set her the task of running two more while he dealt with his emails and phone messages. Before he went back to his office, he hesitated.

'You look great, by the way. Professional. Smart. I'm not wrong about you, Bea. You're going places.'

'Thanks, Gavin – sorry, Mr Howells.'

'Gavin's fine here in the office, Bea. Colleagues, remember?'

He turned to leave, when Bea remembered something else.

'How often do we change the code on the staff door?'

'It's meant to be every month, but that's slipped a bit.'

'I've just seen Dean downstairs. Said he was collecting his things.'

'Ah. Point taken.'

Bea was left with a bright screen, a set of databases, and a rising sense of panic. She tried to remember the steps they had just been through together. There was a paper manual, too. She set it firmly on her desk and started paging through to the right section.

I can do this, she told herself. I'm going places.

She worked through until lunchtime. She had to ask Gavin for a few pointers, but on the whole she was pleased with how she coped. The phone went from time to time, emails pinged into a general branch inbox, but mostly it was quiet, orderly and calm. It reminded Bea of all those years of doing her homework at her desk in her bedroom. She liked it.

At half past twelve she logged out of the computer and switched it off, locked the filing cabinets and walked along to the staff room.

'All right, love. How's it going?'

Bob-on-Meat was by the kettle. He made a 'T' sign with his two index fingers and she nodded. He slung a tea bag in an empty cup and poured hot water onto it.

'It's good, thanks, Bob. Different. Miss my customers, though. Has Norma been in this morning?'

'Yeah, she's fine. And Reg. And Mrs Wills with the tartan trolley. All our regulars are fine.'

'I didn't know you did odd jobs for some of them?'

'Oh. Yeah.' He looked up, tea bag balanced perilously on a spoon in mid-air. 'Who's been talking?'

'Can't remember. Someone said you'd helped them out.'

He dropped the tea bag into the bin. 'Well, I don't broadcast it or I'd never have a minute's peace but I do look after my regulars.'

'Good on you, Bob.'

She added milk to both their drinks and looked round the room. Eileen was sitting close to Kirsty on the sofa. She looked away when Bea caught her eye, then seemed to change her mind. She said something to Kirsty, stood up and started heading towards Bea.

'Have you seen Dot recently?' Bob asked.

'No. I want to visit today, if I can.'

'I saw her yesterday. She's doing really well now—'

'You've got a nerve!' Eileen butted in between them, getting right in Bea's face. 'Coming in here like nothing happened!'

Bob placed his large hands on her shoulders and held her gently where she was allowing Bea to step back.

'Hang on, Eileen,' he said. 'Calm down.'

'She's spreading lies and gossip to the police. That's why they took my Dean in. That's why he's been suspended.'

Deny it, Bea thought. Deny it and keep denying.

'I didn't gossip about Dean, Eileen.'

'Didn't you? Can you swear on your mother's life?' Eileen was jabbing her finger at Bea, and Bea, whose head was suddenly full of Queenie, made a fatal hesitation.

'I didn't mean—' she stumbled.

271

'Oh my God, it's true!' Eileen tore herself away from Bob's grasp and launched herself at Bea. Bea felt a sharp pain as Eileen's nails scratched the side of her face. The staffroom erupted, as people leapt to get them apart or get closer to watch the fun. Bob soon had hold of Eileen again and this time he led her to the far side of the room.

'Let's get you out of here,' a voice said in Bea's ear. It was Ant, and she gladly let him guide her out of the staffroom and down the stairs. Outside in the car park he handed her a tissue.

'You're bleeding. That cow took a chunk out of your face.'

Bea dabbed where it hurt. There were two vivid red lines on the tissue when she held it away and looked. They blurred as the blood soaked into the fibres.

'I'd better go to the loos, sort myself out,' she said.

'Don't go back in there. Go in the café,' said Ant.

'I haven't got my coat.'

'Have mine.'

He took off his parka and draped it round her shoulders. She was so touched by the gesture, she decided not to mind that it smelt a bit musty. She could spritz a bit more perfume on when she got back to the office.

'Everyone knows,' she said, as she watched the steam rise from her mug as they sat at the corner table in the café. 'Everyone knows I'm a grass.'

'So what? It could have been him. And if it was, you'd have been everyone's hero. I hate a grass, I do, but this is murder. This is our town.'

'I don't know how I can go back there.'

'You can do it. Eileen's upset at the moment, but she'll get over it. They all will. Deano's a little shit. I don't mind the egg stuff, it's the nasty stuff, the sly stuff, telling my mum about Dot, setting his mates on you. That's out of order. Hopefully Gavin will do the right thing and sack him.'

'I was starting to believe it could be him, but if it wasn't then it must be someone else. There must be evidence somewhere – the hammer or whatever was used, the clothes the killer wore that night. They'd have bloodstains on them. Where have those things gone?'

'Things like that don't just disappear,' said Ant. 'I suppose he could have burnt the clothes.'

'Yeah, but someone would've seen that, wouldn't they? Seen the smoke from a bonfire. Someone must know, must have their suspicions. It's so frustrating.' She checked her watch. 'Better get back. I'll just fix my face.'

'It's fine. It's not bleeding or anything.'

Bea got her mirror out of her bag. Ant was right. The scratches had stopped oozing. She dabbed on some powder and you could hardly tell they were there at all.

'She's a psycho, that Eileen. I've never liked her.'

'She was just upset. I don't blame her,' said Bea.

'You don't blame her for nearly scratching your eyes out? Who are you, Mother Theresa?'

'It's mums, isn't it? Mums defend their kids. Like yours with Dot.'

Ant rolled his eyes to the ceiling. 'Don't remind me.'

'Are you going to see Dot today?'

He scraped his chair back and jumped to his feet. 'Yeah. Dunno. Maybe. Your coat, Madam?'

He held his coat out and put it round her shoulders again. Bea glanced down. There were some dark spots on the front. *There must be evidence.* Ant headed for the door, and while his back was safely to her, Bea lifted the coat material closer to her nose and sniffed at the stains. There was a slight whiff of vinegar and something sweeter. Ketchup, she thought. Evidence of nothing more sinister than a late-night visit to the chippy.

'Coming?' said Ant. He was holding the door open for her.

'Yeah, I suppose,' she said. 'Back to the coalface.'

Gavin came into her office when he heard her come back. He shut the door behind him. 'I heard about the kerfuffle in the staffroom. Do I need to call Eileen in and have a word?'

Bea was mortified. 'No. No, it's all good. It was a misunderstanding.'

'Really?'

'She thought I was behind Dean being arrested. Thought I'd told the police about Dean.'

'The police? And had you?'

'No. Yes. I might've mentioned something.'

He frowned. 'You rang them up?'

'No, nothing like that. I'm friends with – was friends with – Tom, the copper that's been in here a couple of times. We were just . . . talking.'

'And they acted on your information. Sounds like they haven't got much idea about the case.'

'Yes. I don't think they're making much headway. I wish they would, though. I wish this was all over.'

'We all do. Well, you've done your bit.'

'Yeah. I was wrong though, wasn't I? It wasn't Dean.'

'No, but it could have been. By the way, I've checked the records over lunch and Anna has got a bit behind with the general Health and Safety inspection. Can you look at that, please? I've put the file on your desk. There's a checklist, but do ask if you're not sure about something. Maybe Anthony could help you with it – observe and report back. Might help with his confidence.'

'Okay. Thanks, Mr—' He raised his eyebrows and she quickly corrected herself. 'Thanks, Gavin.'

'And, Bea, if things are still difficult with Eileen, do let me know. All families have arguments, but I don't want this to get out of hand.'

19

'Bea, you'd better come over here.'

'What is it?'

'Come here.'

They'd started their inspection in the bakery. Now, in the butchery, Bob was watching them, standing with his arms folded, but still keeping his distance.

Ant was looking into a shallow drawer. Bea peered in. There was an array of utensils – knives, scissors and a hammer.

'So?'

'Look at the handle,' he hissed.

Bea peered more closely. Against the pale background of the bottom of the drawer she could see a dark strand. A hair. A longish, dark hair. One end seemed to have caught in the seam where the handle met the head of the hammer.

'Shit.'

She glanced behind her. Bob was staring at them.

She straightened up.

'Bob?' she said.

He unfolded his arms and walked towards them.

'I can tell you now, there's a hammer in there. A meat hammer. Is that what you're getting excited about?'

'Bob, is this your hammer?'

'I've just told you. Yes.'

'No, actually look at it.'

Bob glanced down.

'Yes, that's my hammer.'

Ant and Bea looked at each other, at a loss what to do next.

'I'm going to fetch Gav,' Bea said.

'Why?' said Bob. 'What's the problem?'

He stretched his hand out to pick up the hammer.

'No!' Ant and Bea shouted in unison. Ant grabbed his wrist.

'Now, wait a minute—' said Bob, with a warning look in his eye. Ant held firm.

'Bob, there's a hair on there. A long hair,' Bea said.

Bob frowned. He leaned forward and examined the hammer.

'Shit,' he said. 'There's a hair. And it's not mine, is it?' He ran his free hand over the top of his mostly bald head. 'I don't know anything about this,' he said. 'Get Gavin down. Call the police. Do whatever you have to do.'

He started backing away and Ant let go of him.

'Use the internal phone, Bea. It's over there.' Bob pointed to the white plastic phone on the wall further along the counter.

Bea rang Gavin, who appeared soon afterwards with Neville. Gavin took one look, then rang the police on his mobile phone.

'I'm sorry, Bob,' he said, 'but for the time being I need you to wait in my office. Ant, will you go with him please? Take Joe with you. Neville, you and I will deal with the police when they get here.'

'All sorts of people come in and out of here,' said Bea. 'Cara's in here every day.' Cara was Bob's apprentice on the meat counter. With her partly shaved head and round face, she didn't look dissimilar to Bob.

'And the police will need to question her too. In the meantime, I need her serving out on the counter. We need to keep things as normal as possible.'

But when the police arrived, it was clear that nothing was normal any more.

There was an air of foreboding among the staff and gasps when Neville's voice came on the tannoy: 'This is a customer announcement. Would all customers proceed to checkouts. The store will be closing in ten minutes.'

People stood in the aisles and looked up to the ceiling, then started asking any staff they could find what was going on.

Bea logged onto her till to help speed people out of the shop.

Julie was there, with her sunglasses on again, hiding God knows what.

'What's going on?' she said. 'Is it a terrorist thing? A bomb?'

'No, nothing like that,' Bea said. 'It's just routine. They need to clear the shop, but we'll be open again as soon as we can.'

'Is it that girl? The one that was killed?'

'I can't say. They haven't told us anything. We're the last to know!' She tried to make light of it.

'I felt so sorry for that girl. Her family.'

'Yeah, I know. She was great.'

'Oh, I'm so sorry, you knew her, of course. I didn't mean to be . . . '

'It's all right. It's fine.'

'You should feel safe, though, shouldn't you, walking home in your own town.'

'Yeah, you should. They'll get him. Whoever it is. Maybe sooner rather than later.'

Julie leaned forward to grab a tin of mandarin segments

277

which had rolled into the corner of the packing area. Bea glimpsed an angry purple bruise under her left eye.

You should feel safe at home as well, she thought.

She didn't know what to say, how to help. So again, she didn't say anything, and she hated herself as she watched Julie walking out of the store. Gavin stood by the door, ready to lock up. Although he forced a smile at the last few customers, his face was ashen. He came up to Bea.

'We need to get some signs up, apologising for the temporary closure of the store. Say we'll open again tomorrow morning.'

'It's okay. I'll do it,' said Bea.

She hurried up to the office, logged on and composed and printed a couple of signs, then blew them up on the photocopier to A3 size. The staff were filing into the staffroom for a briefing as she finished.

'These okay, Gavin?'

Gavin scanned them and nodded.

'I'll fix them up. Be right back.'

She went out of the staff exit and round to the front door, sticking the paper on with tape. It was clouding over again and she wondered whether the paper would hold out if it started to rain. But they wouldn't be needed for long, would they?

There was a huddle of customers by the door.

'How long is this going on for?'

'What's happening?'

'What's going on?'

'Why are the police here?'

'We don't know yet. It's just for today. We'll be open tomorrow.' Bea put on her best smile and escaped back round the side of the shop as soon as she could. Bob was being led out of the staff door by two police officers as she was going in.

278

'Bob,' she said. 'I'm so sorry.'

He looked at her, and there was no bitterness in his face. 'I didn't do it, Bea. It's fine. It'll be all right.'

She went upstairs. The staffroom was packed, but sombre and silent. She stood at the edge of the crowd, looking in.

'I've spoken to the police. They have a warrant to search the building. Obviously they'll be focusing on the butchery area. I've been advised that the search will take several hours and so I've taken the decision to close the store until the start of business tomorrow. I'll keep a skeleton staff here to advise and help the police, but the rest of you can go home on full pay.'

Someone called out, 'Has he been arrested? Is it him?'

Gavin held both his hands up as if to squash the rumour. 'We mustn't jump to conclusions. Bob has only been taken in for questioning at this stage. He's helping the police with their enquiries, as are we all. We need to get to the bottom of this – we need to do this for Ginny. Perhaps we should have a moment's silence to remember what all this is about, to remember her.'

He bowed his head, and everyone else took their cue from him and did the same. There was complete silence until Gavin said quietly, 'Thank you, everyone. Go home. Keep safe. We'll see you back here tomorrow.'

'Well done, Gav.'

'Nice one.'

People started walking towards the locker rooms to get changed and fetch their coats, but the rooms were guarded by uniformed police. Bea squeezed past the queue only to find Tom barring the way. She felt a rush of embarrassment sweep through her. Infuriatingly, she couldn't help noticing how good he looked in his uniform. She also felt the urge to knee him in the groin. But now wasn't the time for any of these feelings – they both had jobs to do.

He smiled when he saw her.

'Tom,' she said. 'They need their things before they can go home.'

'I know. But we have to search the lockers too, so people will only be let in one by one and we'll observe as they open their lockers.'

'Really?'

'Really. Perhaps you could help marshal them back to the staffroom and we'll fetch them one by one?'

'Yes. Right. Okay.'

There was some resistance but in the end everyone complied. It took more than an hour to supervise the search of the lockers. Bea was the last one in the women's changing room. As she filed out she met Tom in the corridor.

'Any joy?' she said.

'No. A few surprises but nothing criminal.'

'Do I want to know?'

'No,' Tom laughed. 'And I couldn't tell you anyway.'

Bea chewed her lip. 'I wish I hadn't told you about Dean. It wasn't even him and everyone hates me now.'

'You did the right thing. If you know anything else, about Bob or anyone, you should say.'

Bea wrestled with her conscience. She'd been wrong about Dean, but this was different. 'You should check Bob's car,' she said, reluctantly, feeling like she was somehow betraying Bob.

'Yeah?'

She nodded. There was another betrayal gnawing away at her. She couldn't ignore it.

'There,' she said. 'I've told you my secrets. You should tell me yours.'

She felt sure her arrow would have pierced his conscience, but Tom seemed oblivious.

'Great,' he said. 'I'll pass that on. Nice one, Bea.'

He turned away and walked down the corridor. Just like that. *Nice one, Bea.*

'You should tell me yours, Tom,' she called out to him. 'Should have told me.'

He glanced over his shoulder, then stopped and turned round. They faced each other in the corridor, like two gunfighters in a Western.

'Told you what?'

Bea could feel her temper rising. Even now, he was playing the innocent. 'About your girlfriend. Your child.'

He looked quickly over his shoulder, checking for witnesses. 'I can't do this here, Bea. I'm working. This is serious stuff.'

Most of the staff had gone, but Bea was painfully aware that Gavin and Neville were still in the building. She didn't want to do this here either, but she didn't want to let him off the hook.

'Yeah, it is serious. And so am I. I'm not done with you, Tom. I need an explanation.'

'Fine. Okay. I'll text you.'

He turned away and disappeared down the stairs. Bea stood for a moment, then ran after him. 'Tell you what,' she shouted from the top of the stairs. 'Don't text me. Whatever it is you've got to say, I don't want to hear it. There is no explanation, there's nothing, except that you're a cheating, lying shitgibbon.'

He looked over his shoulder. 'Shitgibbon?' he said. '*Shitgibbon?*'

'Yes,' she said. 'A lying, cheating one.'

'Shitgibbon. That's brilliant,' he said and started to grin. 'I think I love you.'

Three little words. They flared briefly in Bea's brain, like fireworks, and then the warmth and light were gone. They didn't mean anything. It was just banter. He was still a cheat. Still a liar.

'You don't know the meaning of the word,' she said. 'You disgust me.'

She turned on her heel and left him looking up at her. Halfway along the corridor she stopped. Her heart was racing, blood thumping in her ears. She realised that her hands were curled into tight fists. When she relaxed them and flexed her fingers, her palms were sticky with sweat.

She wiped her hands on her skirt, took a few deep breaths and went to Gavin's office to see if she was needed. He was standing by the window when she went in, looking out over the delivery yard. Bea noticed why his desk looked tidier – the photo of Stephanie wasn't there.

'You okay, Gavin?' she said.

'It's a bad day for us, Bea.' He faced her. 'Neville said he felt that things were falling apart here, and he was right. We've had to close the store twice in a week. It's unheard of. I don't know how we'll recover from this, get our customers' trust back.'

'They'll come back to us. Let's face it, there's nowhere else for most of them to go except for Poundworld. We've got a captive audience here. Besides, people like us. That's the only thing I missed today, working in the office, my regulars. I like keeping an eye on them, having a chat. Costsave's that sort of place. They'll be back.'

'Be looking for a new butcher tomorrow,' he said glumly. 'I never thought it might be Bob.'

'Now you're doing what you told the staff not to do – jumping to conclusions. Wait and see what tomorrow brings.'

'Yes. You're right, of course. Thanks for today, Bea. Everything you've done.'

'You're welcome,' she said. 'Do you need me to stick around? Will the police need the keys to the cabinets in my office?'

'Lockers and Stores, that's what I was told. You can go, if you want to.'

'Think I'll go and visit Dot. Tell her about Bob before someone else does. They're good friends.'

'Give her my best, Bea. Say we're all thinking about her.'

'Will do.'

She left by the staff exit. It had started raining again so she put up her brolly and tilted it against the onslaught. She almost bumped into Ant, who was sheltering under the parapet at the corner of the building.

'All right?' she said.

'Yeah. Just making sure that you are. Funny day.'

'I'm fine. I'm going to go and see Dot now. You coming?'

'I might go later. I've got a few things to do. Are you all right getting there and back?'

'Yeah, I'll go on the bus. I won't be late. Nice getting off work this early, isn't it?'

'Yeah. See ya then.' Then, 'Bea? Do you think he did it? Bob?'

'It doesn't look good for him, does it?' she said.

'But you said it yourself, didn't you? Anyone could have gone in there.'

'Anyone who works for Costsave. They'll do other tests, won't they? Fingerprints, DNA and stuff.'

'Yeah. Just ... until they're sure, be careful, okay? Oh, by the way, that Kevin's at the front of the store, taking pictures again. Put your umbrella in front of you.'

'Gotcha. Thanks.'

She hurried round the side of the building. Sure enough there was the repeated flash of a camera as she started to cross the car park to the High Street. She held her hand up in front of her face.

'Give us a break, Kevin,' she shouted. 'There's nothing to photograph.'

'Ah, it's you.'

She dropped her hand and he took a photograph full in her face.

'Fuck you,' she said and hurried past him. The bus stop wasn't far along the High Street. She could see a bus coming so she put a spurt on and was relieved to catch it. It wasn't a day for waiting around.

Safely on the bus, she rang Queenie and explained about the store closing and Bob being taken away. 'Not Bob!' said Queenie. 'I don't believe it.'

'I know. We'll have to wait and see what happens, won't we?'

'Dot'll be upset.'

'Yeah, that's what I thought.'

'Give her my best.'

Bea felt anxious about seeing Dot again. She'd missed her so much, but didn't relish breaking today's news to her. She was last off the bus when it got to the hospital and her shoulders were tense, her head down as she walked along the corridors to Dot's ward.

Dot was sitting next to her bed in the blue plastic chair.

'Hi, doll,' she said, and Bea relaxed as soon as she saw Dot's welcoming smile.

'Hiya, babe. How are you doing?'

'A lot better. They're talking about discharging me tomorrow or the day after.'

'Really?'

'Yup. Just need to make sure there's someone to keep an eye on me. I still need a bit of help getting up and down. I can walk, though. Shall I show you?'

'Go on then.'

'Just support my elbow, okay?'

Bea helped Dot to stand up and handed her the metal walking stick with a rubber foot that was leaning by the chair.

'Right, you can let go now. Watch this.'

Bea winced on her behalf as Dot took her weight on her right leg and moved her left foot forward. Dot was too busy concentrating to notice. She took another step and then puffed out noisily.

'I have to keep remembering to breathe,' she said. She shuffled along further until she was level with the end of the bed. 'Not bad,' she said. She was swaying a bit where she stood. Bea lurched forward to help, but Dot waved her away. 'No, no, I'll do it myself. I'll turn round and come back again.' She managed to totter round and make it back to her chair.

'If I can have an arm again, just to get myself safely down – there! Ta, love.'

'You're doing really well,' said Bea.

'You don't have to talk to me like I'm a hundred and three.'

'I wasn't . . . I didn't mean . . .'

'I'm teasing. I feel a hundred and three sometimes, but I'll get there.'

'So who's going to look after you at home? I mean, I could help if Queenie was all right about it.'

'Ah, bless you. I'll go to my Sal's. It's a bit cramped there, with her two little 'uns, but I'll be all right. I think Ant thinks I want him to be my live-in help. He's been a bit funny the last few days.'

'Really?'

'Mmn. He didn't visit yesterday and the day before that he was, I don't know, different. I think seeing me like this has put him off. Made him realise that thirty years is a gap bigger than the Albert Hall.'

'It might not be that. There's been a lot going on.'

'I know, but if he's got cold feet I don't blame him. I never meant it to be a serious thing. I like his company. He's fun.

285

And I'm on my own. It just happened. I wish he'd say something. Be honest with me.'

'Shall I have a word with him?'

'No, I'll sort it out. I'll ring him.'

'He's been really nice to me. I've had a bit of trouble at work.'

'What sort of trouble?'

Bea sighed and ran her hands over her hair. 'I'd better tell you something else first. It's good that you're sitting down for this.'

'What? What is it?' Dot's face crumpled with concern.

'I don't really know how to tell you this. Bob's been arrested.'

Dot's mouth gaped. 'What?'

'Bob's been arrested for Ginny's murder.'

She was expecting shock, tears maybe, but Dot started laughing. Her shoulders shook and she rocked a little in the chair, her hands on her thighs. 'No, no, no,' she said, eventually. 'That's not right. It's not Bob.'

'You don't know that, Dot.'

'He's a lovely guy, a big softy. He wouldn't hurt a fly, well, maybe a fly, but not a woman. He'd never hurt a woman.'

'Wouldn't he?' Bea glanced at the other occupants of the room – two patients on their own, and another with what looked like her husband and daughter visiting – and shuffled her chair a little closer. 'Ginny was hit on the head with a hammer, right? I found the hammer that did it in the butchery. The police have taken it away to look for DNA, but I'm sure it was the one.'

Dot tutted her disagreement. 'He's a butcher, Bea. He has to use tools like that. Tools of the trade.'

'It looked clean, Dot, but there was a hair on the handle. A long black hair.'

Dot put her hand up to her mouth and was quiet for a moment or two.

'Well, I still don't believe it,' she said. 'I won't believe until he's charged, tried and convicted and maybe not even then. I know him. He wouldn't do it.'

Bea sat back a little. The chair dug into her back. 'I know you're friends, but how can you be sure you really ever know someone? What they're capable of?'

'He's a decent man. He helps people in his time off. Odd jobs and that. He's done stuff for me.'

'And maybe that's a smokescreen. So people don't suspect what he's really like?'

Dot shook her head. 'I'm not going to believe it, whatever you say. He's a good 'un, is Bob. What was your trouble anyway?'

Bea groaned. She rested her elbows on her legs and leaned her chin into her hands. 'Come on, it can't be as bad as Bob's, can it?'

Bea groaned again. 'Everyone knows that I told Tom about Dean and he got arrested because of it but now he's out now and he's threatened me and Eileen scratched my face and I reckon I'd just give up if I was still on the till but at least I can hide in the office.'

Dot laughed again and took hold of Bea's hand. 'I only got the first few words of that and then you lost me. Tell me properly. One thing at a time.'

So Bea told her all about her date with Tom – almost all – and Dean's arrest and the aftermath.

'Well, he's always been a bit shifty, to be honest,' Dot said. 'And despite all evidence to the contrary, Eileen thinks the sun shines out of his behind, so you wouldn't expect her to take it well. It'll all settle down. What are you doing in the office?'

'Anna's on secondment. I'm covering.'

'Wow, that's amazing. Is it going all right?'

Bea felt herself relaxing a little. 'Yeah, actually. Gav's been really nice and even Neville's been helping me. Feel a bit out of my depth sometimes, but mostly I really enjoy it.'

'You gonna be leaving us, then? I'll miss you if you do.'

'Nah, it's just till Anna gets back. I miss you, you know. I had Kirsty on your till – not the same at all.'

Dot nodded. She understood.

'Talking of Anna,' she said. 'I remembered the thing.'

'What thing?'

'Last time you were here, there was something I was going to tell you, but I couldn't remember it. It was about Big Gav. Anna told me that he'd been sleeping in his office.'

'Really?'

'She came in early one morning and caught him stuffing a sleeping bag into one of his filing cabinets. He was really embarrassed. Didn't want everyone to know that things were a bit tricky at home.'

'Ah, the photo of Steph's gone from his desk, too. Reckon they've split up?'

'Maybe. He's such a nice man. I wonder what's gone on. You're in the right place to find out now, aren't you? Get me a bit of gossip.'

'I'll do my best.'

Dot's face tensed up as she shifted in her chair, trying to get comfortable. 'Better let you get back to Queenie,' she said. 'She all right?'

'Bit upset. Looks like her benefits might be taken off her. We had a woman round, grilling her.'

'God, I'm sorry.'

'If I can get a doctor's report on her agoraphobia, we might be all right.'

'Here's hoping. And Tom? Are you seeing him again?'

Bea's face fell. 'I shouldn't think so. Ant did a bit of free-lance detective work. Tom's not exactly single.'

'Oh, babe.' Dot's face creased up in sympathy.

'He's got a kid and everything.'

'I'm so sorry. I thought he was all right.'

'Me too. Like I said, you never really know other people, do you?'

'Well, I know you and you're a bloody diamond. You're worth ten of him. I mean it.'

Bea felt the stirrings of incoming tears. She sniffed hard to chase them away. 'Thanks, doll. You too. Can't wait for you to get out of here.' She started winding her scarf round her neck. 'I'll put a rocket up Ant's arse when I see him. Get him to call you – you've got your mobile here, haven't you?'

'Yeah. Don't be hard on him, though.'

'Okay. Let me know how you get on, will you?'

'Yeah, of course. But Bea?'

'Yeah?'

'Bob didn't do it. I know he didn't. So, there's still someone out there. Be careful, babe.'

'All right. I will.'

Bea leant down to kiss Dot's cheeks. Dot reached up and gave her a little squeeze. As Bea was walking out of the ward, she looked back over her shoulder. Dot was looking at her and when she saw Bea was looking too, she blew her a kiss. Bea caught it and held it close to her heart.

Gav wasn't wrong about the Costsave family. There were fallings out and bitching, but there was also loyalty and real love. She didn't know if Dot was another mum, or an auntie or maybe one of the cousins where the generations have got out of kilter – whatever, she was a proper friend.

On the bus home, Bea fished in her pocket and got out her list of suspects. No one who knew him thought it was Bob. But maybe that was how people got away with things – they lived blameless lives and people liked them. Hiding in plain sight. It *could* be Bob, but what if it wasn't?

If that was *the* hammer that she found today, then the killer could only be someone with access to the back rooms at Costsave.

She took out her pen, then put it back in her bag and dug around for a pencil. Too many ifs and buts to take people permanently off the list, but she drew a faint pencil line through Dean, Lee, Kevin and Dave. Maybe the killer was in the police station tonight. Maybe he wasn't.

She looked up. The bus had already turned out of the High Street and was trundling round the estate roads. Nearly home already. She pressed the request bell and gathered up her things. Rain was battering the window, making slanting parallel tracks across the glass.

The bus stop was only a couple of hundred metres from her house, but she felt wary stepping onto the pavement, kept looking behind her as she hurried along. There was very little traffic on the dark street, and so she heard the whirring of rubber bicycle tyres on the wet road while it was still some way away. She turned round again. The bike was bombing along on the wrong side of the road – her side. It had no lights on, and the rider was hooded. Ant?

Instinctively, she stepped back from the kerb. The bike mounted the pavement and sped towards her. She pressed herself into a wet hedge as the bike skimmed past. She felt something hit her face and put her hand up to it. She wiped away a warm, wet, slimy glob of spit.

The bike was back on the road now, disappearing fast. She looked around for something to throw at it, then realised the futility. *Get home. Get in. Shut the door.*

She'd only caught a glimpse of the pale face inside the hood, as it turned her way and launched its loathsome missile. She could be wrong, but she didn't think so. Dean might be off her list, but he wasn't out of the picture.

20

The store was open the next morning but nothing felt normal. The staff were still in shock from the day before and divided about Bob. Most of them had known him a long time. Bea reported for work in the office, and was given a hefty list of things to do. Gavin was edgy, nervous about the effect of yesterday's closure and the press coverage about Bob's arrest. Despite Bea's brave words that their regulars wouldn't desert them, she couldn't help peeping at the CCTV cameras when Gavin went downstairs to unlock the doors. He'd be crushed if there was no one waiting. The image on screen wasn't the best quality, but there was a reassuring gaggle of customers streaming into the shop on the dot of eight o'clock, among them the unmistakeable figure of Smelly Reg. It was business as usual.

Towards the end of the afternoon. Gavin put his head round the door. 'Dean's coming in for a disciplinary meeting in five minutes. Can you hold all my calls while he's here?'

'Yes, of course. Do you want teas or coffees or anything?'

'No, it's a formal thing. Perhaps a jug of water and some glasses. For four – me, Neville, Dean and Eileen.'

'Is there a union rep?'

'Eileen's there as his rep, seeing as Bob is, um, not available today.'

Neville appeared in the corridor behind Gavin. 'They're here,' he said.

'Oh, right. I just need to get some paperwork ready,' said Gavin. 'Can you keep them in here for five minutes?'

Dean, Eileen and Neville gathered in Bea's office. Apart from some terse greetings, no one spoke. Bea made a point of looking Dean in the eye, but the look she got back was so hostile that she quickly looked away and pretended to be busy at her computer. She couldn't concentrate with the three of them crammed into the small room with her, kept remembering the warm spit hitting her face. She put her hand up to her cheek. It was no good. Never mind what Gavin said, she thought, and offered them all tea or coffee as an excuse to get out of the room.

She scuttled off to the staffroom and made up a tray of hot drinks, together with the water and glasses that Gavin had asked for. She'd only just got back when Gavin rang through and asked her to send them in. She led the way with the tray and then left them to it, closing the door behind her.

The meeting lasted for about three quarters of an hour. Afterwards a clearly upset Eileen hurried straight past her door, but Dean paused in the doorway. When Bea looked up he didn't say anything but drew his finger across his throat, then left. Neville and Gavin came in, Gavin tugging at his tie to loosen it, Neville wiping a clean hankie across his forehead.

'Well, that was awkward,' Gavin said.

'These things are never pleasant,' said Neville, 'but they have to be done. Discipline, fairness – they're important.'

'He's gone then?' said Bea, and they nodded their confirmation.

'Do you think Eileen will stay?' Gavin said to Neville.

'She's been here a long time.'

'She will if she needs the money. We're not exactly falling

over job opportunities in Kingsleigh, are we, not since the factory closed,' said Bea.

'I hope she stays,' said Gavin. 'It's not been a good couple of weeks for Costsave.'

He and Neville both looked defeated for a few seconds, then Gavin straightened his shoulders. 'Let's bring everyone together,' he said.

'A staff meeting? Tomorrow morning?' said Bea, reaching for the mouse and clicking on the online diary.

'No,' he said. 'A drink in the Nag's Head this evening. An hour before last orders. I'll get the first round in. How about it, Neville?'

'Well, I could join you. It's Maureen's Brownie night tonight, so I'd be on my own.'

'No, I assumed you'd come. How about buying the second round?'

Neville looked as though he'd just sat on a pin. 'Well I, I don't know . . . '

'Staff morale, Neville.'

Neville's face flushed. 'Well, all right, I suppose.'

Gavin clapped his hands and rubbed them together.

'Great. Put it in an all-staff text and email please, Bea.'

'Yes, Gavin.'

By mid-evening Bea was exhausted. It had all been too much: nights of broken sleep, a romance broken before it had really begun, an investigation that had started out as a righteous cause and ended in a mess of recrimination. All she wanted to do now was go home, put her feet up and watch the TV with Queenie. She certainly didn't feel like going to the pub but she had to go out of loyalty. She'd show her face, be seen, have one drink and go home.

The offer of a free drink was always going to be appreciated by the Costsave crowd, but even so, there was an odd feeling in the pub that night. The last time they'd gathered together here had been the night of the spinathon, and naturally that was playing on people's minds. It was only after the second free drink that things started warming up and the hubbub of conversation reached a more normal level. The subject of most of the conversations was, inevitably, Bob.

Ant found Bea near the bar. He was fetching a pint for Saggy, who had somehow wangled his way into the free round. Bea was frowning.

'I can't find my phone.'

She turned out her pockets and then started rummaging in her bag. She put the contents on the bar. They formed a mountain of odds and ends, seemingly far bigger in volume than the inside of her bag.

'Damn!' she said. 'It's not there. This is stupid. I'm too tired for this. I feel like I'm going mad.'

'All right, all right. Calm down. It'll turn up.'

She filled her bag again with all her essentials and tried her pockets one more time. 'I don't get it,' she said. 'I've always got my phone.'

'Have you put it down in here?'

'No, I haven't had it here.' She carried on patting her pockets. 'What's going on with you and Dot, anyway? She said you hadn't been to see her for a couple of days.'

Ant looked shamefaced. 'I don't know. It's just – well, we'd only just, you know, and it probably wasn't anything anyway. I don't know.'

'She doesn't want to marry you, Ant. She just needs friends right now. That's all. She's not expecting anything from you. Go and see her.'

'Yeah. I should. I will. I'll go tomorrow.'

'You could give her a ring now. She'll still be awake. Clear the air.'

'Yeah, okay.'

'Which reminds me. I reckon I left my phone at work. I definitely had it there. I'll go and get it.'

'It's closed, Bea.'

'Yeah, but I know all the codes and everything. It won't take five minutes. Will you come with me?'

Ant eyed the remains of his second pint longingly. 'Yeah, sure,' he said. He drained the glass.

They were making their way out of the pub when Eileen fell into them, coming out of the ladies' toilet.

'Woah, steady,' said Ant, trying to stand her up straight. She slumped against him, clearly the worse for wear.

'Sorry,' she said. 'Sorry, I didn't mean—'

'You all right, Eileen?' said Bea.

'No. And why should I be? My son's been sacked, thanks to you. Everything's gone to shit. I need another drink.'

She stumbled again and pushed all her weight against Ant, who took a couple of steps back and then propped her up again.

'You need a coffee, Eileen,' Ant said. 'Shall I get you a coffee?'

Bea smiled.

Gavin was working his way towards the bar and over-heard. 'Good lad, Ant. Here,' he dug in his pocket and handed over a fiver. 'Pay for it out of this.'

'Wow, okay,' said Ant.

'I'll just go and get my phone,' Bea said, over the top of Eileen's head. 'I'll leave you two bonding.'

'Are you coming back here?'

'Yup. See you in ten minutes.'

Ant found a spare seat for Eileen and went to the bar to fetch her a coffee. He felt a pang of worry at Bea going out on her own, then dismissed it. Bob was still in custody, after all. They'd had him for over twenty-four hours now. They'd got him.

He looked for Gavin to give him his change, but he was lost in the throng.

When Ant went back to Eileen, she had her head on the table. He gently put the cup and saucer down. 'Here's your coffee, Eileen. Drink up.'

She raised her head slowly. 'Whaa? Oh—'

She tried tearing open a sachet of sugar, but spilled half of it onto the table.

'Here, let me.' Ant added the remaining half and another sachet to her cup and stirred it for her. She watched, silent and glassy-eyed. By the time she'd sipped her way to the bottom of the cup, she was talking again and there wasn't any stopping her.

'I'm sorry, Ant. I got you all wrong. I know you and Dean don't get on, but you're not a bad lad, are you?'

'Well, I try not to be.'

'I don't think you can ever really know someone.'

Ant was only listening with half an ear. He was looking towards the door, trying to see if Bea had come back yet. 'What was that?'

'You think you know someone, live with them, share your days with them, but you don't really know them. Like now. I'm here and I've no idea where my Dean is. He could be anywhere, doing anything. Like most evenings. I haven't got a clue what he's up to.'

Ant stopped looking at the door and turned his full attention to Eileen. 'Like the evening Ginny . . . ?'

'We were all at the pub, weren't we? When it was time to go home, I couldn't find him. Ended up walking back on my own. He didn't get in until gone two.'

She had his full attention now.

'But you told the police he was with you,' he said urgently.

'He's my son. Your ma would do the same for you, Ant. She would.'

'Yeah, but we're talking about murder.'

'He's not a murderer.' Eileen slumped against the padded seat.

'Have you got any idea where he is now?' Ant asked.

She shook her head.

Ant got his phone out and started to dial Bea's mobile. Then he remembered that that was what she was looking for. The phone went to voicemail.

'Bea,' he said. 'Ring me as soon as you get this. It's important.'

She'd check her messages when she picked up her phone, which must be about now, surely. He waited for a few more minutes, then collared Kirsty as she was passing.

'Can you keep an eye on this one, please? She's a bit tipsy.'

Kirsty grinned. 'Sure.' She sat next to Eileen and Ant weaved his way through the crowd and out of the pub. Bea must have found her phone by now, if it was in the office. He tried ringing again with no joy.

He got hold of his bike from where it was leaning against the wall and started wheeling it down the High Street towards Costsave, thinking he'd meet her halfway. He stopped for a minute. Perhaps there'd been a change of plan and she'd found a message from Queenie when she checked her messages. There usually was. On the off-chance, he dialled Bea's home number. It only rang a couple of times before it was answered.

'Hello?'

'Mrs Jordan? Is Bea with you?'

'Who's this?'

'It's Ant. I came to your house?'

'Oh, Ant! How are you , love? Are things a bit better now?'

'Yeah, I'm fine. I'm trying to find Bea. Is she at home?'

'No, but she's on her way here. She texted me to say she was meeting her friend here.'

Ah, she'd found her phone. 'Oh, great.' He felt a bit put out that she hadn't rung him though, when she knew he was waiting at the pub. He wondered who was more important, knowing at the back of his mind that it was probably Tom, despite what he'd told her. 'Um, which friend was it?' He tried to keep his voice casual.

'One of the boys from work. You'll know, I suppose.'

Not Tom then – he felt a little surge of relief. But then he remembered that pretty much everyone from work was at the pub. 'What's his name?'

'Dean, I think.'

The relief turned to something cold and hard inside.

'Dean's coming to your house?' he said.

'Yes.' There was a noise in the background, a doorbell ringing. 'Oh, that'll be him. I'll tell Bea you rang—'

'Mrs Jordan! Don't let him—' Ant was shouting over the top of her, but it was no good. She'd rung off. 'Shit, shit, shitterty shit!'

He rang back and kept it ringing as he turned the bike around and started pedalling the other way. Going past the newsagents, he spotted someone in uniform queuing at the till. Ant checked the traffic and swerved across the road. He bumped the bike up the kerb and rode through the open door into the newsagents. He was aware of people shouting at him, but he ignored that. The officer looked round. It was Tom.

Ant skidded to a halt. 'Mate! Listen!'

Tom looked at him with a mixture of distaste and glee. 'I'm not your mate,' he said. 'And I'm on duty, and this is clearly antisocial behaviour—'

'No! Bea's in trouble! Or her mum is. At her house. We've got to get there now!'

Tom scrunched up his face, trying to make sense of what Ant was saying.

'Dean's up there. He's threatened her. He's there now!'

'Okay, okay. We'll go up in the car. I'll get Shaz. She's just using the bog in the chip shop.'

Ant swore. 'I can't wait for that. I'll see you there.'

He swung his bike around and started pedalling, leaving behind him more shouts of outrage from the shop staff and customers. Ant pedalled as fast as he could. His legs were hurting, it was difficult to catch his breath, but he pushed on. The alcohol was sweeping through him, but it didn't muddy his brain. No, it was all clear now, crystal clear. Dean had no alibi for the attacks and he had a massive grudge against Bea. He pedalled faster.

The police car overtook him at the end of Bea's road. Ant stood up on his pedals and pumped his legs as fast as they would go. When he got to number twenty-three, he jumped off his bike and left it lying on the pavement. He ran through the gate. There were three people in the front garden – the two coppers and Bea's mum. Ant raced up to them.

'Are you okay?' he said. 'Are you all right?'

Queenie looked round. 'Oh, Ant,' she said. 'My feet are freezing.'

'Just step back, please,' said Tom, trying to usher Ant away from them.

'No! Wait a minute. What's going on? Is Dean here?'

'Oh, yes,' said Queenie. 'He's in the cupboard under the stairs.'

'What?' said Ant and Tom together.

'He was saying some nasty things about Bea. I didn't like it. I asked him to leave and he wouldn't.'

'So?'

'So I asked him to fetch us a drink, a bottle of sherry from under the stairs, and then I pushed him in and bolted the door. He was making an awful racket so I came outside and

299

rang the police. I've only just come off the phone. Surprised you got here so fast. Were you in the area?'

'We were on our way here already. Was he carrying a weapon, a knife or anything?'

'A knife?' Queenie suddenly looked alarmed. 'No. Not that I saw.'

'But you asked him to leave and he refused?'

'Yes.'

'That's trespass, at least. And threatening behaviour. We'll get rid of him for you.' The two police officers went into the house. Ant stayed with Queenie. She was starting to shiver so Ant offered her his sweaty hoodie. She looked doubtful, but he took it off and helped her thread her arms into the sleeves.

'Thank you,' she said. 'It is nippy out here, isn't it?'

'Mmn, freezing.' He smiled at her. 'Just realised you're outside. I thought you didn't—'

'Outside seemed safer than in, today, love. I wish I'd put some shoes on, though. The cold's coming through the soles of my slippers.'

Ant grinned. 'We'll sort that out when they've got Dean out of there. Have you heard from Bea? I've been trying to get hold of her.'

'Oh, it's all right. She'll be here in a minute.'

'Did you speak to her?'

'No, she texted. Bit odd, 'cause I thought she would've rung me. She doesn't often send me texts.'

There was some shouting from inside the house, the sound of a scuffle.

Ant whipped out his phone. He found Bea's mobile number in his contacts and pressed 'call'. Dean was being led down the garden path now. He was flanked by Tom on one side and Shaz on the other. Ant could see the glint of the handcuffs joining him to Tom. Dean was mouthing off,

300

protesting against 'police brutality', but he stopped, mid-rant, when he heard the phone ringing. His free hand went to his back pocket and then he looked up, straight at Ant. Ant killed the call and sprinted towards him.

'Oi! What are you doing?' Tom shouted.

Ant made a sort of war cry, a sound of pure fury. He cannoned into Dean and knocked him off his feet. Tom's arm was jerked backwards by the handcuffs and the rest of him followed. He landed awkwardly on the concrete path next to Dean and screamed with pain. Ant balled up his fists and aimed a couple of decent blows into Dean's ribs. 'You thieving little shit!'

He reached underneath him and found the phone.

Tom was writhing on the ground. His voice was surprisingly high-pitched. 'My arm! My arm!' But Ant paid no attention.

'No wonder Bea wasn't picking up. Where did you get this? What've you done to her?'

Dean was still breathless from the punches Ant had landed. 'I haven't done anything,' Dean gasped.

'Liar!' Ant screamed in his face. 'This is her phone. Where did you get this from?'

'Her desk. She'd left it on her desk.'

'Did you text her mum with this?'

Dean didn't answer, so Ant balled up his fist and held it up to Dean's face. 'Did you?'

Dean nodded. Ant was about to pummel Dean's nose when Shaz caught hold of his arm.

'That's enough,' she said.

'He's got her phone. He's done something to her.'

'Shut up, dickhead,' Dean shouted. 'I haven't done anything to her.'

Ant sat back on his heels. Maybe Dean was telling the truth. He'd nicked the phone before they all went to the pub.

301

So Bea was all right. She'd have gone to Costsave, realised her phone wasn't there and gone back to the pub. She was probably in the Nag's Head right now.

The Costsave car park was almost empty. Just a few staff vehicles here and there. Bob's estate car had been lifted onto the back of a police towaway truck earlier in the afternoon. Bea walked round the side of the building, noticing the sound her boots made on the tarmac. Apart from that it was quiet, a heavy, empty sort of evening.

It felt wrong to be here on her own. She wished she'd waited for Ant now. But it wouldn't take long – she'd have a quick scan of the locker room, the staffroom and her office. Her eyes were tired and itchy. She rubbed at one absentmindedly and felt one of her megalashes come free. She thought it was stuck to her hand, but when she looked it wasn't there. It was too dark to see where it had gone.

She punched in the code for the staff door and let herself in, flicking the light switch just inside. She scuttled to the stairs, ignoring the door to the shop floor. The thought of that huge space – devoid of customers, eerie, empty and dark – made her shudder.

She climbed the stairs and checked out the locker room, including the toilet stalls. She couldn't see her phone. The lockers were all tight shut, except for one. The door to Ginny's locker wasn't quite level with the others. There was no reason for her phone to be in there. She hadn't looked inside since the day she found Kevin's card. Even so, Bea bent down and opened the metal door. There was nothing there.

She realised she'd been holding her breath and forced herself to breathe normally. This was Costsave, the same place she came every day, the place where she worked with her mates. But somehow it was utterly different tonight.

302

A quick tour of the staffroom revealed nothing more than some grotty cups that should have been washed out at the end of the day. Bea headed for her office. The harsh strip light made her feel more normal, shutting out the oppressive weight of the darkness in the rest of the building. She was nearly done now and then she could get back to the warmth and noise of the pub.

When the office phone on the desk started ringing, she jumped out of her skin. She knew she should let it go to answerphone. After all, it was way outside office hours and she wasn't on duty any more. But something prompted her to pick it up.

'Hello?'

'Bea!'

She smiled when she heard Anna's voice. 'Hey, Hermione, how are you doing?'

'I'm fine. Missing K-town.'

'Really? It's like *Midsomer Murders* here. You're better off out of it. They've arrested Bob now.'

'Bob-on-Meat? You're kidding?'

'No. He had a hammer in his drawer with Ginny's hair on it.'

'Oh shit. But, really, Bob?'

'I know. You working late?'

Bea scanned the room one more time.

'Yeah, just about to pack up. Thought I'd ring in case you were working late too, needed any help.'

'No, I'm fine. I just came back to the office to look for my phone. Thought I must have left it here, but I can't find it. How are things going?'

She opened her desk drawer with one hand and started scrabbling through.

'It's great. Really interesting.'

'Lucky you spotted the advert.'

'I didn't. It wasn't my idea. Gavin found the advert and put my name forward. I didn't know anything about it until he announced it – it was a done deal by then.'

'His idea?'

'Yeah. I was pretty surprised, but it was really nice of him. It's right up my street. Glad it's only a few weeks, though. Like I said, there's no place like home.'

Bea closed the drawer and looked round the room. 'Anna?'

'Yeah?'

'Did you catch Gavin sleeping in the office?'

'Not exactly, I just saw him stuffing his sleeping bag into the bottom drawer of his filing cabinet. He looked really startled when he saw me looking. I guess he doesn't want anyone to know he's having problems at home. He tried to make light of it.'

'More than problems. Her photo's gone from his desk. Reckon it's all over.'

'Aw, poor Gavin. He's having a rough time.'

'Yeah.'

Bea could hear Anna yawning on the other end of the phone. 'You sound how I feel,' she said. 'Time to go home, hon.'

'Yeah, you too. G'night, Bea.'

'Night, Hermione.'

As Bea replaced the phone in its base, she thought she heard a noise from downstairs. She stood stock still, listening, but no sound came to her.

She must have imagined it. The phone call with Anna had unsettled her. While she was talking she'd had a sense of things starting to fall into place – the pieces of the jigsaw fitting together. What was it? She thought back over their conversation. Anna hadn't found the secondment, Gavin had. He'd practically sent her away. It had all happened so quickly. He'd sent her away because she knew something. She'd seen something.

Oh my God.

Instead of heading along the corridor to the stairs, she walked into Gavin's office, her heart thudding in her chest. She flicked on the light, then tried the filing cabinet. It was locked, of course. She looked around for the key. It wasn't anywhere obvious, but maybe it was . . .

She bent down and felt underneath his desk, smiling as her fingers found the cold, smooth metal of the key embedded in a lump of Blu-Tack. She prised it free and, her hand shaking, put the key into the lock of the cabinet. She couldn't get it to turn, so she crouched down and tried again, and this time it worked. As she slid the bottom drawer out, her mouth was dry and a tight feeling gripped her chest. Dark quilted material ballooned out of the drawer, like it had just been waiting for the chance to expand.

'What are you doing?'

She jumped and looked up.

Gavin was standing in the doorway. Sweat pricked out of the pores on her top lip and forehead.

'What are you doing in my office, Bea?'

'I lost my phone, Gavin. I figured I left it at work.'

'In my office? In my drawers?'

'I . . . I couldn't find it anywhere else. So—'

'What are you really doing here?'

The game was up. Bea had no idea what to do. He was blocking the only way out, apart from the window and a twenty-foot drop. Perhaps she could lure him into the room a little and away from the door.

'I was looking for this,' she said, standing up and pulling the quilted material out of the drawer. She held it up and it unfolded – a hooded jacket, not a sleeping bag after all. 'I knew it had to be somewhere and then Anna said she'd seen you stuffing a sleeping bag away.'

305

Gavin made an exasperated sound. 'Anna,' he said. 'You've been talking to Anna.'

'You knew she'd seen you, didn't you? That's why you sent her away. She didn't find that job, you did.'

'Staff development is important to me.'

'A few weeks,' said Bea. 'Long enough for things to die down – or for you to frame someone else.'

He didn't reply.

'So once Dean had been released you set it up for me to find the hammer in Bob's drawer.'

He snorted. 'You're tired, Bea. I was wrong. This job is too much for you.'

She laid the crumpled jacket on the desk, front upwards. There were darker spots on the navy material, a spatter of them.

'I don't know if you slept here the night Ginny died, but you came back here, didn't you? Did you come back here to think about what you'd done? How you'd cover it up? And then couldn't face the thought of going home, pretending everything was normal?'

'I slept here because things are difficult at home. It's nothing to do with anyone, anything else.'

'Say her name, Gavin. She had a name. The girl you killed was Ginny.'

'I didn't kill anyone. I didn't kill Ginny.'

'So you won't mind if I give this jacket to the police?'

He'd moved towards her, away from the door, but not far enough yet to let her make a break for it. 'You mean your friend Tom – I've heard about you and him. Like I said, people love to talk. Even in front of the boss.' He was standing at the other side of the desk now. He reached for the jacket and picked it up. Bea held onto the hem. 'I'll look after this,' he said. 'Get rid of it properly like I should have done in the first place. And then you've got nothing.

I've been keeping an eye on you. Keep your friends close and your enemies closer. You don't make a very good detective, Bea.'

His voice was colder, harder than she'd heard from him before. He was almost unrecognisable. Frightening. If she could only bring back the Gavin she and everyone else knew. Perhaps she could reason with him.

'I don't get it, Gavin. I really don't. We all like you here. Love you, even. What the hell?'

He laughed. 'Love? Nobody loves me. I've been told. Put in my place.'

'By Steph?'

'Yes, as she was packing her bags and walking out. At first it was "It's not you, it's me", but when I reasoned with her, *pleaded* with her, the truth came out. She didn't love me. Never had.'

'I'm sorry, Gavin. Sorry it didn't work out, but that's no reason to do what you've done. Hurt people.'

'That was an accident. I never meant it. Not to start with anyway.'

'I don't understand.'

'This job, it's all I've got. First to come in in the morning, last to leave at night. No one knew or cared what happened in between. At the end of day, I didn't want to go home. Home to an empty house.'

'So?'

'So I'd drive around town, walk around the streets. I'd follow people, girls. I didn't do anything, was never going to, it was just sport. Something to do. It was a little bit of a thrill. The thrill of the chase. Nothing wrong with it, not really.'

'But chasing wasn't enough?'

'I would never have done anything if that girl hadn't turned round. She looked at me and I recognised her from

307

the shop, realised she'd recognised me too. It was her fault, Bea. If she hadn't turned round . . . '

It was her fault.

With those words, Bea knew she could never reason with him. She would have to escape. He was still holding the jacket. Bea let go of the hem and he clutched it to him.

'You could have stopped then,' she said. 'She lost her memory. You got away with it.'

'I tried to stop. I applied for promotion – a job in Devon. Get away from here. Make a fresh start. But I got turned down. It was a sign. I was meant to stay here. I was meant to carry on. Do it properly this time. Choose a girl. Stake things out. Prepare.'

'And you chose Ginny.'

'She chose herself, Bea. I saw her – Little Miss Perfect – laughing at me during the spinathon. She shouldn't have done that.'

'I'm sure she wasn't. No one was laughing at you. Ginny was a sweet—'

'Ginny was like all them,' Gavin snarled. 'All of *you*. All "Yes-Gavin, No-Gavin" to my face but talking about me behind my back. Looking down on me. Mocking me. *Big Gav*. Do you know how much I hate those words?'

Bea gripped the edge of the desk, braced herself and tipped it towards Gavin with all her strength. As it toppled forward, she darted to the side, but Gavin's bulk stopped the desk going completely over and one of the legs caught her and she stumbled. Gavin swore, dropped the coat and lunged at Bea. She squealed and ran the other way, but he was there and he got hold of her.

'Gavin, stop it!' she shouted. 'Let me go! It's over!'

'It's too late,' he grunted. 'It's too late.'

21

Ant rang Saggy's number. 'Hey, Saggy, is Bea there?'

'It's really noisy. Hang on, I'll go outside.'

There was a pause, then, 'That's better. What did you say, mate?'

'I asked if Bea's there. I need to talk to her.'

'Nah, she's not here.'

Someone needed to go back to Costsave, check it out. 'Can you put me onto the manager, Big Gav? Do you know which one he is?'

'Yeah, okay. I'll go back in.'

Ant could hear all sorts of muffled noises, music and conversation. Eventually, Saggy came back on the phone.

'He's not here either. Someone said he left ages ago.'

'He normally stays till last orders. Look, I'm going to go to Costsave. I think Bea's there on her own. I'm worried about her. Can you come too? Bring Neville with you, the deputy manager – he's sort of stringy looking, not much hair.'

'Oh yeah, I know. He won't come with me, though.'

'Put him on the phone.'

'I'll go back in.'

Another wait and then Ant could hear Neville's distinctive nasal voice, 'Hello, this is Neville Fellows speaking.'

'Mr Fellows, it's me, Ant. Will you meet me at Costsave, please?'

'Anthony.' He said the word as if it tasted bad in his mouth. 'What on earth for?'

'Bea's missing. I'm worried about her. She went back to the shop to fetch her phone.'

'I'm sure everything's—'

'Please. I think she might be in trouble. I'll owe you.'

'Very well.'

'See you in a minute.' Ant scrambled to his feet and sped off down the path. He grabbed his bike and leapt on.

'Where are you going?' Tom grunted. 'Where's Bea?'

'Costsave,' Ant shouted over his shoulder. 'She's at Costsave, of course. Can you drive?'

Tom shook his head.

'No. We've got to take this one in anyway. Shaz'll ring for another car.'

'Whatever. I've gotta go!'

He jumped the bike off the kerb, crossed the street and headed onto the rec.

Gavin put his hands round Bea's throat and squeezed. Instinctively she tried to tear his hands away, but he was too strong, too determined. Leaving his hands, she desperately felt around her for something to hit him with, but she only found thin air.

He was choking the life out of her. She could feel her strength sapping away. In desperation she brought her knee up as violently as she could. It caught him in exactly the right place. He grunted some more and buckled forward a little. He didn't let go, but his grip loosened and that was enough. She punched him in the side of the neck and now she could get away. She bolted out of the room and along the corridor.

She heard him running behind her. She was nearly at the

top of the stairs, when he shouted out. He wasn't shouting at her, though, it was a different noise – pain, surprise. She looked round. Gavin was standing still, holding his chest. Then he sank to his knees.

'Bea,' he gasped. 'Help me.'

She could get away now. This was her chance. But she was torn. He looked like he was in real trouble, having a heart attack right there in front of her eyes. Was it for real? He'd spent months lying, calculating, manipulating. Was this one more play in his twisted game?

She could still feel his hands round her neck. It was too risky to go back. Let the bastard die here if this was for real.

She started going down the stairs.

'Bea! Please!'

He was desperate. She could hear it.

Swearing under her breath, she turned around, went back up the stairs and jogged along the corridor towards him. He was propped up against the wall now, but as she approached he toppled sideways onto the floor and lay there panting

She kept her distance for a moment or two longer, beyond arm's reach, observing.

'I can't . . . catch my breath . . . '

His face was very grey and his breathing shallow. He wasn't faking.

'Oh, Gavin.' She knelt down next to him. 'I need to call an ambulance. Wait here.'

She darted back into her office and called 999. Then, she fetched the cardigan from the back of her chair, rolled it up and put it under his head.

'They're on their way,' she said. 'Hold on.'

It was cold in the corridor, so she took off her coat and laid it over him, tucking it round his arms. He was so helpless now.

'Thank you,' he whispered. He was straining for air,

311

trying to say something else. 'I didn't mean to ... I didn't mean any of this.'

She felt a surge of anger.

'Stop it, Gavin. Save your breath.'

There was a noise downstairs. Someone was rattling the door, then banging on it. They started shouting, and Bea thought she recognised Ant's voice.

'I'd better go.'

Gavin looked stricken. 'Don't leave me. Please, don't leave me.'

'He'll let himself in anyway.'

'I changed the code.'

'Fucking hell, Gavin. I'll just let him—'

'Please. Please. Don't leave me.'

'I'll have to let the ambulance in when it gets here ...'

'Stay until then?'

'Okay. I'll stay.'

At the staff door, Ant was going mad.

'I can't hear anything,' said Neville. 'Is she in there, do you think?'

'The lights are on. Someone's in there.'

Ant saw something on the ground in the pool of light cast through the glass panel in the door. He thought it was a spider at first, was going to squash it with his foot. Then he peered more closely, swooped down and picked it up.

'It's one of her lashes. She's in there. Why won't this fucking door open? We'll have to smash it in.'

He looked around wildly for something to use.

'Have you got a car here?' Saggy asked Neville.

'Yes, good thinking,' said Neville. 'There's a jack in there we could use.'

Neville hurried over to the middle of the car park, where

he'd left his beige Vauxhall. Saggy followed him, while Ant stayed by the door, hammering on it and shouting.

'Give me the keys,' Saggy said.

'What? No. I'll get it out.'

'Give me the keys! Just do it!'

Confused, Neville handed the keys to Saggy, who opened the driver's door and hopped in.

'What are you—? Wait!'

Saggy started the engine and Neville ran round the front of the car and climbed into the passenger seat, shutting the door as Saggy gunned the engine. Ant watched in disbelief as the car disappeared round the side of the store, then it dawned on him what Saggy was about to do and he sprinted after them, shouting and waving his arms.

Saggy drove into the front car park. It was empty. He swung the car round in a big arc.

'What are you doing?' asked Neville.

'We've got to get in there, right?'

'Yes, but— oh no! No!'

Neville held his arms over his face as Saggy put his foot to the floor and drove straight at the front doors. Ant rounded the corner just in time to see the bonnet smash through the plate glass and hear Neville's anguished high-pitched screams. He was still screaming as Ant crunched his way over the broken glass into the store. From the row he was making he assumed that Neville was actually okay, and Saggy gave him a thumbs up and a massive grin as he ran past the car.

He ran through the darkened shop floor with the burglar alarm ringing in his ears and found the door to the staff area. It was locked, but he picked up a nearby fire extinguisher and bashed the door until it started to give way, then kicked a big enough hole to climb through. He raced up the stairs and there he found Bea and Gavin, still sitting in the hallway.

313

'Bea! Are you all right? Christ, is that Gavin? What have you done to him?'

'I think he's had a heart attack. Is the ambulance here yet?'

'No.'

'What was that noise just now?'

'Nev's taken up ram-raiding.'

'What the actual? Oh, never mind. Have you got anything to cover his legs with? It's cold, and my coat doesn't reach.'

'No. I gave my hoodie to your mum.

'What? What are you talking about?'

'There was a bit of trouble at yours.' Bea started getting to her feet. 'It's okay. It's all sorted. Queenie's fine.'

'Really?'

'Really. We'll go there when the ambulance has been.'

'We need the police too.'

'What, to look into the big hole in the front door? Saggy did it with Neville in the car. I reckon that's consent, isn't it? He didn't nick anything. And it's not criminal damage because we were coming to get you. Not self-defence exactly . . . '

'The police will need to interview Gavin, if he . . . ' Gavin was quiet, but not unconscious. 'If he lives,' she mouthed. 'He did it, Ant. He killed Ginny. It was Gavin.'

Ant put his hands either side of his head and squeezed. 'Did he say? Has he confessed?'

Bea nodded. 'I found the coat he was wearing. He attacked me, and then . . . '

Ant got hold of Bea's shoulder and tried to drag her away. 'Christ, Bea, why are you even helping him?'

'Because . . . I . . . I don't know.'

They could both hear the wail of sirens. Gavin's chest was rising and falling in rapid, shallow movements, but Bea started breathing more easily. Help was on its way.

22

Costsave was closed while the entrance was repaired and the police went through Gavin's office for forensic evidence.

Bea had anticipated a deep sleep and a long lie-in at last but she had a fitful night. She saw Ginny in her dreams, felt Gavin's hands around her neck. She woke up gasping for air, too scared to go back to sleep. She got up just after five and made a pot of tea. She was on her third cup when Queenie came downstairs and found her with her laptop open and paper all over the table.

'What's this?' she said. 'I thought you'd sleep in.'

'Me too, but I couldn't. I'm trying to work out why I missed it. Why I didn't see it was him.'

Queenie stood behind her and rubbed her shoulders. 'Nobody knew it was him. Why would they? He is – was – *seemed* a nice man. The police didn't see it, did they? And they were in and out of there ever since Emma was attacked. He fooled everyone.'

Bea started picking at the pattern on her mug with her fingernail. 'But it was so obvious when you think about it.'

'Not obvious at all.'

'And I should've protected you against Dean, too. Can't believe he came round here.'

'You didn't need to protect me,' said Queenie. 'I dealt with him myself.'

'But he was only here, you only let him in because of me. '

'No, he was here because he's a troublemaker. And it was fine anyway. He wasn't going to hurt me, only frighten me. Got more than he bargained for.'

That forced a smile out of Bea. She leaned back and looked up at Queenie. 'You were a hero, Mum. You really were.'

'So were you, love, although I don't know if I'll ever forgive you for going back to Costsave on your own. What were you thinking?'

'I don't think I was thinking, Mum. Not straight, anyway. I was so tired. Still am.'

Queenie cupped Bea's chin and kissed the top of her head. Then she went to fill up the kettle again for a fresh pot of tea.

'Ant said he found you outside?' said Bea.

'I thought it would be safer out there than in here. And it was. I was fine in the garden, waiting for the police. Lovely fresh air and you should've seen the stars, Bea.'

Bea smiled and felt tears welling up. 'You're amazing,' she said. 'Amazing. Perhaps – no, it doesn't matter.'

'What?'

'Perhaps you could try it again sometime. Going outside.'

'Hmm.'

Bea couldn't tell if it was a 'yes' noise or a 'no' noise or something in between. Now wasn't the time to push things.

They pottered around for a while, then went back to bed. Neither got up and dressed until after eleven.

At about quarter past, Bea heard the doorbell ring. She cursed under her breath – she really didn't want to see anyone today. She put the chain on and opened the door a few inches.

Ant was standing there. He had an armful of flowers – ten or twenty bunches, each in cellophane.

316

'Hang on a minute.' Bea closed the door, unhitched the chain and opened it again.

'Who is it?' called Queenie. She came into the hallway and stood beside Bea. Ant grinned at them both.

'For you, and you,' he said, dividing the flowers roughly in two and handing one half to Queenie and the other one to Bea.

'Oh my!' said Queenie. 'Flowers! Again!'

Bea examined the label on one of the plastic wrappers. 'These are Costsave flowers,' she said suspiciously.

'I just went by there on my way. They're clearing up the front. The car smashed into the fresh flowers just inside the door but the buckets at the back were okay. They'll be past it by the time the shop opens again.'

'So you took them, Ant,' she said, reproof in her voice.

'Nah,' he said quickly. 'The Ram gave them to me to give to you. I blagged some extra bunches for your mum.'

'The Ram?'

'Neville's new name. Mr Ram-Raid.'

Bea smiled. 'Not sure if it'll stick, Ant, but it's worth a try. How was he?'

'Actually, he looked well bad. Looked like he was wearing yesterday's clothes and he was pretty pasty. I reckon he's still in shock.'

'Was there anyone helping him?'

'I saw Anna. She came back from HQ as soon as she heard the news. And there were a couple of other people.'

'Do you think we should go and help?'

Ant looked at Queenie and then rolled his eyes. 'No,' he said. 'Really not. It's a paid day off. A day off. With pay. Why would we go into work?'

''Cos they need us?'

He sighed. 'There's something wrong with you, I swear. Your head's not wired like the rest of the human race. You

317

were nearly toast yesterday. And your mum went through the mill, too. Just have a rest. Chill.'

'Point taken,' said Bea. 'Not even sure I could go back. Not for a while.' She shuddered. 'I never thought it might be – well, he was on my list, but really, not Gavin. I just . . .'

'Shh,' said Queenie. 'Don't think about it.'

'Don't know if I've still got a job to go to,' said Ant. 'I was Gavin's pet project after all. Most of the rest of them hate my guts.'

'Not after this, Ant. I'm sure you've got a future there if you want it. Do you?'

He was quiet for a while, thinking hard, while digging in his ear with his little finger. Bea tried not to notice him wiping it on his jeans.

'Yeah,' he said. 'Yeah, I do. Going straight is more interesting than I thought it would be. I reckon I could hack it.'

Bea smiled. 'I didn't think you'd last the first day.'

Ant huffed a bit. 'Shows what you know. So, ladies,' he said, 'cup of tea, feet up in front of the telly today? What are we watching?'

'Actually,' said Queenie, 'I was thinking of going for a walk.'

They both looked at her. 'Really?' they said together.

'Yes. Really. I could go to the corner shop, get that puzzle magazine you usually get me. I reckon I should do it now before I change my mind.'

'Well, okay,' said Bea, trying to stop herself punching the air in front of her mum.

Ant waited in the hallway while Bea put the flowers in a sink of water. She fetched her bag and coat while Queenie went to the bathroom.

'You could've taken some of those flowers to Dot, except she's out of hospital now. She texted me. Bob's giving her a lift to her daughter's today.'

'Saint Bob,' Ant said, with a touch of bitterness.

'No need to be sarky. Turns out he is a Good Samaritan, nothing else.'

'Well, he's nice to most people, but I still reckon he'd put me through his mincer if he got the chance.'

'Better stay clear then. For a while, at least.'

Queenie came downstairs. Bea was keeping an eye on her as she got ready. She seemed quite calm as she fetched her coat from the peg and picked up her bag. She stopped in the hall to check her appearance in the full-length mirror and groaned.

'Oh gawd,' she said, and Bea's stomach flipped. Was she going to have a meltdown? But Queenie was starting to laugh. 'What do I look like? I've done my buttons up all wrong.'

She started trying to undo the buttons, but her hands were shaking.

'Here, let me.' Bea undid her mum's coat, then lined the buttons and holes up and fastened them properly. 'There.' For a moment, she got a flashback to her first day at school, T-bar shoes like shiny conkers on her feet and her mum doing up the toggles on a brand new duffle coat. Mum and daughter. Parent and child. The edges had become blurred, but maybe they were coming back into focus again.

'Okay?' she said to Queenie.

Queenie took a deep breath.

'I can't, love,' she said. 'I'm sorry. I thought I could but I can't.'

Bea felt her shoulders sag. She tried to hide her disappointment.

'Okay,' she said. 'It's okay. Not today, maybe tomorrow.'

Ant was watching from the front door. 'Here, I've got an idea. I saw it on the telly.' He bounded up to them. 'Give us a bit of space,' he said to Bea, who took a couple of steps back. 'Okay, Queenie, press two fingers into the soft bit of your wrist, like this, close your eyes and think of a time when you were really, really happy.'

Queenie looked at him like he'd lost his marbles.

'Honest, Queenie, it's a thing. Trust me.'

She looked at Bea, who raised her eyebrows and hunched her shoulders. 'Don't ask me,' she said. Then she looked at Ant, 'But I— I trust him. I'd trust Ant with my life.'

Ant looked straight at her. His eyes seemed to be filling up and his mouth was gaping unattractively. 'Wow. I—' he spluttered.

'Shut up, Ant,' Bea said, before he could get any more words out and the whole thing got too embarrassing.

He turned back to Queenie who had gripped her right wrist with the fingers of her left hand, and shut her eyes.

'Are you are in a happy place?' he said.

There was no need to ask. The muscles on Queenie's face relaxed. The worry line between her eyebrows disappeared and she started to smile.

'Okay, now open your eyes. Every time you hold your fingers to your wrist now, it'll bring that happy thought back. You can use it when you're worried, when you don't think you can do something.'

The frown was back. 'Just like that?'

'Yeah. Try it.'

She let go of her wrist and then held it again and started to smile. 'It's there,' she said. 'That's bloody wonderful.'

'It'll be there outside too,' Ant said, with a sly look to Bea. 'Try it.'

'I don't know,' said Queenie. 'I've changed my mind about the shop.'

Her fingers went to the top button of her coat, like she was going to undo it.

'You don't have to go to the shop,' said Ant. 'Why not just stand in the doorway, admire the view?'

'I'm not sure.'

'Come here.' Ant put his arm round Queenie's shoulders and Bea left them to it.

She'd seen this too many times before. Almost there, but not quite. Just for a moment, she'd thought that Ant might be onto something, but, of course, it was going to end the same as all the other times.

She walked down the hall, opened the door and leant on the frame, breathing in the cold, fresh air. She could hear Ant and her mum whispering behind her, but she tuned out and stared across the rec, letting her eyes focus on a couple of seagulls, flapping and fussing over a chip wrapper near the kiddies' play park.

A woman, wearing a cream-coloured mac, was inside the fenced off part, pushing a toddler on the swings. Bea could hear the child's happy squeals drifting across in the cold air, but even at this distance she could tell the woman wasn't smiling as she pushed the swing in a weary, almost robotic way.

Bea left the doorway and started jogging towards the park. It only took a couple of minutes, but she was out of breath when she reached the swings.

'Julie,' she called over the fence.

The woman looked up, puzzled at the sight of Bea in her jogging bottoms and oversize sweatshirt, puffing and panting.

Bea lifted the latch on the gate and went in. 'It's me, Bea. I work on the tills at Costsave.'

Recognition dawned. 'Oh,' said Julie. 'Hello. Didn't recognise you without your uniform. You live round here, do you?'

'Mm.' Bea tapped on the screen of her phone. When she found the site she wanted, she held it up.

'Can you remember this number?' she said. 'Or would you like me to put it on your phone?'

'What is it?' Julie screwed up her eyes. Bea shielded the screen with her hand to get rid of the glare. 'Oh. It's all right. I don't need—'

'You should feel safe,' Bea said. 'It's our right. Everyone should feel safe. On the streets. At home. Let me put it on your phone.'

'No,' Julie said quickly. 'No, he'll find it. He—'

'Can you remember it?' Bea read the number out to her. Julie looked at her, but didn't respond. Bea started to repeat the number, but Julie shook her head.

'I don't need it. I'm fine.'

'Humour me,' said Bea. 'Just in case.' She said the number again, slowly.

Julie listened and this time Bea saw her lips moving as she said the numbers to herself.

'I think I've got it,' she said.

'You can search for it online if you forget. Or you know where to find me. Checkout six, day in, day out. If you ever need anything. Anything at all.'

'Right. Yeah. Okay.' She flashed Bea the briefest of smiles.

Tiffany had come to a standstill on her swing. 'Push me, Mummy!'

Julie sighed. 'No rest for the wicked.' She held onto the back of the swing and pulled it up high. 'Thanks, Bea.'

Bea walked across to the gate and headed for home, listening to Tiffany's renewed squeals as she did so.

When she got back to number twenty-three, Queenie was walking down the hall towards the door with a determined look on her face.

Bea stood aside on the front step. Queenie gave her a tight little smile as she paused on the threshold.

'All right, Mum?'

'All right,' she said, and moved onto the step next to Bea. She stayed there for a full minute, just looking. Then she pressed her fingers to her wrist and walked halfway down the path.

Ant joined Bea on the step.

'That's the girl,' he said.

'What the hell did you say to her?' said Bea.

Ant was grinning broadly. 'I just asked her what her happy place was.'

'And?'

'A hotel in Rhyl, apparently, Bea. In bed with your dad. According to Queenie, he was as hot as axle grease.' He clicked his tongue and gave her a cheeky wink.

'Oh Jesus,' said Bea. 'I can never look her in the eye again.'

But she did look. Having put her hand on the metal gate at the end of the path, Queenie turned round and headed back towards them. She was unsteady on her feet, but she was smiling, and, despite wanting to put her mind through a boil wash and rapid spin, Bea smiled back at her.

'That's enough for one day,' said Queenie.

'Yes, Mum, that's enough. That's bloody brilliant.'

Acknowledgements

This book was written while my husband, Ozzy, was waiting for and then recovering from a heart transplant. He read it, chapter by chapter, to start with and then I read it to him when he was very poorly. I'd like to thank the staff and volunteers at Harefield Hospital for keeping him alive, and my family and friends for keeping me going, especially Shirley, David, Ali and Pete.

A big thank you to Kirsty McLachlan at David Godwin Associates, my wonderful agent, and to all at Sandstone Press, who are bringing Ant and Bea to a wider audience.

www.sandstonepress.com

facebook.com/SandstonePress/

@SandstonePress